PENGUIN BOOKS

The Search

ABOUT THE AUTHOR

Howard Linskey is the author of the David Blake series, the first of which, *The Drop*, was selected as one of the Top Five Crime Thrillers of the Year by *The Times*. Originally from Ferryhill in County Durham, he now lives in Hertfordshire with his wife and daughter.

The Search

HOWARD LINSKEY

PENGUIN BOOKS

PENGUIN BOOKS

UK | USA | Canada | Ireland | Australia
India | New Zealand | South Africa

Penguin Books is part of the Penguin Random House group of companies
whose addresses can be found at global.penguinrandomhouse.com.

First published in Penguin Books 2017
001

Text copyright © Howard Linskey, 2017

The moral right of the author has been asserted

Set in 12/14.25 pt Garamond MT Std
Typeset by Jouve (UK), Milton Keynes
Printed in Great Britain by Clays Ltd, St Ives plc

A CIP catalogue record for this book is available from the British Library

ISBN: 978–0–718–18036–2

www.greenpenguin.co.uk

Penguin Random House is committed to a
sustainable future for our business, our readers
and our planet. This book is made from Forest
Stewardship Council® certified paper.

To Alison & Erin

Prologue

My Story
by Adrian Wicklow

I screamed from day one.

I was born screaming, or so my dear mother told me. I screamed from the moment they dragged me into this ridiculous world.

'This one has plenty to say for himself,' the midwife told her, and she was right about that but no one was listening. Nobody paid me any attention. Not for years.

Then I started killing and it all changed. All of a sudden, people cared. I killed again and again. They were desperate to find me then. Some of them became obsessed with me. It felt so good to know I was in everybody's thoughts. You see, everything changed when I started taking their children.

They noticed me then.

I

'I dare you to do it,' she told him, 'I *double* dare you.'

So it was a *double* dare and he couldn't just ignore it.

'Why should I?'

'Because I double dare you,' she repeated, and there was no arguing with that. It was reason enough for a ten-year-old boy to do as he was asked. The fact she was a girl, and he didn't want to look like a coward in front of her, clinched it. If he didn't do this dare, she'd tell all the other girls and they'd flap their elbows like chickens and make clucking noises when he walked by. He couldn't bear the thought of that.

But it was a very long way down.

Maybe she would tell the girls if he *did* do it, and then he'd be a bloody hero. That gave him courage and he took a step closer to the edge, but only a step. He was still a little way back from the perimeter fence, but he could see the great expanse of the old limestone quarry ahead of him. Most of the basin of the huge quarry was flooded, and nature had reclaimed it. Vegetation grew where once bare rock had been, while thick bushes thrived all around the flood water, from the bottom of the slopes until they hugged the steep sides of the quarry, which were covered in moss. Even trees grew out of the ledges here, before stretching upwards, as if trying to climb the cliffs of the quarry so they could haul themselves out and make a break for freedom.

The limestone had been hewn out years ago for building projects, and all that remained was a huge crater. Most of the

3

stone became part of the new houses that widened the village of Maiden Hill on all sides during the boom years of the sixties. These two-up two-downs ringed the village like the circled wagons in a western.

The enormous hole that remained seemed to stretch for miles and miles, but he could still see the other end. It wasn't how wide the crater was that was troubling him; it was how deep it looked. Every kid in the village was frightened of the quarry. They had all heard tales of children who had disappeared out here; swallowed up by the dark water at one end of the crater or dashed to pieces on the rocks at the other. Everyone knew that ghosts lived out here and bogeymen, and there was a grey lady too, who haunted the place after dark and could scare people to death with just one look. You were all right as long as you went in a group or with a friend, but if you came out here on your own those evil spirits would rush out at you and push you over the edge of the quarry just so they could watch you fall and listen while you screamed.

Every kid knew that.

The adults didn't believe it, though. His mum had told him it was all nonsense. 'Don't you think I'd have read about it in the paper,' she asked him, while she was baking in the kitchen, 'if a kid had gone over the edge of that quarry? Don't you reckon we'd have heard about it if someone was missing a child?' And she laughed at his fears and offered him her wooden spoon to lick the cake mix from. Adults didn't understand these things. They had forgotten what it was like to be a child; to believe in something because you just know it deep down to be true. They had to be told things by the TV or newspapers, but they were just stories as well, so how did they know they weren't made up?

He knew the stories were real, so he couldn't understand why the girl wasn't scared, and this meant he couldn't be frightened either. He wasn't allowed to be more scared than a girl. That was another rule.

He hesitated now and looked at the gap in the wire.

'I'll go through the fence as well,' she assured him, 'just to watch you. I'm not doing it, but you can do it. I bet you can.'

He took his time thinking about it then gingerly edged further forward until he was able to stretch out his leg and push it through a gap in the fence. He wondered who had pulled at this first and how long it had taken them to worry away at it until they were able to bend the wire up and apart, forcing a hole in the fence that had been placed here to keep everyone away from the sheer drop that lay beyond it. He wondered how many other kids had gone through it, as he was about to. He had to hold on to the wire and lower himself virtually to the ground so he was almost on his back, then slide his feet through the gap first, his coat catching on the ragged wire until he managed to wriggle free.

Then he was through the gap and he stood up on the other side, a giddy, dizzying feeling sweeping over him, part excitement, part fear.

'See,' she said from behind the fence. 'You did it, and there's plenty of room.'

And there was.

Kind of.

He was standing on a plateau that jutted out into the bowl of the quarry's giant crater but there was nothing now to protect him from a long fall on to sharp rocks. The fence had been placed around the quarry in a large, uneven circle. Most of the time, it went right to the edge, and there was nothing beyond the fence but a sheer drop. The crater wasn't a perfect circle, though, so here and there slabs of land became imprisoned beyond the fence and jutted out into the quarry like jetties on a lake. The bit he was standing on was easily large enough for her to join him, and she wriggled through. On one side, tall, thick bushes created a natural barrier at the edge. The other side of the plateau was unprotected. He felt sick just standing there now. He knew if he were to close his eyes and take three steps he would fall over the edge, then be dead and gone for ever.

'You've done it . . . almost!' she said, but that wasn't true. The really hard part, the bit she had double dared him to do, still remained. She wanted him to hold on to the wire fence from the inside and leave the relative safety of their rocky out-crop to make his way along the edge of the quarry, which had only a small, rutted bit of grassy land against it to keep him safe. He would have to plant his feet on a ledge that wasn't much wider than his shoes while holding on for his life with splayed fingers that clutched the octagonal gaps in the wire as he went hand over hand.

He leaned forward again and looked at the ground far below. 'I don't know,' he said, trying to sound calm. 'What if I fall?'

'You won't fall. Freddie Andrews didn't fall.'

'Yeah, but he's thirteen,' he reminded her, '*and* his dad's in prison.' This meant Freddie had nothing to lose because his life was already horrible and it wasn't ever going to get any better, not never. Freddie had scrambled around that edge from the inside like he didn't care if he fell or not. He'd reached the other gap in the wire, which had to be at least twenty steps along the ledge, before you even knew it. Then he'd climbed out to cheers that must have been the highlight of his sad, young life.

'Naah,' he said. 'I *could* do it . . .' He wanted her to know he was capable of the act. 'I just don't want to.'

'Go on!' she urged him. She smiled then, and the smile seemed to come from deep within and something lit up inside him. That smile made him want to do anything she asked.

Anything.

There was a fire in her eyes when she said, 'I *triple* dare you.'

2

'So I suppose I was the last one to see her alive,' Billy told the awestruck girl in the pub. 'Well, not the *last*, obviously,' and he gave her the grim half-smile he always used at this point.

'Oh my God,' she said. 'That's terrible,'

He was already wondering if he had overcooked it or whether the line had grown stale from repetition over the years. It hadn't quite tripped off his tongue this time. He felt like an old club comedian who has told the same joke once too often.

And he was drunk. Perhaps too drunk.

None of this stopped her from taking his hand in hers and giving it a supportive squeeze, so maybe there was some hope. The barren run had to end sometime, right?

'It's just sooo sad and awful,' she was empathising now, her eyes wide and tears beginning to form in them. 'I don't know how you've coped with this for so long.' She shook her head solemnly and he wondered if she would lean in for the hug, or if perhaps he should risk it, but he hesitated, mindful of the age gap between them. Was it really eleven years? Apparently so. He was thirty and this student just nineteen. It had been so much easier when he was the same age as them. Teenagers were always so emotional with one another and everything seemed huge and overblown. He would pick one who was sitting on her own – the depressed girl at a party who was maybe not as good-looking as her friends, say – then he'd ask her if she was okay. He'd permit her a few self-indulgent minutes to moan about her sadness and isolation while offering more sympathy than it was worth, then he would gradually give up his own tale, one sentence at a time, as if reluctant to do so. This was of course also the story of poor little Susan Verity, and almost everyone had heard of her.

If he pitched it exactly right, the girl on the receiving end of his story would not only feel sorry for him but would usually be mortified at having bothered him at all with her own trivial problems. That would be his 'in'. If things went really well he might even ask to crash at her place for the night and, once he was in her room . . .

Danny called him the king of the sympathy-shag, but Billy wasn't bothered. The notion amused him, in fact, and he had come to think of this as the only perk of the millstone around his neck. Billy Thorpe would always be the last person on earth to have seen poor little Susan Verity alive before she was taken by a monster, and this had stayed with him, as if, somehow, he shared the blame for the village's guilty secret.

Subconsciously, people tended to steer clear of him. Girl-friends, in particular, were always very hard to come by, as if he carried a form of baggage they were unwilling to take on. Billy learned early on that what happened that day held the power to completely overshadow the rest of his life, even though he was only ten years old at the time. So he didn't feel bad using this tale to get his end away. Why should he? What else did he have to offer a young woman like this one? He wasn't tall, he wasn't good-looking; he didn't even have a job. He had no other stories with which to impress her; nothing other than his proximity to that tragic girl on the day she was lost.

'I read about in the paper just this morning,' the pretty student told him earnestly, her eyes wide, and he tried hard to remember her name. She'd told him at the beginning but it had gone from his mind almost instantly because of the drink. 'It's nearly the anniversary, isn't it?'

He nodded sadly. 'Yeah, so it's impossible to forget about it all, even if I wanted to. Which I don't,' he added quickly, in case she thought him callous.

'You poor thing,' she said. 'Twenty years ago,'

'And it still seems like yesterday,' he confided.

'I wasn't even born then,' she said. He could have done without the reminder. He already realized he was punching above his weight with this one. She was not only young but beautiful, with long, dark hair and full red lips he wanted to smother with his own. Her skin was pale and blemish-free.

The girl was back in County Durham from uni and already looking as if she had outgrown the place. The village was no bigger than his own but the pub always attracted a size-able young crowd, which in turn had attracted him, and it was only a short bus ride away. She let go of his hand then; not suddenly or cruelly, but with a sympathetic, 'It must be very difficult.'

He gave her his tight-lipped, I'm-a-survivor smile. 'I have good days and bad days.'

They were interrupted by a great roar from the next room, followed by raucous laughter, which indicated that something was about to get out of hand in the karaoke bar. 'I'd better be going,' she said.

'Me too.'

He followed her out of the pub and, when they were on the pavement, said, 'Where do you live again?' even though she hadn't told him.

'Brook Lane.'

'The new houses.'

'They've been there six years,' she reminded him.

He grinned. 'They'll always be the new houses.' He knew

9

how the *real* villagers here would view outsiders like her parents who'd bought the posh new-builds. 'I'll walk you home.'

'Oh, no. It's fine, honestly.' She wasn't keen on that idea.

'Can't have a young girl going home on her own at this hour,' he said, then looked at her meaningfully. 'Of all people, I'm never going to let *that* happen.'

'Okay.' She was weakening now he had made it all about Susan's disappearance. 'But won't it take you out of your way?'

He hadn't told her where he lived or that the last bus had left ten minutes ago and he faced the prospect of a four-mile trudge home in the dark. He fell in next to her without replying and they walked across the village. 'You can't be too careful,' he said, when he realized she wasn't going to strike up a new conversation. 'They never did catch him, you know.'

'I thought some man admitted it. That's what it said in the paper.'

'Yeah, he confessed eventually, but a lot of people still reckon it wasn't him. That bloke Wicklow killed a bunch of kids, so it made no difference to him whether he admitted it or not. Reckon he just told the police what they wanted to hear. You see, most of his victims were found, except for three other kids and her.'

'God,' she said, suddenly interested again now. 'So you think he's still out there – the man who killed poor Susan?'

It was never just 'Susan'. Always '*poor* Susan' or '*tragic* Susan'.

'Reckon so. He could be dead, I s'pose, but there's more than one other kid gone missing since that day.'

'That's awful. I can't imagine what it must be like for the parents,'

'No one can.'

'And you never saw anyone? You know, following you, when you were with her?'

'That's what the police kept asking, but I never saw a soul.

I was only ten, but I'd have remembered if I had.' He realized she was more than a little interested now. They always were. Once they'd heard the story of Susan Verity, they couldn't get enough of it. They all wanted a few ghoulish titbits to take home with them, something they could tell their pals in the pub. They would boast about knowing him, the last boy to see the vanished girl alive. 'They said he was probably stalking us all that time.'

'Really? Crikey.' She already sounded like some posh southern girl because of that fancy university of hers.

'So they told me. The police said it was more than likely he'd spotted us when we were all playing in the fields together then followed her after we split into smaller groups. They reckon he must have waited till Susan went off on her own before he approached her.'

'What do they think happened then?'

She was hooked, wanting to know every gory detail. 'They don't know,' he said, 'it's always been a mystery'; and he could see she was disappointed: 'But there were several theories that didn't make it into the newspapers' – and that piqued her interest once more.

'Like what?' she asked, and she stopped walking at that point so she could turn to face him.

'Well, I shouldn't say,' he said, and she looked disappointed, 'but if you promise not to tell anyone . . .'

'Of course,' she said.

'Cross your heart and hope to die?'

'What?'

'Figure of speech,' he said, and he jerked his head to indicate they should keep moving. He didn't want to run out of stories before he reached her front door.

'They said he probably lured her away,' he explained. 'Offered to show her something interesting, like puppies or kittens, or maybe he said her mother was ill and she had to come with him.' They were almost at her street now. 'But I reckon he forced her.'

'Forced her?'

'Picked her up and just carried her off,' he said. 'She was only a little thing, barely anything of her, really.'

'But wouldn't she have screamed?'

'Maybe, but if he jammed his hand over her mouth . . .' he said reasonably. 'And anyway, who's going to hear you out there? We were in the fields, remember; miles from anywhere. It was different back then, kids were allowed to roam; their parents didn't realize how many bad people there were in the world.'

'God, that's chilling.'

'Anyway, I don't reckon screaming helps.'

'You don't?' The notion alarmed her.

He shook his head. 'People don't really react, do they?'

'I hope they do.'

'How many times do people hear a shout and think it's someone having a row that's none of their business? No,' he concluded firmly. 'Screaming doesn't help.'

He realized she was looking for something in her bag, probably her front-door key. He needed to think quickly. 'If you've got time for a coffee, I can tell you more.'

She understood that he was inviting himself into her home and looked a little alarmed at the prospect. 'Oh, I can't. I'm sorry. I've got to be up in the morning.' That was a lie, she was a student. What the hell did students have to get up for anyway?

'Oh, don't be boring,' he said.

'I'm not,' she said firmly, 'I just have to go.' She could be formidable when she wanted to be. Sometimes, you could pressure a girl into doing things by making her seem like a dull plank, but not this one. 'But listen, it was great talking to you, and I mean, really, it was all . . . wow.' She had either lost the power of speech or was concentrating on getting away from him as swiftly as possible.

'You, too,' he said quietly, 'and thanks for listening to me. Most people don't understand, but you . . .' He gave her his best sad look then. 'Well, let's just say, you get it.'

'Aw . . . thanks,' she said, and he got the hug he was hoping for then. He held her close and breathed in the sweet scent from her hair and whatever it was she sprayed her body with before putting on her clothes. God, it felt good, and he wanted it to last for ever, or at least until morning.

She broke free then and, even though he knew it was a long shot, he still leaned in for the kiss, because you never knew.

'Let's not,' she said, pressing both her palms firmly against his chest.

'I felt like we had a connection.'

'But I just want to be friends.'

'I understand,' he said, though he didn't, and not for the first time he wondered how she could be so moved by his amazing story – the story of poor, tragic Susan, at any rate – without wanting to be more intimate. What was wrong with him? 'I'll still walk you to your door, though,' he said, but she backed away.

'No, it's fine,' she said. 'I can literally see my front door from here.'

'Well, no, you can't, not really.' He was taken aback by the lie. At best, she could see the start of the cut that would lead into her street, but it seemed she would rather risk walking through that dimly lit alleyway on her own than go down it with him. He felt the anger begin to bubble up inside him, fuelled, as it always was, by booze and the reality of rejection.

But she was gone already. She'd run across the road, as if she had spotted a brief gap during rush hour, even though they hadn't seen a single moving car since they left the pub together. 'Bye!' she called, and gave him a little wave.

He watched the girl go, taking all his hopes with her.

'Bitch,' he said quietly to himself.

POLICE REOPEN BOTCHED MISSING GIRL CASE

By our crime correspondent

Durham police have been forced to reopen the case of a young girl who has been missing for twenty years, following a TV documentary which suggested that officers had acted incompetently. Ten-year-old Susan Verity vanished in 1976 but police botched the investigation into her disappearance, according to the film, which will be aired tonight.

Susan has never been found but, five years after her disappearance, multiple child-killer Adrian Wicklow admitted killing the schoolgirl. He later withdrew his confession, claiming it was beaten from him by detectives.

According to a source close to the production team, the documentary, *Cover-up: The Truth about Susan Verity*, will list a string of errors made by the police. Officers were under huge pressure to find the missing girl and numerous mistakes were made. Detectives are accused of cutting corners and failing to pursue promising leads. The documentary makers allege:

- Valuable time was wasted at the outset when it was assumed that Susan had simply run away and would soon return home. No search was made for the missing girl for several hours.
- There was a 'culture of drink' within the team, with a number of serving detectives accused of severe alcoholism and of being regularly drunk on duty.
- A police appeal for help from the public led to them being bombarded with hundreds of false sightings, a number of malicious accusations made by disgruntled neighbours and

many bogus leads, which distracted detectives. Police received so many calls they had to use card indexes and boxes of files to store the information, but they did not have the necessary resources to question everyone, leaving the case to run cold.

- A sole witness thought she had seen a man who matched the description of Adrian Wicklow in Susan's village that morning. The elderly lady's statement was later discredited and no attempt was made to prosecute Wicklow for any crime involving Susan Verity. He is serving a life sentence for other murders.

- Wicklow's claim that a confession was extracted from him 'under torture' was backed up by witnesses, who observed severe bruising on the killer, which appeared only after he had been detained in custody. At the time, the police dismissed his allegation, claiming that Wicklow had received his injuries while 'resisting arrest'.

- Officers became so desperate to find clues they even turned to a medium for help, a tactic criticized as 'utterly bonkers' by modern-day detectives. 'Psychic Sandra' succeeded only in sending an already overstretched team into meltdown, as they combed large areas of land far away from Susan's village because the medium 'sensed' the presence of the girl at each location.

Susan Verity's disappearance remains on file as Durham Constabulary's greatest unsolved mystery. Current Chief Constable James Newman vowed to do everything he could to discover the truth. 'Mistakes were made, of that there can be no doubt, and I would like to apologize to the relatives of the missing girl. I give my personal guarantee that officers involved in the reopening of this case shall not rest until the truth about Susan Verity's disappearance has finally been uncovered.'

3

'Sir?' Detective Sergeant Ian Bradshaw had been summoned to his boss's office. He was surprised to find Kane reading the paper.

'Come in, lad, sit down,' Kane told him, but he continued to read until he had finished the article. The DCI leaned forward then, as if he was about to betray a confidence. 'You've heard we are re-examining the Susan Verity case?' So that's what the summons was about. 'The brass see this' – and the DCI jabbed a finger at the offending article – 'as a stain on our reputation, something that needs to be cleared up once and for all. The initial investigation was not a particularly thorough one. In fact, I'd say it was scarcely competent.' Kane looked uncomfortable then. 'When it became clear there was unlikely to be a satisfactory resolution to the case, desperation set in.'

'You mean, they pinned it on Adrian Wicklow.'

DCI Kane held up a hand and showed his palm to Bradshaw. 'I'm not saying that.'

'Then what are you saying?'

'Wicklow was questioned about Susan's disappearance at the time, but so were hundreds of other men. He was arrested five years later, but that was for his other crimes.'

'He admitted he killed Susan Verity,' said Bradshaw, 'so why do we doubt that all of a sudden?'

'He confessed as soon as he was arrested then he withdrew that confession and claimed it was beaten out of him. He finally copped for it, years later, long after he was found guilty of the other killings, but he has a history of messing everyone around and the CPS reckoned he'd likely change his tune again once he was in the dock, so he was never formally charged with her murder since he was already serving a life sentence. There was no body, for starters. People forget that Wicklow was found guilty of only three murders, even though we strongly suspect he was responsible for at least seven, possibly eight or nine.' He sighed. 'Maybe even more. The other murders were all left on file, including Susan Verity's. The CPS didn't want to confuse a jury by bringing a bunch of charges that were hard to prove alongside ones where there was a reasonably strong chance of a conviction. Everyone knew that the judge would give him life for one child killing, so there was no need to go after him for all of them.'

'The families of the victims might disagree.'

Kane ignored this. 'In the end Wicklow was found guilty and he did get a life sentence. He'll never be released.' He paused, his face grim. 'Of course, that's when the fun started. He has been running everyone ragged ever since. First, he said he was an innocent man and was working on an appeal. That got him a bit of press coverage, but not much sympathy, so when he was denied the right to appeal he changed his tune completely. He admitted the three murders he was convicted of but said he had nowt to do with the others.'

'The ones left on file? Why would he bother to deny them?'

'To cause us grief. We got him for cases where bodies were discovered and there was physical evidence, but there were numerous other disappearances linked to him. In four of those cases, the bodies were never found.'

'So why the focus on her and not the others?'

'In the other cases, it was pretty clear what had happened. When the kids went missing there were several sightings of a man who looked like Wicklow or of a car that matched his, and he didn't have an alibi for any of them. There was also nothing to indicate that the kids might have been snatched or killed by someone they knew.'

'And the Susan Verity case is different?'

'Only one eyewitness reported having seen Wicklow in the area when Susan disappeared, and she was an old lady.' Kane spread his palms to indicate how unreliable her testimony was likely to be. 'Plus, there were other possible suspects, some closer to home. Read the case files and you'll see what I mean. Now we have this documentary crew raking things up, claiming Wicklow might not have been involved in the disappearance of Susan Verity at all. They think the real culprit might still be out there. Personally, I don't think they have the faintest clue. The producer probably met with Wicklow and fell for one of his lies, but this case always seems to catch the public's imagination; probably because it involved a group of kids playing together and only one of them disappeared, which made it all the more chilling. The killer could have chosen any one of them, but he went for Susan. Anyway, they have stirred up a lot of interest from the press with their bloody documentary and the chief constable wants us to get a result.'

'What does Wicklow have to say about it these days?'

'That usually depends on what mood he is in. *I did it*, then *I didn't do it*,' Kane was impersonating a glib Adrian Wicklow now. '*I did that one but not this one. I know where that body is buried but I really can't remember where that one is, it's too long ago . . . but wait, it's all coming back to me now*.' Kane sighed. 'It's all a sick game to him because that really is all he has left. He's been in solitary confinement for fifteen years with no contact with other inmates; they'd kill him if they got the chance. This is the only thing he has to keep him occupied.'

'Does he get any visitors?'

'His mother used to go all the time, but she died a few years ago. They were very close and she believed in his innocence, apparently, despite all the evidence to the contrary and his numerous partial confessions. It was always, "My little boy couldn't have done this," and she held to that view right up until the end. Other than that, there's been a procession of psychiatrists, psychologists and numerous other head-doctors all trying to get to the bottom of Wicklow's motivation for his crimes and make a name for themselves in the process. A few have even written books about him, but he messed every single one of them around. He'd offer cooperation one minute and withdraw it the next. He enjoyed upsetting them.'

'Is anyone from the original investigation still on the force?'

Kane shook his head. 'All retired or gone.'

Bradshaw was puzzled. 'It wasn't so long ago,' he said. He was thinking that, fifteen years on from Wicklow's arrest, a junior detective on that case would surely still be serving somewhere.

'They all left, Ian.' It was said firmly, and Kane didn't usually use Bradshaw's first name. 'A dozen men worked that case from the beginning to the end. When it was over, they were finished. The senior men stayed on til retirement, seeing out their time, really; no one expected much from them by then. The younger ones got out while they still could and went off to do something else.'

Bradshaw summed it up. 'So the evidence is twenty years old, the original team working on it are all gone, Wicklow probably did it anyway, and there's a hostile press watching our every move. Sounds as if we could be on a hiding to nothing.'

'Not necessarily,' argued Kane. 'We do have one thing going for us. I told you the original investigation was badly handled. I'd say this is a real chance for you to make a name for yourself. I think it's something you could be suited to. You've got results before where more . . . *conventional* detectives have failed. Your career has been a bit patchy but I'm suggesting we play to your strengths. You're bright enough, when you can be bothered to put that academic brain into gear. A lot of good, honest, diligent coppers looked at the Susan Verity case and got tied up in knots. I want fresh eyes on it and a different outlook.'

Bradshaw was used to his boss damning him with faint praise, but at least this time Kane was trusting him with an important investigation, even if it was twenty years old. The chance to make a difference by finding out what really happened to Susan Verity and to bring some closure to her family at last was the clincher. Bradshaw wanted this case. 'I'll start reviewing the evidence right away, then I'll interview everyone associated with her, see what I can come up with.'

'Yes, fine' – the DCI was surprisingly dismissive – 'but I need you to prioritize something else for me first.' Kane seemed almost reluctant to come to the point. 'I need you to go and see somebody. Someone who says he knows the truth about what happened that day, twenty years ago. Possibly, he's the only one who does.'

'Who?' Bradshaw didn't like the sound of this.

'Adrian Wicklow.'

'You're not serious' – he almost forgot to add the word – 'sir?'

'I am.'

'But you've just told me he can't be trusted and the only thing he has left is the enjoyment of running everyone ragged,' Bradshaw reminded DCI Kane. 'What reason could he possibly have for helping us? Why the hell would he tell me the truth now?'

'Because he's dying.'

4

Helen Norton and Tom Carney spent the afternoon in the lounge bar of an old Durham city hotel. The two reporters went there so often they had taken to referring to the place as 'the office'. Tom had partly converted his house so they could work there but the front room was a cluttered and cramped half-lounge, half-office, so they liked to escape from it. The hotel's long and spacious bar was a perfect place to plan their week. They'd sit on its enormous sofas, drinking coffee and eating sandwiches. When Helen queried the financial wisdom of this, Tom told her, 'The cost is nothing like what we'd be shelling out for a real office in town, and we still have to eat, so we might as well do it here.'

Helen had to agree it was a good place to churn over the stories they were working on and discuss new ideas. Helpfully, the hotel provided piles of free newspapers for residents and customers. They could sift through them and discuss possibilities for features or search the local papers for stories they could follow up then sell to women's magazines. 'Miracle babies' were always good, as were articles about people who had survived massive adversity and gone on to do something constructive with their lives.

Working together was meant to have been a temporary arrangement. Helen had been with a Newcastle daily newspaper but then her editor had been killed; run off the road at speed by an anonymous driver she was convinced had been sent by Jimmy McCree, the gangster he and Helen had exposed in a series of damning articles. The shock of Graham's death

22

convinced her to stay away from the newsroom for a while. She couldn't imagine working there without her editor. She knew that every time she saw his office the hurt and the guilt would return: for writing the stories that had got him killed, for being the one who survived while Graham was gone, leaving a widow and children behind; and she knew that everyone in the newsroom was likely to blame her for taking on organized crime in their city without thinking of the consequences.

After a few weeks, it was clear she was never going back to the paper and Tom suggested she work with him permanently instead. He was freelance these days and could use a partner. They had worked together on stories before and it seemed a logical move.

At first, they were ridiculously busy, writing features and news articles exposing local politicians' links to organized crime: backhanders had been given for corrupt land deals, resulting in murder. The stories easily found homes in the tabloids and in magazines and the money had rolled in, but, eventually, interest in those cases inevitably began to wane. A year on, Helen and Tom needed new stories if they were to survive as freelancers, and those did not come from thin air, which was why Helen was avidly watching the local news on the lounge bar's TV while Tom took a call outside on his mobile, trying to persuade a women's magazine to run a piece he had dreamed up. Sandwiched between reports of an aborted strike on the railway and a gale that had felled a dozen trees the previous night was a special report on one of the region's biggest mysteries: the disappearance of Susan Verity.

They were running some archive footage on the screen. The images were faded by time and had a slightly yellowish tinge. They showed a line of uniformed police officers fanning out and trudging slowly across a field near Susan's home as they searched the ground for evidence. There was a close-up of a dark-haired police officer who was asking for witnesses to come forward and help them with any information they might have about Susan's disappearance. The caption on the screen revealed that this was Detective Inspector Barry Meade of Durham Constabulary. Presently, the report moved on to show a mug-shot of Adrian Wicklow, who stared smugly out at the camera while the announcer described his arrest some years after Susan went missing then stated that no one was really sure if Susan Verity's true killer might still be at large even now.

It ended with an appearance earlier today at a press conference by the current Assistant Commissioner, who began by sheepishly admitting that 'mistakes were undoubtedly made during the crucial early hours of Susan's disappearance, which is regrettable.' Helen recalled the image of DI Barry Meade and couldn't help feeling that, wherever he was now, he had just been hung out to dry.

The AC was fielding questions: 'No, we are not saying that Adrian Wicklow is innocent of any involvement in the disappearance of Susan Verity. He has never consistently cooperated with the authorities on this or any of the other cases he has been linked to and his pronouncements must therefore be considered unreliable.'

The camera angle widened as the assistant chief constable took further questions from a raised platform. There were two other officers, one either side of him, and Helen recognized Detective Chief Inspector Kane. Helen and Tom had an uneasy – occasionally, downright hostile – relationship with Kane, but they had at least produced results for him. Kane had hired them before as 'experts' to assist the police with previous 'cold' cases. This could cause friction, if they discovered inconvenient facts that showed the police in a bad light.

'We have agreed to reopen the case under the guidance of a senior officer with a great deal of experience,' said the AC.

'Detective Inspector Kane will carry out a thorough and methodical re-examination of the facts surrounding the disappearance of Susan back in 1976. I can personally assure you that every effort will be made to uncover the truth and bring the perpetrator of this crime to justice.'

So Kane was in charge.

Helen wondered if he might need a little help.

'Billy Thorpe?'

Billy turned to see a smartly dressed, serious-looking woman walking briskly towards him. 'They said I'd find you here,' she said, and sat down next to him without waiting for an invitation. Billy had been enjoying an afternoon of sunshine outside his local pub and her arrival sent a tiny surge of panic through him. Was she a police officer, a lawyer maybe? He was about to go into automatic denial mode, when she said, 'I'm Amanda Barratt and I'm with *North-east News Tonight*' and then when, though his mouth opened, he showed no sign of recognition, she continued: 'The current-affairs programme that airs in the evenings?'

'Right,' he said emphatically, as if he knew what she was talking about.

'We're doing an episode on Susan Verity,' she explained, 'to mark the twentieth anniversary of her disappearance, and we would love to have you on the show. We'd pay you for your time, of course.'

'I see,' he said, a bit narked she'd mentioned money right away like that. Someone must have told her he charged for interviews, but being so upfront about it made him seem cheap. 'Well, I suppose that would be okay, if it's for my time and everything.'

'Of course,' she said.

'So how much would you be paying for that?'

She told him, and he had to hide his excitement. She could have had him for half that amount but, obviously, he wasn't going to let on. In the past, he'd made some good money for his memories, mostly from the big London newspapers. He'd give them a few snippets and they would twist them and somehow exaggerate the hell out of them, turning them into a story that would dominate the page it was printed on. There'd be a big headline like 'MY CHILDHOOD NIGHTMARE' or 'MY LIVING HELL', accompanied by a strap line which told the reader this statement was 'by Susan Verity survivor Billy Thorpe', or 'the last man to see tragic Susan alive'. The story would feature quotes from him about his guilt at not having been able to save Susan or his shock at knowing it could easily have been him who had been snatched and not her. He always made a point of telling reporters that Adrian Wicklow should hang for his crimes against children. They loved that and often ran a phone-in to see if readers thought the time was right for the government to bring back capital punishment for child killers.

After twenty years, though, Billy didn't have much left to say on the subject of Susan Verity that he had not said already and the paid stories had started to dry up. This big anniversary would be a great chance for him to earn some proper money again.

'So when do you want me?' he asked. He was quite comfortable just now, because he'd lifted a tenner out of his mam's purse that morning and had spent some of it on four pints already. The reporter had joined him just as he was sinking the last one.

'Well, now would be good,' she told him. 'My car's just around the corner.' When his face fell, she added, 'You can finish your pint first,' and Billy brightened.

*

'Everything you need is in here somewhere,' the uniformed constable told him, and Bradshaw blinked as the bare bulb flickered on in the small, windowless room. Facing him were three large bookcases full of files, each against a wall. Buried somewhere in among these old cold-case files were the documents on the Susan Verity case and Adrian Wicklow's other terrible crimes. Finding them, though – that was the challenge.

Bradshaw had never been in this room before. It seemed to be a repository for anyone who had the time or inclination to go through the files looking for a lost lead. Each shelf held stacks of bulging manila files. They contained witness reports, police statements, suspect sightings, victim movements and the testimonies of hundreds of innocent men and women who had been interviewed by police but ruled out of further enquiries, explained the constable. It made you realize just how much leg work went into an average criminal investigation, and there was nothing average about Adrian Wicklow. Bradshaw realized he might be spending quite some time here and was glad that there were a small table and a couple of chairs in the centre of the room.

He thanked the constable for showing him in, and the other man made to leave. 'Er' – Bradshaw addressed him as if he had forgotten something – 'which folders contain the Adrian Wicklow case files?' Bradshaw expected that he might at least be pointed in the right direction.

The constable stared blankly back at him. 'All of them.'

5

'How did it go?' asked Helen, but she could guess by the look on his face.

'Not interested,' he said, looking more angry than disappointed. 'You would have thought an article about an English woman working as a nurse and treating wounded children in foreign war zones would be worthy of a few hundred words in a women's magazine, but no.'

'Why didn't they want it?'

'Because she isn't a *celebrity*.' He spat out the last word in disgust. 'Can't we come back with some articles about celebrities?'

'What kind of articles?'

'Doesn't matter. Celebrities going to things, wearing stuff, falling over, getting up again.' He shook his head at the pointlessness of it all. 'Anyway, they weren't interested, so we don't get paid.'

It had been a while since they'd been paid for anything. Helen told Tom about the news item on the reopening of the Susan Verity case.

'I remember that. It was a big story when I was a kid. Poor girl disappeared one day while out playing with her friends.'

'DCI Kane is leading the new investigation.'

'Oh.'

'You could call him.'

'Mmm.'

'Your enthusiasm is infectious. Come on. This is what we're good at, and he has used us before. He'd probably love to have you back on the payroll for a while.'

'I wouldn't go that far. He thinks I'm a massive pain in the arse.'

'Well, you are,' she said reasonably, 'but he's a realist and so am I. We need the money.'

There was too much of it. Far too much. When he was left on his own in the little room full of files, Bradshaw realized just what he was up against. He tried to count the files to see just how much paperwork he would have to plough through but even that proved too time consuming, so he went to the book-case on the wall to his left and took out the first file. It was filled with statements from large numbers of men who had been interviewed by police in connection with the disappear-ance of one or other of the children. They had been spoken to during a sweep that took in every man who lived in the village the child in question had disappeared from. It included huge numbers of adult males aged between eighteen and seventy-five. They had a wide variety of occupations, from school teacher to lorry driver, sales rep and doctor. All gave an account of their whereabouts on the day when the child had gone missing. Some could corroborate this, but many could not, particularly those who worked alone or on the road. It was such a broad sweep, Bradshaw got the impression it had been undertaken in desperation. Officers had been hoping that someone would let something slip, but they had been unlucky. He knew from the dates of this first swathe of interviews that it would be years before the breakthrough, when Adrian Wick-low was pulled over with a girl in his car.

Bradshaw replaced the file and took out another. Its con-tents covered the murder of Tim Collings, a ten-year-old boy who had no connection to Susan Verity. He put that file back too then took out another, then another. An hour and a half later, Bradshaw had a large pile of musty files on the table in front of him, all of which yielded some information but not the overview he was looking for. He needed someone to brief him on the important stuff, rather than sit here for days, going through hundreds of dead-end leads. Bradshaw belatedly realized this was the wrong place to start. 'Sod it,' he said, and left the room then the building.

Moments later, he was in his car, on his way to see a man who might be able to tell him everything he needed to know about Wicklow without having to read thousands of pages of statements. Of course, Barry Meade might not be too keen to cooperate, since Adrian Wicklow had almost killed him.

'Have you got questions?' Billy asked. 'You know, written down and that?'

Billy's eyes were darting around the studio, taking in the bustle as last-minute preparations for his interview were completed. The lighting technician swore at one of the tripods when it stuck and refused to go higher; a young lass with a clipboard marched up to Amanda and said something to her in a low voice, but Billy didn't hear it because he was too busy gazing at her legs: they were long and tanned and barely covered by a very short skirt.

'I don't need to write them down,' she told him.

'It's just I prefer it if I can see the questions in advance, so I don't get confused or take too long to prepare an answer.'

'Don't worry about that. You'll be fine. There's no need to see the questions in advance.' She was smiling at him, but only with her mouth, not her eyes; they remained business-like.

'I suppose it's okay,' he conceded, though he wished he hadn't had four pints before the interview. He wasn't drunk, of course, it was just that the studio was really hot with all of these lights and it made him feel a little woozy. 'I'll get my money as soon as this is over, right?' He'd once had to wait a whole month to get paid by a magazine; there'd been some mix-up because they had been expecting him to send an invoice, which was something he had never had to do before. In the end, he had to phone them up from a phonebox and get in a right radge with the girl from accounts until she agreed to generate him a manual cheque, which was a pain too, as all he ever wanted was cash. You can't spend a cheque in a pub, and his local certainly wouldn't cash it for him.

'You'll definitely get your fee, Billy,' said Amanda, glancing at the cameraman, who was signalling to her. 'Afterwards. We're about to go on soon, so I'll introduce you in a moment, then just follow my lead, okay? Try and relax. Treat this like a conversation between you and me; don't think about the viewers. It's going to be absolutely fine, you've nothing to hide.'

'No,' he said quickly. 'Of course I haven't; nothing at all.'

'Well, then.'

'Okay,' he said. 'Righto. I suppose you can always edit it out if I make a mistake or summat.'

Her eyes widened. 'Oh, no. We can't edit it. This is going out live.'

'Live?' His first reaction was that she must have made a mistake. 'You said it was an evening show.'

'It is, but we're going live for the lunchtime news then we'll air an edited version this evening.'

'You never said it was live!' Billy was panicking now. 'I've never done live –' But Amanda silenced him with a raised hand and looked away from him so she could watch the man standing next to the camera.

'Ready . . . and . . . five, four, three . . .' said the producer.

Billy watched in terror as Amanda spoke into the camera with the practised ease of a professional. With a shock, he realized that, at that moment, she was communicating to thousands of people and was about to start questioning him live in front

31

of them. His entire mind seemed to empty. It was all he could do just to sit there and stare at her as she told the world who he was and why he was here today. He felt as if he were zoning in and out of the room, picking up odd words and phrases like 'twentieth anniversary' and 'tragic disappearance', but the rest of what she was saying seemed to be going straight over his head.

This wasn't fair. He'd had no time to prepare. They'd tricked him. Billy felt frightened and confused. He couldn't cope with this.

He was going to rip off the microphone and run from the studio.

But then he wouldn't be paid and he really wanted that money.

Then, all too abruptly, she had finished her introduction. She turned away from the camera so she could face him and he froze in terror.

'Now then, Billy, in your own time and using your own words, tell us what happened that day . . .'

6

They had pop and crisps and a bag full of kets between them: midget gems, rhubarb and custards, cola bottles; and Billy had stolen some chewy toffees from his mum called 'chocolatey Claires'. They tasted good but stuck their teeth together when they chewed them. Kevin's nana had offered to make the three of them sandwiches, ham ones or jam ones, and wrap them up in brown paper, but they had said, 'Nah,' because sandwiches were boring. They even got the old lady to take a photo of them before they left, because they were explorers and the moment had to be captured.

The thick glass pop bottle was heavy and hung low in the carrier bag so they took turns carrying it then bickered about how long each of them had to spend holding on to it, until someone had a good idea. They took it out, unscrewed the cap and drank the fizzy orange pop as they walked, making sure they didn't wipe the top of the bottle with their hands, because only softies did that and they were already blood brothers. They didn't believe in germs anyway. The pop was meant to last all day but the heat was intense, baking the three boys, so the bottle was empty well before they reached their destination.

The den.

The den is a labour of love. It is the product of hours spent digging out soil from an exposed ridge until it forms a back wall then adding discarded materials that have been foraged from all over the village, to form a structure that resembles a

33

ramshackle shed. The den is a thing of lopsided beauty which has a sheet of corrugated iron for its roof, making it rainproof. This is precariously balanced on walls made up of two sides of the curved ridge plus a couple of heavy wooden pallets which have been leant against a thick clump of gorse, so they wobble alarmingly at times. The corrugated-iron sheet is kept in place above their heads with a tarpaulin, its corners weighted down with half-broken house bricks. The front of the structure is entirely open but that makes it easier to crawl in. Never has a sturdier construction been completed in these parts.

Normally, a den like this one would be long in the making but wouldn't last a week before it was discovered by other kids, who'd play in it for a while then quickly turn destructive through boredom and trash it. The boys would return one day to find their handiwork destroyed, their sacred den violated, and they would be in no mood to rebuild it. This den was different because Danny had a brilliant idea. They had built it far away from their usual spots and camouflaged it well, so it would never be seen by a casual passer-by. 'Not even by a real soldier or big-game hunter,' said Danny. They'd built this den behind a tree line to one side of fields at the very end of their known universe.

Danny's plan was not without its flaws, however; the length of time it took them to walk out there, across numerous fields, being chief among them. Foraging was harder too and it was lucky that the site they had eventually chosen was near a field that had been used by 'a bunch of gyppos', as Danny called them, who were on their way to some horse fair in a place called Appleby. The wreckage of this site yielded the twin treasures of the pallets and the corrugated iron. Smaller items had come from the village, but it was still tough going in the scorching heat. No one could remember a summer like this one, particularly in the north-east of England. It hadn't rained for weeks and the ground they walked on was bone dry and rippled with cracks, like there'd been an earthquake.

Items were chosen for their portability: an enamel mug, some toy soldiers donated by Billy, an ancient football with a puncture that made it flat and a grot mag with nudey pictures of hairy women stolen from Kevin's older brother. He wouldn't miss it, as he was away in Northern Ireland with the army. They tried rolling an old car tyre with no tread all the way down there to make a swing but it was too heavy and they gave up after no more than a few yards.

Going to the end of the universe like this was a scary thing and not to be undertaken lightly. They were several miles from adult supervision, which was gloriously liberating but a bit frightening. They had to cross the churchyard to get into the first field they needed to traverse and they knew it was home to the ghost of the grey lady, whose unfortunate spirit haunted the land around these parts. She came back to the churchyard to rest during the day, so they always ran through the graves in case she heard their footsteps and reached up through the soil to grab them by the ankles and pull them down to her.

Once in the cornfield, they kept on running, being extra vigilant in case the farmer spotted them. He was a vicious old man of at least forty who didn't like the corn in his field being trampled. They always left a new trail as they panted their way through it, crushing the corn stalks underfoot. They never stopped running til they had climbed over the squat, wobbly wooden fence at the far end, because everyone knew the farmer was mad and owned a shotgun. He'd killed loads of trespassers, Kevin had heard, so they always pounded through the corn with raw terror in their hearts.

Beyond the graveyard and the cornfield lay an uncharted world of fields, then rutted tracks with ancient footpaths which ran through the woods and alongside brooks; tributaries of the

River Tees. This uninterrupted countryside went on for several miles, eventually ending at a high wire fence that bordered the abandoned quarry.

The three boys had to look out for children from neighbouring villages, of course, who would surely beat them up for trespassing on the supposedly neutral territory that lay between villages but which had been argued over for years. The older kids carried air rifles and regularly took pot shots at one another from different sides of the railway tracks that marked one of the borders between these territories.

Getting to the den was an adventure in itself, but once they got there, it became their haven, a place far away from the irritations of grown-ups, school or girls, and they could easily lose a whole day playing there. Kevin, Danny and Billy couldn't have been happier. Six seemingly endless weeks of the summer holidays stretched ahead of them and all the adults were saying it was hotter here than in France right now; 'Hotter than the Sahara Desert, prob'ly,' said Kevin. The three boys a shared feeling of joyfulness and endless possibilities.

That was before it all went bad.

That was before Susan Verity.

7

Helen couldn't convince Tom to call DCI Kane but she managed to persuade him to at least look at the case. He would only do this over a beer. They spent a while scrutinizing every newspaper in the hotel lounge. There was plenty about Susan Verity and Adrian Wicklow. Journalists seemed to love this story.

'Do you really think they beat a confession out of him?' asked Helen.

'The police? Maybe. This was back in the eighties, when they were more brutal.'

'You don't sound too concerned.'

'I'm not,' he said, and when he realized she was shocked, added, 'Helen, he is a child murderer. Who cares if they rapped him in the shins with an iron bar or threw him down some stairs?'

'I care,' she said. 'It's illegal.' When he made a scoffing sound, she continued: 'And he might have confessed to a crime he didn't commit, meaning the real murderer is still out there.'

'I suppose,' he said. 'I guess I'm just an old cynic.'

'You've been a crime reporter for too long,' she mock-scolded him. 'Nothing shocks you any more.'

He jokingly went along with that. 'I need a hobby.'

'You need a woman in your life,' Helen told him.

'I've got one.' He grinned.

'Other than me; more than just a colleague or a lodger.'

'You're much more than that,' he explained. 'We argue, we never have sex. It's almost as if we're married.'

'Do you never stop joking around?'

'Who says I'm joking?'

'I just think you need someone outside of this business to –'

'Complete me?' He placed his hands together and brought them to his heart.

'Make you happier.'

'I *am* happy . . . mostly. Do you ever hear the sound of me sobbing through the bedroom wall at night?'

'I don't hear the sound of anything through your bedroom wall at night, and that's my point.'

'Ouch.'

'Sorry. I just think maybe we've become a bit insular since we broke those stories. We spend nearly all our time together and maybe that's not healthy.'

He noticed she had a habit of saying vague things like 'those stories' instead of mentioning the names involved, as if recalling Sandra Jarvis, Callie or the burned girl was too painful – or maybe she just didn't want to think about Graham.

'When did you last take a holiday? You really *should* take a holiday, you know. I can manage on my own for a week.'

'What about you?' he asked.

'What *about* me? We aren't talking about me.'

'We are now. You don't see that much of lover-boy these days.'

'His name is Peter.'

'You don't see much of Peter these days.'

'I do,' she protested. 'As much as I *can* see him, when he lives more than two hundred miles away and is just as busy as we are.'

'Running his old man's carpet business?'

'They're opening a new store.'

'Who knew there was so much demand for shag pile? How many weeks has it been?'

'Since what?' she asked.

'Since you've seen him.'

'Three.'

He shook his head. 'Three weeks ago, we had that thing with the student drug dealer.'

Helen was still fresh-faced and youthful in appearance, so she had been the one to dress younger than she was to look like a student and go along to a party. They'd received an anonymous report that a posh bloke from Durham University had been dealing heroin and coke to his fellow students, endangering the lives of the sons and daughters of several notable people, including two well-known politicians. At the party, the only drug Helen saw all night was a little bit of weed, so they'd put it down to a false and very possibly malicious tip-off. There was no story there; just some rich kids getting off their faces on booze and a bit of dope.

'Four weeks then,' she corrected herself; or was it five? God, had they really gone that long without seeing each other?

The hotel lounge bar was quiet. Most people would still be at work now, but, a few hours on, the streets of Durham would be full of townies, students and out-of-towners all looking for a lively night out. When Tom had almost finished his second drink, he declared his intention to 'get mortal', but Helen was less keen. 'It's not worth it,' she said. 'I hate having hangovers.'

'Well, if you were to get drunk more often, you'd get used to it and you wouldn't have such monumental ones.'

'Oh my God,' said Helen, and Tom frowned at her.

'No, it's true.'

'Not the hangovers,' she hissed.

'What then?'

'Don't look now.' She leaned forward conspiratorially.

'Why do people always say that when it's obviously going to make the other person want to look?' he asked her. 'And how can I know what you're referring to if I don't?'

'All right.' She sighed. 'It's just a figure of speech. If you want to look, then turn your head subtly towards the far window.'

39

Tom twisted his head to allow himself the merest glimpse then turned back to her. 'The girl?'

'The very attractive girl,' she told him.

'In the corner?'

'With the book,' she said significantly.

'What book?'

'Look again,' she ordered.

Tom turned more slowly this time and took a long look at the oblivious but undeniably attractive girl in the far corner of the hotel lobby, then he noticed the book she was reading intently. 'Oh,' he said.

'*Your* book,' she informed him needlessly.

He turned back to Helen. 'Well, that's nice. It's the first time I've seen someone actually reading a copy. Maybe this book will do better than the last one.' Tom's first book, about the Sean Donnellan case, had disappeared virtually without trace, so he had been surprised to be approached by a different publisher to write a new one about the disappearance of Sandra Jarvis and the burned girl.

'I like your writing,' the publisher had explained, 'and I think this story has greater commercial appeal. It's a modern true-crime book, so I think more people will be interested in the subject matter.' He meant that the story involved politics, corruption, gangsters, murder and mutilation, along with some awful crimes of a sexual nature. In short, more people would like it.

'Well, go on then,' Helen urged.

'Go on what?'

'She's reading your book.' She spoke as if it were obvious. 'That's your *in*. Go and say something.'

'Don't be daft,' he said. 'Say what exactly?'

'Something like, "Excuse me, but I couldn't help noticing you were reading my book."'

'Give over,' he countered. 'And?'

'Then she'll say something like "Oh my God! You wrote this?"' Helen shrugged helplessly. 'I don't know . . . that ought to be enough to strike up a conversation, surely?'

'Well, yes, but to what end?'

'To what end? Have you been working too hard? Is this the famous Tom Carney? She's beautiful, or haven't you noticed?'

'Hang on,' he said dryly, and he turned to look again at the girl, who was still reading intently. 'Yep, she's very beautiful,' he agreed. 'But I can't just go over there and talk to her like that.'

'I bet you do that sort of thing all the time.'

I used to, he thought.

'It's just a bit . . . flash, that's all.'

'So it's okay to chat a girl up for no reason but when you clearly have something in common –'

'An interest in crime? How romantic –'

'Your book,' she said. 'You wrote it; she is reading it. You'd be the first to admit you're not a famous name, so what are the odds? This is fate. It was meant to be. Now, go on over. I'll be fine.'

'No,' he said firmly.

Helen sighed again. What was it with this north-east thing of not wanting to seem too big for your boots? 'Then I'll go.'

'You will not . . .' but she was already up out of her chair. 'Are you drunk? . . . Helen?' he hissed, but it was too late; she was gone. He experienced an unfamiliar flush of embarrassment as he waited for her to cross the room. Maybe this was a wind-up. Perhaps she was just going to the bar or the loo.

'Excuse me.' He could hear Helen's voice now. It wasn't a wind-up. 'I couldn't help noticing that you're reading my friend's book.'

'Oh Christ,' he whispered to himself, then brought his hand to his forehead and covered his eyes.

8

'Two heart attacks,' muttered Barry Meade, once the introductions were over. 'They reckon three strikes and you're out.' He called that last bit over his shoulder by way of explanation for the slow progress he was making as Bradshaw followed him into the little bungalow where he lived, on his own these days. 'I've had to give up the fags,' the retired detective said. 'God, I miss them.' He showed splayed fingers to Bradshaw. 'Never know what to do with my hands. I'm not supposed to have a drink either,' he added, and there was something about the way he said 'supposed'. Bradshaw reasoned that abstaining from drink on top of giving up cigarettes was a bridge too far for the former detective inspector. The older man confirmed this when he added, 'But I'll make an exception, since I have company.'

'Don't go to any trouble on my account,' Bradshaw said. In truth, he didn't really want a drink, but Meade was so old school he just assumed the younger man would join him in a whisky if they were going to talk over an old case.

Bradshaw noticed how badly Meade's hand shook as he poured scotch for them both. He shuffled into the kitchen and re-emerged with a small milk jug into which he had poured a little water. He set this down on the table between them but did not add any to his own drink. 'Well, sit down, lad. We don't stand on ceremony here,' he said, and lowered himself carefully into an armchair while Bradshaw took the seat opposite. Bradshaw poured a generous measure of the water into his scotch and they raised a glass to one another and sipped.

'So you've news of Adrian Wicklow?' asked Meade. Bradshaw

had been deliberately vague on the phone about the reason for his visit. 'I suppose it's too much to hope that he's dead. I still want to outlive the bastard and one day raise a glass to his demise, but that's looking like a forlorn hope.'

'Don't be so sure about that.' Bradshaw told him about Wicklow's terminal illness.

The old detective snorted. 'He's having them on. Probably nothing wrong with him at all. You can't believe a word that comes out of that man's mouth, believe me.'

Bradshaw was surprised that Meade could be so dismissive of this news. Did he really believe that Wicklow was capable of conning the prison doctors into believing he had a fatal disease? 'It's not just Wicklow's word,' he said. 'They've done tests; it's lung cancer, he's riddled with it. It's inoperable and terminal. He has months, possibly only weeks, left.'

The older man considered this for a moment, frowning suspiciously at Bradshaw as if he was in on Wicklow's latest trick. Then he brightened. 'Bugger me,' he said. 'Cigarettes?'

'Presumably.'

'Ha!' and he laughed at this. 'Who said they weren't good for you? That's the best news I've had in years. You can come again, son. You've brightened my day and no mistake. To think of all the people who wanted to get their hands on that evil bastard and do him in, then he gets finished off by cigarettes. They've only gone and done the job for us. Bloody marvellous!' He raised his glass to Bradshaw and drained it, as if in toast to cigarettes. 'I hope you'll come back here and tell me when he's finally gone. Do you know what I'm going to do when I get that news?'

'No.'

He smiled. 'I'll dance the soft-shoe shuffle on my own doorstep and I won't care who sees me.'

Bradshaw said nothing. Meade noticed this and frowned once more. 'Please tell me that's the only reason you're here;

43

a courtesy call to let me know he's a dead man, so I can enjoy my remaining days.'

'Not quite.'

'Oh no,' said Meade, shaking his head emphatically. 'No, no, no. I don't care who sent you, the answer is no.'

'Just hear me out, sir, please.'

But the retired policeman had already made up his mind. He was convinced he knew why Bradshaw was there and he was having none of it. 'When that evil bastard finally dies, I'll read all about it in the papers, but I want nothing more to do with him. I won't write to him, talk to his solicitor or speak to the bloody press about him, and I will not' – he took a rasping breath then repeated for emphasis – '*will not* go and see him. I don't care if you've been sent here by the chief constable, the Home Secretary or God Almighty Himself, I won't do it. Got that?'

He pointed at Bradshaw. 'You can finish your drink,' Meade told him, his voice trembling with suppressed anger, 'then sling your hook and don't ever come back.'

Billy got his money. In cash, just the way he liked it. It was in a little brown envelope in his inside jacket pocket and he could feel its weight pressing against his chest. He took it out now and lifted the flap of the envelope. A sizable pile of small-denomination notes like he'd asked for. The woman who had sorted out his fee was going to give him fifty-pound notes – as if anyone would change those in the village; not bloody likely – and he'd insisted on fivers or tenners. She wasn't very impressed by that but he got what he wanted – eventually.

But Billy wasn't happy. The interview had gone on a while longer than he was expecting, considering it was for the lunch-time news, where you usually barely had time to understand a story before they were on to the next one. They explained afterwards that it was a very slow news day and not much else was going on, so they'd decided to 'major' on the reopening of the case and the recent criticism of the local police force.

Now he was in the back of a car the producer had organized to take him home from the studio in Newcastle and, normally, that would have been a right treat. Billy had assumed he would have to wait for a bus in Worswick Street station, but here he was, being driven by a proper driver who worked for the TV production company, not just any old cab whistled up on the street outside their offices.

But still Billy wasn't happy, and he wasn't really sure why. Now that he thought about it, he couldn't really remember the questions that reporter had asked him during the live interview, nor the answers he had struggled to provide. A combination of the heat in the studio and the beer in his system had made him feel light-headed and he had lacked the concentration he normally brought to these things. You couldn't be too careful where the press was concerned. They were always trying to catch you out and make you look guilty, even when it really wasn't your fault.

None of it.

It was being live that did it. He had quite literally forgotten to breathe at one point and his words came out too fast; in a rush, as if they were trying to catch up with each other and the air he expelled along with them. He spent the last few minutes of the interview feeling like he was bursting for the loo and wishing he'd gone for a slash before they'd started.

He just hoped he hadn't sounded too terrible but anyway, so what? He'd been paid, and that was that. They couldn't have their money back now. It was too late.

Still, Billy couldn't shake the feeling that something had gone badly wrong.

The producers hadn't said anything. They'd seemed happy enough with his contribution, but Billy had a feeling deep inside him that he couldn't quite explain or even properly understand. Billy didn't know the word 'foreboding' but that was exactly what he had a sense of right now.

And all because of Susan.

It was nearly always all because of Susan.

'Tom!' called Helen, and he winced. 'Tom!' Louder this time, at a volume he could no longer ignore. 'There's someone here who would love to meet you.'

Tom planted a rictus grin on his face to mask his true feelings then turned to face them, silently resolving to kill Helen once they were alone again. He was taken aback by the smiling face of the beautiful young woman sitting opposite her. He hadn't had a proper look at her to begin with but, now he could see her clearly, his mood began to soften. Maybe it was the way that little black dress seemed to cling to her. Perhaps there was no real harm in saying hello. He walked over.

'I can't believe it,' said the young woman. 'I am so engrossed in your book. It's brilliant.'

'Thanks,' he said, then added truthfully, 'You're the first person I've ever seen reading it.'

'It's had great reviews,' said Helen encouragingly, 'and Tom's been profiled in a national newspaper as a rising star of investigative journalism.'

'Really?' The woman sounded very impressed.

'Well, it *was* August,' said Tom, and because she looked as if she didn't understand, added, 'No news in August. Even terrorists are on holiday.' When he realized she might not be used to his brand of gallows humour, he went on: 'All I'm saying is, it must have been a slow day for news.'

'As you can see, Tom finds it hard to accept his own success.'

'And you too,' prompted the woman. 'Assuming you're Helen?'

'That's me,' she admitted.

'You're in his book as well.'

'She's the brains behind the outfit,' said Tom. 'I just make the tea and do most of the driving.'

Helen screwed up her face at him for not making enough of an effort. The woman didn't notice. She was smiling at Tom. It was a warm, bright smile and it was beginning to win him over. That, and the undeniable fact that she was a striking-looking woman, with auburn hair down to her shoulders and piercing green eyes that seemed to lock on to his.

'Sorry,' he said. 'I didn't ask your name.'

'Lena.' She must have realized that her London accent sounded out of place in a Durham hotel, so she added, 'I'm up here for family reasons.'

It was a pretty vague explanation, but it was none of Tom's business why she was in the north-east. Strangers didn't have to reveal their secrets.

'It's my round,' Helen announced enthusiastically. 'Can I get you one, Lena?'

'That's very kind of you, but I don't want to intrude if you guys are working.'

'There'll be no more work today,' Tom told her.

'Well, okay, if you're sure you don't mind.'

'I insist,' Helen told her, and asked Lena what she'd like. 'Sit down, Tom, and tell Lena all about writing the book.'

Tom narrowed his eyes at Helen to show his displeasure, but he had to admit the prospect of another pint and some female company as easy on the eye as this one would deaden the pain of a very bad week. He sat down across from Lena.

While Helen was gone, she asked him how he had come to be involved in the Sandra Jarvis case and just how he could even go about solving something that complicated. She seemed so interested in his answers he felt completely disarmed by her.

'My job is pretty dull,' she explained. 'I'm an investment

47

analyst. It's well paid but nowhere near as interesting as your line of work.'

'Don't knock well paid,' he said ruefully. 'There's a lot to be said for it.'

Helen returned then, carrying the drinks.

'Why are there only two?' asked Tom.

'Because I have to go,' she said, hoping he wouldn't press her.

'Why do you have to go?'

'I've got that thing.'

'What thing?'

'That thing I told you about,' she said, and he frowned at her. She turned to Lena, smiled and said, 'Lovely to meet you, Lena. I'm sorry I have to dash, but I'll leave you two to get acquainted.' Then she spoke to Tom again, 'I'll see you later, but I'm likely to be a while.'

'Doing that thing?'

She ignored this but put a supportive hand on his shoulder as she walked past him on her way out of the hotel.

Tom watched her go then looked at Lena. Her eyes widened.

'I am so sorry,' he said, but Lena just laughed, causing him to laugh too.

'Is she always so –?'

'Mad? No, not usually.'

'I was going to say supportive. She's like . . . what do guys call it? . . . your wing-man?'

'Helen is lovely, but she thinks I need a woman in my life.' He added quickly, 'But not just any woman, so you should take it as a compliment. Please just enjoy your drink then feel free to leave. I won't tell her.'

Lena leaned forward to pick up her glass. Her eyes left Tom's for a moment and instead she looked into her drink. 'Who said I wanted to leave?'

9

It took Bradshaw a while to calm Barry Meade down.

'I am not going anywhere near Adrian Wicklow,' he told the detective sergeant, 'and neither you nor piggin' DCI Kane can make me. That . . . *man* . . . cost me my health, my marriage and damn near took what was left of my sanity . . . so the answer is no, and it will always be no!'

Bradshaw shook his head. 'You've got this all wrong. You don't understand.'

'I bloody do. Kane sent you here to get me to visit Wicklow again and I won't effing-well do it!'

'No one wants you to see Wicklow.'

Meade looked exasperated now. 'What?' he faltered. 'Then what do you want?'

'I just need your help. I want to hear your side of it. Of all the people involved in this case, living or dead, you are the one who knows the most about it. That's what they told me.'

'It's what *Kane* told you. Your DCI was a wet-behind-the-ears detective constable when I knew him. They say cream rises to the top' – he snorted – 'but shit floats.' And he stared hard at Bradshaw to see if he was going to challenge his opinion of Kane. Bradshaw said nothing. That seemed to calm Meade.

'Is this for him or for you?' he asked.

'It's for me, sir.'

'You seem like a decent lad,' Meade told him. 'Respectful.' He nodded his head slowly. 'But do yourself a favour and don't get involved.'

'I've been ordered to become involved, which is why I need

you to give me some inside information, basically, anything you can tell me about Wicklow: what he did, what he didn't do but claims he did, everything . . .' he said. 'Anything.' Bradshaw shrugged helplessly. 'Please.'

'Why?' demanded the older man.

'Because they want *me* to go and see him.'

'Oh, Jesus Christ,' said Meade, in a tone that did nothing to calm Ian Bradshaw. 'Don't do it,' he urged. 'Tell them no. Tell them to shove it. It might set your career back a bit but, believe me, that's nothing compared to . . .' And he left the alternatives unsaid.

'Is he really that bad?'

Meade took a deep breath, 'I have met a lot of criminals in my time. Some of them were okay, really. Maybe they had a bad start to their lives that got them going down the wrong path early on. Others were naturally mean. They liked to do bad things and enjoyed hurting people, but there was still a bit of human in there somewhere, deep down, if you looked for it hard enough. I've interviewed my fair share of murderers an' all. Most people kill because they lose control and lash out at someone they know. The vast majority don't do it twice. You can release them back into society after their sentence on the fair assumption that they are never going to hurt anyone again. Some people do kill more than once, but it is rare. Sometimes it's gangster stuff, one crew eliminating another one. If it's killing for kicks, you can get a quack in who'll tell you the bloke is a paranoid schizophrenic, or he hates women for some reason, or he has warped sexual needs so he rapes then kills to avoid leaving a witness behind. There's usually a reason – an awful one, more than likely, but a reason.' Then he paused. 'No one has ever discovered why Adrian Wicklow does what he does. He has been interviewed by dozens of people: police officers, lawyers, doctors, psychiatrists – you name it. They have all sat down with him at one time or another. Know what they found? Nowt. He is a completely closed book. He has not let a single thing slip in all of that time. One day he will say one thing and the next something completely contradictory. In fifteen years, he has run everybody witless.'

'Why do *you* think he did it?'

'I haven't the faintest clue,' said Meade. 'No, really, I haven't. It has kept me up at night and occupied many of my waking hours, but I cannot get my head round him, except maybe . . .'

'What?'

'. . . he might just be a one-off.'

'In what way?'

'You really want to know what I think?'

'Yes,' urged Bradshaw. 'Please. Tell me.'

'It stays between us, right?'

'I swear.'

'All right,' said Meade, and his whole body straightened as he continued: 'But you won't like it.'

'Try me.'

'I am not a religious man,' said Meade, 'but there are some mysteries that are hard to explain rationally. I think Adrian Wicklow might just be the nearest thing there is in this world to pure, undiluted evil.'

Billy ordered his pint, and the landlord of his local looked at him as if he had just crawled out of the cheese but served him anyway, without a word. Billy took his beer to the corner of the room. Was it his imagination or were there eyes on him as he sat down? No one said anything, but maybe that was the point. Perhaps he *had* imagined it, but he felt as if the room had gone quiet when he walked in, and that strange sense came over him again; a feeling like he'd messed up, let something slip, said something he shouldn't . . . but he couldn't quite put his finger on what it was.

Flush with the television money, he'd planned to pass the afternoon here but now he was having second thoughts. The atmosphere wasn't exactly hostile but it did feel frosty. He'd experienced this before when he'd talked to the press. Danny had warned him. 'What do you expect? People get narked when you discuss Susan's disappearance. It's a very sensitive subject.'

That was true enough, but people also knew that Billy didn't have a job and couldn't hold one down. He was just not built for work and had a doctor's note to prove it. The GP called it acute anxiety but Billy told people it was on account of his nerves and left it at that. For this reason, he reckoned most people understood why he talked to the newspapers. It was the only money he could get, apart from the social and the few quid he pinched off his mother to fund his drinking.

Today, though, it was as if the whole village had a cob-on with him. Well, then, Billy knew when he wasn't wanted. He would sup up and catch a bus to one of the other villages, maybe even go to Darlington. It had been ages since he'd been out in Darlow, and that hundred and fifty quid was burning a hole in his pocket.

It hadn't taken Helen long to find what she was looking for. There wasn't just one book about Adrian Wicklow, there were several. He was the pin-up boy of true crime, with writers queueing up to tell his story. Helen leafed through four books before selecting one. The thickest was an academic study of the man and his murders, which might have helped a student of criminology, but she wanted something less wordy that would give her the bare facts about the man and everything he had done.

The second title was a much slimmer volume, penned by a reporter from the cheapest and most sensational tabloid in the country. The title was in lurid red letters that dripped like blood and there was a photograph on the cover that had been snatched by paparazzi through the window of a police van as Wicklow was taken into court. The killer was actually grinning in the photograph. The book was entitled 'The Mickle Fell Murderer', as if this was a nickname everyone knew Wicklow by instead of just one of the locations where the body of a child he had murdered was found. Helen didn't even bother to open it and examine its contents.

She looked more closely at the next two books and settled on one written by a broadsheet journalist who had reported on the earliest child murders then attended every day of Wicklow's trial to write about it for his newspaper. That was more like it.

Helen went home, curled up on the couch and began to read. She was still reading an hour later when the phone rang.

Peter was not in a good mood. He wasn't in a bad mood either, but he did sound mightily stressed when he called her.

'Your folks *are* coming, right?' he asked, once the initial hellos were out of the way.

'What?' She must have sounded preoccupied because he sighed then.

'Your parents,' he said, slowly and deliberately, 'are they coming to my mum and dad's twenty-fifth wedding anniversary party or not?'

'They say they are,' she told him.

'They *say* they are,' he queried, 'but are they *definitely* coming?'

She wanted to say no, because she had barely spoken to her mother lately and couldn't understand why this silver-wedding party was such a big deal, but she supposed everyone had to play happy families from time to time. Her parents had accepted the invitation more enthusiastically than she had, to be honest.

'They are definitely coming.' And she prayed they were.

'Good,' he said, 'and you are, of course?' When Helen didn't immediately answer him, he blurted, '*Please* tell me you're coming.'

'Of course I'm coming. I've already said I'm coming.'

'So there's not going to be any last-minute crisis that prevents it?'

Helen sighed again. 'Well, I can't tell that, can I? If there's a hurricane, or I'm run over by a van or something . . . I can't predict – what do the insurance companies call it? An act of God.'

'I meant work-related things. You know what I mean.'

She did know what he meant. More than a couple of times in the past year she had been forced to postpone visits to see him because she was working on a story that couldn't wait. These admissions had provoked arguments, followed by stony silences, and Helen was careful never to mention Tom, because she was under the distinct impression that her long-term boyfriend loathed her journalistic partner, even more so since she had 'shacked up with him', as Peter described it. Helen had assured Peter that their living arrangements made sense, because they were inexpensive and efficient. 'You do have your own bedroom?' he'd asked then.

'Of course!' she'd told him, and immediately felt a pang of guilt because, when she had first stayed with Tom, her life had been in danger and there was only one bed in his home. He had taken the couch, but the house had no heating at the time so, rather than let him freeze, she had invited him to share the double bed with her, which they had done for several nights, until a new bed was delivered and a spare room prepared for her. Nothing had happened but she still felt guilty that she hadn't told Peter about it. She had lied and said she had stayed with a female colleague from the newspaper.

She wasn't lying these days, but she was guilty perhaps of lying by omission, which was almost as bad. She hadn't told Peter that the main reason she lived in Tom's house was that she felt safe there.

'I'll be there,' she assured him.

'Good.' His tone softened. 'It's just I want everything to be perfect for them both – twenty-five years, and all that. So have you bought your train ticket?'

'Yes,' she said, without hesitation.

'Good, excellent, nice one.' He seemed to calm down then.

The rest of their conversation passed without incident and there were no further stress points. After Helen had said her goodbyes and hung up, she went straight to her notebook and turned to the back, where she kept a daily to-do list. She took a pen and wrote 'Buy Train Ticket' in big letters at the top.

'It was a terrible time,' Meade told him. 'Kids were disappearing. It seemed like every other month another one just went' – he clicked his fingers to illustrate the suddenness of it – 'gone; into thin air.'

'How wide an area?' asked Bradshaw.

'All over County Durham and into Northumbria, but mostly it was small towns and villages round these parts. Parents were terrified, understandably, and every time we lost another little boy or girl the tabloids piled the pressure on us.'

'You were a DI at the time? How come they put you in charge? Wouldn't it usually be a DCI or even a detective superintendent?'

'No one wanted to do it. There, I'm being honest. I don't think they gave it to me because they considered I was the best officer on the force. I think they realized we could be on a sticky wicket, and no one wanted the level of abuse I got from the gutter press. You know, they took to following me around off duty. If I went for a few pints, they made it sound like I was an alkie. They even stopped my wife in the street to ask her about me – what kind of man I was, whether I was a good husband and father – as if any of that had any bearing on my ability to catch the evil man who snatched those kids.'

'But you didn't catch him,' said Bradshaw. 'Not at first.'

'No, we didn't,' Meade admitted. 'We kept drawing a blank, time after time. We hauled in every paedo and nut-job in the county, and beyond, but one by one we ruled them out. With every new disappearance, we were able to say it can't have been *him*, or *he* couldn't have been there because he had an alibi.'

'Including Wicklow?'

'Wicklow had an alibi for Susan Verity all right; someone he described as a friend. Years later, we arrested him, too, for interfering with kids. At the time, he seemed like a legitimate person, and so did Wicklow. Turned out they were two evil bastards who met somehow and covered for each other. We soon ran out of obvious suspects. Trouble was, there was no real evidence. Most of the time, when a kid went missing, the body was never found, at least not at first, and when we did have a body it didn't yield us much in the way of forensics. We never got any prints, the kids were never messed with, you know' – Bradshaw knew he meant there was nothing sexual in the attacks – 'there was no real pattern or motive, except the children were all aged between seven and ten and lived in small communities. We didn't know if we were dealing with one man, or several, or possibly different groups of men who weren't even linked but took advantage of the confusion of multiple disappearances. At one point, we got paranoid that maybe one or more of the killings were perpetrated by close family members who were using the existence of this serial killer as a smokescreen to get rid of unwanted children. I mean, we had no bloody idea what was going on, so we did the only thing we could do.'

'The broad sweep?'

'Interview everyone, suspect everybody, speak to as many people as we can, throw bodies at it. We were all just praying someone would slip up or they would know something that might lead us in the right direction, but instead –'

'You ended up with too much information. I've seen the files.'

'There might have been gold in there somewhere, but it was buried under a heap of shit. Hundreds of statements, witness reports and uncorroborated alibis, which took up hours and hours of our time and yielded nothing significant. Then the press got hold of some stats.'

'Someone leaked them, you mean?'

'It could only have come from someone on my team.' It looked as if the admission hurt Meade even now. 'It was front-page news: "Bumbling police interview hundreds of innocent men but get nowhere". "Keystone Cops", they called us, as if we couldn't tie our own shoelaces in the morning. They had no idea of the time and dedication that went into trying to find the man who did these terrible things. For more than five years we worked on the suspicious disappearances of seven children that were eventually linked to Wicklow and investigated numerous others that turned out to be runaways or children killed by people who knew them. We had officers who became obsessed with the cases, and I was one of them. I realize that now. People were working all hours, not sleeping or eating properly, drinking too much because of the . . .' He fell silent for a moment while he tried to find the right words. 'Do you know what it's like to deal with parents whose kids have just . . . gone? There's nothing worse than looking a mother in the eye and admitting you have no idea where her child is and that you can't bring them back for her, and every now and again there's another one gone . . . and another . . . and another. We were all very damaged by it, even before the tabloids stuck the knife in.'

'In the end, it was through luck that you caught him.'

'Yeah,' said Meade ruefully, 'it was. There was no great breakthrough. Not me, nor one of my lads, ever had the satisfaction of working it all out.'

'That must have been tough.'

By way of explanation, Meade said, 'You know how they caught the Yorkshire Ripper? Thirteen women he murdered, and that investigation went on for five years too. Hundreds of men interviewed, including Peter Sutcliffe, who was allowed to go free. They only got him because they found him sitting in his car with a prostitute and, when they checked the licence plates, they found out it was a stolen car. He had weapons on him, which he managed to dump while he was taking a leak, but they found them later, and he confessed. Simple as that. No massive breakthrough, no super-sleuthing from a senior detective, just a couple of vigilant coppers in a patrol car doing their duty. It was like that with our case. Adrian Wicklow was stopped in his car because of a faulty tail light. When they pulled him over there was a young lass lying on the floor by the back seat.'

'The one that got away,' recited Bradshaw, because that was how everyone described her.

'And only by the skin of her teeth. She was going to be next, and she would have been too, if it hadn't been for a sharp-eyed bobby who'd been on the force for a matter of weeks. He was out with his sergeant in a patrol car, learning the ropes, when he spotted it. A faulty tail light.' He snorted. 'Hundreds and hundreds of leads, and he was stopped because of a broken bulb and that keen new bobby who thought they should maybe have a word.'

'Wicklow didn't try and drive off or resist arrest?'

Meade shook his head. 'He pulled over, right enough, and got out of his car. The young PC must have shat himself when he saw what was inside it, but he retained the presence of mind to grab Wicklow and get some cuffs on. Apparently, he went like a lamb.'

'I wonder why.'

'I've often wondered that myself. Maybe he thought there was no point. Perhaps he had always expected it to end that way. Maybe he was tired and wanted to be caught. They do sometimes, you know. They want it to be over.' He reflected on this. 'Trouble is, with Wicklow, it's never over.'

'I read somewhere that one of the victim's parents went to see him.'

Meade nodded grimly. 'Angie Ferris wanted to know what had happened to her little girl, Milly. Everyone begged her not to go and see him, but she was a Christian; said she would forgive him if he saw her face to face and told her where she could find her daughter. She wanted a proper burial, see. Nobody wanted that meeting to happen, but she was poorly and the press kept reporting it as her dying wish. Eventually, the authorities, under considerable pressure, relented. It took months of negotiations before he would agree to it. He demanded all sorts of things, a lot of which he got: privileges, books, time alone in the exercise yard, certain foods he wanted . . .' Bradshaw could tell by the look on Meade's face that he strongly disapproved of these concessions. 'Finally, the meeting went ahead, but no details of it were ever reported. The press was informed that the outcome was inconclusive and that the search for young Milly was ongoing.'

'What really happened?'

'Wicklow sat down with Mrs Ferris and heard what she had to say. He listened politely while she told him she knew he couldn't help himself when he killed her daughter. She told him only God could truly judge him, so she wouldn't, and she had forgiven him for killing her child. Mrs Ferris said she knew he had some decency deep within him and begged him to grant a dying woman's wish to find the body of her daughter and bring it home.'

'What did he say?'

'"*I'd love to help you but there's nothing I can do.*"' Meade shook his head. 'When he got up to leave, he had a big smirk on his face, by all accounts. He told them to take him back to his cell,

60

leaving that poor woman . . .' Meade's anger left the sentence incomplete, but he didn't need to say any more.

'He had never intended to help her,' observed Bradshaw.

'No, he hadn't. He enjoys suffering. Seeing it in another person's face sitting opposite him was meat and drink for Wicklow. He'd been looking forward to it for weeks.'

Bradshaw shared Meade's anger and disgust, but he had never been in a room with poor Mrs Ferris, like Meade had. He could only imagine the sense of impotent rage Wicklow's dismissive stunt had caused him.

'What happened with the psychic?' asked Bradshaw. 'That your idea?'

'Jesus Christ,' hissed Meade, irritated by the notion. 'No, it bloody wasn't, but muggins here took the flak for it. If you must know, we had an assistant commissioner back then who was a proper God-botherer. He had all sorts of helpful ideas to solve the case, including prayer.' He shook his head at the folly of this. 'Then he contacted me personally to say he was sending me some help and he would appreciate it if I kept a positive outlook. I said, "Of course, sir," and she turned up.'

'Psychic Sandra?'

'Yep, we used to call her Claire Voyant behind her back. Strangely enough, she never knew about *that*.' He raised his eyebrows at her lack of supernatural perception. 'We wasted a lot of time running around after her and her bloody ESP. She was convinced Susan was speaking to her via her spirit guide, an elderly Victorian lady, no less, and would suddenly announce that voices were guiding her to locations that could be Susan's last resting place. I'm telling you, man, none of us believed in her, except the AC, who we all thought was a bit puddled. We called him Jesus's little sunbeam. Of course, when the press got hold of it, I got all the blame and he kept his head down. Everybody thought it was my idea.'

This clearly still pained Meade, and Bradshaw could sympathize.

'I do have one last thing I would like to ask you,' he said.

'Fire away.'

'Adrian Wicklow confessed to the murder of Susan Verity, and others. He later recanted and claimed to be innocent of all charges.'

'Well, he wanted his day in court, didn't he? He's a show-off and they like an audience. What's the point of being a notorious child killer if no one sees you in the stand?'

'You think that's why he changed his mind?'

'That and his mother. He didn't want to admit he was a murderer to her. Poor woman was blameless, as far as I could see. She brought him up right, made sure he never wanted for anything, that he never went without a meal, and she got him to school on time every morning. Basically, she was a respectable member of the community.'

'What about his father?'

'Died in a car crash when he was young; a formative experience, according to one of the many head shrinks that have hung on Wicklow's every word. You can speculate all you like as to whether that sent him crazy, but there's many folk lose parents and grow up fine. They don't kill kids.'

'How did his mother take his arrest?'

'How do you think she took it? She was devastated and never accepted he was guilty. Always thought it was a big mistake or that we had stitched up her son somehow.'

'How did she explain the girl in his car?'

'He was giving her a lift out of the goodness of his heart,' he said dryly. 'The girl only thought otherwise afterwards because we told her Wicklow was a bad man.' He shook his head at the enormity of Mrs Wicklow's self-delusion. 'In my experience, when it comes to our children, we see what we want to see,' said Meade, 'and Mrs Wicklow did not want to acknowledge that she had given birth to a monster.'

'Once he was convicted, he cooperated,' said Bradshaw. 'At first.'

'Up to a point, yes. He gave us some information and a body, but only one.'

'If he had given you all of them, you would have stopped paying him any attention.'

'Exactly. We should have realized that from the beginning. His only currency was the truth. It was like he was drip-feeding us information one little piece at a time, so we kept coming back to him.'

'Couldn't you play hard ball with him, tell him the game was over and he either fessed up to it all straight away or you wouldn't continue to play?'

'I wanted to do that, but there was no way. You have to understand the scrutiny and the level of pressure on us. It never let up. The newspapers wouldn't let us leave him alone. They'd write articles about him all the time. It was like he was a celebrity or something. It was sickening. Every once in a while, I'd pick up a paper and see some poor bereaved parent staring out of it, clutching a photograph of their lost son or daughter. *I just want my baby back so I can bury her.* Every time that evil bastard remembered something or pretended to, it was national news, often front page, and he enjoyed every minute of it. There was a whole industry around him. The papers paid prison guards for titbits about him: what he ate, what books he read, the fact that he liked to watch *Pebble Mill at One* on the bloody TV, which other notorious prisoners were his best buddies. Most of it was complete bullshit. He wasn't allowed anywhere near another inmate. He wouldn't last two minutes with them.'

'A few years back, he changed his story about Susan Verity?'

'Initially, he confessed to her murder, along with all of the others. He admitted to being in the area and seemed to know her whereabouts on the day, though, to be honest, he could have got that from the local news or the papers. He said he strangled her but couldn't remember where he buried her. Then he changed his story, said it wasn't him, and he was jailed for the other murders instead, and that was that,' said Meade. 'For a couple of years he admitted the ones he'd been found guilty of but denied he'd ever made a proper confession about Susan. He said he only confessed to her killing because we made him say it. He claimed he was tortured' – Meade snorted – 'but everything that man says is a lie. A few years later he admitted he did kill the three other kids he'd always denied murdering, but then he said Susan wasn't one of his victims.'

'Why would he do that?'

'To spite us. He liked the idea of the real killer evading justice. Someone who could kill again and again.'

'You believe him?'

'I didn't believe him then and I don't believe him now.'

'And was he? Tortured, I mean? Before that first confession?'

'What do you think?'

'I don't know. I wasn't there.'

'Been reading the papers, have we?'

'Sorry?' Bradshaw didn't understand.

Meade picked up a copy of that morning's *Sun* and handed it to Bradshaw. It was open at page nine and the headline was 'CHILD-KILLER COPS COULD FACE CHARGES'. Bradshaw read the article while Meade chipped in with his own commentary.

'Lies, all bloody lies.' But there was something in the desperate way Meade was denying it all that did not quite ring true. The truly alarming part for Meade was the mention of criminal negligence on the part of the officers who investigated

Susan Verity's disappearance and the determination of the chief constable to 'get to the bottom of this', according to a police source. 'If it is proven,' the anonymous source was quoted as saying, 'that Adrian Wicklow was coerced into admitting a crime he did not commit, enabling the real perpetrator to walk free, then criminal charges will be brought against any officer who abused their position in this manner.'

They are stitching him up like a kipper, thought Bradshaw, *and Meade knows it*.

'They've been calling up former colleagues,' Meade told him, 'trying to get them to say we tortured Wicklow on my orders.' He snorted again. 'Anyway, I've nothing to hide.' But he looked worried, and well he might. They both knew how hard prison time was for former police officers.

'I guess it must have been tempting, though,' said Bradshaw, 'knowing what he had done and being unable to prove it at that point. If I was in your shoes, I might have arranged for Mr Wicklow to fall down a couple of times or walk into some doors.'

'Would you?' Meade gave Bradshaw a look of disgust. 'Is this how you always extract confessions, Detective Sergeant, by pretending to empathize with your suspects?'

'I'm only saying —'

'I know what you're saying,' interrupted Meade, 'and here's my answer: no comment.' Then he scowled at Bradshaw. 'I think you'll find I have the right to remain silent.'

11

Helen read a hundred pages of the book that evening. She learned all about Wicklow and his victims and pored over the details of his case. She was already aware of the man, but the level of detail was useful and the specifics of Wicklow's deeds truly shocking.

The photographs in the middle of the book showed that this monster had enjoyed a surprisingly normal childhood; the black-and-white images of trips to the seaside, with donkey rides and ice creams on the prom, could have been from her own past or anyone else's. They must have been taken by Wicklow's mother, Helen reasoned, for his father had been killed in a car crash when he was still very small. Wicklow and his mother were close, but not unnaturally so, claimed the author. His mother was a good woman who kept her house clean and neat, worked hard and went to church on Sunday. There were no clues to be found here and no way that anyone, let alone his mother, could have foreseen Wicklow's crimes back then. This only made them even more chilling.

Helen grew tired and was about to stop reading when she reached a new chapter entitled 'The Curse of Susan Verity' and her curiosity got the better of her.

Six children went out to play that day, but only five returned. They were the lucky ones; Susan Verity was not so fortunate. Adrian Wicklow came to Susan's village that morning, intent on murder. He was seeking his next victim and poor Susan was exactly what he was looking for. She was the right age: his previous victims had all been between nine and eleven years old. She was small and slight, which appealed to Wicklow, even though he was an immensely strong man who could have easily overpowered an older child. He liked to stalk his victims, sometimes for hours, but when he finally struck he didn't care for complications. A struggle was distracting and could alert passers-by. Wicklow liked to dominate his chosen targets completely.

An eyewitness saw Wicklow leaving the village that day, heading in the direction of Marsh Farm. Susan was last seen not far from the hedges that marked its boundary. Lilly Bowes, the elderly lady who reported seeing him there, was not called to testify in court and Wicklow was never charged with any crime in connection with Susan. She simply disappeared, and her body has never been found, but it is generally accepted by police that she was one of Adrian Wicklow's unfortunate victims.

What is less widely known, however, is the fate of the surviving children, those 'lucky' ones who returned home that day without their playmate. Each one can tell a story of missed opportunities, ill luck, severe illness or fatal tragedy. Many people from their village, including the children themselves, routinely refer to them as 'cursed', as if the price they were all forced to pay for escaping the clutches of this modern-day bogeyman was to have their own lives ruined in the process.

Helen stopped reading for a moment while she let that sink in. She had been unaware that there had been talk of a curse involving Susan Verity and would have dismissed this out of hand. Helen was a practical and rational person. There were no such things as curses. There was only bad luck. Sometimes it visited a number of people and came in large quantities but that did not make it a curse. She was surprised a journalist of such renown would bother to detail this in his book, but she supposed he was pandering to the fears of his readers.

She managed to read to the end of the chapter but then her eyes began to feel heavy and she closed them for a moment to rest before falling asleep on the sofa with the book still in her hands, waking only when it slipped from her fingers and hit the floor, making her start.

Helen glanced at her watch. It was late, so she went to bed, noting that Tom had still not returned.

'Where to next?' Lena asked.

'Blimey, you're amazing,' he told her. 'We've been drinking for hours, and you still want more?'

'Okay, perhaps we shouldn't drink any more,' she agreed, though she didn't sound any the worse for wear. 'Take me dancing instead, Tom.'

'Dancing?'

'I like to dance.' She showed him some moves right there in the street which involved holding both her arms high above her head and shimmying to imaginary music.

'Bloody hell, girl!'

'What?' she asked, as if she didn't understand the effect these moves were having on him.

'You . . . that dress . . . everything,' he managed.

She moved towards him then and wrapped her arms loosely around his shoulders. Her voice was a parody of pretend-innocence. 'What about . . . me . . . this dress . . . everything?'

'It's distracting.'

'And you don't like to be distracted?'

'I don't mind it.'

She leaned in then and they kissed in a drunkenly uninhibited way, not caring about passers-by heading for clubs or taxis.

When they broke free from the kiss, he said, 'So you want to go dancing, Lena?'

'Maybe.'

'I've not been clubbing in Durham for years. There's Klute, under the bridge, which is tiny and very hot but a little bit legendary, but we'd be the oldest ones in there by a mile.'

She kissed him again, 'I've changed my mind.'

'Already?'

'We don't need to go dancing,' she said, and they kissed again.

'So what *would* you like to do?'

'I don't know.' She brought her hand higher and traced his top lip with her finger. 'What would *you* like to do?'

'Well . . . I suppose . . . we could go for a coffee.'

'But where could we get coffee at this hour?' She frowned, as if this were an impossible request.

'I have coffee at my home,' he told her, 'and a kettle.'

'You have a kettle?'

'I do. It's a particularly fine kettle, though I don't like to brag.'

'Really?'

'Yes,' he said, then added with mock-seriousness: 'It's cordless.'

'My God!' she gasped, as if he were describing a new Lamborghini. 'Then you must show it to me right away.'

Ian Bradshaw wasn't sleeping. He was watching a mindless Hollywood buddy movie involving two cops trying to capture a Colombian drug dealer, by crashing a lot of cars and destroying a great many shop windows during shootouts. The two policemen in the film did not get on at first but gradually grew to respect each other's abilities. One of them was young and reckless, the other old and jaded. Bradshaw found it much easier to identify with the older man.

When the younger detective ended up in bed with the drug lord's stunning girlfriend, receiving intelligence about a forthcoming consignment of heroin from her at the same time, Bradshaw lost interest.

'Not usually the way it's done round here,' he muttered, and wandered off to get a beer from the fridge. Of course, his day had also been anything but normal. His mind kept going back to DI Meade.

Was Adrian Wicklow a sad and pathetic example of a man whose brain was simply wired very differently, or was he, as Meade maintained, the distillation of pure evil in human form? Should Bradshaw really go and see a man who had been responsible for the downfall of Meade, and many of the men who had worked with him, or could he just turn his back on the case? Should he tell his DCI to stuff it, in other words? And if he did, what impact was that likely to have on his career?

Then Bradshaw thought further. Did he really even have a career, or was he simply tolerated in the force? If he left Durham Constabulary tomorrow, would anyone really miss him? Had he achieved anything at all while he was there? Not for the first time, Ian Bradshaw considered his options. What could he become if he just jacked it all in and stopped being a detective? Would he be happier without the burdens of this job, or would his fragile mental health worsen if he didn't have the distraction of detective work to busy his troubled mind?

The film continued in the background. The older detective was shot and nearly killed by the drug lord while saving his partner's life. The younger detective, who had seen his new girlfriend brutally slain by the villain's henchman, went on a killing spree Rambo would have been proud of, despatching criminal after criminal while oozing blood from several gunshot wounds that didn't seem to trouble him unduly. He then threw the drug lord off a high building rather than arresting him and resigned, throwing his badge at his incompetent superior: the only part of the movie Bradshaw genuinely enjoyed.

As the credits rolled, he still hadn't made up his mind. Meade's assurance that he should walk away, no matter what the cost, had got to him but, if he did refuse to take on the case, who would find out the truth about Susan Verity?

Then there was Wicklow himself. He didn't want to admit it, but the child killer had got inside Bradshaw's head already.

Didn't he deserve to be out-thought and out-fought, for once? Wouldn't it be great to be the man who finally outwitted Adrian Wicklow, to make sure he was brought to justice for all of his crimes? Bradshaw had made his decision.

Helen woke from a light sleep to the sound of scratching at the front door. Her immediate reaction was panic. Someone was trying to get in. They were going to kill her, just like they had killed her editor.

The digital alarm clock told her it was long past midnight. She hadn't heard Tom come in but if she went to his room she could wake him and they would at least be able to fight together against this intruder.

Then she heard another sound. Keys hit the ground outside, and this was followed by giggles.

Female laughter, then a man's voice: 'Hang on a sec.' Relief flooded through Helen. It was Tom, but he wasn't alone. 'There!' He must have found his keys. He was a bit loud, considering he must know she would already be in bed and it wasn't like him to be inconsiderate, so he must be drunk, but who was he with? Had he gone out and picked up some random girl and brought her back here? She was not jealous, of course, and it was *his* home, but she did live here, after all. But then he was single and it was his business what he did.

Was he with Lena?

She looked at the clock in disbelief. Had he been drinking with her all this time? Had Lena come back to his home, even though she had known him only a matter of hours? Helen told herself not to be such a prude, but a lingering sense of disapproval remained.

'Tea or coffee?' she heard Tom say as they belatedly gained entry to the house.

'I like coffee,' was the reply.

That was Lena all right.

She heard Tom and Lena's voices drifting up the stairs and strained to listen. Were they about to end up in bed together?

Helen climbed out of her own bed. Her room was at the top of the stairs, and she slowly eased the door open so she could hear them better, first in the kitchen then in the lounge. She couldn't make out much to begin with, so she padded out on to the landing, where she picked up more than she would usually have done because they were both quite drunk and loud. They must have been in a pub that played music at a volume high enough to deaden their hearing. They were almost shouting, in fact, and there was a lot of laughter. There were also intermittent silences during which Helen got the distinct impression they were kissing.

Helen felt glad that her matchmaking seemed to have been so successful. She told herself this was a good thing and that it was a positive development that Tom might start a relationship with this girl.

It would stop him thinking about Helen.

It would stop Helen thinking about him.

She told herself this more than once.

She was still telling herself this when she heard the creak of footsteps on the stairs. Panicking, Helen bolted back to her room, praying they hadn't heard her. She would be mortified if they discovered her eavesdropping.

Helen managed to close her door, without a sound. For a second, she wondered if Tom was coming to bed on his own but she hadn't heard a taxi arrive for Lena. Perhaps he was letting her sleep in his bed and he would take the couch, like he had done the first time Helen stayed with him.

Then she heard Tom's voice. It was low and indistinct, so she couldn't make out the words, but Lena answered him with a giggle and a shushing noise. 'She's asleep,' Tom assured Lena, and Helen realized he meant her when he said *she*. It upset her a little that he hadn't said '*Helen* is asleep,' and she knew this was silly but she couldn't help it.

She held her breath as Tom's door opened and closed then tried not to imagine what they were doing in his room together, though she did imagine it, the whole time it went on, and the sounds coming from his room didn't help. Mostly, she could hear Lena, and she seemed to be having a very good time.

Billy was drunk.

Billy was very drunk.

He had almost fallen out of the last place when he was asked to leave it. He had assured the bouncer he was fine and could definitely handle yet another pint, but even he knew he couldn't really and, in the end, he went without too much fuss.

He'd been drinking on his own the whole time. Drinking and thinking. Just like always, with the familiar feelings of hurt and anger at the unfairness of it all. How had his life worked out like this? Self-pity consumed Billy then, and he drank more to overcome it.

He was swaying along the path, heading for the taxi rank now. It would be an expensive ride home but there were no buses at this hour. He reached into his trouser pocket and pulled out a wad of crumpled notes. There were plenty left – even Billy couldn't drink a ton-fifty's worth of beer in a day – but when he looked at the pile of notes it was much smaller than he was expecting.

'Fuck.' He was shocked by how much he had gone through.

Then he remembered that he had more money, piles of coins in his coat. Every time Billy ordered a drink he had paid with a fresh, crisp fiver or tenner then stuffed the change into his pocket. He could feel its weight now and, as he drew nearer the taxi rank, he delved into his coat to grab a handful of coins. He would use them to pay the taxi driver and keep the notes for another day.

Billy pulled his hand out of his pocket and the movement threw him off balance and he whirled slightly. That and his extreme drunkenness made him trip and fall sideways. He crashed to the ground, landing heavily on the pavement, the mass of coins knocked from his hand tumbling and rolling in all directions. The pain he should feel was deadened by drink, and he attempted to get up to chase after the coins, but the world seemed to spin then and he decided he needed a moment.

He'd cut the palm of his hand on something, and he must have banged his head too, because there was a bump on his forehead and some blood on skin that had been scraped raw by the impact. Billy managed to haul himself to his feet, then he bent low to pick up the coins. He got some of them back in his pocket but they were tricky little buggers and he kept dropping them back on the pavement. He settled for the ones that hadn't rolled too far. He gave up on the others.

Stuffing the money back in his pocket, Billy stumbled on until he reached the front of the taxi rank. He took a deep breath, concentrating hard, and bent low so he could speak through the passenger window. He made a massive effort to pronounce the name of his village clearly, but the taxi driver looked at him in disgust.

'You must be joking, bonny lad.'

'No,' protested Billy, 'I've got money, honest,' and he showed the taxi driver.

The money didn't seem to interest the man, which puzzled Billy. He swayed and leaned on the taxi's passenger-side mirror. Then he realized that the mirror might very well be the reason the bloke wouldn't take him. The driver would have seen Billy fall and decided he wasn't worth the trouble.

'Fuck it, I don't care,' said Billy to himself. It was warm enough. He'd find a quiet doorway and sleep in that. It wouldn't be the first time.

12

Cross my heart and hope to die
Stick a needle in my eye

The den had its rules.

Chief among these was: no girls. They weren't allowed anywhere near the den, but Danny seemed to have forgotten that rule where Andrea, Michelle and Susan were concerned. Mostly, Billy suspected, it was because of Susan.

Andrea was more like a boy than most boys and Billy was secretly afraid of her. He was pretty sure she would be able to fight him too, though he wouldn't admit that to his friends and was careful never to give her an excuse to challenge him to a scrap. If that ever happened, he would just have to take her blows while proclaiming loudly he would never hit a girl, no matter how much he was provoked. Receiving two or three punches from the tall and muscular Andrea would be a small price to pay compared to the abject humiliation of publicly losing a fight, and one in which he was seen to be trying but was beaten anyway, to a girl. Just the prospect made him shudder.

But that summer, if you wanted to play with Susan Verity, you had to play with Andrea and Michelle too, for the three were inseparable, thrown together by the proximity of their houses and the fact that other girls were away on holiday or had been packed off to grandparents because their parents worked during the day.

That morning the girls stopped by the broken swings and the merry-go-round because Danny, Kevin and Billy were lounging there listlessly due to the heat. Kevin was making it go slowly back and forth, powering it with his foot against the ground. He stopped when the girls arrived.

Susan spoke first. 'What ya doing?'

'Nowt,' answered Danny, and Billy was glad he had, since he himself would have struggled to answer Susan without becoming nervous and sounding stupid, 'but we're going off later.'

'Off where?' asked Susan, interested now.

'Never you mind,' cautioned Danny.

'We don't care where you're going,' sneered Michelle.

'Shut your mouth, Specky,' Kevin told her, and Michelle said nothing more. No one chastised Kevin for saying this to the bespectacled girl. This kind of talk was allowed.

'Go on,' urged Susan. 'Tell us.'

Danny looked at her for a moment. 'We've built a den, and it's ace.'

'But it's not for lasses,' Kevin warned her.

'Show us then,' said Susan.

'I've just told you, it's not for –'

Susan rounded on Kevin furiously. 'Shut up, Sammy Shrink. I wasn't talking to you!'

And that did shut Kevin up. He was the smallest boy in his class, and some said he might even be the smallest person in their year, though he maintained he was a good inch taller than Stephanie Malcolm and it was only her frizzy hair that made her look taller. Susan calling him Sammy Shrink, after the tiny cartoon character from the comic *Whizzer and Chips*, was a crushing blow.

'We can't just show you,' said Danny. 'You're not in our gang.'

'What do we have to do to join the gang?'

Danny thought for a while, and everyone watched him closely.

'You have to kiss us,' Danny blurted finally, and Billy gazed at him in astonishment. Did he just say that out loud? Did he really just ask the girls to kiss them? Billy was amazed he had managed to form the words. They weren't supposed to want that sort of attention from girls. Not yet. Lasses were soft. Real boys played football, swapped stickers, went on bike rides and built dens. They did not kiss girls.

But the question was out there now and, so far, there had been no hysterical reaction from any of the girls. They merely stared back at Danny. Billy felt a potent combination of fear and excitement he had never experienced before; it looked like this might actually be about to happen.

Billy Thorpe had a secret he had kept hidden from all his friends, a secret so shameful he had managed never to tell it to a soul: not his best friend, not his parents – *especially* not his parents; not to anyone, in fact.

Billy was in love with Susan Verity.

Now he was staring at her intently with his mouth open, for a number of possibilities were racing through his fevered mind. Susan would get angry with them and storm off, taking her less beautiful friends with her, in which case Billy would have to pretend it was just as well, because nobody wanted to see stupid girls at their sacred den anyway. He knew he would then have to spend the entire day trying not to think about the soft-peachy skin on Susan's face and her strawberry lips, her honey-coloured hair and her eyes, as dark and wide as Bambi's.

There was another possibility. The girls would agree to kiss them. He would tolerate Andrea's kiss. It would be worth it. He would accept Michelle's kiss uncomplainingly but without much enthusiasm. Then he would finally be granted his most fervent and desperate wish. He'd get to kiss Susan Verity.

It wasn't quite true that he had told no one about his love for

Susan. God knew. Billy had told God about it on a number of occasions: in the village church during the Easter services, when they were asked to bow their heads in prayer; and in his bed alone at night when he wrestled with sleep, trying to work out the meaning of this love and how it would change him.

Billy would also tell God about his love while out on solitary walks across the fields. When he knew no one could possibly hear him, he would dare himself to say, 'I love Susan Verity,' out loud, quietly at first, in case the bushes and the trees had spies lurking in them who would report back to his friends. He would slowly and steadily increase the volume of his mantra. 'I love Susan Verity,' he would say, as if in conversation with an imaginary best friend. 'I love Susan Verity.' He could feel the skin on his face prickle with heat as he admitted this deeply embarrassing fact a little more loudly. Billy would tell the trees and the fields and the air around him. 'I . . . love . . . Susan . . . Verity,' he would say it gleefully to the scarecrow on Marsh Farm, 'but you'd better not tell.' He'd jab a finger at it for emphasis. 'I – love – Susan – Verity.' The volume would go up as he revealed his deepest secret over and over again until, eventually, he reached the edge of the abandoned quarry.

Billy would stand at that sacred place and shout out, *'I love Susan Verity!'* He'd be hoping for an echo and, when none came, he'd shout it louder, spooking himself as he did so, for his voice must have carried miles. The words would surely have been transported all the way back to the village, where Susan and her friends would hear them, and they would laugh at him for the rest of the year. Struck by the enormity of this, he would turn for home and run.

Now, there was a chance he could kiss her.

God really had been listening to his prayers.

Abruptly, the spell was broken. 'We're not doing that,' Susan told Danny firmly.

'I was only joking anyway,' flushed Danny. 'We don't want you to kiss us. I just wanted to see if you'd do it,' he stammered. 'And you wouldn't, so you passed the test.'

Everyone knew he was lying. And Danny knew they knew he was lying, but no one said anything. The other girls just looked to Susan as their leader, and she didn't pursue the matter with Danny, sparing him further embarrassment. Billy loved her a little more for that.

'So you're in the gang,' blurted out Kevin.

'Who said?' Danny was angry, and Billy knew why. He was supposed to be the one who decided who was in the gang.

'If Danny says so,' added Kevin quickly, 'I was going to say.'

'All right, you *can* be in the gang,' said Danny, and the tension lifted, 'but that doesn't mean you get to see the den.'

'Why not?' asked Andrea.

'Because you haven't earned it.'

'We don't want to see your stupid den,' said Michelle, who, like Kevin, was forgetting her place, as she wasn't the leader of their group. 'Do we?' she implored Susan.

'Well, go home then,' sneered Kevin.

There was silence for a moment and all eyes turned to Susan, who was regarding Kevin calmly, as if weighing him up.

Billy was praying she wouldn't leave, but if there was a moment when she could do so without losing face, this was it. He expected she would snort impatiently and lead the other two away to play house or dollies or whatever it was that girls of his age did when they were on their own, but it already felt like a long, hot summer and everyone was desperate for some new form of entertainment. Something different, something grown-up.

'So what do we have to do then?'

Kevin offered up a solution.

'Don't be so disgusting, Kevin Robson. We're certainly not

doing that,' said Susan, and Kevin realized he had really over-done it and flushed a fierce red.

'I was only joking, like,' he stammered.

'No, you weren't,' Michelle told him. 'Dirty boy!'

Then Andrea delivered the nuclear option. 'I'm going to tell your mum on you.'

She was serious too. Kevin had clearly forgotten that Andrea's family lived only two doors down from his, so mum involvement was a strong possibility, 'I don't care,' he said, but he did care, and everyone knew it.

'All right,' said Danny. '*One* of you,' he said, 'has to –'

'What?' challenged Susan.

'. . . kiss *one* of us . . .' And, as if he had suddenly found his bravery, he added with great emphasis: 'On the lips.'

Susan Verity thought for a long, long while. Billy Thorpe was holding his breath. He felt he might pass out from sheer hopefulness alone. Her silence meant she was actually consid-ering it, but who would do the kissing and who would be the kissed? What if she ordered Andrea to do it? What if Andrea chose him? He wouldn't be able to trust Danny and Kevin to keep quiet about it, and then the whole pigging school would know, but there was always the possibility Susan would do the kissing and maybe, just maybe, she would choose him.

Susan looked at her two friends but did not consult them. 'All right,' she said, and Billy wanted to faint right there and then, just like Paul McIlroy always did at school during over-long assemblies. He'd go spark out then tumble over without even putting his hands out to protect himself, dropping to the ground with a loud slap, and a teacher would have to pick him up.

Then Susan said, 'After you show us the den.'

'No way,' protested Danny. 'You won't do it then.'

'We will,' promised Susan. 'Won't we?' She was addressing her friends now, and they both mumbled their agreement, though neither of them looked thrilled at the prospect.

'Okay, then,' agreed Danny after some considerable time. 'We'll take you there, but you can't tell anyone, ever.'

'I won't,' she agreed.

'Not anyone!' The boy shouted it for emphasis and the girl's reply matched his volume.

'I won't!'

'You'd better not, Susan,' he warned her.

'I've said, haven't I?'

The three boys looked at each other. Nothing was spoken between them but they all understood. It wasn't enough; not nearly. Extreme measures were needed here. 'Cross your heart,' Danny told her.

'And hope to die,' added Kevin, to back up his friend.

The girl closed her eyes and screwed them up. 'I cross my heart and hope to die,' she chanted, and opened her eyes again to stare back at the boys. 'Stick a needle in my eye,' she offered, and that finally sealed the deal.

'All right,' said Kevin.

'Okay,' said Danny. 'We'll let you see the den.'

'What's the matter with you?' demanded Andrea, who was staring at Billy now. 'Catching flies?' Billy realized he was standing there with his mouth wide open.

13

Tom woke to sunlight streaming through the windows and the sound of muted sobbing next to him. Groggily, he rolled over to Lena as she tried to stifle her crying.

'Hey, what's the matter?'

'Nothing,' she told him.

She looked and sounded as if the world were about to end, and Tom wondered if he could be the cause of this distress. He thought they'd had a great evening. Surely they must have, if they ended up back here together. Then he thought he understood.

'You're not married, are you?' She wasn't wearing a ring, but her tears could have been guilty ones.

'No,' she said firmly, and before he could press her further she started sobbing uncontrollably.

'Hey, hey, it's okay. What's wrong? What's the matter? Just tell me.'

'She's gone,' she cried, and he could barely make out the words. 'She's gone, and I can't bring her back. I've tried, but I can't.'

'Who?' He had no idea who she meant. 'Who has gone, Lena?'

'My sister.'

'Your sister?' This was the first time she had even mentioned a sister.

She stared at him intensely, as if urging Tom to understand. 'I tried to bring her back, but she's gone. She's gone for good. My baby sister,' she said. 'Jess is the reason I am here, in the north-east.'

'Your baby sister? How old is she?'

'Twenty,' she said.

'You think she might be in Durham?'

She nodded. 'It was her last known location.'

'And she ran away?'

She nodded again. 'Just disappeared one day. Left, no note, no clue . . .' Her words trailed away, as if she no longer had the energy to explain further.

'When did you last see her?'

'Weeks ago . . .' Then she corrected herself: 'Months.' She looked desolate.

'And you've had no word from her in all this time?'

She shook her head. 'No. Oh, Tom, I'm so scared. She's my baby sister and I'm frightened something really terrible has happened to her.'

'I'm sure she'll be fine,' he reassured her. 'Thousands of people disappear every year, and the majority of them come home,' he said. 'Eventually.'

She shook her head violently. 'No, that's not it! You don't know about her. You don't understand.'

He was starting to sense that Lena's sister's disappearance wasn't the usual missing-person's case. 'Why did she leave, Lena?' he asked. 'Why did she go?'

Lena began sobbing again and her breath came out in short, sharp bursts, so he could barely understand the words. 'Bad men,' she managed. 'Bad men.'

Bradshaw was admitted into Durham jail, but not before undergoing a variety of security checks, involving the confirmation of his identity, a close examination of his warrant card, the production of a letter from DCI Kane that he had been told to bring with him, a search of his person, which involved turning out his pockets, to ensure he was not carrying a recording device or a weapon of any kind, then a detailed briefing on what was deemed to be acceptable interaction with the prison's most infamous inmate. This included the order not to touch Wicklow. Bradshaw assured the prison guards he had no intention of laying a hand on the child killer, but they did not seem convinced by his sincerity.

'Wicklow has the ability to push buttons,' one of them informed him. 'He likes to provoke. He is after a reaction, but if you make a lunge, if we have to drag you off him, then you will never be allowed within these walls again and he will bring another case before the European bloody Court for assault and violation of his human rights.'

'I am a serving police officer and not in the habit of assaulting criminals, no matter how notorious.' The prison guard did not seem convinced. 'Now, can I see him?' asked Bradshaw.

'There's someone who wants to see you first,' said the guard, and when Bradshaw bridled at the further delay he added, 'If you don't mind.'

Bradshaw was expecting a pep talk from the prison governor or possibly one of the numerous psychiatrists or prison doctors who had seen Wicklow during his years of incarceration. He certainly hadn't been expecting a priest. Father Noonan was waiting for him in an anteroom.

'I don't mean this in any way disrespectfully, Father,' Bradshaw told the priest, 'but why exactly are you here?'

'I am here because I heard you were visiting Adrian, Detective Constable.'

Bradshaw was tempted to correct the priest on his rank but decided to let it slide. 'I am here to question Wicklow,' Bradshaw said, 'about events that occurred some years ago.'

'I know, and when I heard you were coming' – the priest's voice was almost a whisper, as if Wicklow were in the room with them already and he was worried the prisoner might overhear them – 'I must admit, I was more than a little concerned.'

Bradshaw regarded the priest, a man in late middle age with a gentle face but intense eyes. 'You were worried about me?'

'About Adrian,' said the priest, as if he were discussing a small, vulnerable child.

'I don't follow. Why would you be worried about a murderer?'

'I have known Adrian these past fifteen years now,' said the priest, 'and he is a complex man. I think if you were to look beyond his crimes for a moment you would see a level of intelligence and sensitivity you might be surprised by.'

'A level of sensitivity?' Bradshaw could not quite believe what he was hearing. 'The man murdered several children. How *could* I look beyond his crimes and why the hell would I ever want to?'

'Since those dark days, Adrian has come to understand that what he did was wrong.'

'Oh,' said Bradshaw dryly. 'Well, that's all right then. We should probably let him out, I suppose.'

There was a flash of irritation in the priest's eyes then, but he calmed himself. 'I'm not suggesting that. Though, I must say, I would be in favour of releasing Adrian back into the community eventually.'

'I'd be in favour of that too,' said Bradshaw, attempting to control his fury.

'You would?' The priest brightened. 'Really?'

'Yes,' Bradshaw assured him. 'He wouldn't last two minutes out there. Someone would beat him to death on the day he was released. Of course, we'd never catch them, because there'd be about a hundred thousand suspects and, even if we did, I doubt any jury in the world would convict the man who killed Wicklow.'

'I thought you were an officer of the law.' The priest looked mightily offended now. 'I must say, I am disappointed by your attitude.'

'And I thought you were a man of the cloth and I am astounded by yours. You've been visiting Adrian, as you call him, for fifteen years? What about the families of his victims? How many times have you visited them, to get their perspective on *Adrian*?' The priest looked hurt and angry. 'What's the matter, Father? Are you judging me? Is that what you're doing? Perhaps you had better think about the company you've been keeping before you do that. I'll say a few Hail Marys at the weekend if it makes you feel any better. A man kills children, and you're worried about his feelings and my hostility towards him? I think you've got your priorities all wrong.'

'That man is gravely ill,' the priest reminded him. 'He has months, perhaps only weeks, left to live. I believe that God will judge him then, as He does us all, and I think he will find a regretful man, a repentant sinner.'

'We are not talking about a fella who has robbed a bit of lead from a church roof and sold it. This is a child murderer. Can't you see that?'

'This is a man who was driven by a demon inside him.'

'A demon? You really believe that?'

'Yes, I do, and when he passes from this world I intend to be with him to ensure he is finally at peace, which is why I do not want to see his mind disturbed by yet another reappraisal of deeds committed long ago.'

'Then what would you have me do, Father? Should we just not bother the guy?'

'I'd like you to focus on the man you find today rather than the man he was before. That would be more productive, don't you think?'

'Unfortunately, the man he was before is the one who knows what happened to poor Susan Verity and several other missing children who have never had a Christian burial. Perhaps your energies would be better spent focusing on persuading

Wicklow to help you find them. Their souls are more important than his.'

'We are all of us equal in the eyes of the Lord.'

'Really? Well, that's reassuring to know. Perhaps your Lord won't judge me too harshly for upsetting Wicklow if I bring up events he would rather forget. I guess you have your job to do, Father, but now I'd be grateful if you would let me get on with mine.'

'I'm sorry,' Lena said, as she dried her eyes.

'Don't be. Your sister has gone and you are worried about her, that's totally understandable, but I'm sure you'll find her.'

'But . . . she doesn't want to be found. Not by me, not by anyone. Otherwise, I would have done it by now. Jess was the reason I bought your book. It was about a missing girl, so I thought I'd see if I could get some ideas on how to find my sister. I couldn't believe it when Helen walked up to me and said you'd wrote it.'

'Why didn't you say anything then?'

'I was too shocked, I suppose, and I just thought you would be working on other things and that I shouldn't bother you about it. Then we got on so well, and I really didn't want to exploit that. It wouldn't be fair.'

'You daft thing. I would have been happy to help you,' he said. 'I *am* happy to help.'

'You're busy, and Helen won't like it.'

'She'd understand, and it sounds like you need help.'

'I figured I'd find her on my own, but it's all been dead ends and now I don't know what to do.' She dabbed at her eyes. 'We had a great night together and I haven't had fun in such a long time. I didn't want to spoil it.'

'It hasn't spoilt anything,' he assured her, 'so tell me what happened. Did you report your sister's disappearance?'

'To the police,' she told him dismissively, 'but they don't care. They're not even trying to find Jess. *Maybe she just doesn't want to come home*, they told me, like I don't know that already. They are no help.'

'Did you tell them about those men you mentioned?' he asked, because he was curious about that himself. 'The ones your sister was running away from?' Her face told him she had not.

'These men,' she began hesitantly. 'It's hard to explain. They own the police.'

'That sounds a bit dramatic.'

'I knew you wouldn't understand,' she flared.

'Woah, hang on, I'm trying to,' he assured her. 'Why don't you tell me about them?'

'Why do you want to know?'

'Maybe I can help.'

'How?' she asked. 'How can you help?'

'Your sister is missing,' he said. 'And missing is what I do.'

14

Bradshaw was still not yet allowed to see Adrian Wicklow in person. Instead, he was intercepted again by a prison officer. 'You've got to get past the governor first. Those are the rules when it's Wicklow,' he was told as they escorted him to the governor's office.

He sat down opposite the man, who regarded him doubtfully. Sir John Rawlins was a small, stout man in late middle age, dressed in a dark suit and tie that made him look more like a senior civil servant or businessman than the custodian of a thousand prisoners.

'Are you sure you know what you are doing, Detective Sergeant?' was Rawlins's opening line.

'I beg your pardon.'

The governor held up a hand. 'Forgive me, that was clumsy. I meant, have you been fully briefed about what to expect when you meet Adrian Wicklow?'

'I think so, yes,' answered Bradshaw, but it crossed his mind that he couldn't possibly know if he had been *fully* briefed or not.

'You've heard about his little . . .' The older man was searching for the right words: 'mind games?'

'I've heard about them, yes.'

'It isn't just that he likes to mess people around and waste their time. It goes much deeper than that.'

'How do you mean?'

'It's more like psychological warfare. With some prisoners, if they get a life sentence, our biggest problem is to motivate them at all. It's quite a challenge to convince someone there is any point in going on, of even getting out of bed, if all we can promise them is that they are very likely to grow old and die within these four walls.'

'I can see that must be difficult.'

'With Adrian Wicklow, things were different. I became governor here just before he arrived. I was a relatively young man for the position but even I had enough experience of the prison system to realize there was something unique about him. He seemed – how can I put this? – almost to come alive at the prospect of incarceration or, more accurately, the attention that came with it. His crimes were so abhorrent and his reasons for committing them such a mystery that he has attracted something of a cult following among psychologists and criminologists, all of whom seem to think finding out why he did what he did is the holy grail of their profession.'

'He's not the only person to have murdered children.'

'True, but in many cases the motivation for targeting a child is a sexual one. The killing comes afterwards, as a need to keep the other crime a secret. In the cases where a criminal is motivated purely to kill and gains satisfaction from that act alone, it is often quite easy to understand why. Some show psychopathic tendencies from an early age. They started out killing animals and gradually gravitated towards human beings, or showed symptoms of schizophrenia and were motivated by *voices* in their head urging them to kill, or they were abused as children themselves and went on to abuse others, as if this were somehow a natural progression. I could go on . . .' he said, by way of showing that he would not. 'There are numerous reasons for killing, but no one has ever got to the bottom of why Wicklow does what he does.'

'Why?'

'Because he won't let them. You want to know my theory? You know he is an intelligent man, right? He has been put through all sorts of tests and come out with a higher than average IQ rating, but he seemed to lack the social skills needed to get and maintain a more illustrious position in the outside world than the menial jobs he managed to hold down. For years, Adrian Wicklow was ignored. Only after his arrest did he start to feel some sense of his own importance.

'He finally mattered,' said Bradshaw.

'Precisely. I'm sorry to have to say it, but I think incarceration for life was almost the making of him. Most of the time, he appears perfectly content to be in here. I'd even go so far as to say he is quite happy.'

'That's a depressing thought,' said Bradshaw, 'for the families of his victims.'

'Indeed it is. He worked out quite early on that if he gave up everything he knew, if he cooperated fully with the police and all of the doctors who came to see him, if he helped them find the missing children, ultimately, they would –'

'Lose interest in him?' Bradshaw completed his sentence for him. 'I spoke to the senior investigating officer on his case and he is of the same opinion.'

'He'd be just another prisoner on C wing in solitary confinement: no friends or visitors, no one expressing an interest in the workings of his tortured mind. He'd be an unimportant figure once again, just as he was in the real world. I believe he plays his little mind games to maintain his feelings of importance. I would go so far as to say that running you, and everyone else, ragged is his *raison d'être*, Detective Bradshaw.'

'You're saying he gets off on it.'

'I wouldn't put it quite like that, but yes.'

'That why you wanted to see me before I see him?'

'That, and to warn you.'

'About what?'

'A lot of people have sat down with Adrian Wicklow over

the years. I've seen many of them come and go. Obviously, none of them has ever discovered the fate of those missing children, or you wouldn't be here now, but you should set your expectation levels low on that score. He won't tell you.'

'I'll bear that in mind.'

'You should bear this in mind too: no one who visits Wicklow for any length of time is unaffected by the experience. We've had several reports of people suddenly resigning from their jobs; I'm talking about experienced and skilled professional people here who abruptly decided they did not want to carry on with their work because of their experiences with Wicklow. One went off to the Highlands of Scotland to live on a croft' – he paused for a moment – 'and we had a suicide; a psychiatrist who dealt with Wicklow for a year slit his own wrists with glass from a broken bottle, and he cut them like this.' He mimed a slashing motion on his forearm from his hand right up to his elbow. 'Not like this.' He then mimed the action of someone slashing from one side of their wrists across to the other side. 'This was not a half-hearted attempt or a cry for help. The cuts were deep. He meant to do it.'

'Because of his experience with Wicklow?'

'That was never proven, but neither did the police ever uncover any other plausible explanation. The man's life was unspectacular in every other way.' He looked meaningfully at the detective.

'So bearing in mind I have no choice but to see him, what exactly are you saying?'

'I'm telling you to take very great care in there, Detective Bradshaw. *That's* what I'm saying.'

'I have a picture,' Lena remembered, and she retrieved her handbag and delved into it for a photograph of a young woman and handed it to him. Tom examined it.

Jess didn't look exactly like her older sister but they shared some features and she was undeniably attractive. 'Some sisters look alike,' said Lena, as if she knew what he was thinking, 'but we are quite different. Our personalities too; Jess was always wilder, she took risks.'

'What kind of risks?'

'Nothing crazy, but she travelled on her own, all round Europe, and not just the tourist places. She would throw in jobs without caring if she could get another one and she had boyfriends I didn't like. They were into things.'

'Such as?'

'Drugs, sometimes.' She said it reluctantly, as if he might judge her sister because of this.

'And was she into drugs?' he asked reasonably, as if she might well be, considering the company she kept.

Lena took a while to answer. 'I think she experimented, but nothing too hard. She's not an addict.'

'Where was she working when she disappeared?'

'A bar in London called Shelley's. She danced sometimes and worked at the bar.'

'She was paid to dance there?' he asked. 'Was it just dancing or was it, you know, a lap-dancing bar?'

'No,' she said, 'it was just dancing.' Then she added, 'In a cage.'

'In a cage? She was a' – he was trying to remember the phrase – 'go-go dancer?' It seemed a ludicrously old-fashioned term.

'Yes,' Lena said. 'That's what she called it. She told me there were two cages high up on platforms so everyone could see the girls from the dance floor. She had to dance really fast to get people fired up. That's how she described it.'

'I've seen that kind of thing in Newcastle.' He remembered a bar with a dance floor, girls in tiny pairs of shorts and T-shirts gyrating above everyone to create an atmosphere. It

93

was very retro, a sixties gimmick that had suddenly come back into fashion.

'She did that on the busy evenings and worked behind the bar when it was quieter. That's how she met Aidan.'

'Her boyfriend?'

'I never met him, but he didn't sound like a good guy –' He indicated that she should go on. 'It wasn't what she said about him. It was what she didn't say. When I asked questions, she was vague. I couldn't seem to pin down what he did. He had some link to the bar but didn't officially own it or work there. He had a stake in it, but it was unofficial.'

'Right.' Tom was beginning to get the idea.

'He was in there every night, and he must have seen her dancing, then he asked her for a drink. She started seeing him and carried on for months before she disappeared.'

'Was this guy a gangster?' he asked outright.

Lena blinked, as if the question was too direct for her. 'I think so, maybe, yes,' she admitted. 'He hung out with some people Jess didn't like. She once told me she was afraid of his friends. He was a big guy too, and she said no one messed with him.'

'So what happened?'

'She went to work one night but we never saw her again. We've been able to confirm that she worked her shift, she was still there when the bar closed and the bar staff left, but no one has seen her since.'

'What makes you think she might be in the north-east?'

'Her family' – she corrected herself – '*our* family, originates from here. Our grandfather left the area as a young man looking for work and never went back. We used to visit relatives years ago. We thought she might have tried to contact them for help. If she really wanted to get a long way from London she might choose here,' she offered helplessly.

'And you say you involved the police?'

Lena nodded. 'Yes, and as I said, they weren't much use. They asked about her, but people just said she must have gone home. Her boyfriend said he had left before her that night because he had business to attend to. And he had an alibi.'

'They always do,' said Tom.

'The police told us there was nothing they could do unless there was evidence that something bad happened to Jess. She's a grown woman who can come and go as she pleases, and many people just disappear.'

'About a quarter of a million every year,' he told her.

'So many? I didn't realize.'

'Most of them come back after a while,' he explained, 'but some stay missing. I'm going to have to ask you this, Lena: what do you think has happened to your sister?'

She hesitated for a second. 'I think if something terrible had happened to her we would know. If Jess had been killed, wouldn't we have found her by now?' Tom wasn't convinced. Criminals who murdered their victims preferred it if they were never found. Without a body, it was very hard to get a conviction.

'Then there was the private investigator,' she said, as if Tom already knew about him.

'You hired a PI?'

'Yes,' she said. 'We thought it might be our only chance of getting her back.'

'There are some good private investigators,' he offered cautiously, 'but it's an unregulated profession, so just about anyone can set themselves up as one. Did he find her?'

'He claims he did, but when he approached her she got scared and disappeared again. We can't be sure if what he told us was true. I never really trusted him. He was expensive and he took a long time to get anywhere. In the end, he somehow managed to see her bank accounts. I don't think that was legal but we were desperate, so we didn't complain. He found she had taken money from a cashpoint in Durham city on several occasions, but nobody had seen her. The private detective spoke to all the family members. Jess knows the region, but she hasn't told anyone she is here.'

'Why do you think your sister wants to disappear?'

'I'm convinced she must have seen something or heard something she shouldn't. Maybe she found out something about the club or the people behind it. Why else would she leave so suddenly without getting in contact with us since? If she had gone off on one of her trips to Europe, she would have let us know she was okay – a phone call, a letter, something. She's obviously frightened and trying to get away from the life she was leading.'

'Too frightened even to call you or her mother?'

Lena nodded. 'It must be something big, or she would have been in touch.'

'And your mother has no idea where she might be?'

'My mother has gone to pieces. She's in a bad way and has been ever since Jess disappeared. I know, normally, you'd want to speak to her, but I don't think that would be a good idea. She just gets too upset when we discuss Jess, and she knows way less than I do about the life she was leading or the company she was keeping. I'm trying to keep that from her, to be honest.'

'Don't worry,' he said. 'I won't bother your mother.'

She seemed relieved to hear that. 'If you do find Jess, can you tell me before you approach her? I don't want her to run away again. I don't think she trusts anyone right now.'

'Sure.'

Lena looked relieved. 'There is one other thing you should know if you are going to help me.' She looked worried then. 'The private investigator we used' – she hesitated – 'he got hurt.'

'Hurt how?'

'He was beaten up,' she admitted. 'Badly. He ended up in hospital with two broken legs.'

'Jesus,' hissed Tom. 'Is it too much to hope he was working on another case and that led to the beating?'

'Honestly? We just don't know, and neither does he for sure, but I don't want you to be in any danger, so if you find anything out . . .'

'I won't do anything crazy. I'll tell you about it first.' She seemed reassured by this. 'You think the men your sister was involved with did that to your PI?'

'I think so, yes.'

'Then they must be looking for her too.'

'Maybe,' said Lena, 'that's why I want to find her. To make sure she's okay. I'm sorry I was so emotional. I'm just so exhausted,' she said. 'I've spent all my time these past few months either working or looking for Jess. There was no room for anything else.'

'Sounds like you need a break.'

'I do. As soon as I know she's okay, I'll take one . . . *if* she is okay.'

'She will be.' He squeezed her hand.

'Thanks, Tom.' She looked at him closely. 'When did you last have a holiday?'

'Me? Oh, ages ago,' he admitted.

'Knew it,' she said. 'You're pretty driven. aren't you. Mr Rising Star Journalist.'

'It's not that. In my defence, I've had a pretty weird time of it for quite a while now.'

'Don't you think you should take some time off?'

'Probably,' he conceded, remembering that Helen had advised him to do the same thing.

'When I know for sure that Jess is alive and well, I'm going to fly off somewhere very warm and just lie on a beach for a week.'

'That sounds good. Where did you have in mind?'

'I don't care. I'll just walk into a travel agent and book the first place I like the sound of.'

'That's impulsive.'

'I like impulsive. It's good sometimes to drop everything and take off.'

'I wish I was more like that.'

'You could be.' She climbed out of bed then and started to pull on her clothes. 'And I'll need someone to rub the oil into my back, if you'd like to apply for the job.'

15

She was draped on him. They somehow managed to get down the stairs despite this, though Lena stopped to kiss Tom before they entered the kitchen, then she looked up and noticed Helen sitting at the table watching them, her hands around a mug of tea.

'Oh hi,' she said breezily, letting go of Tom.

'I thought you'd have gone out by now,' said Tom, excusing their public show of affection.

'I might go out later,' said Helen. 'I'll go now, if you like.'

'Don't be daft.' Tom flicked the kettle on and started pulling things out of the fridge.

'Have you had breakfast?'

'Ages ago.'

'Okay,' he said. 'Looks like it's bacon sarnies for two then.' He smiled at Lena, as if she'd landed from the heavens, and she gazed back at him adoringly, like he'd just promised her the moon.

Helen wanted to say, *It's only a bacon sandwich*, but instead she asked, 'Did you have a nice time?' When Lena's eyes widened questioningly, she added quickly: 'In town, after I left you. You must have done,' she concluded, and felt immediately foolish again.

'Oh yes,' Lena responded brightly. 'He took me everywhere, didn't you?' And she smiled up at Tom again while he cooked the bacon.

'Only the good places,' he told Helen. 'What did you get up to?'

'Research. Into the Susan Verity case. I bought a book.'

He laughed. 'You know what they say about all work and no play, Helen.'

'I am *not* dull,' she answered, and even she realized this made her sound like a petulant child.

'I'm only pulling your leg,' he answered needlessly. He was in an irritatingly good mood. 'Did you find out much?'

'I'll tell you later if you are interested.'

'Of course I'm interested.'

Lena looked uncomfortable then. 'I'm heading off after this.' She meant the bacon sandwich. 'You can have him back then.'

The room set aside for Adrian Wicklow's visitors was small and bare, with grey breezeblock walls and barred windows. It had a door at each end and Bradshaw was shown into it through one of them. He sat down at a small table facing the other door and waited. There was a second chair, but no other furniture.

The delay was unsettling. Bradshaw had conducted prison visits before to follow up on leads – he recalled Tom Carney coming to Durham jail repeatedly to speak to a convicted murderer – but this was different. Richard Bell had been found guilty of beating his lover to death with a hammer and that must have been disconcerting for Tom, but Bell hadn't murdered children. Bradshaw wondered what kind of man could not only do that but actually take some form of twisted pleasure from the act.

The second door opened abruptly and Adrian Wicklow stepped through it, followed by two prison guards. He was a huge man: tall, with a powerful, muscular frame; and Bradshaw couldn't help but look at him from the perspective of his tiny victims. They must have been terrified, he reasoned, when this enormous man bore down on them. Wicklow was completely bald but Bradshaw couldn't tell if he shaved his head or if it was due to the cancer treatment.

Wicklow looked at Bradshaw and surveyed him without comment, then he crossed the floor to the chair reserved for him and pulled it out, before sitting down opposite the detective. He stared at Bradshaw silently for a while before asking, 'What rank are you, Officer?' His voice was deep, his tone immediately combative.

'I'm a detective sergeant.'

'Only a DS,' Wicklow did not bother to hide his scorn. 'I thought they'd send at least a DI. In the old days, I'd have got a Detective Super, at least.' Then he thought for a moment. 'Unless it was Meade. They often sent Meade.' He sounded almost wistful, as if his adversary were an old friend.

'Yes, well, you've wasted a great deal of police time in those intervening years, Wicklow,' Bradshaw told him. 'You should be grateful we bother to send anyone at all.'

'Got the short straw, did you?' Wicklow asked amiably. 'Or were you the only one they could spare? How does that feel, I wonder, knowing you're not really needed? How long have you been a DS? Must be frustrating – seeing brighter, younger men leaping ahead of you, leaving you behind?'

'I came here because I have been asked to reopen the Susan Verity case. My DCI reckons you have something to say about it. Since you previously claimed to be her killer, before repeatedly changing your story, it seemed sensible to take a few moments of my time to drive down here and speak to you about it.' He locked eyes with Wicklow. 'Frankly, though, I have many better things to do with my time than have my career limitations critiqued by a man who shits in a bucket in his cell every morning and hasn't had a stroll in the park for at least fifteen years.' Bradshaw got to his feet. 'so I think I'll just leave.'

'Don't be so hasty, Detective,' the killer said. 'Or so sensitive. I'm only seeing if you can take it *and* dish it out.' Wicklow smiled without humour. 'As for shitting in a bucket, we don't do that any more, thanks to me. You may have read about my campaign in the newspapers. I took it all the way to the European Court of Human Rights, and I won. Slopping-out has ended here, and who could possibly deny that's a good thing? It was degrading. I believe you can tell a lot about a society from the way it treats its prisoners . . . but I digress. We haven't even been properly introduced.'

'I know your name is Wicklow; mine is Bradshaw. Now, do you have anything relevant to tell me or am I on my way?'

'I didn't kill Susan Verity,' Wicklow said abruptly. 'Is that relevant enough for you?'

'Then who did?'

The child murderer smiled again. 'I might be able to help you with that,' he said archly, 'so why don't you sit down?' Bradshaw hesitated for a moment. He'd been on the verge of leaving, he'd very much wanted to turn his back on this madman, but where would that get him? He pulled his chair back and it scraped jarringly on the floor, then he sat down again.

'I can read you like a book,' Wicklow said. 'You don't keep anything back, do you, Detective? I know exactly what you're thinking.'

Bradshaw folded his arms. 'What am I thinking?'

'You don't want to be here, for starters. You look as if you'd rather be anywhere else but sitting opposite me. Should I take it personally, Bradshaw? Speak freely. Do I disgust you?'

'I will,' said Bradshaw evenly. 'You do.'

Wicklow's face changed slightly, a combination of anger and disappointment, perhaps, but he soon recovered. 'And yet here you are. Most people who visit me are courteous, at least, and do you know why? Because they want something from me.'

'I was sent here,' Bradshaw began, 'because we heard you

were seriously ill and there might be some things you wanted to get off your chest. I was told you were dying.'

Wicklow's voice was steady, his words calm. 'I am. Lung cancer. I blame all those dirty roll-ups we make in here. No proper filters. They tell me I have weeks, but it could be months.' Then he seemed to brighten, as if it were amusing: 'Though I could even drop down dead tomorrow, so they said, when I pressed them. Truth is, the doctors really don't know. They're like the weather men, who make forecasts based on all that scientific knowledge and years of training but are still wrong at least half of the time.'

'And do you think they are wrong this time?'

Wicklow shook his head. 'I *am* dying,' he confirmed. 'They just don't know when.' And he laughed without humour. 'So you'd better hurry up and tell me what you want, hadn't you, before it's too late.'

'You know what I want.'

Wicklow sighed. 'You would like to hear about Susan Verity and you want to know where the bodies are buried. That's all police officers ever want to know. The doctors, the criminologists, the psychiatrists – at least I can have an interesting conversation with them about my motives, my background; even Father Noonan and I can pass an interesting hour together. We discuss faith, God, the prospects of an afterlife. But I get none of that with you people. Police officers are so boring.'

'I am not here for your entertainment.'

'Those children are dead and gone, you know. Finding their rotted corpses won't bring them back or provide any comfort to their families. They think it will, but it won't.'

'It might,' said Bradshaw, 'if they can give them a Christian burial. You would understand that if you had genuine religious faith and weren't just stringing Father Noonan along.'

Wicklow chuckled. 'I have faith,' he said, but he didn't

elaborate. 'And Father Noonan loves coming here. He's trying to save my immortal soul. It's a big job, and it's going to make his name. God's going to reserve a special cloud for him when he goes; a nice big one with a sea view. What about you, though? Don't you want to make a name for yourself too?'

'Not particularly.'

'Isn't that why you are here? You say it's for the families but, really, it's so you and all the people above you can have a career. If you dig up those children, you'll probably get a promotion, a few extra bob in your pocket on pay day, your name in all the papers. That's the real reason, isn't it?'

Bradshaw said nothing.

Wicklow let out a breath. 'You're a real live wire, you are.' He looked bored now, as if the game were no longer to his liking.

'Susan Verity,' said Bradshaw. 'Tell me about her.'

Wicklow immediately re-engaged with him. 'Why her? Why Susan in particular, and not the others?'

'Because some people are saying you didn't do it. *You* even said you didn't do it, but then, you've said a lot of things.'

'Well, if you're not going to believe me, why should I bother to tell you anything?'

'Because you're dying,' Bradshaw reminded him, 'and this is the very last game you get to play. If you die before you give up the bodies or admit what happened to Susan, you'll go down in the files as unfinished business, and you wouldn't want that. Better to tie up the loose ends, don't you think?'

'Maybe I'll go down as an enigma.' He smiled. 'Like Jack the Ripper. Everyone still talks about Jack, because nobody knows who he really was.'

Bradshaw nodded. 'But even the real Jack died without getting the credit for his notoriety. His own neighbours wouldn't have known who he was. What's the point of that? You've been caught and jailed these past fifteen years and you admitted you killed children. You're not trying to maintain your innocence or get yourself parole. No Home Secretary was ever going to release Adrian Wicklow. We both know that was never going to happen, even before your latest diagnosis, which ensures that it won't. If we finish your story here today, then all the head doctors and criminology students will carry on talking about you for years –'

'They'll do that anyway.' Wicklow seemed bored again, or at least disappointed that this was all Bradshaw could offer him.

'Yes, but they'll never understand,' said Bradshaw, 'will they?' Wicklow turned his head slightly so they had eye contact again. He was interested in that, Bradshaw could tell.

'Go out on a high, Wicklow,' Bradshaw urged him. 'Give us the bodies of the kids and tell us what happened to Susan, and you can put it all down, chapter and verse. Tell them your story so no one can distort it. Wouldn't you like that? Wouldn't that finish things off neatly?'

'Funny you should say that,' said Wicklow, 'but I've been working on my story, day after day, in my cell.'

'You've written a book?'

'Not written,' Wicklow corrected him. 'They wouldn't let me have a pen.'

'Because you stabbed a fellow inmate with one,' Bradshaw reminded him. 'In the neck.'

Wicklow was dismissive. 'That was years ago, when I first arrived here and I still had some contact with other inmates around the place – in the dinner queue, on the way back from the showers. *He* wanted to kill *me*.' He shrugged. 'It was self-defence.'

'He tried to kill you?' pressed Bradshaw. 'It didn't say that in the report.'

'He *wanted* to kill me,' Wicklow said again, more firmly this time, and Bradshaw wondered if the murderer had convinced himself of this in his own crazed mind then struck first. No wonder they'd kept him in solitary ever since. Bradshaw had assumed it was for Wicklow's own safety, but perhaps the other inmates were the ones at risk if Wicklow was allowed to mingle with them.

'They let me have a dictaphone, though,' said Wicklow, 'so I could record my thoughts. The doctors loved that. They thought they could evaluate me without even being in the same room. I didn't mind. I wanted to set the record straight, you see, just like you said, but they won't let me publish it. They won't even let me send it to a publisher for consideration.'

'Well, they wouldn't, but I'm sure they'd let students and academics hear it.'

'They have,' confirmed Wicklow, 'but not a single one of them understood me. They were too scholarly, you see, they saw things that weren't there, like critics staring at modern art and seeing great hidden significance in a blob of paint.' He shook his head. 'That's what you get when you deal with someone who's not from the real world.' Then he regarded Bradshaw archly. 'You, on the other hand, Detective – well, you've walked those mean streets, haven't you? I'm sure you've probably got a couple of A levels, but you didn't waste years of your life cooped up in a library studying for a PhD on serial killers.' A frown appeared on his forehead. 'That's a thought, you know.' He contemplated it for a moment before revealing it to Bradshaw: 'How would you like it if I made a deal with you?'

'No deals,' Bradshaw was experiencing a rising sense of alarm. He could guess what was coming next.

'I'll give you what you want to know if you can tell me what I want to hear. How does that sound?'

'Why don't you just stop pissing about, Wicklow, and tell me what happened to Susan?' Bradshaw was feeling desperate now and flailing. He knew he was losing. 'If you even know?'

'Oh, I know all right,' said Wicklow, 'and I'll tell you all about it, but I'm not going to make it easy for you. You have to prove yourself worthy. I can't just give up my biggest secrets to the first DS who walks through the door. This will make you famous, Bradshaw, and everyone will want to be your friend, but I need to know you are good enough. You have to earn the right.'

Bradshaw didn't reply. He was feeling cornered, fenced in with nowhere else to go. Wicklow spelt it out for him. 'Listen to my story.'

Ian Bradshaw shook his head. 'No.'

'Why not? What are you afraid of? It's only words. What could possibly lie between those pages that can harm you, a grown man, a police officer who says he wants to understand the truth? Well, it's all in there – most of it, at any rate – and if you can tell me one simple, little thing after you've read it all, then I will give you what you crave the most: the truth, every last bit of it.'

Bradshaw could tell by the sinister smirk on Wicklow's face that there was more to it than that. He did want to know the truth, but it was facts he was interested in, not the lurid and self-justifying description of a monster's life. He could tell just by looking at Wicklow right there and then that his autobiography would be riddled with things Ian Bradshaw did *not* want to know.

'Not interested.'

Wicklow looked smug. 'Well, you say that now, but I've got a very strong feeling you'll be back, Detective.' He smiled. 'Because it's the only way you'll ever learn what really happened to Susan.'

16

'So,' Helen said when they were alone, 'you obviously hit it off with Lena.'

'That was what you wanted, right?'

'Of course,' she said. 'I'm pleased for you.'

'You don't sound pleased,' he said. 'You practically threw us together, remember? I didn't even want to go and say hello, but you engineered it.' Then he added, 'For which I am, obviously, grateful.'

'She seems like a very nice lady,' said Helen primly. 'I was just a bit surprised . . .'

'By what?'

'Seeing her this morning.'

'Oh,' he said. 'Why?'

'I thought you might take her number, ask her out. Not just –'

'Sleep with her?' Tom was irritated by her tone now. 'So now you're disappointed in me?'

'It's your life,' she said breezily.

'Yes,' he said, 'it is, and you've been banging on at me to get a girlfriend, and when I do –'

'She's not exactly your girlfriend, though, is she? When I said you needed someone in your life, I didn't mean just for a few hours.'

'It wasn't a one-night stand. If you must know, I'm seeing her again,' he said.

'Oh, I thought . . .' She hesitated. 'I didn't realize.'

'Let's talk about something else,' he said, resolving not to tell her about Lena's missing sister, assuming she wouldn't be happy about that either, if it took him away from the work they were doing together.

'Okay,' she agreed gratefully. 'What do you want to talk about?'

'That book you're reading,' said Tom. 'Any good?'

'It's interesting,' she said cautiously. 'There are some good bits and some not so good bits. Then there's the part I'm reading now. It's all about the kids who went out to play with Susan Verity and survived.'

'What about them?'

'They're cursed,' she told him. 'According to this book.'

'How so?'

'One of them died young, another lost his partner in an accident, one of them had a complete nervous breakdown just before taking his final exams and another has apparently been so convinced she will become a victim of this so-called curse she has vowed never to marry or have children, because she doesn't want her husband and kids to be afflicted by it too.'

Tom snorted. 'That's ridiculous.' He thought for a moment. 'That's four of them. Didn't the documentary say six children went out to play that morning? If Susan Verity makes it five, then who was the sixth?'

'Billy Thorpe – and that's another story.'

Tom sat down next to her. 'Go on, then,' he urged. 'Tell me about these cursed children.'

17

1976

> *All the boys in our school aren't very nice*
> *Except Danny Gilbert, he's all right*
> *He took me to the pictures*
> *He sat me on his knee*
> *He said, 'My duck, my darling, will you marry me?'*
> *'Yes!'*
> *'No!'*
> *'Yes!'*
> *'No!'*
> *'Yes!'*
>
> *— Skipping song*

'It's all right, I suppose,' said Susan doubtfully. The girls were surveying the den.

'All right?' Danny was amazed. 'It's the best. It took us ages.'

'It's a good den,' Susan conceded, and her seal of approval was the signal for everyone to enter it and begin playing together.

The trouble was, nobody could agree on what to do. The boys wanted to play a Second World War game they called Japs and English, which involved hiding, then jumping out on each other and shooting with guns made out of sticks. The girls wanted to play a game with Michelle's skipping rope called Spanish Lady, but the boys wouldn't do that because it was 'soft', and no boy round here wanted to look soft.

In the end, they settled on a game that involved the boys

going off together 'hunting' while the girls played house. Playing separately in and around the den seemed to be the best option at first. Later, they played A Bottle of White Medicine together, where each kid had to hold a finger of the person who was *it*, then that person listed a bunch of stuff that Dr White had, ending up shouting, '*White medicine!*' Then everyone had to scatter because that was the signal for *it* to try and catch everyone else. After a while, though, everyone agreed it was far too hot to be running around. They tried more children's games, until they got bored because they'd been playing them all summer, then the conversation turned back to the dare. It was Danny who mentioned it, but Billy listened intently because he couldn't imagine any way Susan could wriggle out of this after she'd sworn to do it.

'We're not kissing you,' said Susan flatly.

'You swore,' Danny reminded her. 'You crossed your heart and hoped to die.'

'Yes, but that was before we saw the den,' said Susan, as if their handiwork had not lived up to the girls' expectations and now the dare was off. Susan didn't seem to understand the sacred nature of these things. She had sworn to do something, and now she said she wouldn't do it. You weren't supposed to just change your mind like that. Billy didn't understand how girls could see things so differently to boys.

'We'll do another dare,' she said firmly, 'but not a kissing one.'

And that was that. Somehow, nobody could challenge Susan Verity when she was like this. Billy concentrated on hiding his disappointment.

'We'll do a truth instead,' said Michelle, but the boys didn't understand what she meant. 'Truth or dare,' she explained, along with the rules, which involved pulling straws to see who would go first. She plucked some blades of grass and made sure they were different lengths before offering them.

Kevin got the shortest straw so he had to go first. Michelle asked him, 'Who do you love?'

'I love Sarah Morgan,' he replied, without hesitation.

Billy scoffed, 'She's eighteen!' He couldn't see how Kevin could possibly end up going out with the prettiest girl in the village.

'I don't care,' said Kevin, 'I can still love her.' And he did some maths to back up the feasibility of his passion. 'When I'm eighteen, she'll still only be . . . twenty-six.' He nodded firmly, as if this made it all right and he could still marry the girl of his dreams. 'What about you then?'

Billy flushed and stammered, 'I – I'm not next.'

Andrea was. It was decided that everyone should answer the same question. 'Who do you love?' repeated Michelle.

There was a gap while Andrea composed herself then, almost defiantly, answered, 'Danny.' Everyone shrieked and fell about laughing. Andrea flushed bright red. It was hard to tell whether Danny was flattered or embarrassed.

'And who does Danny love?' asked Michelle in a teasing tone, hoping it would be Andrea.

'It's not my turn,' he answered.

'But does Danny love Andrea back?' Susan Verity's tone was mocking.

'Course I don't,' snapped Danny, and even Billy felt for poor Andrea then. Her head went down, but she said nothing.

'It's Billy's turn!' said Michelle gleefully, as they had decided to go boy–girl no matter who had the shortest straw.

Billy's mouth felt very dry and he shuffled his feet.

'Go on then, Billy,' Michelle urged. 'Who do you love?'

Before he could allow himself to consider whether this was a good idea or not, he blurted out the word, 'Susan,' then stared at her hopefully.

There was further hilarity at this, but it was more muted,

and Billy realized this definitely wasn't a good thing. It was as if his dream was somehow ludicrous. Only Kevin was rolling around on the floor, clutching his sides and laughing loudly in an exaggerated way Billy found excruciating.

'And does Susan love Billy?' asked Michelle, through her own muted laughter.

'Don't be stupid!' snapped Susan, and Billy's long-held dream died in that moment. It was the anger in her response that was most hurtful. Billy loved Susan, but Susan could not even entertain the idea of loving him back.

Billy looked down at the ground and wondered if he could think of an excuse to leave soon and go home.

'It's Susan's turn,' said Michelle.

'I don't love anyone,' said Susan firmly.

'That's not fair,' said Danny. 'You have to say someone. That's the game. You shouldn't have played it if you weren't going to say someone. *They* all did it.' And he pointed towards Kevin, Billy and Andrea.

'If you want to play,' sneered Susan, '*you* say someone then.'

'There's no one,' he said quickly, and Billy wondered if he would have mentioned Susan when it was his turn, had she not refused to play.

'Well then, Danny Gilbert, you're just the same as me. It's a stupid game anyway.'

'Then we'll stop playing it,' snapped Michelle.

'It isn't fair,' said Andrea. 'We all had to.' But no one was listening to Andrea. No one ever listened to Andrea.

'You won't do *any* dares,' grumbled Danny.

'I will,' said Susan.

'I know a great dare,' continued Kevin, 'but none of you girls will do it.'

'We will,' Andrea told him. 'There's nothing you can do that we can't.'

Kevin smiled then, because he knew he was about to shock them. 'The hay bales.'

'What hay bales?' asked Michelle.

'There's only one load of hay bales,' said Kevin, 'and they're in Marsh's barn.'

Billy panicked. The boys had played in the bales before and been chased away from them by the farmer, who had gone mental. 'I know who you are! I know where you live!' he had roared and Billy had believed him. He ran as if the Grey Lady were chasing him. And now Kevin wanted to go back there?

'Why do you want to play in some stupid bales?'

'They're brilliant,' said Kevin. 'You can build dens and everything.'

'You've got a den here,' said Susan.

'You're only saying that because you're too scared to go on Marsh Farm,' said Kevin. 'Because the farmer has a gun.'

'Who wouldn't be scared?' asked Michelle. 'What if he shoots us?'

'I know summat you don't.' Kevin was enjoying himself now. 'The farmer is out in his fields, 'cos he has to kill all the weeds. My dad said that's what he does. He sprays pesky-sides on them for hours and hours. We can play in his barn and he won't even know about it.'

There was silence then, while everyone considered the serious nature of this dare. It saddened Billy deeply to think Susan might be actually contemplating doing something this scary as an alternative to kissing him.

'Told you you wouldn't do it,' said Kevin smugly.

Susan was defiant. 'We will if you will.'

18

'So you've just got to read his book then?' asked Kane when Bradshaw had briefed him, as if this were a simple, not entirely unpleasant, task. 'Or listen to it, at any rate?'

'And come to some sort of deduction about the motivation for Wicklow's crimes,' Bradshaw reminded him. 'He wants me to tell him why he did what he did.' He shook his head at the lunacy of the idea.

'Well, I would have that thought much was obvious, wouldn't you?'

'Really?'

'Yes, he's a bloody madman.'

Bradshaw sighed. 'I don't think that's the answer he is looking for, sir.'

'Maybe not,' admitted Kane. 'So have you got this book of his, then?'

'No.'

'Why not?'

'Because I don't actually want to hear it.'

'I don't understand,' said Kane, 'I thought you had to.'

'That's what Wicklow is saying, but I don't have to do everything he asks, sir.'

'But how will you work out why he does his crimes if you don't? It's in there is it, his justification?'

'He says it is, but a number of people with letters after their names have heard it and they couldn't answer the question, so I'm not sure I'll be able to.'

'How do you know if you won't try?' snapped Kane.

'Sir, I don't want to try.'

'Why not, man?'

'It's his life story. Presumably, much of the text refers to his twisted mind and goes into graphic detail about the killings.'

'Well?' Kane didn't understand. 'What's the difference between that and questioning a murderer? They often go into graphic detail once they've admitted what they did. It's a bit late in the day to suddenly turn squeamish, Bradshaw. You're a detective. You've got to be a man about this and just get on with it.'

DCI Kane's argument may have been unsophisticated, but it was hard to challenge. All Bradshaw could manage was 'This feels different somehow.'

Kane grew impatient then. 'Look, all we need to know is what the bloody hell happened to young Susan Verity and where those other bodies are buried.' He fixed a steely gaze on Bradshaw. 'Is this because you're in – what-you-call-it . . . therapy?' He almost spat the last word.

'Counselling,' Bradshaw corrected him. 'And it wasn't my decision. I don't want to go, but it's obligatory. They made it conditional when I was made a DS. If I wanted the rank, I had to keep seeing Dr Mellor.'

'It's all bollocks, anyway, isn't it?' queried his DCI.

'You'll find no disagreement from me on that score, sir.'

'So,' said Kane, 'what then?'

'I'm just not sure I want to delve that deeply into Wicklow's mind.'

'Well, delve you must,' ordered his senior officer. 'I chose you for a reason, Bradshaw. You're a bright lad – you've got qualifications most of my men wouldn't have a snowball's chance in hell of attaining – I thought this would be right up your street . . . but all of that is by the by.' He waved his hand dismissively. 'If you won't do it for the challenge then do it for Susan Verity . . . or do it for me.'

'Sir?'

'I gave the chief constable your name. I told him you were on the case, I assured him you were the best man for the job, and he wants this solved. He's gone on the record on TV about it, and so has the AC, so it must be done. Otherwise, we'll both be for the high jump, you understand?'

'I think I do, sir, yes.'

'Good. I hope you do. So start listening to this bloody book, work out whatever it is Adrian Wicklow wants to hear from you and do it quickly. We've got to find out where the bodies are buried before they bury *him*, you hear?'

'Yes, sir,' said Bradshaw, without enthusiasm, then a thought struck him. 'There's a lot of paperwork in the case files. I could use a bit of help there.'

'I'll bet there is. They were getting calls from all over the country.' He frowned. 'I don't know who we can spare, though. We've got a double murder to solve, and everyone else is on that.' Two men had been found dead from gunshot wounds in a car parked in a rural area. Both had previous convictions for supplying drugs, so the most likely reason for their deaths was a turf war between dealers. Proving who had lured them out there and pulled the trigger, or who it was that gave the order, wouldn't be easy, however. Until the perpetrator was brought to justice, the newspapers would portray County Durham as a lawless place gone bad, so the force had put virtually every available man on it until they could make an arrest.

'I was thinking, since the chief constable and the AC are so committed to solving this one, perhaps a little outside help might be useful?'

'What did you have in mind?'

'Helen Norton is an excellent researcher. She could probably wade through that archive in no time, and since there's door-knocking to be done . . .'

'Tom-bloody-Carney,' sighed Kane.

'Might be simpler than taking detectives away from live investigations. We've still got money in the budget to fund the hire of experts and consultants.'

'I'm not sure Carney qualifies as either of those things.'

'Maybe not,' admitted Bradshaw, 'but he solves cases. You can't deny that.'

'I just wish he could manage it without causing absolute chaos in the process.'

'You know what they say about omelettes and eggs,' Bradshaw reminded him.

'All right. I'll allow them back on the pay roll, assuming you can persuade them to help you. They're probably minted these days, from selling stories to the *Sun*. Just make sure this frees you up to study Wicklow's memoir.'

'Okay.' It seemed a fair enough deal under the circumstances. 'There was one other thing,' he told his DCI. 'On the way in, I was accosted by a priest.'

'Oh Jesus,' said Kane. 'Father Noonan.'

'You know about him?' asked Bradshaw.

'Lord Longford in a dog collar.' He nodded. 'Thinks there is good in everyone and nobody is beyond salvation, as long as they see the light and turn towards God. I'd have warned you about him if I'd realized he was going to try and get in your way. I assume he gave you a speech about his pet project?'

'How do you mean?'

'Saving the soul of Adrian Wicklow,' announced Kane grandly. 'He's been trying to convert Wicklow to Catholicism for years. Father Noonan has become obsessed with it, in fact. He no longer even has a parish. I think he's an embarrassment to the Catholic Church, and that's saying something these days. They've moved him on and sidelined him. He doesn't take Mass with a congregation any more, just undertakes church work in the community and visits Wicklow on an almost daily basis. The man's delusional but, since he learned his favourite prisoner has terminal cancer, he'll be even more determined than ever to ensure he is ready to enter the kingdom of heaven.'

'He sounds unhinged.'

'He is a bit, I think,' agreed Kane, 'but Wicklow seems to bring that out in people. The good father wants to hear the killer's final confession so he can absolve him of his sins and send him on his way to heaven with his slate wiped clean. Don't worry about him. Was there anything else?' Bradshaw shook his head. 'Good,' said Kane. 'And, seriously, this Wicklow thing' – his DCI tried to finish on an upbeat note – 'it's only a bloody book. What's the worst that could happen?'

I could end up topping myself, Bradshaw thought, or living in a croft in Scotland.

19

Ian Bradshaw hadn't been to Tom's house in a while. The place had changed. Sure, he had spent time, effort and not a little money turning it from a run-down, ramshackle old wreck into a modern house with a new kitchen, bathroom, floorboards, doors and windows, but it wasn't just that.

It was the outside that was really different.

Where there had once been an open driveway, a high metal gate now filled the gap between the thick hedge at the bottom of the front garden and the house next door, and there was tall fencing on all sides. You couldn't just open this gate and walk in, either. You had to press a buzzer and wait for someone to come out and admit you. When they did, a motion sensor triggered a light that shone from the house down on to the driveway and illuminated it. A closed-circuit video camera situated next to a top-of-the-range burglar alarm pointed at you. The windows had discreet bars on them. The place was a bloody fortress.

Tom's original plan had been to do up an old house and sell it for a profit. Now it was his home, his office and his castle all rolled into one.

It was true that a really determined attacker could still break into this house, but they would have to be very good indeed to manage it without alerting Tom or Helen or leaving traces of their presence. The investigative reporters probably managed a decent night's sleep here, and that wasn't easy when you were on Jimmy McCree's hit list.

McCree was quite probably the most dangerous man in

Newcastle and, thanks in large part to Helen, Tom and Bradshaw himself, the notorious gangster had recently been convicted for the first time and was currently serving a three-year custodial sentence. It should have been a lot longer, Bradshaw recalled resentfully. If there had been any proof of his involvement in several murders, which everyone knew he had played a part in, it would have been life. As Bradshaw buzzed at the gate at the foot of Tom's driveway, he wondered if all of these security measures would really be enough to protect them, once Jimmy McCree was released.

'Hello.' The disembodied voice did not sound alarmed at having a day-time visitor.

'It's me.'

'Who's me?'

'Stop mucking about. I know you can see me on your big-brother-is-watching-you machine.' He waved at the CCTV camera.

'I'm sorry,' said Tom. 'No traders, no hawkers, no rag-and-bone men, no Jehovah's witnesses and, definitely, no detective sergeants.'

'Open up, you bastard, or I'll have you arrested on trumped-up charges.'

'Wouldn't be the first time,' said Tom's robotic voice.

There was a buzzing sound, and the gate unlocked and opened slightly. Bradshaw pushed it open fully and made a point of carefully closing it behind him til it clicked securely back into place.

'This is good,' said Bradshaw, surveying the office-cum-lounge where Helen and Tom did most of their work. He peered at the two large personal computers and the printer wedged between them, the fax machine and the several in-trays full of paper.

'Yeah,' said Tom. 'It certainly cost enough.'

'It's an investment,' protested Helen. 'We can do our own DTP on this.'

'Really?' said Bradshaw, even though he had no idea what 'DTP' actually stood for.

'Yes, look. I'm doing newsletters for businesses when we have quiet times.' She showed him one of the in-house magazines she was in the process of producing, for a catering company, with dozens of employees kitted out in matching uniforms and unflattering hairnets. They were smiling and raising triumphant fists in the photograph, as if they had each landed the best job in the world.

'Nice,' was all Bradshaw could think to say about it.

'If you need a parish magazine at short notice, Helen's your girl,' said Tom, and Helen gave him a dirty look. Bradshaw was detecting more tension than normal between these two today. Maybe they spent too much time together.

'It pays the bills when we're not working on something bigger,' Helen told Bradshaw.

'Which is most of the time,' said Tom ruefully. 'I still think the salesman saw me coming. He was banging on about how you can't afford to be obsolete in a high-tech age, and we were flush at the time so I went along with it, but he was a proper zealot. He told me that, one day, computers would do everything for us – play music and films, find us friends, or a girlfriend, even buy our groceries.'

'That'll never happen,' said Bradshaw. 'Only saddos sign up for dating companies, and people like to see and feel the things they buy.'

'That's exactly what I told him,' said Tom. 'I'll put the kettle on.' He tapped the PC. 'Our whizzy computer hasn't worked out how to do that yet.'

*

When Tom returned with three steaming mugs of tea, Bradshaw asked, 'Did you see that documentary about Susan Verity's disappearance?'

'No, I missed it,' said Tom, and when Bradshaw seemed surprised, he added, 'I was out.'

Did Bradshaw spot a slight look of disapproval from Helen? He fished into his bag and withdrew a blank video cassette. 'Just as well I recorded it then,' he said, and handed it to Tom.

'I recorded it as well,' Helen said. 'I thought we'd watch it together.'

'Anything earth-shattering on there?' asked Tom.

'Nothing we didn't expect, but why not see for yourselves?'

'So why did your big chief come out so strongly to reopen the case?'

'He's on the shortlist.'

'Oh,' said Tom.

'What shortlist?' asked Helen.

'The Home Secretary might be looking to appoint a new head of the Metropolitan Police,' Tom explained. 'There are a few suitable candidates and it seems our local chief constable is one of them, though I'm surprised by that. Durham isn't exactly a tough proving ground.'

'Rumour has it the Home Secretary is considering a low-profile appointment this time,' said Bradshaw carefully. 'An uncontroversial, safe pair of hands.'

'Otherwise known as someone who can be easily controlled,' said Tom.

'With no skeletons in the cupboard to embarrass him – which is why he wants to be seen to clear up an old cold case his predecessors cocked up.'

'So they handed you this golden opportunity?' asked Tom, and Bradshaw nodded. 'But you have limited resources?'

'How did you know that?'

'You're here, aren't you? And it doesn't feel like a social call. What do you want from us?'

'The same as before: help me solve another cold case.'

'How would that work,' asked Helen, 'in practice?'

'You'd come on to the payroll again, as experts, bringing specialist skills to assist us with our enquiries.'

'Is this because Kane really rates us or because you can't spare any extra manpower?' asked Tom.

'Both. Kane *does* rate you, or he wouldn't have agreed to it but, I'll be honest, if you say no, I don't know where I'll turn to next.'

'I'm not sure, Ian,' said Tom. 'We'll have to think about it.'

Bradshaw sighed, then Helen said, 'Don't wind him up.'

'What do you mean?' asked Tom.

She turned to Bradshaw. 'We were going to call you,' she said, 'to see if you needed any help.'

'Great,' said Bradshaw. 'So you'll do it?'

Helen shot Tom a look that was loaded with significance.

'She normally plays more hard to get,' he said.

'So,' said Helen, 'where do we begin?'

Bradshaw walked towards the television and slotted the video cassette into the VCR. 'With this, for starters.'

20

The programme began with a pre-title sequence involving images of County Durham countryside, then a photograph of a smiling ten-year-old girl was superimposed on it while a dramatic voiceover informed the viewer that a scandal was about to be uncovered.

'This is the last picture of Susan Verity, taken days before she vanished, almost twenty years ago. Her disappearance from the village of Maiden Hill in the north-east of England was eventually blamed on a notorious child killer, almost five years after she went missing.' There was a pause and the screen changed to a shot of the man doing the speaking, investigative reporter Craig Hughes. 'But was Adrian Wicklow really guilty or simply a convenient scapegoat for an under-pressure police force mired in incompetence, alcoholism and corruption?'

'Wanker,' hissed Bradshaw.

'Tonight, *Nothing but the Truth* examines the case of tragic Susan, who went out to play with her friends one summer's day and was never seen again. We uncover the mistakes and lies of Durham police as they failed to find the girl and struggled to solve the case that became known as "the Maiden Hill Mystery".'

'Never heard anyone call it that before,' said Bradshaw contemptuously, but Helen hushed him.

'It was the morning of 30 August 1976,' continued the reporter, 'a day like any other during that long, hot summer, when Susan Verity left her house to see two friends, Andrea Craven and Michelle Dutton. Those of us who can remember that far back will recall a Britain gripped by heatwave, a year of severe droughts and record temperatures.'

The reporter went on, 'The girls met up with three boys their own age and went to a den they'd made at the edge of some fields approximately three miles from their village. In the course of that day the six children played together before splintering into smaller groups and finally heading home. Only five of them would make it safely back to their parents. Susan Verity was never seen again.

'Her disappearance triggered the biggest police search in the history of the county, but no trace of Susan was ever discovered, apart from a red hairband found on a local farm. This crucial evidence was largely ignored by the police.'

'No, it wasn't,' said Bradshaw.

'Sshh,' hissed Helen, but it was a half-hearted intervention.

The voiceover resumed. 'The farm belonged to Colin Marsh, a man with a troubled history. Police had been called to his farm previously on a number of occasions . . .'

'And *he* usually called them,' Bradshaw reminded them. Tom and Helen were starting to get used to Bradshaw's cynical interjections now and Helen no longer bothered to try and prevent them.

'. . . Despite this, Farmer Marsh retained a firearms licence for a shotgun which he kept at the farm. He claimed this was merely to drive away foxes . . .'

'Virtually all farmers do that,' said Bradshaw.

'. . . but we have uncovered the truth. An unstable Colin Marsh waved the shotgun at local children before and, in one instance, actually discharged it above their heads. Police reprimanded Marsh for this shocking behaviour but, for some unknown reason, did not take his shotgun away from him. Marsh was a near-neighbour of former Chief Superintendent Grant Taylor, and it is claimed the two men knew each other socially.'

'Claimed by whom?' asked Bradshaw. 'And what do they mean by *knew each other socially*?'

'Presumably, the Masons or the local Tory party,' offered Tom, but Bradshaw didn't bite.

The reporter continued. 'Were local magistrates perhaps influenced by Marsh's powerful friends? Far from showing remorse for discharging the shotgun, the introverted loner showed signs of bitterness over his treatment, witnesses claim, and planned to take the law into his own hands to prevent trespassing on his land.'

'If he was an introverted loner, how would they know?' asked Bradshaw.

'Susan Verity was last seen by two of her friends, Billy Thorpe and Kevin Robson, taking a path home that would have crossed Farmer Marsh's land. The missing headband was found a hundred yards inside the boundary fence that marks the perimeter of Marsh's farm, but Farmer Marsh, who died four years ago, denied having seen the girl or any of the other children, despite claims that they had all crossed his corn fields on their way to the den that day and that he had chased them from a barn where he stored his hay bales earlier that afternoon. Marsh was noted for his hatred of trespassers on his land, particularly young ones, who trampled his crops on their way to play in the countryside.'

'So the poor bugger is dead,' said Bradshaw, 'which gives him no right to reply. The programme is making him look like the killer because her headband was found on his land.'

'That and the fact he had a shotgun,' Helen reminded him, 'and he fired it at children.'

'Technically, he fired it over them,' said Tom, 'which may be a mightily irresponsible thing to do, but it doesn't sound like he was actually trying to kill them. I'm pretty staggered that the police didn't take his gun off him, though. Friends in high places?'

'Possibly,' conceded Bradshaw, 'but Superintendent Taylor died a while back too, so we won't be able to ask him if he and the late farmer knew each other, let alone if they were friends. It's a bit bloody convenient to make your viewers suspicious of people who are no longer around to deny your claims.'

The documentary then explored the areas of countryside the children had played in that day and recreated the sequence of their movements. There were comments from villagers on the terrible shock Susan's disappearance was at the time and an interview with a retired journalist who covered the case for a local newspaper. His main contribution was to say that he wasn't convinced about Wicklow's involvement in Susan's disappearance and that something 'never felt right' about the case.

'Well, that's helpful,' said Bradshaw, in response to the journalist's vague observations.

They fell silent again then because the reporter was now standing in the heart of the village. 'Others were questioned but ruled out on various grounds. It is this programme's view that these people should have been questioned further at the time, and doing so would have saved suspicion falling on those who had nothing to do with Susan's disappearance. These innocent people have ever since been linked to local gossip which refuses to go away. One such person is Susan's father, Paul. Later in the programme, we'll be exploring Susan Verity's troubled home life and her father's history of alcohol abuse, his life of petty crime and the sudden, untimely death of her mother.'

Stirring music signalled the commercial break and Tom fast-forwarded through the adverts for bleach, washing powder and a supermarket that claimed to be cheaper than all the others. Then the reporter reappeared and Tom set the video to Play. On the screen, Hughes explained that he was standing outside the house where Susan had once lived.

'When Susan Verity's mother, Jennifer, got engaged to Paul Verity in 1964, she kept one important fact from her parents. He was a criminal with a number of convictions for burglary and assault. Paul Verity swore he would mend his ways and, at first, it did appear that he was going straight, holding down a job at a local timber yard and keeping it when his only daughter, Susan, was born. After the shock of Susan's disappearance, he quit his job and started seeing old associates. Paul was soon back in trouble again and was sentenced to a year in prison for a series of break-ins. Shortly after his return from jail, his wife died prematurely. A coroner reported the cause as chronic alcoholism.'

'He said that as if he's implying that her death might have been caused by something else,' observed Helen.

'Paul Verity has never spoken publicly about his daughter's disappearance and has refused to discuss the events of that day with this programme. He would neither confirm nor deny that there was a loud argument on the morning Susan left their terraced house for the last time, but neighbours told us they heard shouting coming from the house and a series of crashes and bangs. Paul Verity was not at work that day and has never accounted for his whereabouts.'

'He must have done it then,' observed Bradshaw. 'That's concrete evidence right there that he murdered his own daughter.' His words were dripping with sarcasm.

'Yeah, a minute ago it was the farmer,' said Tom. 'Now, it's the dad. Who's next? I wonder.'

The reporter answered Tom's question with a ten-minute segment about a group of known north-east paedophiles who had been in contact with each other in the mid- to late-seventies before being driven underground by police attention. At least two of the group had gone on to murder children, and neither of them had an alibi for the time when Susan disappeared. One of them was the friend of Adrian Wicklow who had vouched for him in the very early days of the investigation, when neither man was known to or suspected by the police.

The programme then used a simple map formed from a computer graphic showing distances and angles of elevation to show how unlikely it was that the elderly eyewitness, Lilly Bowes, now deceased, could have clearly identified the man later claimed to be Adrian Wicklow.

Helen, Tom and Ian watched the remainder of the documentary. It continued to peddle unsubstantiated theories, rumours and half-truths as reasons why the probable killer of Susan Verity might not be Wicklow.

'They're tying themselves up in knots,' said Tom, who was unimpressed by the programme.

The final word went to the reporter. 'One thing is certain, however. We may never learn the truth of what happened that day or discover the real fate of poor, tragic Susan Verity.'

'At last, he says something sensible,' said Bradshaw, as the pulsing theme music signalled the end of the programme.

'That provided more questions than answers,' said Helen.

Tom was irritated. 'All those claims about police incompetence, all that hype about finding out the truth, then they admit at the end that they don't know anything. That wasn't journalism, it was gossip.'

'So where do we go from here?' Helen asked.

'We should start from scratch and go in with an open mind. Let's speak to everyone we can in the village who can shed some light on the case.' Tom turned to Bradshaw. 'What about the case files?'

'There are tons of them.' The detective told them about the roomful of documents. 'Actually, I thought Helen might –'

'Oh, thanks,' she said.

'. . . since you are so good at research,' he offered, to placate her.

'He's right,' said Tom. 'You have an uncanny knack of finding a diamond in a pile of coal.'

'Do you really believe that?' she asked him. 'Or do you just not want to be the one who has to wade through the files yourself?'

'It's a bit of both,' he admitted.

'I'll take a look,' she told Bradshaw sternly, 'since you're putting us on the payroll.'

They talked for a while longer about Susan Verity and the best way to combine their resources, then split the tasks that lay ahead.

Tom took out his notebook and started to jot down the names of the people they needed to speak to about Susan's disappearance. They would have to track down family members in cases where the witnesses were already dead. He read the list back to Bradshaw and Helen. It included the four surviving childhood friends of Susan Verity.

- Adrian Wicklow – (Ian dealing with)
- Paul Verity – Susan Verity's father
- Colin Marsh – farmer (deceased)
- Lilly Bowes – witness (deceased)
- Billy Thorpe
- Danny Gilbert
- Kevin Robson
- Andrea Craven
- Michelle Dutton (deceased)
- Matthew Green

'Who's Matthew Green?' asked Helen.

In answer, Tom picked up a copy of the local paper and handed it to her. 'A good place to start, I would say.'

The newspaper was open at the relevant page and Helen read the cutting aloud for Bradshaw's benefit.

TEACHER TO RETIRE

Maiden Hill teacher Matthew Green is to retire from Plum Lane Church of England School after twenty-three years.

Headmaster Anthony Holt said, 'Robert has been part of our school over three decades and has taught hundreds of children from this village. Staff and pupils in Year 6 will miss him greatly, and we thank him for his years of service to the community.'

'Twenty-three years,' said Tom. 'So he started teaching at Plum Lane back in 1973 and would have taught Susan and all of her friends.'

'Are they on your list as witnesses?' asked Bradshaw. 'Or suspects?' He was wondering why Tom wanted to speak to their teacher.

'Always keep an open mind,' Tom said. 'Susan's friends were very young when she disappeared but, if Wicklow wasn't responsible for her death, then someone else was.'

'Tom, they were ten years old.'

'They may not have had anything to do with her disappearance themselves, but they might know something the police may have overlooked. I'd like to know a little bit about Susan's playmates when they were children before we speak to them now, as adults.' No one protested.

When they were finished, Bradshaw asked, 'You going to watch the match then?'

'Does the pope shit in the woods?' answered Tom.

'I hope he doesn't,' said Helen. 'Not very dignified for a man in his position. What match?'

'What match?' Tom was incredulous. 'Did you hear that, Ian?'

'I did,' he said sadly. 'And Helen just went down a notch in my estimation.'

'I don't follow football.'

'Helen, this is Euro '96, the first tournament England has hosted in thirty years – since we won the World Cup, in fact – and you are completely unaware of it?' He was aghast.

'No,' she corrected him. 'I am vaguely aware of it. How could I not be, when it's on the news all the time and every guy out there with a pick-up truck has the flag of St George stuck on it? I just didn't know exactly when it started, or who is playing, that's all.'

'Doesn't your boyfriend watch football?' asked Bradshaw.

'Thankfully, no.' They both regarded her suspiciously, as if this couldn't be true. 'So who *is* playing?' she asked, to avoid further speculation on Peter's dislike of football, for which she had always been grateful, until now.

'England are playing Switzerland,' Tom told her in disbelief.

'So they should win, right?' she asked cautiously.

'I don't know about that,' said Bradshaw. 'Shearer hasn't scored in twelve matches.'

'I've heard of *him*,' Helen said brightly, 'but I still don't want to watch it.'

'Don't write him off, Ian,' cautioned Tom, 'and keep the faith. England will win and Shearer will score.'

'Want to bet?' Bradshaw asked him.

Tom thought for a moment. 'With actual money?'

Bradshaw nodded.

'No.'

21

Billy didn't like the looks he was getting from his fellow drinkers but, now that he thought about it, maybe he had always been getting those looks and this wasn't something new; he'd just never noticed it before. Had they always looked down on him because of who he was? Billy had always thought he had been let off the hook after what happened, as if proximity to that kind of tragedy somehow gave you a bye. He'd seen, and taken, his opportunity to drop out, to give up and not have the usual peer pressure to get a job or settle down. He'd always thought people didn't mind that all he really did was piss about and drink in the village's pubs. With one friend likely murdered, another dead and one bordering on unhinged, he assumed that was enough to prove that all the children who'd been there when Susan had disappeared had been badly affected by the experience.

Only Danny appeared to be immune from it all, at first glance anyway. He had lived as close to a normal life as possible – had a good job, a nice wife, a couple of nippers – but Billy knew the truth. Danny had suffered through it too when he was still a young man and Billy wondered where he had found the strength to carry on. His friend had been in bits after the tragedy. Susan disappearing was one thing, but losing your first serious girlfriend in an accident was in a different league. He didn't know where Danny had found the strength to pick himself up and continue after that but, somehow, he had done it. Billy wouldn't have known how to describe the respect he had for his oldest friend after that.

Billy often thought about death and whether there was anything after it. The shock of knowing the person was gone for ever, that you could never bring them back, no matter what you did, was what made death so final, which was why Danny had been so lost for a while. They called it grief but it seemed such a small and inadequate word to Billy. He had seen his friend up close and witnessed the affect it had on him, and it was more like the death of hope.

Billy looked around the pub again but, for some reason, no one was watching him now, and he began to doubt himself. Was he really getting dirty looks from the other drinkers in the pub or was this some new rising paranoia caused by his inner feeling of wretchedness? On a bad day, he too believed in the curse and felt like one of its victims. Sitting here now, he simply felt unwelcome. He finished his pint and left. He was crossing the car park when a familiar shape moved into focus.

'You leaving?'

'Yeah,' shrugged Billy. 'Bit dead in there tonight.'

'That the only reason?' Sometimes, it was as if Danny could read his mind.

'Yeah.'

'But the football is about to start,' Danny reminded him. 'You want to watch England, don't you?'

'S'pose.'

'We can go back in there together, if you like?'

His old friend's words were reassuring. 'Yeah, Danny. That'd be great.'

Danny grinned. 'We'll probably be sorry after,' he warned his friend. 'England are always shite.'

'I told you they wouldn't win,' said Bradshaw as he drained his pint. 'Can't even beat a nation that prides itself on staying neutral. Not a good start.'

'And I told you Shearer would score,' Tom reminded him. 'Which he did. I also said to keep the faith. It's early days.'

'All right,' conceded Bradshaw, pulling on his coat. 'I'll watch the next match with you and we'll see if we get any better.'

'Er, Ian . . . before you go. I've got a bit of a favour to ask . . . if it's all right with you?'

'Go on,' said the detective, then he realized from the look on his face that Tom had more to say, so he took off his coat and sat back down.

'I've met this woman . . .' Tom began.

'And you want me to be best man, since you have no other friends?'

'How did you guess?' deadpanned Tom.

When Ian Bradshaw returned to his flat, he found a parcel waiting for him. It was propped up against his front door and must have been there since the morning. He wondered why delivery drivers did that when packages could so easily be stolen and figured it was because most of them didn't give a shit.

He picked up the parcel and looked at it. It was wrapped in thick brown paper and tied with string. The name and address were his, but he had no recollection of having ordered anything, and it wasn't his birthday, so what could it be and who could have sent it?

He went inside, placed the package on the kitchen worktop, cut through the string with a knife, tore open the brown paper, and out fell a dictaphone, along with a handful of tiny cassettes. This was Adrian Wicklow's book: part autobiography, part confession. The child killer had sent it to him, which meant he somehow knew where Bradshaw lived. That alone was a chilling thought.

There was a compliment slip too. The typed portion detailed the name and address of a firm of solicitors that represented

Adrian Wicklow. Then there was a handwritten part which read, 'Detective Sergeant Ian Bradshaw. Please find enclosed Adrian Wicklow's memoir, which we are sending to you in accordance with our client's wishes.'

Helen was reading the book again. She looked up when the front door opened.

'England didn't win,' she said, 'but Shearer scored, so you were half right.'

'How do you know?' he asked. 'I thought you weren't interested.'

'I'm not, really, but I know you are so I watched it on the news, in case you wanted to talk about it. People who work together do that, don't they? Talk about football, I mean. So what do you think about this new diamond formation?'

Tom stared at Helen to see if she was winding him up. It appeared she wasn't and was merely making an effort, presumably to make up for her earlier frosty mood, but England's performance had been depressing enough without re-examining it.

'You find anything else in there?' He nodded at the book.

'It's mostly what we know already, except he interviewed one of the kids,' she said, 'about what happened when they trespassed on the farm.'

22

1976

It was a huge, open-ended barn with a metal roof, and large rectangular hay bales filled most of it. The bales were tied in the centre and the straw neatly compacted, making them firm and easy to clamber on. They formed a natural series of steps that took the children higher into the barn, and there were gaps between the bales which they all squeezed between.

'Wow,' said Susan, wide-eyed at the sight that greeted them. Beyond the first pile was a tiny room, formed by bales in the middle rolled by other, bigger kids who had invaded the silo while the farmer was elsewhere. The heavy bales had been piled up on the sides to create a space that was now a cosy den. The farmer wasn't even aware of its existence.

Susan thought it was magical but Billy didn't enjoy being enclosed like this. It felt even hotter in here, and airless.

'I don't like it in here,' said Michelle. 'It's scary.'

'Nowt scary about it,' scoffed Kevin.

'What if the farmer comes back?' she pleaded. 'What then?'

'I'll keep watch,' said Billy, happy to find a reason to leave the confined space. 'I'll be our sentry.' And before anyone could contradict him he was out of there.

'I'll watch too,' said Michelle, and followed Billy gratefully.

'Get out of there, you little bastards!' roared the farmer as

138

soon as Billy and Michelle emerged from the barn. He was coming out of the farm house and heading straight towards them. Michelle screamed, Billy screamed, there were screams from inside the bales, and all the children fled from the barn and scattered as the furious farmer pursued them.

23

Bradshaw struggled to sleep again that night. He lay in bed, hoping to doze off, but he couldn't and he knew why. Try as he might to ignore it, that bloody book of Adrian Wicklow's was in his home, and it was taunting him. What if it really did contain a clue, some valuable piece of information no one else had been able to understand or decipher? Perhaps what was needed here wasn't the eye of a psychiatrist or an academic but some old-fashioned common sense. Bradshaw ignored the voice in his head telling him that his superiors all seemed to think he lacked that.

He gave up and rolled out of bed. He went downstairs and made himself a coffee, picked up the dictaphone, placed it on the table next to his armchair and pressed play.

My Story
by Adrian Wicklow

I screamed from day one.

I was born screaming, or so my dear mother told me. I screamed from the moment they dragged me into this ridiculous world.

'This one has plenty to say for himself,' the midwife told her, and she was right about that but no one was listening. Nobody paid me any attention. Not for years.

Then I started killing and it all changed. All of a sudden, people cared. I killed again and again. They were desperate to find me then. Some of them became obsessed with me. It felt so good to know I was in

everybody's thoughts. You see, everything changed when I started taking
their children.

They noticed me then.

Christ, thought Bradshaw. He'd only heard a few words and he was already filled with disgust. Was this honestly the reason for Adrian Wicklow's killing spree? Did he really murder children just so society would finally notice him? It seemed more than extreme, but Wicklow's brain wasn't wired like other people's. That much was already clear.

My mother loved me, though. I should make that point early on, in case anyone was to get the wrong idea. She doted on me. I never wanted for food, clothes, toys or parental affection, even when my father was killed so abruptly when he drove his car into the back of an articulated lorry. I don't remember him, not really. He's just a blur, but my mother meant everything to me. I rarely lose my temper, but a young man from some university psychology department tried to tell me years ago that my so-called crimes may have somehow been due to my upbringing. It was the first time I found myself desperate to kill again in almost seven years. I caused him some damage. He was lucky they managed to drag me away before I could end him. Needless to say, I never saw him again.

My mother wasn't to blame for anything. If my crimes are actually crimes at all, they are down to nature and society. It's in everyone's nature to kill. Civilization doesn't change anything. There is still a bit of wolf in the dog. It cannot help but bark at the moon or hunt a rabbit. In the same way, a man can't be expected to forget thousands of years of his killing instinct just because he puts on a suit in the morning and heads to an office. And society? I do blame it. I turned my back on society because it turned its back on me. I was a bright boy, but I couldn't take to their exams, didn't fit in with their world of questions and interviews. I left school without a qualification to my name and, since I couldn't abide the thought of working with other people, I used my hands to fix things, when all I really wanted to do was destroy everything.

Bradshaw listened to passages on teachers who had been cruel or who had misunderstood Wicklow, failing to spot his precocious intelligence. Then there were recollections about a friendless boy who was teased by the little girls in his class and tormented by bullies, until one day he stabbed one of them in the arm with the sharp end of a compass and *was caned brutally but at least the bullying stopped.*

It was almost an hour before Bradshaw reached the section where the adult Wicklow started to follow children.

Immediately and instinctively, he switched the dictaphone off. He didn't want to hear this. It wasn't a made-up story by some writer of grim fairy tales. This was all too real.

But how was he going to discover the truth about Susan if he didn't listen to it?

Bradshaw got out of his seat and went into the kitchen. He reached into the fridge and withdrew a bottle of vodka, unscrewed the cap and poured a very large measure into a glass before adding an equal amount from a bottle of tonic. He went back to his chair, sipped his drink and hit play again. Wicklow was talking about Tim Collings, his first victim. His voice changed as he remembered stalking Tim. Bradshaw could hear his excitement.

Tim was a loner, like me. I could tell. He never saw me, not once, but I saw him. I stayed in the background and watched from a distance. He wouldn't play with anyone else, didn't seem to have any friends at all. Other kids just walked by. I understood that. I wanted to give his young life some meaning – by taking it. They'd remember him then. Everyone in his village would talk about him for years.

Bradshaw listened while Wicklow described Tim's home life, or at least the one he imagined the boy having. He explained how he lured Tim away by pulling over in his car and asking him his name.

'Tim,' the young lad replied.

'Thank God I found you, Tim.' I made myself sound breathless and agitated. 'It's your dad. There's been an accident at work. He's had a bad fall and I have to take you to the hospital.'

He fell for it so easily. It was a fair assumption he had a father and that the man was working, but if he had told me he was fatherless or his daddy didn't have a job I'd have told him I'd got the wrong boy. As I drove him away, I wondered if his parents had told him not to go with strangers and whether that thought flashed through his mind as we sped out of his village.

I took him to a nice quiet spot.

Bradshaw listened for the next ten minutes without noticing the world outside his flat. He didn't hear the drunken couple arguing or the siren of the police car that sped by moments later. Instead, he became entirely caught up in Wicklow's account of the murder of his first victim: how the boy's uncertainty had turned to fear, how he had pleaded to be taken home once he realized that was not going to happen. He heard the vivid description of the last moments of that poor, desperate boy's life and, when he stopped listening, he realized he was shaking and there were tears in his eyes.

Bradshaw went to the bathroom, ran the cold tap and put his wrists under the water, letting it cascade down on to the pulse points, cooling his blood, then he cupped some in his hands and splashed it hard against his face. He shocked himself back into his own reality and left Wicklow's sick world behind.

He looked up to see his pale, dripping face in the mirror, and exclaimed, 'Oh, dear God.'

24

Helen rubbed her eyes before opening yet more files. The ones she had already read had been placed to one side so she knew not to examine them again. Bradshaw had arranged for Helen to have full access. He had warned her about the sheer number of files and the disorganized mess that awaited her. She had been prepared for it, but it was still a shock.

'Needles and haystacks,' she said to herself as she pulled down half a dozen more dusty folders and placed them in a neat pile on the table in the middle of the tiny room. She sat down again, selected the first folder and opened it.

Unlike most of the others, the newest file contained something of interest: a map of the outskirts of Maiden Hill. Curiously, this had been hand drawn; neatly, and with an attempt at scale. Helen realized it must have been completed by a diligent police officer, as it showed areas not normally marked on conventional maps, presumably to aid those searching for Susan.

The map began where the village ended, with the church-yard and the lanes near Marsh Farm, then the corn fields the children had crossed to get to the woodland and their den. Clumps of trees represented the woodland and every track, footpath, gate and stile was marked. The railway was repre-sented by a long, bold line with marks across it to signify the tracks, and the tributary of the river with its name between two lines. The quarry was a large oval and there were two smaller ones that were noted as 'gravel pits – flooded'. Every building on the farm was on the map and each of the abandoned buildings of an old factory not far from there, marked with the words, 'Halliwell's Factory – site abandoned 1961'.

This detailed map helped Helen understand the problem that had faced the people searching for Susan. When she first heard about the disappearance she had assumed someone must have taken Susan somewhere else; otherwise, her body would have been quickly discovered. Now she realized just what the police had been up against: Maiden Hill itself was not a large place, but the surrounding countryside was vast and full of sites where a body could have been lost.

'You listened to my story then?' Wicklow asked hopefully.

'Yes.'

They were seated opposite one another again, the same guards keeping watch over Wicklow. Bradshaw felt deeply uncomfortable sitting with this man. He had to fight a strong impulse to leave the room and never come back.

'What did you think?'

'You don't want to know what I thought.' Bradshaw told him.

'Oh, but I do. I need to know I'm trusting the right man. I want to be sure I am giving a precious gift to someone who is worthy of it, and not just some time-serving dullard.'

'A precious gift?' asked Bradshaw. 'You mean, the bodies of the children you murdered?'

'And all that comes with it, Detective. If I tell you where they are' – his eyes glistened and he almost sang the last four words – 'it'll make you famous.'

'I'm not interested.'

'Really? I find that hard to believe. You'll be a hero . . .' He paused deliberately then enunciated the next words slowly and clearly: 'All . . . over . . . again.' A chill seemed to run through Ian Bradshaw then. The killer had researched him. Wicklow knew who he was and what he had done.

'Oh yes,' Wicklow went on, 'I've heard all about it. I asked my solicitor to check you out. He made a couple of phone calls, looked at a few of the old press cuttings. Rescued a little girl, didn't you, Ian? You're a role model, according to the chief constable, a man prepared to put his life on the line to serve the public.'

Bradshaw did not bother to reply, so Wicklow continued, 'If you think you got a bit of positive press when you did that, imagine what will happen when I hand you those little angels for burial?' He made a fake, sad face then; the kind a clown might put on to pretend he was on the verge of weeping. Bradshaw wanted to strike him, hard. 'The gratitude of those relatives' – Wicklow made his voice take on a tearful note – 'thank you, Detective Bradshaw, you've given me my baby back.'

Bradshaw was trying to keep his cool, but he shifted in his seat now. It was an instinctive movement, but Wicklow noticed it. He held up a hand, as if seeing the words on a front page in front of him. His voice was filled with awe. 'Hero Solves North-east's Greatest Mystery.' He went on: 'Detective Sergeant Ian . . . no . . . Detective *Inspector* Ian Bradshaw modestly refused to take any credit for finding the bodies of the children who have been missing all these years.' He returned to his normal voice. 'After all, promotion would be a doddle after that and you'd be able to name your next posting.'

'Are you finished?'

'Maybe,' said Wicklow, 'if you can convince me you have actually listened to my story.'

'How can I do that?'

'I told you.' He seemed disappointed. 'If you can tell me why I did what I did, then maybe I will tell you what everybody wants to know.' And he folded his arms, as if to illustrate that he would not be saying another word until Bradshaw answered him.

146

'Power,' said Bradshaw simply.

'Go on,' said Wicklow. 'What makes you say that?'

'The Tim Collings' murder.' Bradshaw felt his voice crack as he remembered Wicklow's deeply disturbing account of the final hours of that poor young boy. 'From the way you . . . subdued him . . . ignored his pleas to be released . . . kept him alive . . .'

'You think I did that because I enjoyed having power over him?' asked Wicklow reasonably.

'Yes.'

'You didn't think there was a sexual connotation in that one?'

'No.'

'Why not?'

'Because everything you wrote about your earlier life leads me to believe you are an asexual person.'

'Interesting,' said Wicklow. 'There was one psychiatrist who said I killed the children because of a deep-rooted hatred of my own sexuality. He seemed to have a theory that their pre-pubescent bodies turned me on in some way.' Wicklow frowned, as if the man's theory was nonsense. 'Personally, I think *he* might be the one with the fixation on children's unde-veloped bodies, not me.'

'No,' said Bradshaw. 'You find sex disgusting.'

'I do,' he admitted. 'And why is that so strange? I'm cer-tainly not the only one. Why would you want to push yourself inside another person's body and be exposed to all their germs?' He gave a little shudder. 'No, I've never had any incli-nation. So, you're right, it wasn't sexual, but what about Milly Ferris? I didn't prolong that encounter.'

'No, but . . .' Bradshaw hesitated.

'And you surely can't compare either of those to my final encounter with Elizabeth Mason? Were there any similarities?'

'Some . . . perhaps . . .'

'And now you're bullshitting and hoping I won't notice.' Wicklow's tone was hard now, but the words were true. Ian Bradshaw desperately wanted to carry out the assignment he had been given. He hoped to learn the truth about Susan Verity and the other children then locate the missing bodies; he just didn't want to have to hear Adrian Wicklow's deranged, self-justifying account of his awful acts. The description of his first victim's fate had been enough to disturb Bradshaw thoroughly, and he hadn't been able to listen to any more of it.

'I'm very disappointed,' he said. 'You didn't listen beyond my encounter with Tim, did you?' He sighed, as if he'd thought better of Bradshaw. 'Don't you have the stomach for it, Detective? Is that it? Well, I'm sorry, I'm not going to indulge you until you know my whole story. This is my legacy to the world. When I am gone, they will want to study my work so they can better understand me and, when they do, they will acknowledge the man who first unlocked the mystery, the one who deduced my true motivation and was rewarded with the locations of three missing children. Sadly, it does not look as if that person will be you.' He shook his head. 'What a lazy pupil.'

'I'm not your pupil.'

'Just a figure of speech. You haven't been doing your homework, Detective, and I'm afraid I can't reward you if you are not prepared to put in the hours. I'm sorry.' He got to his feet. 'Take me back to my cell,' he ordered his guards, then he turned back to Bradshaw. 'Come and see me again when you have listened to the whole story, Detective . . . or don't come at all.'

25

He supposed he could have called ahead and made an appointment but, in the end, Tom elected to turn up on the doorstep of the school unannounced, as the kids were streaming out at the end of the day. The playground was full of parents meeting their little ones. Tom turned to a mother who was checking her son's school bag to see if he had forgotten anything. He chose her because she looked distracted.

'Excuse me, I'm looking for Mr Green's classroom,' he said.

She twisted her body partially away from her son and pointed at an outer door, one of five that had been pushed open to allow the pupils to escape. Tom thanked the mother and walked up to it. He leaned in and saw a man with greying hair sitting behind a desk. The teacher didn't notice Tom. He was too busy examining exercise books, marking them with ticks at a speed that said *I'm about to retire and don't really give a stuff.*

Tom watched him for a moment then said, 'Sorry to interrupt, but I was hoping to have a word,' before introducing himself as an investigator working with the police on the Susan Verity case.

'Why are you asking *me* about Susan?' The teacher sounded as if he were on his guard.

'You taught her,' Tom said. 'And the others.'

'Well, yes, but I taught every other child in the village too.'

'Retiring soon, I hear?'

'That's right.'

'Isn't it a little early?'

'If you had taught young children for as long as I have, you wouldn't be saying that.'

'Could you tell me a little bit about Susan and her friends?'

'Why would my opinion of the children matter?' He frowned. 'How could it help you?'

'I don't know,' Tom admitted. 'It might not, but you never know.' He couldn't really explain it but he wanted to start with the opinion of someone who had known the children but wasn't too close to them.

'It was twenty years ago,' Mr Green protested.

'It's a long time,' admitted Tom, 'but I would imagine those kids stayed in your mind since they were involved in such a tragedy.'

'They did,' he conceded.

'Well, then,' Tom prompted gently, 'what do you recall about Susan?'

'Bright kid,' he said. 'Very bright, considering her family; must have got it from her mum. Polite, well turned out, always did her school work.'

'The kind of child you would notice?'

'How do you mean?' Mr Green was immediately defensive.

Tom shrugged. 'Some kids sit at the back of the class and hardly say a word, others contribute.'

'She did have her hand up a lot,' he said cautiously, 'which is always appreciated, so in that sense, I'd say yes, I noticed Susan.' He thought for a moment. 'I can't really think of anything else I'd say about her, though.'

'What about the other girls? Michelle and Andrea?'

'Michelle was very quiet, not very academic or involved in lessons. Nothing wrong with her, really, but probably not destined to set the world alight.'

'She wasn't,' Tom said. 'She died.'

'Oh my God. I had no idea. What happened?'

'Breast cancer.'

'That's terrible.' He seemed genuinely shocked.

'Do you remember Andrea?'

'Yes, bit of a tomboy, that one, a little boisterous, but no trouble really.'

'What about the boys?'

'Billy was a lazy lump. I'm not sure if he was bright or not, because he simply would not try.'

'Was this before Susan's disappearance or after?'

'I don't think her disappearance made a lot of difference to his attitude. It affected the other boy more.'

'Kevin Robson?' Tom guessed he was not talking about Danny.

'I got the impression he was really traumatized by what had happened to Susan. You'll have heard the story, no doubt.'

'I haven't heard much,' said Tom, since he was keen to hear it in Mr Green's own words, and not simply from a passage in the book Helen had been reading.

'Coasted along right through secondary school and was just about to do his O levels in . . .' he thought for a second '. . . '82, it must have been, then it all went to pot.'

'What happened?'

'He walked into his first exam, turned over the paper, took one look at it, turned it back over again and ran out of the hall. They found him later, in the toilets, on the floor, sobbing – complete breakdown.'

'How do you know about that?'

'Well, I wasn't there, obviously, but it's what I heard. This was at the secondary school, of course, so you might want to try the head there, or the counsellor.'

'Kevin had a counsellor?' asked Tom. 'At the school?'

'Not just him,' said the teacher. 'The school had lots of instances of kids not coping, for a variety of reasons – home life, bereavement, exam pressure – so they hired a counsellor; Mrs Rees, I think she was called. It was one of the new head's big initiatives and was meant to be progressive. Anyway, it got him in the local paper. She's still there, as far as I know.'

Tom wrote this in his notebook, 'Do you really think Kevin's breakdown had anything to do with Susan?' asked Tom doubtfully. 'It *was* six years later.'

'No one really knows what prompted it. Maybe it was just pressure of exams. I understand he hasn't been able to hold down a job since then, and he did get into quite a bit of trouble.'

'What kind of trouble?'

'Violent outbursts. Fighting, mostly. Getting drunk in the pub then starting arguments with the nearest bystander. Been arrested a few times.'

'What about Danny Gilbert? What was he like?'

'Oddly enough, I can't remember much about Danny, which probably means he was no trouble. I understand he is doing quite well for himself. At any rate, he's the only one of the boys who's working.'

'So he was unaffected by what happened?'

'I think people are affected by things in different ways,' concluded Mr Green. 'Danny was probably just stronger than the others.' He peered at the journalist, as if looking for a clue. 'Was that any help at all?'

'Maybe,' Tom said. 'Thanks for your time.'

Bradshaw didn't want to be seen by anyone at first, so when he drove away from Durham jail he did not immediately return to headquarters. He wasn't even sure where he was going and, as he drove around, he found he still couldn't banish the sight of Wicklow's smug face, the memory of his sneering manner and mocking tone from his mind. Meade had warned him about the man, had told Bradshaw he was evil, and maybe the retired detective was right. How could there be people like Adrian Wicklow in the world? What went wrong with their brains to make them do the things they did and enjoy them so much, without even a glimmer of remorse?

Bradshaw drove for an hour before he could clear his head enough to go to HQ. He wasn't sure why he knocked but he did it anyway, and Helen answered with a 'hello'.

He opened the door and was greeted by the sight of large piles of files on the floor near Helen's chair.

'I was going to ask how it's going, but I think I can guess.'

'I'm a little tired. I've spent the whole day wading through this lot.'

'I don't envy you that. Did you find anything?'

'Possibly. I'm not even halfway through, but there were a number of interesting things in there. What I *didn't* find was most revealing, though. I discovered a letter from that documentary crew that was written about six months ago. They asked to see the notes from the questioning of Adrian Wicklow about the disappearance of Susan Verity. They were told they couldn't, that this was not a matter of public interest and the notes were private, but the crew didn't let it lie there. They got a local MP on their side. I know him. He's the campaigning sort and likes to see his name in the paper in connection with miscarriages of justice or any quest to uncover the truth.'

'So he couldn't really be ignored then, if he's a member of parliament, I mean.'

'Your top brass couldn't ignore him for ever but they chose to at first. He sent three letters on House of Commons notepaper before the force formally replied to him and, when they did, it was to tell him that they were unaware of the existence of any notes.'

'Did he believe that?'

'No, he wrote again, a fourth time, telling them that the senior investigating officer had previously stated that notes were taken during the interview with Wicklow.'

'I'd be curious to read the reply.'

'The correspondence is all in the files, including copies of the letters the police sent back to him. They told him that, if there were notes, they must have been lost or destroyed during a big restructuring at headquarters at the end of the eighties, because they couldn't be found now. They apologized for the oversight.'

Bradshaw thought for a moment. 'Things do get lost,' he offered.

'They do, but the reply was sent within twenty-four hours of the MP's letter landing here. Are you really telling me the force deployed sufficient resources to go through this entire archive in such a short space of time?'

'It sounds highly unlikely.'

'And why keep everything else? Every lead and witness report, every possible sighting of Wicklow or Susan in the intervening years. Every crackpot theory phoned in by a member of the public appears to be here, but not the notes from a hugely important interrogation at the very heart of their investigation? It doesn't make sense.'

'Unless you wanted it to be hard to find?' suggested Bradshaw.

'Exactly. The archive is huge. Why keep it all unless you wanted to bury something in here?'

'You think it's in there somewhere?' he said. 'Wouldn't it be simpler just to destroy something incriminating rather than leave it here?'

'I've thought about that,' Helen said, 'and that might be breaking the law. You'd be destroying evidence, causing obstruction, possibly perverting the course of justice. This way, you're simply adding piles and piles of rubbish to the files and hoping nobody can be bothered to look for the one piece of evidence that might point you in the right direction.'

'Who signed the letter replying to the MP?'

She slid a piece of paper out from a pile and handed it to him. 'Can you decipher that signature?'

Bradshaw looked at the squiggle on the bottom of the letter. 'No one could.'

'Exactly – and there is no typed name or job title underneath. The only way you'd know it was even from this force is from the letterhead at the top.'

'Someone didn't want to be identified and, if that's the case, you need to be careful,' Bradshaw told her.

'I doubt I'll be murdered in the police station.'

'We do that all the time,' he told her, deadpan. 'We just don't tell the public.'

'Your secret's safe with me.'

Bradshaw looked again at the piles of files she had been through. 'Are you nearly done for the day?'

'I was thinking of calling a halt for now.'

'Good, because I have a better idea.'

'Is it a lead?'

'No, it's a calzone. I thought we could go for a pizza. Figured I owed you one after the day you've had.'

Tom's first notion was to follow up his meeting with Mr Green by knocking on the doors of each of the surviving children, but he decided against it. Not without Helen. If he was going to speak to them all face to face, he wanted her with him. Tom trusted Helen's judgement and her instinct. She was also more measured and less impetuous than he was. Until he worked with Helen, Tom had simply trusted his own feelings and acted accordingly, but Helen invariably had a different outlook and she was right a lot more often than she was wrong. He wanted her to read the faces of everyone who had seen Susan on the day she went missing.

There was another reason. Guilt. Helen had been handed the decidedly unglamorous job of wading through the case files at police HQ, which made sense with her research skills, but she was right, he didn't fancy the job and neither did Ian. Palming it off on Helen was the kind of thing her lazy, old editor on the *Durham Messenger* would have done and Tom had despised Malcolm.

Tom resolved to take Helen away from those files and out into the real world. In the meantime, though, her absence did afford him an opportunity he wouldn't normally have. He had been thinking about Lena. He'd been thinking about her a lot, in fact, and not just about her. This missing sister obviously meant a great deal to Lena and he desperately wanted to help her, but finding a woman who did not want to be found was not going to be easy. It was likely to be a slow and frustrating process, and he would have to explain the situation to Helen eventually if he was going to be able to devote sufficient time to it. Since they were already working on a case together that was meant to be taking up all their energy, he wasn't relishing that prospect so, he reasoned, he might as well make a start now, while Helen was busy elsewhere.

He wasn't sure where to begin but he had to start somewhere, so he took the photograph of Jess into town. He didn't bother with the electoral roll. If Jess had been looking to escape, she was hardly likely to register to vote. When you wanted to disappear off the grid, there was no signing on for social security, no jobs with regular companies which needed to see ID before they would take you on. Any work would have to be casual and cash in hand. This would present problems for anyone seeking to find you. In theory, Jess could be anywhere in the country and had almost certainly left Durham after the private detective had found her, but he could at least start with her last-known whereabouts and begin his search from there.

Tom went to the cash point in the city centre. According to Lena, Jess had withdrawn cash from the same machine on several occasions and, when she turned around, she would have been presented with the same view of the city he had now:

Durham's Victorian marketplace, with its statue of the Marquess of Londonderry on horseback in the uniform of a hussar at its centre. Tom had told Helen about the sculptor, Raphael Monti, who had boasted that his statue was flawless, challenged any man to find fault with it. No one had been able to until, one day, a blind man was hoisted up so he could run his hands all over the statue, and he found an error. The horse had no tongue. It was said that Signor Monti was so distraught he killed himself by jumping from the top of the cathedral.

'That's a great story,' Helen had said when he told her, 'but is it actually true?'

'No.' And Tom had laughed. 'It's utter bollocks. The horse does have a tongue, apparently, you just can't tell from street level. You know what I really like, though? The story is just plausible enough. I still hear people telling it.'

Now, in his line of vision stood the town hall, the guild hall and a tiny church, along with a building that was of far more interest to Tom: the Market Tavern pub – but, for once, he wasn't going there for a pint.

Tom had a theory, based on Jess's desire to disappear and her need to survive while she was in hiding. She would need money, and it would have to come from a source where the work was casual or temporary. There weren't many places like that, where you could come and go without creating too many ripples.

What would he have done if he had been in Jess's shoes when she first arrived in Durham? She could have gone anywhere in the county, but he reckoned she was far more likely to stay in the city. It was packed with students her age, so she could easily blend in. There were opportunities for work here that smaller places couldn't offer and Jess had worked in a bar before. Tom was going to work his way round every pub in the city in the hope that someone remembered her.

'Worse ways to spend my time,' he said as he walked into the

Market Tavern. Immediately, he felt guilty as he recalled Helen wading through all those files. She was probably still there, diligently ploughing through every piece of paper. Poor lass must be bored out of her mind.

'Cheers,' said Ian, and he clinked his bottle of beer against Helen's wine glass.

Moments later, the pizzas arrived. 'Thanks, Ian,' said Helen, 'I didn't have any lunch.'

'How can you survive without lunch?' He couldn't imagine it.

'I'm used to it.' Helen had started to cut into her quattro stagioni when she remembered something, 'I found some stuff in the case files about Colin Marsh this morning.'

'The farmer?'

'The documentary was accurate. He was well known to the police,' she said, 'because people kept trespassing on his land, particularly kids. They visited Marsh Farm on several occasions in the months before Susan disappeared. Sometimes he called the police; on other occasions it was the parents of the kids he tangled with. Usually, by the time they showed up, the kids had run away, but he seemed to get increasingly irate.'

'You mean he took the law into his own hands and gave the kids a leathering.'

'It was alleged that he hit an eleven-year-old boy round the head. The boy's father took exception to this –'

'As you would,' said Bradshaw.

'– and he marched up to the farm to have it out with Marsh.'

'Bet that was interesting.'

'A fight ensued, leaving both with minor injuries,' Helen said, 'but neither man felt the need to press charges.'

'They sorted it out the old-fashioned way, by knocking seven bells out of each other,' said Bradshaw. Then he asked, 'Was the farmer ever convicted of anything?'

'No, but he did end up in court when he discharged that shotgun near the kids.'

'So he was a bit of a nutter,' said Bradshaw, 'but is there any evidence linking him to the disappearance of Susan Verity?'

'The police questioned him, because Susan was last seen walking off towards his land, but he denied ever having laid eyes on her. He said he was off on his tractor in a field some way away at the opposite end of his farm at the time she went missing.'

'He also admitted chasing the kids out of his barn earlier because they were playing on his hay bales, but he maintained they were all perfectly all right when he shooed them away. The kids confirmed that. His fields and every building on the farm were searched, and the entire village and miles of land surrounding it on all sides. There was no trace of Susan, apart from that hairband in a field. It could be evidence of foul play or it may have been dislodged that morning or as she ran from the hay bales,' concluded Helen.

'So, no reason to suspect him,' said Bradshaw dryly, 'apart from his hair-trigger temper, an aversion to children on his land and previous evidence of violent behaviour, plus the discharging of a shotgun near kids?'

'I think they treated him like a village eccentric who couldn't possibly be responsible for Susan's disappearance. From day one, it was as if she couldn't have been harmed by anyone she knew. The investigation always focused on the likelihood that a stranger had taken Susan. The police questioned everyone who had ever committed an offence against a child for miles around.' She added, 'It would have been useful if we could have questioned the farmer.'

'But Marsh Senior died four years ago.'

'And took his secrets with him,' said Helen wearily, then she stopped. 'Did you say Marsh *Senior*?'

26

The guy in the Market Tavern explained that even casual bar staff would have to show some ID or supply an address if they wanted to work there. The picture of Jess looked vaguely familiar but they got two or three queries a week from impoverished students desperate for work – 'Not all of them are minted, you know' – and he couldn't remember them all, especially if it was months back.

Tom thanked him and moved on to the next pub. It was a similar story in the Shakespeare and the Fighting Cocks, but a girl behind the bar at the Coach and Eight on Framwellgate Bridge thought she did recognize her. Jess had been looking for work but they had nothing for her at the time. Buoyed by this, Tom continued his trawl, convinced he was walking in her footsteps.

Everywhere he went, he said the same thing. His girlfriend was worried about her sister and he was helping her to find the missing girl. This was the first time he had considered Lena to be a girlfriend, but this felt like more than just a casual thing. It was, in fact, the first time he'd had feelings for anyone since the early days with Helen. Of course, he still cared about Helen deeply, but that ship had sailed long ago when he had been unable to prise her away from her idiot boyfriend. He told himself it was all for the best. Helen was happier with Peter and he was probably better off with Lena.

Tom trudged around more than a dozen pubs that day, showing the photograph of Jess and asking questions, receiving little more than blank looks in return for his efforts. Maybe the girl at the Coach and Eight had been wrong. One young woman could look very like another, after all. No, he decided, if he were in Jess's position, this was what he would have done. It had turned cold and was getting late so he would stop for now, but he would pick up the trail again another day.

'So there's a Marsh Junior?' he asked, when Tom and Helen were both back home and able to compare notes from their respective days. 'That's interesting. Why don't you give the files a miss tomorrow,' he said, 'and come to Maiden Hill with me instead. I was going to try and speak to the surviving children after I met with their teacher, but I wanted you to be with me.'

'Why?'

'What do you mean, why?' He laughed. 'Because I trust your judgement and we're a team.'

'Are we?'

'Of course we are.'

'It's just, sometimes, it doesn't feel like it.'

'What are you talking about? We share everything: the work, the writing, and the money when it rolls in – *if* it rolls in.'

'I know we do, but even the office is your home.'

'Yours too,' he reminded her.

'I'm just staying here. It feels like it's your business and I'm just helping out.' She shrugged. 'I can't help the way I feel.'

'I can't help the way you feel either,' he told her, 'but you are an equal partner in this business in every way. We're Norton–Carney, and that's what I tell everyone.' He smiled at her encouragingly.

'Okay,' she demurred.

'So you'll come with me tomorrow?'

'All right.'

'We can talk to this young farmer too,' he said, 'to see what he thinks of his old man.'

Bradshaw knew he was stalling, delaying the inevitable, putting off a deeply unpleasant task for as long as humanly possible. It was part of the reason he had gone for pizza with Helen; anything to postpone his time alone in the flat with Wicklow. That was how it felt when he was sitting in his little lounge with the curtains drawn against the outside world, a drink in his hand, because he always needed a drink the second the tape from the dictaphone whirred softly and the child killer's gravelly, hypnotic voice poured out of it. All day he had been telling himself that this was not something to shy away from, that it was the only way to help the families of Wicklow's victims, that the result justified a few hours of unpleasant testimony, but now, while he listened to the excitement in Wicklow's voice rise as he described the manner in which he had stalked poor Milly Ferris, he was struggling.

She was a very small thing, little more than a scrap of skin and bone, looked like a doll, one of those old-fashioned china dolls from an antique shop, with a pale face and dark, wide eyes full of wonder and life. I took that life and I enjoyed having control over her but I didn't keep her with me for too long. I took a big risk already on the journey from her village. Anyone could have stopped us in the car, but she didn't try and signal or cry out as we sped along, even though she must have known by then that she was with one of the bad men her parents had warned her about.

At this point on the tape, Wicklow let out an involuntary sound at the memory that was something between a gasp and a sigh. It made Bradshaw shudder.

I spoke to her as I drove. 'I'll tell you a story,' I said, 'all about a little girl just like you who was dressed in a red hood, and do you know what that silly little girl did? She went out all by herself, into the wood, and walked through it alone until she met a big bad wolf . . .'

Wicklow fell silent then for a few moments, and all Bradshaw could hear was the sound of the tape whirring in the background. Trying not to imagine what had happened to that poor little girl, he was desperate to banish the images that were swirling around in his brain: of poor Milly, of her devastated mother, and of Wicklow, delighting in her murder at the time and now relishing the tale as he retold it. The silence on the tape was proof that he was reliving the feelings of euphoria that had swept over him back then.

It didn't take very long at all. She had such a tiny neck.

27

The two reporters went to Billy Thorpe's house first and knocked, but there was no sign of anyone there. Tom stepped back from the front door and looked up. 'Bedroom curtains are drawn,' he noted, but there was no way of knowing if anyone was still up there. 'No point hanging around,' he observed.

Danny Gilbert was standing on his driveway when they arrived at his home minutes later and, for a second, Tom had the bizarre notion that he'd known they were coming and was waiting there for them. Then he spotted the chamois leather and watched as Danny lovingly caressed the bodywork of his impressive German car with it. The man was dressed casually for a working day, in an open-necked shirt and jeans, and Tom wondered if he had been recently laid off. Jobs always seemed to teeter uncertainly around here, no matter what the state of the economy; if there was a downturn, it was always one of the regions to be hit first when government cuts were made.

They introduced themselves as investigators re-examining the Susan Verity case, a description they had agreed on because it might trigger less opposition than stating that they were journalists working with the police.

'How can I help you?' asked Danny. 'I don't think there is anything about poor Susan that I haven't said before at least a thousand times.'

'Maybe not, but it would be a great help to us if we could just ask you a few questions about what happened that day,' explained Helen. 'We're coming in with fresh eyes, and that can be confusing.' Then she added: 'Please.'

Danny smiled at Helen. It was a warm, almost flirtatious smile and, even though Danny's house looked like it probably contained a wife and family, Tom couldn't help wondering if Danny was a bit of a player when it came to women.

'Of course,' said Danny. 'I'd be happy to help. Come in and I'll make you both some coffee.' His eyes didn't leave Helen's when he said that.

'Not working today?' asked Tom when they were seated at Danny's kitchen table with their coffee a few minutes later.

Danny looked puzzled. 'Oh,' he said, realizing that the way he was dressed and the fact that he was at home made it look that way. 'I work from home sometimes – perk of being a regional manager. I live on my patch and all my sites are nearby, so it's easier to get the paperwork done here. I'll head out for meetings later.'

Tom smiled. 'You didn't look as if you were doing the paper-work when we arrived.'

'I get to skive off now and then, when I need to.' He gave a guilty smile. 'I think I've earned the right. I have had to work bloody hard to get this far.'

'What does your company do?' asked Helen.

'We supply stationery and office equipment for the home and for businesses. I look after eight retail sites across the north-east.'

'Sounds like you landed on your feet,' said Tom.

'I'm doing okay.'

'I've been reading a book about Adrian Wicklow,' Helen explained. 'The chapters on the Susan Verity case make it sound as if she wasn't the only victim that day.' When he didn't contradict her, she continued, 'Some of your friends have struggled since then.'

'And you think I haven't? I just choose not to let it destroy me. That's the only difference. What happened that day was a terrible thing. Our friend just disappeared, with no explanation, then years later we were told she was probably killed by a maniac. They caught him, but it never ends.'

'Why not?' asked Helen.

'Because she was never found and everyone has an opinion. They all reckon they know what happened to Susan: she was killed by Wicklow, or Wicklow is lying; she was taken by the farmer or by a stranger; her dad killed her; her mum killed her; the milkman killed her; she had an accident somewhere miles from the den so they couldn't find her body; her corpse was eaten by a wild puma that escaped from the zoo years ago; her teacher was a pervert, aliens swooped down and spirited her away; she's still alive somewhere but being held by a maniac; or she's alive and free but can't remember who she is or where she's from; she has a husband and children of her own now but doesn't want to go back home because her father interfered with her when she was little. Do you get it?'

And they did. Every journalist, police officer, friend, casual acquaintance or pub bore Danny Gilbert had ever encountered had a theory, and poor Danny had heard every single one of them.

'I understand it must be very difficult for you, Danny,' Tom conceded, 'but what do you think happened to Susan?'

'I don't know. I wish I did.'

'What do you remember from that day?' asked Helen.

'I was out with Billy and Kevin, and we bumped into the girls – Andrea, Michelle and Susan – and we went off together to play in our den.' She could tell by the way he was recounting the story that he had told it many times before; his voice had become monotone. 'We played for a while there, then someone said it would be a good idea to go and play in the farmer's hay bales. We went there, then, afterwards, we split up.'

'Wait a second,' urged Helen. 'Why did you split up?'

'We didn't have any choice,' he said. 'The bloody farmer chased us. We ran in all directions.'

'Fair enough,' said Tom. 'Scary guy, was he?'

Danny nodded. 'When you're that age. Most of the kids were shit-scared of Farmer Marsh back then.' Tom took a sip of his coffee and Danny used the gap to ask his own question. 'So why start with me? Am I a suspect?'

'God, no,' said Tom. 'You were only ten years old, and we haven't started with you. We are talking to lots of people, including all the surviving children.'

'Good luck with that,' said Danny.

'How do you mean?'

'Have you been to Billy's house?'

'We went first thing this morning,' confirmed Helen.

'Any response?'

'No,' admitted Tom.

'He won't be out of bed before noon. Billy isn't like normal people.' He went on to explain that his friend had never really held down a job and how the man's mother somehow allowed this situation to continue.

'And this is all down to what happened that day with Susan?' asked Helen.

'Well, it's a convenient excuse, isn't it? Look, I don't want to be harsh here – Billy is my friend, always has been, always will be – but what he really needs is a kick up the arse. He's a lazy sod, and if it was up to him, he'd be in the pub every day.' He laughed. 'But that doesn't mean I wouldn't do anything for him, and him for me. We've been through a lot together. That's how it goes.'

'Was he there for you after the accident on Mont Blanc?' asked Helen.

The question seemed to throw Danny at first. 'You know about that?' he said, and he wrapped his fingers around his mug, as if shielding it. It was a defensive gesture they both picked up on. 'Yes, he was, and I'll never forget it. I was a wreck for quite a while but, in the end, you have to pick yourself up and get on with it, don't you? Life is for the living. What choice do you have?'

'You could sit in the pub all day, like Billy,' offered Tom amiably.

'Not much future in that,' said Danny. 'And not really my style.'

'That day on the mountain?' Helen asked gently.

Danny sighed. 'You want to know what happened? Though I don't see what it has to do with Susan Verity . . .' There was a flash of anger in his look, but he seemed to force himself to calm down. 'My girlfriend Victoria was a climber, and she persuaded me, a complete novice, to go up Mont Blanc with her.' He took a breath and explained, 'It's not like Mount Everest, you can walk up it almost to the summit, but the weather can change like that.' He snapped his fingers. 'That's what happened to us. One minute we were trudging along at nine thousand feet in beautiful sunshine – tough going, but I could handle it – next moment the storm clouds dropped over us, the wind started howling, the temperature fell below zero and snow started falling so thick you couldn't see your hand in front of your face. We turned back and struggled along for a while, but we weren't roped together or anything.' He stopped, as if he was trying to find the right words to describe what happened to Victoria. 'One moment she was there, the next she was gone. I didn't even hear her call out.'

'She fell?' asked Tom. Danny just nodded.

'I'm sorry,' said Helen, for she could see the effect recounting this story was having on him. It was as if he had been transported back to that moment almost a decade ago now.

'I looked for her,' he told Helen. 'Even though I knew it was hopeless, I went back up and down for ages, trying to find her

168

or see if I could spot where she had fallen, but in the end the hypothermia got to me and I had to go back down.' He sighed. 'We were young, and we were fools. We didn't respect the mountain. Neither of us was prepared and we didn't have the proper equipment.' He looked tragic and helpless. 'Victoria slipped, and that's all there is to say, really.'

'And she wasn't found,' observed Helen. 'That's awful. You've experienced a hell of a lot,' she said. 'All of you.'

'The curse?' he said mockingly. 'Is that what you think it is?'

'No,' she assured him. 'But I've read about it, and I know a lot of people do believe there is a curse on you all. Some of your friends believe it too.'

'Well, I don't. Have I been unlucky? Yes, but not as unlucky as poor Michelle and Susan. I picked myself up and worked hard. I have a good job. I love my wife and kids.'

'How long have you been married?' asked Tom.

'You mean how long did I wait?' he snapped, meaning after Victoria died. 'Long enough. I couldn't imagine seeing anyone after her, so I didn't bother, not for a long time. Then, a few years after she died I met Janine. We've been married nearly five years now. Our girl is four and our little boy is coming up to twelve months. I count myself fortunate. I can't really speak for the others.'

'We'll let them speak for themselves,' said Tom. 'We're going to try Billy again and, of course, Kevin.'

'Kevin?' He looked sceptical. 'You'll not get much out of him.'

Bradshaw didn't know it, but he was standing in almost the exact same spot in the shop where Helen had bought the book about Adrian Wicklow. He wasn't looking for another biography of the man, though. He was searching for something more scientific.

He passed the rows and rows of true crime volumes with

their lurid covers and sensationalist titles and eventually found a shelf at ground level where the books were thicker and more academic. He perused them until he found a couple of titles that seemed promising. *The Science behind Psychopathy* was written by a doctor with a great many letters after his name. Its chapters contained graphs and statistics to back up the author's findings. *Why Killers Kill* was an academic study based on hundreds of interviews with convicted murderers in the US prison system. It purported to be the one book to shed light on the numerous reasons why men – for it was nearly always men – were driven to commit murder.

Bradshaw examined the prices on the back of the books and winced. He bought them anyway.

He was hoping to put some distance between himself and Adrian Wicklow's life story. The night before, he had woken abruptly from a night terror of which he had little or no recollection. Whatever he had been dreaming was instantly lost to him when he opened his eyes, to find his bed sheets tangled around him. He must have been thrashing about in his sleep; his body was covered in sweat. He felt trapped and helpless, and a strong sense of panic. He kicked the sheets away violently and stumbled from his bed. It wasn't hard to link these feelings of fear and disgust to the book he was forced to listen to. Every time he heard one of Wicklow's accounts of the stalking and murder of a child it seemed to lodge deep in his subconscious. Every night since he had sat down with the child killer in Durham jail, he had experienced bad dreams, some more vivid than others, but none as intense as this one. Maybe he was wrong about his encounters with Wicklow; perhaps it wasn't possible to come out of this whole thing undamaged. Buying the books was an act of desperation. Suppose he could find out what motivated a man like Wicklow by reading them, instead of listening to this insane murderer tell his own twisted story? It was a very long shot, he knew, but Bradshaw grasped at it anyway.

'Looks like he might finally be up.' Tom noticed that the bedroom curtains had been drawn back. He knocked on the door of Billy's house.

Then he knocked a second time, but there was still no answer.

'Do you think he's gone out?' asked Helen.

'Let's try round the back.'

They went to the side of the house and followed a sloping road that took them up a hill, towards another street with newer properties on it. They made the older houses, like the one Billy and his mother lived in, look grey and shabby by comparison.

Halfway up the hill they were granted a bird's-eye view of Billy's backyard. Music was coming from what sounded like an ancient transistor radio but they could still hear Billy's hacking cough. Tom climbed over a tiny wall on to a small patch of common land by the road and peered down into the yard below.

Billy Thorpe was sitting on an old deck chair, cigarette in hand, smoking it between coughs. He was a stick-thin man dressed in tracksuit bottoms and a knock-off 'designer' T-shirt.

'Mr Thorpe!' called Tom. 'Can we have a word?'

Billy gestured for them to climb down, so Helen joined Tom on the far side of the little wall, then they walked back down the hill until the high wall adjoining Billy's yard turned into a low one which they could climb over without difficulty.

When they approached Billy, he said, 'Who are you with? I'm only talking to a few this time, so if you are wanting something to quote –'

Tom interrupted him before he could start naming his price.

'We're investigators, Mr Thorpe, assisting Durham police with the reopening of the Susan Verity case.'

Billy's face fell visibly. 'Let's go inside,' he croaked, looking around to make sure no one else was peering down at them.

They followed him into the kitchen. 'Are you wanting a tea?' he asked, and they politely declined. 'Well, I'm having one,' he said, and they had to wait while he filled the ancient kettle and placed it on the gas ring.

He didn't offer them a seat; he just sat on the edge of the tiny kitchen table and asked them what they wanted.

'We're talking to everyone connected with the case to see if we can gain new insight,' said Helen.

He looked at her as if she were speaking a foreign language so Tom intervened. 'It's in case anyone remembers something new that might help us to find Susan.'

Billy seemed happier with that explanation. 'I can't think of anything I haven't said over and over again, to the police, to reporters.' He shrugged helplessly. 'There's no doubt in my mind that he did it.'

'Who did it?'

'Wicklow, of course. Who else?'

'Well, you say that, Billy, but a few people think he didn't do it, including the makers of a recent TV documentary I'm sure you're familiar with.'

'I missed that,' he said, as if it were just another TV programme. 'I was out.'

'You were out?' asked Helen. 'Where did you go?'

'Pub,' he said, as if it were obvious.

'I thought you might have been interested to hear what they had to say,' she told him.

'Not really. I've been hearing this shite for twenty years, pet. He did it. Nowt else to say, really.'

'You seem very sure,' Tom probed.

'Who else could it be? Oh, I know what people say – one of us kids hurt her, or her dad came looking for her, or the farmer caught her in the bales and turned her into silage? No, there was only one maniac in our village that day, and it still chills me that it could have been any one of us he chose.'

'We don't know for sure that Wicklow *was* in the village that day,' Helen reminded him. 'There was only ever one eyewitness, although she did describe someone who looked like Wicklow.'

'But her testimony was discredited,' recalled Tom.

'That Lilly Bowes might have been old,' Billy said, 'but my mam reckons she was as sharp as a tack. She saw him all right, and he took Susan. The only question is what he did with her.'

'What do you reckon he did?'

'Buried her somewhere, I s'pose. Isn't that what he did with all the others?'

'We don't know,' Helen said, 'because they haven't all been found.'

To begin with, Bradshaw's new books did not enlighten him. Instead of helping him to define what Adrian Wicklow was, they merely succeeded in highlighting what he was not.

Psychopaths usually lacked empathy, but Adrian Wicklow not only felt his first victim's pain but he could sense his sadness and isolation, even though he was only a child. Wicklow felt sorry for Tim and anger towards his parents and friends for not caring enough about the youngster. He killed the boy anyway.

Stranger-killers who committed more than one crime were sometimes motivated by rejection, but Wicklow was loved by his mother, even after she learned of his crimes, and he claimed to feel no need for romantic interaction with either men or women, so rejection could not have been his motivation. Sex with a victim was often a prime factor, according to the doctor with the letters after his name. He even cited examples where killers had sex with the victim after they were dead, but Wicklow had no interest in this and had never assaulted any of his victims in this way.

Bradshaw turned to the other book and read accounts of the imprisoned murderers. Some killed out of anger, but Wicklow's accounts of his murders were free of that emotion. He held no particular grudge against children or towards any ethnic group or religion. He didn't torture his victims for his own pleasure, preferring a clean kill by strangulation. He did not see his victims as evil or sinful, he wasn't preventing them from growing up into something that would eventually become vile. He had never received any form of insult or been slighted by any of the children he had murdered.

Just when Bradshaw had begun to question whether he would find anything in these books comparable to Wicklow's crimes, he came upon a passage which stemmed from an interview with a former factory worker turned serial killer in the States. The man had a grudge against society and, the more Bradshaw read about him, the more he began to see parallels between this white, blue-collar worker from Michigan and Wicklow. It was the man's state of mind when he carried out his murders and the way he explained and justified the reasons for his spree that intrigued Bradshaw. He wondered then if he might be stumbling closer to an answer.

28

Danny was right. They didn't get much out of Kevin. Not at first. Calling at the home he shared with his grandmother, they were greeted by the elderly lady, who told them, 'He's away over the fields again, or fishing down the lake.' She nodded firmly towards the land at the rear of the allotments, which were adjoined to the little terrace of one-storey houses.

'The lake?' queried Helen, who had not seen this marked on the map in police headquarters.

'Yes, the lake.' The old woman said it again, as if Helen might be simple-minded.

'It's an old gravel pit,' Tom told her, 'flooded when the river burst its banks thirty years or more ago. People fish in it.' And Helen wondered if there was a village in the whole of County Durham he didn't know everything about.

'He'll be back for his tea in fifteen minutes,' said the old lady.

They decided to wait in the car, 'So, how's it going with Lena?' Helen asked Tom, making it sound like casual conversation.

'Good.'

'It's just you haven't mentioned her much.'

'I thought it was a sore point.'

'Of course not. I'm sorry if I sounded –'

'Like my mum?' he offered.

'I am *not* your mum.'

'Can I have that in writing?'

They sat for a while, watching the land Kevin would have to

cross to get home for his tea. They talked about the case and being back on a job with Ian Bradshaw.

'I like Ian,' Helen said.

'He doesn't change,' observed Tom.

'How do you mean?'

'Always looks like he has the troubles of the world on his shoulders, and he's so bloody tenacious. Give him something to investigate and he doesn't ease up on himself until it's done.'

Helen gave him a significant look.

'What?' he asked.

'You could be describing yourself.'

He wasn't sure how to respond to that, so instead he asked, 'Do you miss Newcastle?'

'A little, but I can still go there and I like Durham. It's funny, I didn't know anything about the place when I was growing up, apart from the song.'

'Oh yes,' he said. 'The song.'

'Dad used to play it incessantly in the car. He liked Roger Whittaker,' she explained. 'A lot.'

'Yeah, well, he got that wrong, didn't he?'

'My dad?'

'No, Roger Whittaker. There's a line in the song about sitting on the banks of the River Tyne when he was a child.'

'I remember.'

'It's the bloody Wear, not the Tyne. Newcastle's on the Tyne,' he explained needlessly. 'Durham's on the Wear.'

'Another childhood illusion shattered. Is there anything in this world we can rely on?'

'Kevin's grandma,' answered Tom, and when Helen looked puzzled he pointed towards a figure heading their way across the fields. 'Here comes Kevin, home for his tea, and he's right on time too.'

Helen and Tom watched as Kevin trudged through the

allotments towards them. He was dressed in an old army jacket, carrying his fishing gear in one hand, and on his shoulder was slung a long, slim package wrapped in cloth.

'Jesus,' said Tom quietly as they got out of the car to meet the man. 'We'd best not fall out with him.'

'Why not?' asked Helen.

'Because he's got a gun.'

29

They interviewed Kevin by their car. Tom didn't want his grandmother standing over them, influencing what he said. Kevin was a surprisingly open subject but he spoke very little sense. He seemed quite jumpy, tense and talkative but with a low span of attention and a habit of going off on tangents.

'It was just a shame I didn't have my gun with me that day, else Susan would still be alive.'

'You owned a gun?' Helen was shocked.

'Yeah, course. Always had one. Me fatha taught us.'

'But you were only ten,' she reminded him.

'So?'

'Was it an air rifle, Kevin?' asked Tom, as much for Helen as for himself.

'Course it was,' said Kevin. 'They wouldn't have let me own a shotgun back then. Still won't,' he added significantly, as if this were a huge injustice, ''cos of me script.'

Helen looked at Tom, who explained, 'His prescription. They won't let him have a gun licence because of his medication. Is that right, Kevin?'

'Aye, 'cos of the pills. I have to take them, though, so.' He shrugged in a what-can-you-do? gesture.

'But you still have an air rifle?'

'Oh, aye,' he said. 'Always had one. Used to gan out spuggy-hunting when I was a bairn, like.'

'Spuggy-hunting?' Helen was at a loss once again.

'Aye,' he said. 'Spuggies are hard to get, 'cos they're arnly little, like, but I could knock one out of a tree from yards off.'

Helen looked at Tom for a translation. 'A sparrow,' he said. 'He used to shoot sparrows.'

'Really?' asked Helen, who was shocked by this. 'Why would you do that?'

'Why not?' asked Kevin. 'It doesn't do no harm.'

'It harms the sparrows,' said Helen. 'Is it legal to shoot them?' She was looking at Tom again and, though he understood her disgust, it seemed a little irrelevant. It was time to steer the conversation back to the more important matter of Susan Verity.

'Not really,' he said. 'Anyway, Kevin, we've been asked to talk to anyone who knew Susan Verity back in 1976 when she disappeared, so we're speaking to lots of people.' He wanted to put the man at his ease. 'It's purely routine, going over old ground, and nothing you haven't been asked before by the police or the newspapers.'

'I don't talk to them,' said Kevin emphatically.

'The police?' asked Helen.

'No, the papers. I don't talk to *them*. The police are all right, 'cos they're only doing their job. If you've done wrong, you'll get wrong.'

Tom knew Helen would be baffled by that phrase. 'If you *get wrong*, it means you get told off.'

'Oh.' Helen wondered how many years she would have to spend in the north-east before she understood everything.

'Aye, so I divvent mind that, like.'

Tom had realized that Kevin was one of those blokes who knew the difference between right and wrong but did the wrong thing anyway. Subsequently, he accepted the consequences, which often included arrest. It was quite refreshing that he refused to blame the police when this happened.

'So who are you?' asked Kevin. 'Police or the papers?'

Before Helen could answer, Tom said, 'We are working with

179

the police. And we just have one or two questions for you about what happened the day Susan went missing.'

'I know what happened to Susan,' he said, 'but you won't want to hear it.'

They had to persuade Kevin that they really did want to hear it. He seemed reluctant to give up the truth. He appeared to believe it would be too shocking for them.

'That's why we're here, Kevin,' Helen assured him. 'To discover the truth. What happened to Susan? If you think you know, please tell us.'

'It was the farmer that did it,' said Kevin, with great conviction.

'Did what?' asked Helen.

'Took Susan.'

'Farmer Marsh kidnapped Susan?' asked Tom.

'Aye, and everybody knows it round here.'

'What possible motive would Farmer Marsh have for abducting Susan?' asked Helen, and when Kevin looked blank, she put it more simply: 'Why would he do that?'

''Cos he hated kids. Wanted to stop us playing in his bales and messing up his corn in the fields. He was always going on about it? Kept dobbing us in to the police. Threatened to shoot us with his shotgun. Him and Lenny Butler had a brawl ower it once. Lenny blacked his eye but he got a bust nose. Marsh had enough of kids messing about so he took one to scare the others away.' When neither Helen nor Tom seemed convinced by this argument, he added, 'Well, it worked, didn't it? No one ever went on his land again, did they?'

'That may be true, but it seems a bit extreme to kidnap a child to keep others away,' Helen said. 'And the police searched his farm, Kevin. They went over it.'

'Aye, but they didn't know where to look, did they?'

'How do you mean?'

'No use to just search his farmhouse and look in his fields.'

'Why not?'

''Cos he had a barn and outbuildings, and there was all the other places that used to belong to him.'

Tom frowned. 'What other places?'

'Well, his fatha sold a field, didn't he, years before, so they could build that factory on it, but when it closed down the buildings stood empty for years and years. He started to see it as his land again. He was always prowling round it, taking things.'

'Taking things? What things?' asked Helen.

'Owt he could get his hands on, man. He called it salvage, but if any other bugger tried to take owt he'd go mad and that bloody shotgun would come out again.'

'Are you saying Farmer Marsh imprisoned Susan Verity in one of those old factory buildings?' asked Tom.

'Aye.'

'But the police searched them,' said Helen, 'and they didn't find her.'

'No,' said Kevin smugly. 'They didn't, did they?' And he tapped his nose conspiratorially.

'All right, Kevin,' said Tom. 'Enough's enough. If you know something, then out with it. We haven't got time for games.'

'I'm not playing games. All those buildings had . . . what-you-call-em?' He stopped to think, and he didn't make it seem an easy process. 'The underground things,' he said impatiently.

'Cellars?' said Helen.

'Aye!' confirmed Kevin. 'But they all got flooded an' that 'cos of the rain and the fields being marshy, then the buildings were falling apart, so they just locked the doors up when they left the place. Me and my mate were out snaring rabbits and we went down there once, but you couldn't get in to them all 'cos no one had a key any more.'

Kevin was talking in such a rush it was wearying to keep up with his train of thought. Tom knew the likelihood of Susan Verity having been imprisoned in the cellar of one of the old factory buildings without anyone noticing was close to zero.

'You seem pretty sure Susan was kept there,' said Helen. 'What makes you think that?'

'Because I heard her.' His voice was a conspiratorial whisper now.

'You heard her?' Helen was shocked.

'One night,' said Kevin, 'I heard her moaning.' He nodded emphatically to show the truth of this statement.

'When was this, Kevin?' asked Tom, and his tone indicated that he wasn't taking the man very seriously.

'Last year,' said Kevin, as if this were an entirely reasonable notion.

'Last year?' He looked at Helen significantly.

'It was our fault she died,' said Kevin suddenly.

'What?' asked Tom.

'Our fault,' repeated Kevin. 'We caused it.'

'What do you mean?' asked Helen. 'How did you cause Susan's death?'

'Because we made her,' he said. 'We made her do it.'

'Do what?' asked Tom.

'Swear out loud,' he said sternly. 'To die. We made Susan cross her heart and hope to die,' he said reasonably. 'And she did.'

30

They could have been back in the seventies. The singer was asking them if they happened to have seen the most beautiful girl in the world and Tom wondered if the landlord had ever changed the records on the ancient jukebox.

'Kevin Robson lives in his own world,' Helen explained to Ian Bradshaw, who had joined them in one of Maiden Hill's two village pubs for an evening meal and a debrief.

'The poor, daft bastard,' added Tom.

'I don't know,' said Helen. 'It could all be an act.'

'You think that wasn't for real? Robert De Niro couldn't have faked that, Helen. Kevin Robson is puddled.'

'I'm not saying he isn't disturbed, I think he very probably is. I'm just saying that the bit about the farmer taking Susan could have been made up for a reason.'

'Meaning what, exactly?' asked Bradshaw.

'A boy who grows up shooting birds and snaring rabbits is used to killing. He thinks it's normal.'

'It doesn't mean that he killed Susan, though, does it?' asked Tom.

'That's how serial killers start,' she told Tom, 'by torturing then killing animals, then they move on to humans. It's well documented. They don't have any empathy for the thing they are harming. Kevin Robson doesn't seem to care about the tiny little birds or the cute little bunnies he's murdering.'

Tom laughed. 'Cute little bunnies? That's hilarious, Helen. Just because he enjoys snaring rabbits for sport doesn't make him a murderer.'

'For sport? Do you think it's acceptable to catch wild rabbits and kill them?'

'I don't, no, unless there are too many of them and they're causing a nuisance.'

'Well, then.'

'But he doesn't think like that. His dad was into it, and his grandparents, I should imagine. Back then, they will have caught rabbits for the pot. Round here, it doesn't mean what you think it means.'

'Round here?'

'In the north-east.'

'Oh, so this is something I'll never understand, is it? Because I am not from this part of the world. I'm just a southern princess?'

'Christ, I can't believe you're still chucking that one back at me. I hadn't even met you properly, it was a stupid, throw-away line, I was a bit drunk and I didn't mean it. Most importantly, you know how I feel about you!'

There was an uncomfortable silence between them for a moment and Bradshaw made a point of gazing at his pint, until Tom added somewhat sulkily, 'If I didn't rate you, I wouldn't be working with you, I mean.' He sighed. 'Think bull fighting or, closer to home, fox-hunting,' he said. 'They're also barbaric and inhumane, but lots of people still hunt foxes. They put on their posh red jackets, climb on their horses and go chasing after foxes with packs of dogs. Sometimes the foxes get ripped apart by the dogs and the hunters smear the blood on their kids afterwards. I, personally, cannot imagine doing that to a child, but lots of people do and it's been going on for centuries. Those horsey types are no more likely to murder a human being than you or me, though, or Kevin Robson for that matter.'

'Maybe not,' said Helen, 'but something happened to Susan and, if it wasn't Wicklow, we need to explore every other possibility. That's all I'm saying.'

Their meal arrived then and Helen was taken aback by the amount of food on her plate. 'I won't need to eat for a week,' she said, once the landlady had retreated.

'Northern portions,' Tom explained. 'People expect it. If you tried to do nouvelle cuisine up here, you'd be lynched.'

A new record came on the jukebox. 'Can you believe this?' asked Tom. Both Helen and Ian looked at Tom's dinner to see what was amiss, but it wasn't the food he was referring to. '"Tie a Yellow Ribbon", for fuck's sake,' he said, and shook his head in irritation. 'It's like the land that time forgot in here.'

'I quite like it,' said Bradshaw. 'It's better than Oasis.'

'You're not serious?'

'If I hear "Wonderwall" one more time, I will not be responsible for my actions.'

Helen did not bother to express an opinion on the musical merits or otherwise of 'Tie a Yellow Ribbon'. 'When Kevin Robson had that breakdown during his exams, his teacher told you he had a counsellor for a while, didn't he?'

'That's right,' said Tom.

'Do you think you could track her down and speak to her?' she asked Bradshaw. 'It might reveal something.'

'It might,' agreed Bradshaw.

Tom had his notebook out now and was leafing through it to get to the right page.

'It was a Mrs Rees,' he told the detective. 'She dealt with a number of cases of child mental health problems at Kevin's secondary school.'

'Then maybe she can shed some light on how a normal schoolboy could suddenly lose the plot and end up . . .' She was momentarily lost for words.

'Hearing ghosts,' said Tom.

'Exactly,' said Helen.

'I'd have said he had a pretty good reason,' observed Bradshaw.

'The upset caused by the disappearance of Susan?' asked Tom. 'Maybe, but the others didn't react like he did.'

'So what are you saying?' asked the detective.

'Perhaps he had more reason to feel traumatized than they did.'

'Why?'

'I don't know why,' admitted Tom, 'and that's what we should try and find out.'

'Okay,' agreed Bradshaw, 'I'll give it a go. Oh, and before I forget, I checked out that name for you.'

'Right, thanks,' said Tom, so quickly that Helen noticed.

'No one of that name was ever officially reported missing,' he told Tom.

Helen could tell he was surprised to learn this, but he quickly hid his feelings. 'Who's that?' she asked.

'Nobody,' said Tom. 'I'll tell you later.' He got to his feet. 'My shout,' and he gestured towards their drinks.

As he went to the bar, Helen wondered why he would bother to tell her about it later if he and Ian really were talking about a nobody.

As Helen emerged from the bathroom the next morning, she could hear Tom taking a phone call in the hallway, but she couldn't make out what he was saying or who he was saying it to. She dressed and walked downstairs.

'Okay, no problem,' Tom was saying. 'Just give me a call when you're coming back and we'll meet up.' He stopped talking as Helen reached the bottom of the stairs, and she passed him and went into the kitchen to make coffee.

'Was that Lena?' she asked when he appeared moments later.

'Yeah.'

186

'When is she due back?'

'A couple of days,' he said, but she got the impression he still wasn't comfortable discussing his new girlfriend with her and reasoned this was her fault.

Tom made himself a mug of coffee and some toast and glanced at the papers. She decided not to interrupt his train of thought but, moments later, he left his seat, crossed the room and looked out of the kitchen window intently.

'What's up?' she asked.

'Weather's not too bad,' he said brightly. 'How do you fancy a day at the seaside?'

They were sitting in her office, because the counsellor had a private practice and went into the school only when required. 'I can't tell you anything that Kevin and I discussed in a session,' said Angela Rees firmly. 'That wouldn't be ethical.'

'I understand,' Bradshaw told the counsellor, 'but I'm trying to rule him out of a murder enquiry.'

'A murder?' she asked. 'I thought they never found that girl?'

'Which is why we have to assume she was murdered,' he told her, 'or had some inexplicable accident, which I have to say is a pretty slim possibility.'

'Even so, I work on the basis of complete confidentiality. Imagine if you came to see me with a problem, you poured your heart out and I told your innermost secrets to the first policeman who happened to come along and ask me about you?'

Bradshaw wished she hadn't used that example, since it was a chilling possibility for a man who had been in counselling himself. 'I get it,' he assured her. 'You can't tell me anything he told you directly, but I'm more interested in your professional opinion about the day Kevin Robson had his breakdown. What happened to him? Was it real? Was it fake? Is that kind of thing rare, or commonplace? Is it triggered by stress, or could it be guilt? Was he all right that morning and suddenly flipped when he turned over his exam paper?' He shrugged helplessly. 'I just need some help because I'm floundering in the dark here and all I've got is gossip and whispers.'

'Kevin Robson did not go mad. He isn't some crazed lunatic. He simply had what we should probably term a complete nervous breakdown.' The counsellor sighed, as if she would probably get nowhere explaining this to a police officer. 'Are you familiar with mental health issues?'

'I know a little about them, yes,' Bradshaw admitted reluctantly.

'Many people in this world are silently suffering from mental disorders, often caused by extreme stress. A nervous breakdown can result if they reach a point that really is their limit. That day, Kevin reached his.'

'His first exam?'

'It was the trigger, yes, but not necessarily the cause.'

'Sorry?'

'The stress of his exams might well have been the final straw for Kevin. He wasn't particularly academic and may have worried about that at the time. He might even have built this worry up into a phobia or felt he just couldn't go on, but it is rare for us to see someone break down like he did over an exam.'

'So what are you saying?'

'I'm saying it could have been a number of factors. He might already have been severely depressed, he could have been struggling to perform the most basic of functions, he might even have had difficulty getting out of bed. There were reports that he had been withdrawn for some time.'

'Right,' said Bradshaw. He was trying to sound as if his interest in this topic was entirely professional, even though he recognized quite a few of those symptoms. 'Could this have been due to events long ago that somehow didn't fully affect him until the day in question?'

'You mean, did he snap because of that girl's disappearance? I can't talk about his sessions with me, but I will say that, in general, it is not uncommon for events to be suppressed for years but then they can suddenly bubble up to the surface one day and feel like fresh trauma.'

'And I understand he ran from the exam?'

'I was told he simply put down his pen and walked out. That alone would attract enough attention in an exam room. Over the years, it probably evolved into a tale involving his running from the room screaming. You know how these stories can be twisted.'

'But didn't they find him in a bit of a state?'

'A teacher went to look for Kevin and eventually located him in the boy's toilets. He was sitting on the floor, weeping. When the teacher tried to comfort him, he lashed out and screamed to be left alone. It took some time to calm him and, for the sake of caution, an ambulance was called.'

'He must have been in a really bad way.'

'He was, by all accounts.'

'Poor little bugger.'

The counsellor was impressed. 'I'm surprised, Detective Bradshaw.'

'By what?'

'Your empathy. Most police officers I've dealt with think people with mental health problems are either faking it or completely gaga and should be locked away. There isn't a lot of understanding, usually.'

'I've seen colleagues go through a bad time. Police officers have to deal with some pretty horrendous things, but if someone is struggling they tend not to talk about it. There's a lot of gallows humour, and the expectation is they should just get on with it, but some experiences leave scars.'

'I suppose the police do see disturbing things that members of the public never encounter.'

'We do.'

She slid open her desk drawer, took something out and handed it to him. 'My card.'

'Oh, I wasn't talking about me,' he said quickly.

'Even so,' she said carefully, 'you never know when it might come in useful.' She pressed the card into his hand before adding quickly, 'For you *or* your friends.'

31

'Why the big mystery?' asked Helen as Tom drove north up the A1.

'What mystery? I told you we were going to the seaside.'

'But you haven't told me why. I'm guessing this is not a day off.'

'Well,' he admitted, 'we might call in on someone while we're there.'

'Who?' she demanded. 'And where is *there*?'

'You don't like surprises, do you?'

'No,' she conceded. 'I really don't.'

'You prefer to be in control,' he observed.

'That's not the same thing.' The sky brightened then, but the sun was still low in the sky. Tom started scrabbling around in the driver's door compartment. 'What are you looking for?'

'My sunglasses.'

'You're always losing them.'

'And I always find them again.' He thrust his hand deeper in among the debris and a CD fell out on to the floor by his feet. Tom swore.

'You should really clean out this car.'

'Any other helpful suggestions?'

She ignored that. 'You still haven't told me where we're going.'

'Seahouses,' he said.

'Where's that?'

'You see, you're none the wiser for knowing, are you? Can't believe you've never been to Seahouses. You haven't lived. It's a fishing village on the Northumbria coast. My dad used to take us there sometimes, but when he did he would never tell us where we were going. He just said, "It's a mystery trip," even though we always knew it was Seahouses, because it was *always* Seahouses. Somehow, pretending it was a mystery trip made it more fun.' He glanced at her dubious face, then assured her, 'Anyway, you'll love it, trust me.'

'But who are we going to see?'

'Andrea Craven. She lives there now.'

'Susan Verity's friend?'

'Susan Verity's last surviving female friend,' he corrected her. 'Since Michelle Dutton is already dead.'

Andrea Craven lived alone in one of a long line of small terraced houses that overlooked the bay. The view was spectacular, but the tranquillity was repeatedly shattered by the insistent cawing of rogue bands of seagulls scavenging the harbour nearby, looking for scraps from that morning's catch or poking their beaks into last night's fish-and-chip wrappers.

Tom knocked and a woman answered. She looked a good deal older than her thirty years. Her face was lined and there was a dullness about her features. Life had knocked the stuffing out of Andrea Craven.

'Miss Craven,' he began, 'my name is Tom Carney, and this is Helen Norton. We are here because –'

'I know why you're here,' she said flatly. 'Come in, if you must.'

Bradshaw's backside had barely touched the chair in the canteen before DC Malone appeared and joined him. She didn't usually do that.

'Where have you been?' she asked, as if he had been skiving this past week.

'Out and about, following things up.' She already knew he was working the Susan Verity case, but he had no desire to discuss his sessions with Adrian Wicklow with her.

'DI Tennant's been looking for you.'

'What did she want?'

'How should I know?' She managed three bites of her dinner before she could no longer resist the temptation. Malone had a sly look about her, as if she had been looking forward to this moment. 'What do you think about your ex then?'

'Karen?' he asked dumbly, because whatever she was about to say would be news to him. Karen didn't speak to him any more. She had ignored Bradshaw from the minute she stormed out of his apartment, when he'd told her he no longer wanted her to move in with him. Occasionally, he would see her at headquarters, when one of them was going into the building and the other walking out. The last time that happened she blanked him while simultaneously ensuring that he overheard her tell her friend where she and the boyfriend were going for their holidays – 'Two weeks in Tenerife, and I cannot wait!' – as if this would be crushing news to Bradshaw, which, strangely enough, it was.

Whatever he had thought of Karen, whatever his doubts about moving in with her and her not being 'the one', they had spent months together as a couple. Now she was back with her old boyfriend and that occasionally stung, particularly as he was still single.

'You know,' Malone prompted him, 'getting married.' She said this as if he was obviously aware of it already. Bradshaw could tell by her face she knew it was news to him and couldn't wait to be the one to tell him. It was like a dagger in the ribs.

'Really?' he said brightly. 'Well, that's great.' He smiled, as if this news had cheered up his entire morning. That ruined the moment for DC Malone, who could not fully hide her disappointment. She must have assumed Bradshaw would be gutted, but he was determined not to give her the satisfaction. 'Good for her!'

'You and Susan were close friends?' Helen asked Andrea, when the explanations and introductions were concluded.

'We were *best* friends,' Andrea Craven corrected her, as if the distinction mattered just as much now as it would have done at the time.

'Along with Michelle Dutton.'

'She used to tag along too, yes.'

'But you and Susan were closest,' Helen reiterated, so Andrea knew she understood just how close they were. 'And I understand Michelle died some time ago.'

'A few years back; three, maybe four. She was no age.' She shook her head at the injustice of this. 'I'm the only one of us three left. I suppose you'd call me the lucky one.' Andrea didn't look as if she felt lucky. Instead, she said solemnly, 'We were cursed that day. When Susan disappeared, it was as if we were all to blame. That's how it felt, anyhow. You could see it in the eyes of the adults, like they were accusing us of something.'

'I don't think anyone seriously felt the other children were responsible for Susan going missing,' said Tom. 'You were all just ten years old. From the beginning, they were looking for a man and, in the end, they convinced themselves it was Adrian Wicklow.' He wanted to steer her back on to more solid ground than an ancient curse. 'We are less convinced.'

'I'm not saying they thought we did it,' she corrected him. 'I'm saying we were cursed.'

'But,' Helen began, 'how could you have been?'

'Susan disappeared,' she said needlessly, 'Michelle died in her twenties, Danny's girlfriend was killed in an accident,

Kevin had a breakdown, and Billy . . . well, he's just Billy. Nothing's ever gone right for him.'

'Billy flunked a bunch of exams and struggles to hold down a job. Does that make him cursed?' asked Tom.

'He used to be a bright lad,' she said firmly, as if this were some form of explanation.

'But you seem to be doing okay.' Andrea's eyes widened, as if Helen had decided to bring the curse down upon her there and then. Her fingers slapped the coffee table in front of her.

'Touch wood,' she said earnestly. Helen got the impression that Andrea thought the god of misfortune was watching her every move, waiting to pounce.

'Is that why you moved away?' Helen asked, and she had to make a conscious effort not to sound incredulous when she added: 'To escape the curse?'

'Why else would I leave my village?'

'Right,' said Tom. 'But if you think bad luck haunts you all, then how would living here make any difference? I mean, Danny's girlfriend died on a mountain in France.'

The look she gave Tom was so harrowing it quite startled him. Her stare was accusatory, as if she were demanding to know why he would remind her of this unpalatable fact. She finally settled on: 'I feel safe here.'

'By the sea?' Helen smiled at the woman, hoping to calm her. 'It is beautiful.'

'I can be on my own up here.' And that was explanation enough, it seemed.

'What happened that day?' asked Tom abruptly, because he was growing impatient with her superstition.

'What?'

'When Susan disappeared' – Helen was trying to speak gently so she could coax the woman back on track – 'you were playing together in a *den*?' She emphasized the final word to turn it into a reminder.

'Yes,' agreed Andrea, and Helen rewarded this admission with a smile. 'Three of us and three of them.'

'Three boys and three girls,' said Helen. 'You, Michelle and Susan were playing with Danny, Billy and Kevin.'

'That's right,' said Andrea. 'To begin with.'

'For most of the day, we understand,' said Tom. 'Then there was an argument.'

Andrea said nothing.

'What was the argument about?' asked Helen, and Andrea immediately sounded evasive.

'Stupid things,' she said, and when they stayed quiet she must have felt pressured to fill the silence with words. 'I can't really remember it, after all these years.'

Liar, thought Helen, *you remember right enough.*

'It was all over some silly game,' the woman went on, 'of truth or dare. You had to admit who you liked. You had to admit which boy you liked the most.' The nervous woman's expression softened. 'I was worried about that. No one could keep a secret back then.'

'So who did you like?' asked Helen. 'I promise I'll never tell.' And the two women laughed. Tom let Helen talk, because he could see a bond was beginning to form between them.

'It was a very long time ago.'

'Bet you still remember, though. We always do, don't we?'

'Yes, I suppose we do.' She hesitated for a second. 'I liked Danny. He was more grown up than the other two, and kinder.' She felt the need to clarify. 'Kinder to me, at any rate.' Helen was left with the impression that the other boys in the village had been far from kind to Andrea.

'And better-looking too, I shouldn't wonder. I've seen him recently.'

'Well' – the woman actually seemed to blush a little then – 'we were only ten but, yes, I suppose he was.'

'Was that when the arguments began? Were the other boys jealous of Danny?'

'It wasn't just that. It took everyone ages to agree to play the game. We were all very shy about it. Admitting you liked some-one was a very big thing. It sounds stupid now, of course, but –'

'We can all remember what it was like to be that age,' said Helen, and Tom found himself trying to picture her as a young girl.

'I went first ... or was it Kevin? I don't remember what he said. Anyway, I picked Danny and everybody laughed at me. I don't know why.'

Tom thought he knew, though. The kids had all judged the likelihood of Danny liking her back as slim, so they thought it was hilarious. By the age of ten, poor Andrea had been found wanting on the prettiness scale and been publicly humiliated for liking a boy who was out of her league.

'Then it was Billy's turn and, of course, he said he liked Susan, and there was more laughter.' *And I bet you joined in too*, thought Tom, *grateful to distract them from picking on you.*

'He must have been upset,' said Helen.

'He was.'

'How did Susan take that admission?'

'In her stride,' said Andrea. 'She was used to it. All the boys loved her. Billy was just daft enough to admit it. So then it was Susan's turn.'

'Who did she like?' For some reason, Helen was under the impression that this mattered. It may have been a simple chil-dren's game, its consequences completely overlooked by the adults at the time, but Helen could remember what it was like to be a child, how important it was to fit in and not be excluded, how every word you uttered was pounced upon.

'She didn't, or at least she wouldn't admit it. Of course, everyone was outraged. You must like someone, and you have to play the game because we all did, la di da di da.' She added the last bit to be dismissive of it all, but both of them could understand how annoyed the other kids would have been by Susan's silence. They had admitted their deepest secret in a game of huge consequence, and had been betrayed. 'We all moaned at Susan, but you could never get her to do anything she didn't want to. Danny refused to take his turn, probably because he would have said he liked Susan. All the boys liked Susan.' There was resentment there still, even after all those years.

'Did it become a big argument?'

'It was probably forgotten in ten minutes. That's how kids are, isn't it? Then we played on the hay bales.'

'Until you were chased away by the farmer?' asked Tom.

'Yes.'

'I've read the case files,' Helen told her. 'You ended up in the woods with Danny after that?' She was trying to confirm the chronology of events that day.

'For a little while,' said Andrea.

'Then Susan found you,' Helen said, 'but she only stayed with you and Danny for a while. She went back across the fields, presumably heading home, and the last people who saw her alive were Billy and Kevin. When she left them she was heading towards the farm, and they watched her go. No one ever saw her again,'

Andrea nodded. 'That's how it was.'

'Do you still see them?' asked Helen. 'The boys, I mean.'

'I haven't seen Kevin in years. There's something badly wrong with him. I used to see Billy around, usually in the pub, when we were younger, but not for ages.'

'What about Danny?' she asked Andrea, who flushed again.

'Danny and I have a connection,' she said, as if this was

something she was proud of. 'He still comes round, now and then.' Her words hinted his visits to her had become less frequent, as you would expect from a family man. 'I was there for him when he lost Victoria, and he never forgot that. His job takes him all over the north-east, so he used to pop by when he could. Sometimes, he'd stay over.' She blushed at this admission, but Helen could tell there was pride in it too.

'We didn't learn all that much,' said Helen as they walked away from Andrea's home, after a further half-hour of Andrea's thoughts on Danny and who had murdered Susan. 'Adrian Wicklow, obviously,' she had said.

'I don't know,' he offered. 'I think we learned quite a lot about the kids and how they interacted with one another. We know what prompted their argument and the fateful decision to go and play on the hay bales, where it all went badly wrong. We also learnt Andrea had a big crush on Danny,' he reminded her. 'And still does, seemingly.'

'I'm not sure it was worth the drive out here,' Helen concluded.

'Not worth the drive? Look at this place. Breathe in the sea air. Let that bracing north-east breeze put some colour in your cheeks as you walk along with an ice cream.'

'An ice cream? Are you serious?' she asked, as if he had just suggested eloping.

'Perfectly. I'm going to buy you one; a ninety-nine, with monkey's blood.'

'With what?'

'Monkey's blood,' he repeated, and when he realized she had no idea what he meant he groaned, 'Gaah, you've never lived, pet. Come on.' And he was off towards the nearest ice-cream van.

32

Monkey's blood turned out to be strawberry sauce, and it was put on Helen's 99 before the Flake. She and Tom ate their ice creams as they walked along the seafront.

'I haven't had one of these since I was a kid. Why do they call it monkey's blood, though? I mean, why specifically a monkey? Why not some other unfortunate animal?'

'No idea. I've never given it a moment's thought. It was just something we grew up saying round here, like "spelks" or "kets".'

'What are spelks and kets?'

'You get a spelk in your finger. It's a . . . what-do-you-call-it?' He clicked his fingers twice as if trying to conjure up the word.

'A splinter?'

'Yes. And kets are sweets,' he told her. 'Don't ask me why. I obviously don't have your enquiring mind, Helen.'

'You do have an enquiring mind. You're obsessed with finding things out.'

'Important things, like who murdered who or why somebody disappeared, yes, I'll grant you that. But the origin of "monkey's blood"? Who cares? Just enjoy your ice cream.'

'I *am* enjoying my ice cream. Where are we going, by the way?'

'Bamburgh Castle. You can't come to Seahouses without walking down to Bamburgh Castle, particularly if you haven't been here before.'

'Aren't we supposed to be working?'

'We're always working. Let's have a couple of hours off, live a little.'

*

They chose a spot in the grounds of Bamburgh Castle, close to the huge cannons which pointed out to sea, ready to repel any invader. Ahead of them was a wide, sandy beach and a becalmed North Sea, under a deep blue sky.

'It's beautiful here,' Helen said.

'It is. Just don't tell anyone about it.'

'Why?'

'Look at this beach. It's gorgeous, and there's hardly anyone on it. Let's keep it that way. On a day like today, Brighton beach will be packed, and it's nowt but shingle. Imagine if people down south knew how good it was up here? You'd not be able to find a patch of free sand.'

And with that they sat for a while in what Helen would later think of as a good silence, which gave her a rare sense of contentment.

'Do you reckon he was shagging her?' Tom asked after a while. 'When Andrea was *comforting him*, I mean.'

'Danny?'

'Yeah.'

'Perhaps. She's always been smitten with him – that's obvious – and he might have been lonely. What do you think?'

Tom thought for a while. 'I can't see a man like Danny sleeping with a girl like Andrea.'

'Why?' It was a challenge. 'Because she isn't good-looking enough for him?'

'It's not that. She'd be a difficult one to extricate yourself from. I can't imagine Andrea as the casual lover happy to step aside when Danny found himself a proper girlfriend.'

'Fair point,' she admitted.

'I reckon that's the way Danny would think. I'm guessing that, when he stayed over, it meant just that. He probably kipped on the sofa, though she probably wished it otherwise.'

'Well,' said Helen. 'We managed just over an hour.'

'What?'

'Without talking about murderers or missing people.'

'I thought we were talking about shagging,' said Tom, 'but we can stop talking about that too if you like.'

They watched the waves roll for a while, then Helen said, 'Do you ever wonder what would have happened if you'd taken that job?'

'With the magazine? Not really.'

'You'd be in London now, interviewing celebrities.'

'Celebrities are boring. All they want to talk about is themselves. I had six months of wannabe pop stars and MAWs when I worked for the paper down south.'

'MAWs?'

'Model-Actress-Whatevers,' he explained. 'People with no discernible talent who just want to be famous.'

'But I hear that lads' mag is doing really well.'

'People are bound to get tired of reading about celebrities eventually. Anyway' – he glanced at Helen – 'I'm happy here.'

Their eyes locked, but only for a moment because, abruptly, Tom's mobile phone began to ring.

He reached into his pocket and silenced it. Helen thought he'd just turned it off and, normally, she would have disapproved – they were professionals, after all; but today, she wouldn't have minded for once – then he brought it to his ear and said, 'Hello.' He listened for a while, then said, 'Great. I'll meet you there then,' and laughed at some comment or other. 'Me too.'

When he said his goodbyes and hung up, he was smiling. 'That was –'

'Lena,' she interrupted. 'I gathered.' She got to her feet. 'We'd better head back then.'

He followed her and, when they had gone a few yards, she glanced back to the bench where they had been sitting. 'You left your sunglasses behind,' she said.

*

'Come in, Ian,' DI Tennant told him. 'And don't give me that look.'

'What look, ma'am?' he asked, from the door of her office.

'The smacked-arse face you're wearing right now,' she said. 'This isn't a bollocking.'

'I didn't think it was,' he answered, but he had wondered if it might be.

'I'm just enquiring as to your wellbeing.'

'Sorry?' he asked as he sat down.

'Are you okay?' She spoke the words slowly, as if he were a dim child.

'I'm fine, ma'am.' When she said nothing to that, he added, 'Why do you ask?'

'No reason,' she said. 'Apart from the fact you were pulled off my squad by DCI Kane in order to spend some time face to face with a maniac.'

'All part of the job, boss,' he said chirpily.

'Not usually,' she replied, 'but I'm glad you're taking it in your stride.' She looked at him closely. 'You *are* taking it in your stride?'

Bradshaw nodded. 'Absolutely.' He saw no reason to enlighten his DI about the night terrors, or his general, ever-present and heightened sense of anxiety these days. What good would that do? She might be more sympathetic than most, but the top brass wouldn't be. *Tell him to pull himself together*, would be the reaction and there'd be another black mark on his record.

'And how's it going with Dr Mellor these days? You're still going?'

Bradshaw frowned. 'I am going, yes, ma'am, but it's a waste of bloody time, frankly, all that navel-gazing. I don't think I'll keep on with it.'

'Well, you have to,' she reminded him. 'Your offer of promotion was conditional on it.'

'Yes, but it wasn't open-ended, was it? I mean, how long have I got to keep doing this? For the rest of my career?' He laughed. 'I ran out of things to say to him months ago.' Bradshaw had another good reason to avoid the intrusive Dr Mellor. At some point in every session he asked Bradshaw about developments in his private life, and the detective had absolutely no desire to reveal to the doctor that his ex was getting married. Mellor would ask him how this made him feel, but how could Bradshaw answer that when he wasn't sure himself? He didn't really want Karen back, but he couldn't help but feel a jolt when DC Malone had informed him that she was soon to be wed to another man. 'The truth is, I have tried to be more positive about the sessions, ma'am, but I honestly never feel any better when they are over. If anything, it makes me more gloomy knowing I have to see Mellor for an hour every week.'

'You're sure you want to stop seeing him?'

'I am.'

'All right,' she said cautiously. 'I'll have a word with DCI Kane about it.'

'I doubt he'll object to me finishing. He thinks –'

'– it's a load of old bollocks,' she interrupted. 'I know; he told me. Leave it with me then. How long are you going to need away from the squad to sort this Wicklow business out? I'd much rather have you back on my team, if that's what you want.'

'That is absolutely what I want. I'm not sure how long I'll have with him anyway, since he's terminally ill, but if it were down to me I'd report back here tomorrow.'

'Unfortunately, it's not down to you, or to me either. The chief constable has a personal interest in this particular cold case, I understand.'

'He's determined to solve it,' said Bradshaw, 'for the sake of the families.'

'I thought it was because he wanted to be the next chief of the Met.'

'That might have something to do with it, ma'am.'

'Very diplomatic, Bradshaw,' she said. 'Just make sure this Wicklow business doesn't derail you.'

'Derail me?'

'I think you know what I mean.' And he did, sort of. Everyone seemed to know the cost of dealing with Adrian Wicklow. 'Tidy up the case if you can but don't get drawn too deeply into it. Don't play any of his games. You might not be able to make a difference in the end, but don't take it personally. Just get back here afterwards and help us with this double murder.'

'Yes, ma'am.'

33

Victoria Cassidy's parents weren't hard to find. They had set up a trust dedicated to the memory of their daughter following her death on Mont Blanc and wanted people to get in touch with them if they wished to make a donation. Helen had called them once already, before she and Tom had met with Danny Gilbert. She had left a message but got no response.

Helen left a second one on their answerphone now, explaining once again who she was, along with a polite request to call her back. She had a few questions for them about the circumstances of their daughter's death on the mountain. She did not mention that what she was most interested in was their opinion of Danny Gilbert.

Tom popped his head around the door then. 'Listen, do you think you could go and see Paul Verity on your own today?' he asked her.

'I could,' she replied, 'but why do you need me to do that? Have you got another lead?'

'Kind of,' he said. 'There's just something I need to do and I figured it would be quicker if we split up. You know' – he smiled sheepishly – 'like those famous crime fighters.'

'Which ones?' She was wondering if he meant the FBI.

'I was thinking of the gang in Scooby Doo. They always split up. It seems to work for them.'

'True.' Did he never stop joking? 'Do you think we should get a dog as well?'

'I reckon we have enough on our plate already.'

'So I'll see you later then?'

'Yeah, just don't go exploring any haunted cellars on your own.'

'I'll try not to.'

It was only as Helen was driving away that she realized Tom still hadn't told her what he was up to.

Normally, one of them did the driving, leaving the other to navigate. In Newcastle, this was particularly useful once they were outside the city centre they both knew well and criss-crossing the myriad streets filled with houses and flats that housed a city of a quarter of a million inhabitants. Paul Verity's home was easy enough to find, though. He lived in a fourteen-storey high-rise in Denton that had been thrown up in the sixties. Helen checked the numbers and was relieved to discover he was on the ground floor. The place was quiet now and didn't look too bad in the daylight, but she wondered what it might be like round here after dark.

Helen knew it was unlikely Paul Verity would speak to her. According to the documentary, he had never spoken publicly about the death of his daughter. He was also a convicted criminal who had returned to his old ways once his family was gone.

She rang the doorbell and waited. A shadow crossed the frosted-glass window as a figure moved behind it. It was too late for second thoughts now. The door opened to reveal a slight man in late middle age with greying hair turning to silver. He didn't look angry to see her, just exhausted.

'Who sent you then, pet?' he asked. 'The social?'

'I'm not Social Security,' she explained, and he seemed relieved. She told him why she was there, expecting the door to be closed in her face.

'Oh, right,' he said placidly. 'Howay in then.'

Helen followed Paul Verity into his tiny flat. There were no pictures on his walls and no ornaments or keepsakes. The place was bare, apart from a battered sofa and armchair and a small coffee table with a newspaper on it. He didn't even own a TV.

'So you want me to talk about Susan?'

'If you don't mind,' she said. 'I know you don't normally do that.'

'I don't talk to the newspapers,' he corrected her, 'but you said you're helping the police?'

'That's right,' said Helen.

'So what do you want to hear?'

'Your side of it,' she said simply. 'I understand you aren't from the village originally.'

'I'm from Newcastle.' He gestured for her to sit down, then shrugged. 'And now I'm back in Newcastle.' He sat down as well and must have realized she was expecting some sort of explanation for his move to Maiden Hill.

'Before I met Barbara, I was a mess,' he explained. 'I was drinking a lot, hanging out with a bad crowd, and she made me realize that if I wanted a decent life with a job, a family . . . with *her* . . . then I had to sort myself out. I had to stop drinking all the time, pack in the thieving and nicking cars and grow up.' He paused, as if remembering that pep talk, from long ago now. Helen stayed silent and let him continue. 'She talked to me, and I listened, for once, and I did stop. I ditched the friends who were into all the same stuff I was doing, even my own brother, and we moved away from Newcastle to Maiden Hill. It was the quietest place I'd ever seen. I got a job, and I held on to it' – he sounded genuinely surprised by this – 'because of her, because, more than anything in the world, I didn't want to let her down, or our daughter when she came along. I had responsibilities and I held it together.' Then he added quietly, 'For a while,' and there was such sadness in those last three words that Helen's heart went out to the man.

'And that's how we were for years. If Susan hadn't disappeared, we would have gone along fine. I even went to church. I knelt and prayed and swore to God I would become a better man if he would let me keep Barbara.' He sighed. 'And of course we were blessed. Susan was so beautiful people used to say she couldn't possibly be mine' – he was smiling at the memory – 'but she *was* mine . . . and Barbara's, of course.' Then the smile left his eyes. 'When we lost her it was as if we both lost everything right there and then.'

'You've never spoken about this before,' Helen said. 'Publicly, I mean.' She was wondering why he was being so open now.

'Not to the newspapers, no, I haven't. Why should I? It's private, but you're trying to get to the bottom of what happened,' he said. 'You're working with the police. That *is* what you said?' he challenged her.

'I did, and we are,' she assured him. 'You can phone Detective Sergeant Bradshaw if you like.'

'I'll not be doing that. You're not like those others – the ones from London who want to put my troubles on their front pages. Why should I speak to any of them?'

'Perhaps to get your side of the story across, to stop some of the accusations?' she began, trying to be delicate.

'Do you think I care what they say about me? Do you reckon any of that actually matters?' He meant by comparison to his loss.

'They said there was a row that morning in your house.'

'There was a row every morning in our house,' he conceded. 'There were three of us and only one bathroom,' he explained as if that was the cause of most of their arguments. 'It was never anything more than that: a family all trying to get ready at once.'

'But you didn't go to work that day?'

'I was sick,' he said. 'People do get sick now and then. I had a stinking cold, and the police knew about it at the time. I still had it when they first came round about Susan. It was no great mystery. I just didn't feel the need to tell the papers.'

Paul Verity looked like a man who had given up long ago. Maybe that was why he really didn't care what was written about him.

'Mr Verity,' she asked, 'do you believe Adrian Wicklow took Susan?'

He stared right back at her then and seemed almost to be looking through her. She wondered for a moment if he was about to lose his temper, then he started shaking his head slowly from side to side. 'Do you think I know anything more about it than you do?' he asked her. 'For twenty years I've been wondering, was it him or someone else like him? Maybe it was someone closer to home – the farmer or somebody else. Did she walk over those fields and meet someone from the village coming the other way? Did he hurt her, then carry on with his life like it was a normal thing to do? I don't know, pet, and I never will. I had to get away. The most difficult thing was other people. They don't mean it, but they all knew Susan and what she meant to us. Not one of them knew what to say to me. They always looked panicked, as if they might make it worse – as if *anything* could make it worse. There were others who would go out of their way to avoid us,' he said, 'and I can't say I blame them. They felt guilty see, because it wasn't them suffering. I couldn't bear it. So, after a while . . .' He shrugged.

'You started seeing your old friends.'

'They were all back here in Newcastle, pretty much the way I'd left them. They were a bit funny with me at first, but they knew about Susan. It was in all the papers.' He let out a bitter laugh. 'I mean, these people were no saints – I can tell you that for nowt – and I hadn't seen them in thirteen years, but I felt like they were all I had and they let me back in.'

'How did Barbara take that?'

'She said a leopard never changes its spots, but she didn't really care that much. She thought her life was over by then anyway. She started drinking. Never touched a drop before, and I thought nowt of it. I figured if a glass or two eased her pain then why not? But she couldn't control it, started hiding booze all round the house. They do that,' he said, 'proper alcoholics, I mean. I drink, but I can stop.' He looked Helen in the eye. 'Barbara couldn't. Then I went away for a year' – they both knew he meant to prison – 'and when I came back she was in a very bad way. She died a year and a half after I got out of the nick. I moved away then.'

He told his tale matter-of-factly, but Helen shuddered inwardly at the pain that had caused these two people to fall apart like that. How different their lives might have been if only Susan had come back to them.

'You know, there's something about that village,' said Paul then. 'I mean, all small places have their secrets, but Maiden Hill . . .'

'What about it?'

'The villagers there . . . we never felt accepted. Even after ten years, I always thought it was them and us.' He was struggling to explain himself.

'They closed ranks?' Helen suggested.

'How did you know?'

'It can happen,' she explained. 'I've seen it before. In a village where everyone knows everyone else and families go back for generations, they keep things close.'

'Why do you think I got so much grief and no one else did?' he asked. 'I wasn't the only one there who did bad things, but I was the one who got to read about it over and over again in the papers.'

This intrigued Helen. 'Who else did bad things, Paul?'

He snorted. 'Kenny Gilbert, for one.'

34

Danny Gilbert loved his dad, but he was a *chancer*. Young Billy knew this because his own father had said so.

'Kenny Gilbert's a right chancer.' The words came from the kitchen but, with the door open, Billy could clearly make them out, and his ears had pricked up when he heard the mention of his best friend's father. 'He could sell snow to the bloody Eskimos.' There was lightness and humour in his father's voice, and the words were addressed to Billy's mother. It sounded at first as if his father was impressed by this, but then his tone seemed to darken. 'But he's in a lot of bother now. Wouldn't want to be in his shoes if he can't fool the jury.'

Billy only half understood what his father meant but he knew some of the words he was using. Chance was a game of cards, but he didn't reckon that's what his dad meant by a *chancer*. It sounded like a bad thing. And Billy knew what a jury was because his nana liked to watch *Crown Court* on the telly in the afternoons. It bored Billy, who usually played on the carpet while it was on, but he would hear phrases like 'Ladies and gentlemen of the jury' spoken by posh southern men in white wigs and black or red gowns before someone was either let off or sent to prison.

Billy walked into the kitchen to find his father standing there, looking at the local paper.

'Is Danny's dad in trouble?' asked Billy.

His father was immediately evasive. 'No,' he said sharply.

'Never you mind.' And he shooed Billy out of the kitchen and into the backyard. Billy decided it was best to stay out of the way and kick his football against a wall for a while. His dad was in a bad mood already, because the beer at the White Horse had gone up again, to twenty-five pence a pint; he had threatened to stop drinking there, but they all knew that was never going to happen.

Billy waited til his father went off to the pub and his mother was busy upstairs changing the beds. He went back into the kitchen and skimmed through the paper til he found the article that mentioned Danny's dad. He read it carefully, not understanding all of it but working out that Kenny had been accused of selling something that didn't belong to him. It was something about land being leasehold and not freehold, and Danny's dad had 'misrepresented' something, which Billy worked out was a posh word for telling fibs. There was a lot of money involved and, if found guilty, the accused was 'likely to face a custodial sentence', according to the lawyer who didn't like Danny's dad. The other lawyer, the one who did like Kenny Gilbert, said that it was all a misinterpretation, a word so hard to read that Billy had to say it aloud as he went through the article and it took him three goes to get it right.

Later, he would foolishly ask his friend outright if his dad was going to jail and Danny would react furiously, kicking out hard at Billy's shin and shouting at him to shut up. Billy never mentioned the subject again.

35

Helen left her interview with Paul Verity with some interesting family history concerning Danny Gilbert, but there had been no call back from the parents of the girl killed on Mont Blanc. If they suspected Danny of any wrong doing, surely they would have called by now. Helen wasn't content to leave it at that. She went to the library and looked at its newspaper archive. She and Tom often used it to examine the press coverage at the time of a case they were looking in to.

It took Helen half an hour to find the pages she was looking for. The newspaper archives were useful but unwieldy, their enormous, leather-bound covers containing dozens of editions, which made finding references to a particular story difficult. Armed with the date of the accident on the mountain and knowing that a British national dying in a climbing expedition would be newsworthy enough to make the tabloids, she selected a few binders and went through them methodically until she finally found what she was looking for. There were several stories, spread over four days. They began with the disappearance of twenty-two-year-old Victoria, then covered her family's gradual loss of hope that she would ever be found alive and the reaction of her grief-stricken boyfriend, Danny.

Helen jotted down key facts. Victoria had been a keen climber and was the veteran of several such adventures, it was her boyfriend's first time on the mountains, so she had been the one in charge of their climb. Their original intention on setting off, he explained, was to go only the distance they were both comfortable with then turn back. Victoria was conscious of her boyfriend's limitations as a climber and wouldn't put him in jeopardy. She had been pleasantly surprised at Danny's ability to keep up and, encouraged by his girlfriend, he had continued long past the point where they should have turned back. However, it had never been their aim to attempt the mountain's summit. They were at nine thousand feet when the storm hit.

'Mont Blanc has the highest death rate of any mountain in Europe,' an anonymous guide explained to one reporter, adding, 'It is not to be climbed by casual tourists. If the lady persuaded her boyfriend to follow her so far up without a guide, then she paid the ultimate price for her mistake. It is a tragedy, but not a surprise. The weather on Mont Blanc can change in an instant.'

'One hundred hikers a year die at Mont Blanc,' the article continued. It was a staggering statistic and one which gave Helen pause. She had gone into this investigation thinking Victoria's death might have been suspicious and her boyfriend somehow responsible for it. Dying from hiking on a French mountain had seemed an absurd notion, but it was far more commonplace than she could ever have imagined.

Nor did Victoria's family appear to lay any blame at Danny's door. Her father even thanked the man for trying to find his daughter; Danny had been treated for the effects of hypothermia afterwards. It seemed obvious now why Victoria's parents had not bothered to call Helen back. Gordon Cassidy was quoted as saying, 'Victoria lived life to the full and we knew we could never talk her out of doing something once she set her mind on it. Victoria loved climbing and it is a very small consolation to us all that she died doing something she loved so much.'

The more Helen read, the more she understood the reality. Victoria Cassidy hadn't been killed by her boyfriend. She was killed by the mountain.

*

Tom visited eleven more pubs that day then found one that was tucked away in a side street some way from the city centre. He could easily see its appeal to a woman on the run. It looked like the kind of place mostly populated by regulars.

The guy behind the bar was a grumpy-looking soul in his thirties with a beard, a Clash T-shirt and an attitude. When Tom showed him Jess's photograph and told him he was looking for her, his reply was, 'And who might you be?'

Tom explained this also, sticking to the truth. The man behind the bar folded his arms and looked at Tom as if he had just made up the whole story. 'If this woman is so close to her sister, how come she hasn't heard from her?'

'It's out of character,' said Tom, who had taken an instant dislike to the barman. 'That's why she's worried. They *are* close. Lena just wants to know that Jess is all right.'

'If a woman wants to disappear, that's her business, surely?'

'Of course. Her sister just wants to be sure she's okay.'

'Well, I'm sure she'll get in touch at some point then.'

'Look, *mate*,' said Tom, in a tone that made it clear they weren't mates, 'do you actually know this girl, or are you just messing me about?'

The barman planted a forced smile on his face but didn't answer. It was a smug and aggressive gesture. He was deliberately trying to infuriate Tom, and he was succeeding.

'So, you're not going to tell me anything?'

'Why should I? You could be anyone. If that lass doesn't want to be found, it's up to her.'

'Well, you obviously do know her and I'm assuming she worked here.' Again, the stupid, humourless smile from the barman. 'Okay, if that's the way you want to play it. I'll be back in half an hour.'

'That would be pointless.'

'I won't be alone.'

'Oh, so you're threatening me now.'

'Not in the way you imagine,' said Tom. 'I'll be back with the police.'

'The police?' scoffed the barman, but there was a look of slight panic in his eyes. Significantly, one or two of the bar's customers looked up when they heard him use that word and seemed noticeably uncomfortable.

'A young woman has disappeared. It's clear that you know her, but you won't cooperate. Her family are extremely worried about her well-being. That makes you a suspect in her disappearance.'

'A suspect? Give over!'

'All along, the family has feared foul play, but they were hoping for the best. They thought Jess might turn up or get in touch, but it's becoming clear to me that something terrible must have happened to her, and you seem to know all about it. At the very least. the police will want to take you in for questioning. I'll be bringing a Detective Sergeant Bradshaw with me and he will take a very dim view indeed if you are not waiting right here for him when we return.' Tom put the photo in his pocket and made to leave.

'Now wait a minute,' said the barman. There was something about his appearance and attitude that had led Tom to assume that he wouldn't relish dealing with the police, and that instinct had been proved right.

'I don't have a minute,' said Tom, 'not when you refuse to help me. We'll see if you can convince a police officer you had nothing to do with Jess's disappearance.' And Tom turned to go.

'Eva!'

The word was shouted after him, and Tom turned to see the barman's hopeful, desperate features staring after him. 'That's what she called herself, not Jess. She told us she came north to get away from a boyfriend who hit her. She left a few weeks back, for the same reason. I was only trying to protect her, mate. You could have been the boyfriend. You still could be,' he cautioned.

'Would an abusive ex-boyfriend threaten you with the police?' asked Tom, but the man didn't answer. 'Okay, have it your way.' He took another couple of steps towards the door.

'Wait,' pleaded the barman. 'I'll get Sally. She works here. She might know something.'

The barman was right. Sally did know something. She was the bar supervisor, responsible for paying the staff, all of whom had to at least provide an address, so she had one for Jess, which she gave up reluctantly, because the woman she had known as Eva had asked her to keep it to herself. Only the assurance from the barman that Tom was 'okay' persuaded her to hand it over. How easy it had been to pressure the barman into giving her up. He couldn't help wondering what the man had to hide if he was that keen to stay away from the boys in blue.

Tom went straight to the address Sally had given him, but there was nobody home. It was a house in Gilesgate with a poster in the window urging passers-by to 'VOTE DAVIS' in the local elections as their Green party candidate.

After traipsing around the city for much of the day, Tom was tired and hungry, so he decided to come back another time. He was certain Jess wouldn't still be living there. If she had felt the need to quit her job at short notice because of the unwelcome attention of a private investigator, she was unlikely still to be in the area, but at least he now knew where she had been living and working, and that was a start.

Helen arrived home in a good mood. The sun was shining above her and she'd found what she was looking for. Using her usual diligent methods, combining hard work and research, she had managed to get to the bottom of the accident on Mont Blanc, banishing her suspicions of Danny Gilbert along the way. He had been just as scarred by Susan's disappearance as the others, and this trauma had been compounded with a tragedy of his own, but he had somehow found the strength to pick himself up and carry on. Helen admired that quality. He was the only one of the gang with a partner, children and a career – a normal life, in other words.

The house was empty. Whatever Tom was up to, it was taking him all day. She cooked some dinner and was just sitting down to eat it when he walked in.

'I'm bloody starving,' he said by way of greeting.

'I'd have made you some,' she said, 'but I didn't know if you were going out with Lena.'

'I'm in tonight.' He started to get food out of the fridge to prepare his own dinner.

'What have you been up to then?' Helen asked.

'I just had something I needed to do.' He grabbed a saucepan and poured water into it.

'Is it connected to the Susan Verity case?' Tom lit the gas ring with a match and placed the pan of water on to boil. 'I wondered if you're coming back out with me in the morning?'

'I'll be back out with you in the morning.'

She regarded him suspiciously.

'Don't look at me like that.'

'You're normally an open book, Tom,' she said. 'I just want to know you're okay.'

'I'm all right,' he said, and sat down opposite her, 'I was just trying to help Lena, that's all.'

'Oh,' said Helen, 'you were busy because of your girlfriend.'

'It wasn't like that. We weren't out on a date or anything.' And he explained about Lena's sister.

'And Lena has asked you to help her to find this sister?'

'No. I offered. She didn't want to bother me because we're busy.'

'We are, and this is a paying job.'

'I'm not ducking out of it, Helen. This was just one day when I figured you could handle things on your own while I did a bit of digging.'

'Did you get anywhere?'

'I got some leads, but nothing concrete.' He told her about the pub Jess worked in.

'So what's next?'

'I'll keep on digging,' he said, 'but I won't let it get in the way of our case.'

'It's bound to,' she said, 'if you're going to be devoting time to it.'

'Then I'll do it in the evenings. Jesus!' he snapped. 'She said you wouldn't like it.'

'Did she now?'

'I told Lena you'd understand. Her sister is missing and possibly in danger. For God's sake, Helen, you've got a sister.'

'I have, and it's worrying for her that she has gone missing, but does it have to be you who goes looking for her?'

'The police aren't interested, and they tried a private detective, but he didn't get anywhere.' *Except the hospital*, he thought to himself, but he wasn't going to share that with Helen.

'If you're determined to help her, then fine, but you don't know Lena, not really. Are you sure you know what you're getting yourself into?'

'Bloody hell, Helen! What did we say about you not being my mum? How do you think I managed before you came along?' She resisted the temptation to remind Tom that he had just been suspended from the tabloid newspaper he was working on and was being sued by a Cabinet minister when she first met him. 'Give me a break, will you? I'll be back on the Susan Verity case tomorrow, and I'll handle this one in my spare time.'

Helen almost said, *We never have any spare time when we are working on a case*, but instead told him, 'Okay, fine.'

He got up from the table and carried on preparing his dinner.

'Don't you want to know what I found out today?' she asked.

'If you want to tell me?' he said, without looking at her. 'What do you think about Paul Verity then?'

'No way did he kill his daughter,' said Helen.

'From what we heard, the man's whole life unravelled after she'd gone. That could be guilt, of course, but I don't think so.'

'The mother too,' said Helen. 'Barbara Verity turned from a virtual teetotaller into a raging alcoholic and died of liver disease.'

'It can happen,' said Tom. 'Ann Best.' When Helen didn't recognize the name, he went on: 'George Best's mother. Everyone knows George is an alcoholic, but his mum was too. Anne Best never touched a drop of alcohol til she was forty-four and she still died from liver failure.'

'My God.'

'None of us knows how we will react if we are put under a lot of pressure until it happens,' he reminded her.

'Which is why we should never judge?'

'I didn't say that' – he didn't want to sound preachy – 'but you have a point.'

'I think we're all the same,' she said, 'plodding on with our lives, just one tragedy away from a complete meltdown.'

'Now that's a cheerful thought.'

There was a buzz and Tom left the room to peer at the CCTV monitor. Bradshaw was standing by the gate. 'Talking of cheerful!' he called to Helen, and she guessed it had to be Ian.

36

Tom made enough pasta for two and handed a bowl to Bradshaw.

'I discovered something interesting today,' said Helen. 'According to Susan's father, Danny Gilbert's dad had a criminal streak. Kenny Gilbert never served time but his crimes were, arguably, more damaging than Paul Verity's. I checked him out while I was looking at the newspaper archive. Kenny persuaded people to part with their money for various investments – in land, property, villas in Spain – but a fair number ended up with less than they hoped for and blamed him for misrepresenting these opportunities.'

'Was he bent?' asked Tom. 'Or just good at selling thin air?'

'Hard to say, but the judge at his trial, which finished a few months after Susan went missing, concluded that he had been, at the very least, economical with the truth and was a living embodiment of the maxim *caveat emptor*.'

'Let the buyer beware,' Tom translated. 'I wonder if his son inherited his economy with the truth or his persuasiveness. What happened to Danny's old man?'

'Like I said, he avoided jail, just. He got off with a suspended sentence that time. Kenny Gilbert had a few more brushes with creditors and angry investors during his lifetime but managed just about to stay one step ahead of them. He died two years ago.'

'That's the trouble with looking into these cold cases,' said Tom. 'As soon as we hear something interesting about someone, we find out they're dead.'

'I don't think Kenny Gilbert had anything to do with Susan's death,' said Helen, 'but it does seem as if lying came easy to him and he didn't have a lot of compassion for others.'

'So now you're wondering if Danny has inherited his father's qualities?' asked Bradshaw, between mouthfuls.

'Maybe. It sounds silly, I know.'

'What about that ex-girlfriend?' asked Tom. 'The one who disappeared on the mountain?'

'I researched that too. It wasn't Danny's fault. A storm came down unexpectedly and they were caught in it.'

'What a horrendous way to go, falling like that from such a great height,' said Bradshaw. 'Imagine what must go through your mind on the way down.'

'I don't think I want to,' said Helen.

'So, the death of Danny's ex wasn't suspicious, but it does add to this kind of aura Susan's friends have. Or am I just imagining that?' asked Tom.

'No, there's definitely something there. They share a . . .' She couldn't find the word.

'A bond?' asked Bradshaw.

'It's not that,' she said, 'Danny and Billy are close, but they always have been. Danny still sees Andrea. She might be a little bit in love with him,' said Helen. 'But Kevin isn't close to anyone and Michelle died. Andrea escaped to the coast so she could leave it all behind.'

'What if it was more than the trauma of Susan's disappearance they shared?' Tom asked. He was intrigued by Helen's comment because he agreed with her. 'It's just a feeling I get from the way they speak about it and how their lives all seem to have been derailed in one way or another. What if it isn't a bond they share,' he asked, 'but a secret?'

'What are you getting at?' she asked Tom. 'Do you actually think the children could have been responsible for Susan's death in some way?'

'I'm not saying they killed her,' he clarified, 'and it's not much, just a feeling I've got, like they're hiding something. What if, out on their own, miles from the adults, things got out of control? Maybe something really bad happened that day and, somehow, Susan ended up dead.'

'I wouldn't rule that out entirely,' said Bradshaw, 'but are you really saying that five children could be involved in the death of one of their friends without once letting slip that it was them? These were ten-year-olds, remember, and they would have been subjected to endless interviews about Susan's whereabouts and what they got up to that day. Do you honestly think one of them wouldn't have cracked and spilled the beans before now if they had hurt Susan?'

When Tom listened to Bradshaw's argument, he had to concede. 'You're right. It's probably a stupid idea.' He felt foolish for even mentioning it now. 'I just keep coming back to this nagging feeling I have that they're not telling us everything. Maybe one of them . . .' He shook his head 'I don't know,' he admitted.

'I do know one thing,' said Bradshaw. 'If a group of ten-year-olds were involved in a death of any kind, the body would have been found.'

Helen and Tom were back in Maiden Hill the next day. Tom parked the car on a street of old terrace houses that had been washed clean by a rainstorm during the night.

He got out of the car and surveyed them.

'Doorstep scrubbers,' he said absent-mindedly to himself.

'Pardon?'

He pointed to the thick, shiny steps by each door. 'They used to scrub their doorsteps round here, and I mean, literally. My nan would do it in her village too, even when she was well into her seventies. She'd be out there with a bowl of hot water and a scrubbing brush and she'd make her doorstep shine. You know the phrase "the devil finds work for idle hands to do"? So everybody was always working away at something. Imagine a world with no washing machines or tumble dryers, no dish-washers or microwave ovens and still taking the time to scrub your bloody doorstep. Come on, this is the one.' He walked up to the front door and knocked firmly on it.

When Lilly Bowes's sister answered and Helen explained who they were, she looked at them sceptically. Her face did not soften when Helen told the old lady of their interest in her late sister's eyewitness testimony that Adrian Wicklow had been in the village on the day Susan had disappeared. She heard them out then admitted them both with the words, 'About blooming time.'

Helen and Tom exchanged glances behind her back and fol-lowed her into her home. She switched off the television, which was showing an Australian soap, and cleared playing cards from the table by her chair. Ivy had been playing Patience. They politely declined the tea and custard creams she offered them, but when Tom brought the subject round to the reliabil-ity of Lilly Bowes as a witness she became frosty.

'My sister was not decrepit,' Ivy told him firmly. There was a touch of the school ma'am about her.

'I never said she was.'

'The police did.' Ivy took an exasperated breath, then her tone softened slightly. 'They didn't use those exact words, but they certainly implied it when they came to see her.'

'Lilly was living with you at the time?'

'She never married. When I was widowed, it seemed a sen-sible arrangement for both of us.'

'And you were fond of her?'

'Of course. She was my sister.'

'That doesn't always follow,' he explained, 'but you got on?'

'We had our disagreements,' she said primly, 'but I would say we muddled along quite well, considering.'

Tom wondered if the *considering* was a reference to her sister's personality. Bradshaw told him she had been described as both difficult and prickly.

'Why don't you tell me what happened that day, back in 1976?' he said gently. 'I believe your sister went for a walk?'

'As she often did.' Ivy seemed eager to prevent him from thinking this was somehow out of the ordinary. 'She liked to walk the lanes. Hardly the pastime of someone you might describe as *elderly*, like they did in that bloody documentary. She was barely sixty at the time.'

She was sixty-three, thought Tom, but he let this pass. 'Wasn't it a bit hot for a walk? It was scorching that day by all accounts; towards the end of the famous heatwave.'

'Lilly wouldn't care about that. She went out in all weathers.'

'And she was on her way back when she saw him?' asked Helen.

'That's right, and she got a good look at him too.'

'She described Adrian Wicklow to a tee.' Helen confirmed.

'Well, she was an observer, which the police and those fools making that documentary seem to have completely discounted.'

'An observer . . .' Helen queried.

'My sister was the first woman in the area to join the Royal Observer Corps.'

'Sorry, when was this?' asked Helen.

'It was 1942,' said Ivy as if this were a recent occurrence, not something that happened more than fifty years earlier.

'Right,' was all Tom could think to say in reply.

'Well, don't you see? She was a trained spotter. She'd always been an observant girl, but they taught her how to do it properly in wartime, when people's lives depended upon it. If she let a German bomber pass overhead without being intercepted by our fighters, it could destroy streets full of houses. That's some responsibility.' Perhaps Tom and Helen didn't appear impressed enough, because she continued: 'How easily people forget what we went through. Thousands died in our cities during the bombing.'

'So she was trained to notice things,' Tom began gently, then reminded her, 'but that was quite a long while ago, even in 1976.'

She bridled at that. 'Mr Carney, if my sister was capable of telling the difference between a Spitfire and a Messerschmitt at two thousand feet on a stormy day with just a pair of binoculars, I am bloody sure she could accurately describe a large man across a field on a clear day, even thirty years later!'

Tom realized that she was furious with him now. 'Point taken,' but she had not finished yet.

'There used to be a team of three people manning the observations posts, morning, noon and night, in all weathers, scanning a ten-mile radius. They had a machine with a sighting arm they used to zero in on a plane that was nothing more than a tiny dark shape in the sky. They had to work out its height, speed and direction from the ground. Do you think you could do that, Mr Carney?'

'I'm sure I couldn't.'

'Well, my sister could. She would contact the Operations Room in Durham and they would scramble fighters to intercept enemy planes on her say-so. Her corps was known as the eyes and ears of the RAF.'

'Yet the police didn't take her seriously?' asked Helen gently.

'Oh, at first they did. To begin with, it was all *you've been such a great help, Mrs Bowes, we can't thank you enough, Mrs Bowes, we'd love another cup of tea, thank you, Mrs Bowes.*' She ground her teeth at the recollection. 'Then, later, it was *you couldn't really have got a good look at him, Lilly, not from that distance, Lilly, not at your age.*' She shook her head. 'It was scandalous.'

'What changed?' asked Helen. She had her own theory but wondered what the old lady thought.

'I can't imagine. One moment they couldn't hear enough about it; the next they were so dismissive. It never even went to court. I don't know,' she said. 'You're the one doing the investigating. You tell me.'

'I think it was because they had no other evidence against Adrian Wicklow other than your sister's testimony,' Helen told her. 'If it hadn't been for that, they wouldn't have been on to him in the first place, but they couldn't prove he abducted Susan Verity and they were reluctant to put an elderly lady in the witness box. They would have been worried that an acquittal on one case might jeopardize a guilty verdict on the others.'

Her whole face seemed to brighten then. 'Do you really think so?'

'I do. I also think that if they had taken the trouble to explain this to you and your sister, you would both have been perfectly capable of understanding and accepting it. Instead, they took the easier route and dismissed her as a batty old lady, which, of course, we all know she wasn't.'

The fight seemed to go out of her then. 'My sister went to her grave still angry at the way they treated her. *I did see him, Ivy,* she would tell me every time that evil man's face was on the television.'

'And I don't blame her.'

'Then *you* believe her?' she demanded. 'You think she saw Adrian Wicklow that day?'

'Yes,' said Helen, who had been swayed by Ivy's description of Lilly's war work. 'I believe she did.' But if Adrian Wicklow really had been in the village that day, Helen wondered, how could he not have been responsible for Susan Verity's fate and why would he claim otherwise, except to create mischief?

'I did hope you might have worked it out by now, Detective. I could drop down dead at any moment,' Wicklow reminded Bradshaw cheerfully when they had discussed the passages of his memoir Bradshaw had listened to, 'and then where would you be?'

'You can choose to end this at any point,' Bradshaw reminded him. 'Just tell us where the bodies are buried.'

Wicklow appeared to think about this, then he said, 'I don't think so. Knowledge is power, Ian, and power must be earned. The glittering prizes await you.' He was taunting Bradshaw. 'All you have to do is engage that brain of yours and tell me why I did it.'

'It was payback.'

'What was?' asked Wicklow. 'Do tell.' He seemed excited now, leaning forward in his chair, eager to play his little game once more. It made Bradshaw feel sick, indulging him like this.

'The murders. No one recognized your intelligence or your talents before. You grew frustrated and wanted to punish society. The best way to punish anything is to take from it what it values most. That's why you took the children.'

'Interesting theory. What made you come up with it?'

'A case I read about. A blue-collar worker in America with a very high IQ but unimpressive prospects took his revenge on the world by murdering seven college-educated women. At first they thought he had some obscure sexual motive, but it turned out he killed them out of spite. If he couldn't have a good life, he would rob them of theirs. He claimed he was taking something valuable from a world which had ignored him.'

'I'm glad to see you've been working hard, Ian. You're reading around your subject, and that's gratifying. That, perhaps, could have been my reason. It's plausible enough, I suppose.' He leant back in his chair and his face darkened. 'But, alas, you are no nearer the truth now than when you first walked through that door. An effort point for trying, though,' he concluded.

'How would I know?' challenged Bradshaw, 'if I was correct? You could tell me I was wrong no matter what I said.'

'I won't do that. I promise.'

'Your promises aren't worth much. I'm not sure I want to keep playing this twisted game with you, Wicklow.'

'I didn't think you had a choice. They do keep ordering you back here,' he observed. 'There must be something resting on it. Some big careers, I should imagine. I think you're pretty much trapped with me until this is over.' He grinned. 'Or I die. You're a prisoner too.'

'I don't have to do anything,' Bradshaw told him. 'I could walk away at any point, and bugger the consequences. I'm not the one who's on death row.'

'What a poetic turn of phrase you have,' said Wicklow. 'I'll swear it then. I swear that, if you discover the truth, I will admit it.' Bradshaw's eyes told Wicklow that the detective was unimpressed by this. 'All right then. I swear it on the grave of my dear, departed mother, who meant more to me than anything else in this broken, morally bankrupt world. There, how does that sound?'

It sounded serious, but Bradshaw didn't want to admit it so he said nothing.

'Back to the drawing board then,' Wicklow informed him brightly. 'But keep at it. The truth is in there somewhere –' he meant his book – 'and I'm sure you'll find it eventually.' He smiled at Bradshaw, making the detective instinctively want to move away from the killer. 'I've got a very good feeling about you, Ian.'

37

When Helen walked into the house, Tom was hanging up the phone. From the contented look on his face, she assumed he'd been talking to Lena – again. Their long chats had been a feature of virtually every evening since Helen had pushed them together in the hotel bar. But she was wrong.

'I just spoke to Marsh Junior,' Tom said. 'He finally picked up the phone.' They had been trying to get hold of the man for days, calling him or simply turning up, but whatever he did on that farm of his, it certainly kept him away from the house most of the time.

'The farmer's son?' asked Helen. 'What did he have to say?'

'He's agreed to talk to us about his father.'

'Great.'

'But it has to be at the weekend because he's *too busy grafting.*' Tom laughed and mimicked the gruff voice of the farmer: *'My land doesn't know what day it is* – which is his way of saying that our investigations are not even a close second to his labours. He's agreed to see us after his tea on Saturday. It was either that or Sunday morning. That okay with you?'

'Sure,' she said, and then she remembered where she was supposed to be. 'Oh, no. Actually, I can't. I've got to go and see Peter.'

'Oh, right,' he said without, enthusiasm.

'It's important.'

'Of course.'

'No, I mean, it really is. It's his parent's silver-wedding anniversary, and I'm expected to be there.'

'To play the dutiful daughter-in-law.'

'No,' she said again. 'I'm his girlfriend, which is why I've been invited to their party.'

'And you've been his girlfriend for how long now?'

'You know how long.' He was beginning to get on her nerves now. 'Since we met at university.'

'Right,'

'What does *right* mean?'

'It means that, by now, they will assume you are the future daughter-in-law, that's all. I'm not having a go, Helen, I'm just saying that I understand why they want you to be there and why he expects you to be there. You're practically family to them . . . but that's no bad, thing though, right? I mean, as long as you're comfortable with it.'

'Of course I'm comfortable with it. I've known Paula and Ray for ages, but it's not like *that*.'

'Like what?'

'That! We're not married . . .' She was going to say *yet* but thought better of it, because she knew Tom would press her on when they might be. 'It's not that full on. I live up here, for starters, and we are taking things slowly. We're both still young.'

'You're in your mid-twenties, Helen,' he announced solemnly. 'I bet his parents were married before they were that age, if they're celebrating their twenty-fifth anniversary.'

'People married younger back then and, anyway . . .' She was going to protest further, then she saw the gleam in his eye. 'You are such a wind-up merchant.'

He grinned. 'Go to their anniversary party. You might even have fun.'

'I didn't say I would definitely go,' she lied, without really knowing why. 'It's not that big a deal.'

'Okay, well, if you don't make it there, then maybe you could go and see young farmer Marsh with me instead?'

'Maybe I will,' she said.

When Ian Bradshaw arrived back at his desk that afternoon, something was waiting for him: a plain brown envelope with no stamp, address or even a name on it. Bradshaw could only deduce it was meant for him because it had been placed on his seat. He picked it up but, before he opened it, he looked about him for any clue as to its origin. No one was paying him the slightest attention.

Bradshaw opened the envelope, slid out the photograph inside and surveyed it. He recognized the original image, sure enough, but there was something different about it. The photograph had been taken at a leaving do years ago. It had been a raucous affair, and the laddish image featured him and the man who was leaving that day, arms around each other and shouting drunkenly into the camera. Seeing that old photograph would not have bothered him; it was the fact that someone had doctored the image.

The other man's face had been obscured by another. In its place was a shot of a smiling Adrian Wicklow. Now the photograph appeared to be Bradshaw with his arm around the child killer, both of them smiling, like they were the best of friends.

Bradshaw realized it must be a joke played by his colleagues and knew he was meant to laugh at it, engaging in a bit of laddish banter along the way, before consigning it to the waste bin, most probably with a concession that this had been 'a good one, lads'. He knew there was little or no point complaining about it or trying to make the culprit feel bad.

He knew all this, but he couldn't help himself.

When he looked up and saw that everyone was still sitting at their desks, ignoring him, something inside Bradshaw snapped.

'Think this is funny?' His words were loud enough to make everyone in the room turn towards him. 'Do you?'

No one spoke.

That just made it worse.

Bradshaw felt as if he was about to lose it. He wanted to smash the room up, overturn desks and throw hard objects at the lot of them. That would show them. Most of all, he wanted to get hold of whoever had played this sick prank and beat him to a pulp.

'This man,' he reminded them, 'murdered children.' He let that sink in. His colleagues looked at him, seemingly at a loss for words. 'He killed little kids, and I have to sit opposite him and listen to him, and you think that's funny? What is wrong with you people?'

From the way they were gazing at him, it became clear that at least some of them hadn't the faintest idea what he was talking about and the ones who did were not going to let on. He held the photograph higher so they could all see it.

'How would you feel about this if it was your child who had been strangled and dumped somewhere?'

Silence.

It was the silence that really pushed him over the edge.

'Who did this?' he demanded. 'Who took time out of their working day to make this? If you're proud of your handiwork, then admit it!' He challenged them with his eyes but got no reply. 'Come on then!' he roared.

'Bradshaw.' The single word was not shouted but it stopped him in his tracks. Kate Tennant was framed by her office doorway. 'Could you come in here, please?' she said calmly.

He looked at her, but did not reply. He turned away and surveyed his colleagues, people who, up to this point, he had had a modicum of respect for. Now he felt as if every single one of them must be in on the joke, and if that was how they treated him, they could all go to hell.

Bradshaw walked into DI Tennant's office. She was already sitting back behind her desk. 'Close the door,' she told him.

He did as he was asked but immediately felt like a caged animal, and full of adrenalin. Outside, the detectives were all just getting on with their work, as if nothing had happened.

'Bastards,' he hissed, then he turned back to Tennant, who was watching him. He jabbed his finger at his DI. 'Don't you dare try to give me a bollocking,' he told her, not even caring how that sounded. In his eyes, his outburst had been fully justified.

'I wasn't going to.'

He remembered he was still holding the photograph then and made a point of placing it on the desk in front of her so she could share his sense of outrage.

'It's in poor taste,' she admitted evenly.

'Is that all you're going to say?' He had expected better from her.

'Calm down, Ian.' That was like pouring petrol on the flames.

'I can't,' he told her, and began pacing round her office, at the same time looking out through the window for any sign of who had done it. Was anyone laughing? Did anybody look guilty?

'You can,' she assured him, and when he turned towards her she wasn't even looking at him. Instead, she was signing paperwork, waiting for him to cool down.

'Are you not appalled by it?' he asked.

She sighed. 'A little. It's a crude, unfunny, slightly pathetic attempt to rattle your cage. Mostly, I'm disappointed it succeeded' – he opened his mouth to protest, but she put up a hand to prevent him – 'though I understand it.'

'Sit down,' she said, and he complied. Kate Tennant put down her pen and gave him her full attention. 'In my old squad I was the first female DS they had had, and I was so proud. I'd climbed the greasy pole. I walked in that day feeling like a million dollars. It caused a bit of consternation, though, among the old guard, who thought being a detective was an all-male preserve. Know what they did?' She didn't wait for Bradshaw to guess. 'Sent me a doctored photograph a bit like this one. Only it was from a porn mag. They put my face on the body of a naked woman being taken from behind over a desk and put the face of our DCI on the man who was doing the taking. It wasn't just an obscene image. They were making a point. To be promoted like that must have meant I was shagging him. That's how I got the job, they reckoned, not on merit.

'I was furious,' she admitted. 'I wasted the first morning in my new job raging about it. I couldn't decide whether to report it, or do what you just did and let rip at the whole room. I wanted to take it to my DCI to see if I could get him on my side. I wondered if we could find the culprit; perhaps we could test it for fingerprints. Then it finally dawned on me that the very best thing I could do –'

'You're going to say, *ignore it*,' he said.

'I am.'

'But that –'

'Is precisely what they don't want you to do,' she assured him. 'Where's the fun in going to all the trouble to manufacture something like this' – she held up the photograph – 'if the person on the receiving end doesn't even bother to react?' She allowed Bradshaw some time to think about it.

And, to his extreme irritation, she was right. He'd just played into the hands of whoever had left that photograph for him. They'd be in the pub later, bragging about it to their mates. 'Did you see Bradshaw's face? Priceless!'

'Christ,' he said, but he was annoyed at himself, not Tennant, and she knew it.

'Take a moment,' she said. 'Calm down. Go and get yourself

a coffee . . . better still, get yourself off home early for once. It's almost the weekend, and tomorrow's another day.'

He let out a long breath. 'Thanks,' he said, then asked, 'Did they accept you in the end? Your old squad?'

'I didn't give them a choice,' she replied, and he realized the obstacles she must have faced at the time.

'Did it get any better?'

'Oh yes,' she said. 'When I was promoted to DI, all they did was take an old photograph of me in a posh frock at some black-tie do and draw a massive cock and balls on it to signify that I was really a man, not a woman. I told myself it was actually a massive backhanded compliment in their idiotic eyes, then I threw it in the bin. There will always be some Neanderthals, Ian. Just don't let them win.'

38

It was an afternoon match, and they had some time before England kicked off against Scotland, so they took their beers to a quiet corner of the pub.

'I can only have one,' Tom told him. 'Got to drive later.' But Bradshaw didn't appear to be listening.

'How did you get on with Miss Marple?'

'Who?'

'Ivy Bowes. I was told she hated coppers and journalists.'

'You didn't tell *us* that.'

'I knew you'd win her over.'

'I used my charm.'

'You mean Helen got it out of her.'

'Yes. Her sister was an extremely reliable witness and Adrian Wicklow was very likely to have been in Maiden Hill on the day Susan Verity disappeared.' Tom explained Lilly Bowes' war service with the Royal Observer Corps.

'Bloody hell, really? So where does that leave us?' asked Bradshaw. 'Wicklow denies killing Susan, but it looks like he was there that day. When he said he knew what really happened to her, I thought he was implying he knew who had killed her.'

'Meaning it was some lunatic he'd met inside nick,' agreed Tom, 'or out in the real world before he was arrested – but if he didn't kill Susan, the fact that he was there that day means he could have been –'

Bradshaw nodded. 'A witness.'

*

Peter was waiting when she stepped down from the train. As soon as she saw his face she felt guilty for even having contemplated not coming. Then she noticed what he was wearing.

'What's the matter?' he said. 'You knew I'd be here to meet you.'

'It's just . . . er . . . I'm not sure about that jacket.' And she really wasn't.

'It's Harris tweed,' he said, as if this were explanation enough. 'What's wrong with it?'

'I'm not saying there's anything wrong with it, as such, but it does make you look older.'

He brightened then. 'That's no bad thing. I have to manage people who are almost twice my age. When the new store opens . . .' And as they walked from the station and headed off down the high street he started to regale her once again with lengthy explanations of their plans for the new carpet store. His words just seemed to wash over her.

'Sorry, what?' She realized he had stopped talking and was expecting an answer.

'I said, I'm so glad you're here. I must admit, even this morning, I half expected to get a call from you to say you couldn't make it.' He laughed, as if this was an absurd notion. She was saved from having to give an answer by a great roar coming from a nearby pub.

'What's going on?'

'It's the football,' he said disdainfully, 'England were winning two–nil when I parked the car. It must be over now.'

'Great,' she said.

'What do you care?'

'I don't, really, but some people do.' And she thought about Tom and Ian in the pub enjoying the result and tried not to wish she was sitting with them.

*

'What a bloody goal that was from Gascoigne!'

'Careful, Ian,' warned Tom. 'You sound almost happy.'

'I *am* happy. That was a great match and worthy of celebration. You ready for a proper drink yet?' He frowned at the glass of coke Tom had insisted on after his first pint.

'I'd really like to, but can you give me an hour?' And he explained that he had arranged to meet the farmer.

'That's pretty bad timing, Tom. I wondered where you had to be and why you weren't drinking. All right, you have an hour. I'll hold the fort.'

Tom got to his feet. 'Don't get too pissed without me.'

Tom had to park his car on a grass verge. He couldn't drive into the farmyard because the road leading to the farmhouse was blocked by a sturdy wooden gate of about chest height. He got out of his car, only to find the gate was locked. He cursed and muttered, 'You're expecting me,' as if Robert Marsh were standing by the gate, but there was no one around. Unsure of his next move, he finally made a decision and climbed over the gate.

As soon as his feet hit the ground a dog started barking. It sounded big and vicious and nearby. He moved gingerly towards the farmhouse, praying the dog was behind a large door or chained up somewhere. He didn't have to knock. A man in his late twenties emerged, looking as if he were about to tackle a burglar.

'Robert Marsh? I'm Tom Carney. We spoke on the phone.'

'Finally,' said Marsh Junior. 'I thought you weren't coming.'

Tom bit his lip. He was less than ten minutes late. Obviously, Robert Marsh wasn't a football fan. The farmer went back inside and closed the door, leaving Tom standing outside to wonder why he had not been invited in. The dog continued to bark with enthusiasm. Marsh came back outside again, wearing a coat this time, and he strode off with Tom following him, having evidently decided they would walk while they talked. Marsh shouted a command and the dog instantly fell silent.

'Has he sent you to apologize?' asked the young farmer facetiously.

'Who?'

'The chief constable,' he said, as if it were obvious. 'If he has, it's long overdue.'

'You know why I am here, Mr Marsh. I told you on the phone.'

'You want to know if my dad killed Susan Verity?'

Tom exhaled. 'I didn't say that.'

'But it's what you meant.'

'All I'm wondering is why so many people even bother to put your father in the frame for this, when there are more obvious suspects, one of whom is currently serving life in prison for very similar offences?'

'Well, at least we can agree on that. It's ridiculous,' said the farmer, 'but it never goes away. You have no idea what my father went through. It was five years before they arrested that bastard and, even then, it didn't stop. Dad thought he would get his day in court. He reckoned there'd at least be a trial and an accounting for Susan Verity would be part of it, then at the eleventh hour they took her name out of the proceedings and tried Adrian Wicklow for his other crimes. It was like she never existed.'

'They didn't have enough evidence against him to try him for Susan's murder,' said Tom.

'There was no evidence against my father!' snapped Marsh. 'But that didn't stop the gossip. You know why? Because Susan was last seen heading towards our farm and her hairband was found in one of our fields.' He looked incredulous. 'That was enough for some people. No smoke without fire, isn't that what they say?'

His anger and bitterness were undimmed. Helen had told him that Paul Verity looked worn out by the disappearance of his daughter and the death of his wife. He was ground down and exhausted, but the sense of injustice at his father's torments burned as brightly as ever within Robert Marsh.

'It was a little more than that,' he countered gently. 'There was history between your father and the kids in the village.'

'They were trespassing! It was never-ending and it drove Dad to distraction. Every time he went out to the fields, they would be there, trampling the corn and messing in the hay bales. How would you like it if, every time you went out, someone broke into your home and caused chaos?'

'I hear you,' said Tom, 'and I'm sure he was right to be aggrieved, but some say he took the law into his own hands.'

'The police wouldn't do anything,' protested Robert, 'so one day a kid got a clip round the ear.'

'And your father ended up brawling in the street with the kid's dad.'

'He was defending himself. What was he supposed to do, just stand there and take it? He fought back.'

Tom could see that Robert Marsh was getting more and more irate. He had a short fuse, and Tom wondered if he got that from his father.

'I do feel some sympathy for your father, Robert, genuinely I do, but not to the point that I think firing a shotgun over the heads of some children is acceptable.'

Robert looked helpless then. 'He told me about that. The gun went off by accident.' He didn't sound convincing. 'He was trying to scare them.'

'He certainly achieved that. So the police were called ... again,' Tom recalled, 'but he was allowed to keep his gun. Why was that, do you reckon?'

'Because they realized he wasn't actually a danger to the community. That's why!'

And Tom wondered who *they* were.

'What do you think happened to Susan?' he asked.

'How should I know? I wasn't there. You should be speaking to the ones who *were* there.'

'We are.'

'Have you asked them why they lied?'

Up til now, Tom had questioned the wisdom of coming here. He had known he was never going to get a balanced view of Colin Marsh from his son and, so far, all he had witnessed was the man's anger. This was the first time he had said anything of interest.

'Who lied?'

'All of them,' said Robert. 'The little buggers.'

Tom tried to be patient. 'What did they lie about?'

'Where Susan went!' snapped Robert, as if Tom must already know this.

Robert had the exasperating trait of giving his listener only a small part of the story.

Tom had lost patience. 'Robert, if you have something you want to tell me, then get it off your chest, but I need more than *where Susan went*. What, specifically, do you mean?'

Marsh glared at Tom, then seemed to come to his senses. When he started to speak again his voice was more measured.

'Susan was last seen heading towards the farm. That's what everyone always said. Billy bloody Thorpe watched her walk away and swore time and again that was the direction she was going in. Kevin Robson backed him up, and Danny Gilbert reckoned the last time he saw Susan she was going in that same direction before she bumped into Billy and Kevin.'

'Correct,' confirmed Tom.

'Then why did Billy suddenly change his tune?'

'When did he do that?'

'The other day,' said Robert. 'On that TV interview he did.'

'What TV interview?' Tom had seen the documentary, but he knew nothing about this.

'It was on the daytime news. I pop back to the house for my scran and to let the dog out, so I usually watch it. He was on there, banging on about the anniversary.'

'And he altered his story?'

'The reporter asked him to recall what had happened that day and, when he got to that bit, he said, "I was the last person to see Susan Verity alive when she walked away from us, towards the woods."' He paused to make sure that Tom understood the significance of this. 'Not the farm, the woods!'

The twenty-fifth wedding anniversary party was more fun than she had expected. There was a well-stocked bar, the hotel venue had spacious and scenic grounds and, best of all, Peter had been allowed to populate two long tables with friends from school and university, so Helen was able to catch up with people she hadn't seen in years. To her surprise, she was having a nice time.

Peter's parents had made a real effort and had obviously spent a lot of money on the event. It was like an actual wedding, in fact. There was a cake, food was served to the guests, there was even a microphone so Peter's dad could make a speech about their twenty-five blissful years together. Thankfully, his parents and Helen's parents got on and wanted to spend time together, so Helen was free to see her old mates, avoiding her mother's fussing and her father's questions about 'this freelance business', which he was less than impressed with. He had liked to tell people his daughter wrote for a newspaper but was less sure how to describe what she and Tom 'got up to these days', as he put it.

The hours passed in a pleasant enough blur of chat accompanied by food and drink and everyone seemed to be in a good mood. Helen felt guilty for having dreaded the occasion and resolved to listen intently to every tedious word Peter's father uttered during his ill-prepared and slightly rambling speech. Eventually, and not before time, he handed the microphone to his son so that Peter could say some kind words about his parents and raise a glass to them. Everyone applauded the end of Peter's speech.

But Peter wasn't finished yet.

'Helen,' he said, and he turned to face her. For some reason, he looked nervous, and Helen had a terrible premonition. 'We have been together for some time now . . .' The whole room fell silent at this point and everyone was looking at either Peter or Helen. 'Our relationship has survived distance and quite long spells apart, but I think we are stronger now than we have ever been, which is why . . . in front of my parents, your parents and all our friends and family . . . there is something I want to ask you . . .' There were excited gasps and more than one young woman brought her hands up to her face in surprise. Helen felt a shock of realization as Peter fumbled into his pocket. She looked quickly around and took in the sea of expectant faces. Peter managed finally to retrieve the little felt-covered blue box in his jacket pocket. He opened it so she could see the ring, took a step forward and actually went down on one knee in front of her and everyone else in the room.

'Helen Norton' – his voice was trembling – 'will you marry me?'

39

Ian Bradshaw was drunk. He'd had a few pints during the match that afternoon, sunk a couple more while he waited for Tom to return from the farm, then drank with him steadily for the rest of the evening.

Initially, they had talked about the case and whether Tom's break from the pub had actually been worth the trouble. Tom told him about Billy's slip during the TV interview.

'I should challenge him on that,' said Bradshaw, and for a moment Tom wondered if he meant right then.

'Might not be a good idea for you to turn up on his doorstep after a few pints,' Tom told him.

'You could go,' offered Bradshaw.

'Do you think Billy Thorpe will be any more sober than you? He'll have been on the beer all day too because of the football. I suggest we corner him when he's at least partially sober or he'll mumble some excuse about it being a slip of the tongue and we'll be no further forward.'

'Maybe,' conceded Bradshaw. 'It's a good one to keep in the back pocket til he's off guard.'

'Robert Marsh did say another interesting thing. He told me the children were all liars, as if they had cooked up the false story together.'

'I cannot believe five ten-year-olds killed their friend and covered it up,' he said. 'Can you? It's ridiculous.'

'No, I can't,' said Tom, 'but *something* happened that day and it's driving me mad not knowing what. I can't stop thinking about it.'

'Me neither,' admitted Bradshaw.

In the taxi home that night Bradshaw did some thinking of his own. He decided he was in the mood to make some decisions. He was sick of coming home on his own to the same poky little flat, watching the same programmes on TV, before going off to sleep in the same bed, also on his own, then waking at the same time to go off to the same job he had always done.

He'd been thinking about Karen in the taxi and how seamlessly she had transitioned, from being on the verge of moving in with him, to taking back up with her old boyfriend and a year later announcing they were going to be married. He supposed that if their first few months together in his apartment had gone well, then he might have been the one looking for a wedding suit. He couldn't understand how she could so effortlessly change direction like that. He wondered if Karen ever thought of him and, if she did, if those thoughts were ever kind. It still pained him when he recalled her summation of him as a coward when she broke up with him, which was ironic, because he was being hailed as a hero when she had first met him.

Then he wondered if Karen and her fiancé ever talked about him together. Did they share jokes at his expense and laugh about him? Bradshaw told himself this way of thinking was futile. The truth was, he didn't want Karen. They had very little in common and she used to drive him a bit mad, so he had no right to be in any way jealous or begrudge her her happiness. Still, her impending wedding did put his own insular life in perspective.

This couldn't go on. The visits to Adrian Wicklow had made him realize the futility of it all. He told himself he wasn't like the others who had done battle with Wicklow and come out so scarred they jacked everything in. Wicklow hadn't caused his gloom and depression. Bradshaw had been suffering from that for some time. No, this was different. He felt a sudden urge to change things, to alter his life in ways he had never seriously contemplated before. He wasn't trapped here and he didn't have to comply with DCI Kane's every wish. He could just walk away. He was an adult, living in a free society. He was single, had no family or dependants and was beholden to no one. The thought cheered him.

Change was possible, and he was going to start on Monday morning by making a bloody big one.

Helen was still in shock. Oh God. What had she just done? What had she actually said, and how many people had witnessed it? Virtually everyone they knew was there: her parents, his parents, his entire extended family, including aunts, uncles and cousins, and every friend they had made at university. Now she knew why Peter had been allowed to invite so many of their friends to his parents' silver-wedding anniversary party. He must have been planning this for ages.

Helen had a choice.

Option one was to accept a marriage proposal she was not even close to expecting, let alone ready for, from a man she had been dating for a long time but wasn't entirely sure about marrying. That thought struck her in the moment after his proposal. Helen had always visualized a future with Peter, but it was always way off somehow, in a mythical time when he had grown up a lot and she had fulfilled all her ambitions in journalism. She wasn't yet ready to say yes to marriage.

The alternative was to turn him down flat in front of everyone they knew and subject Peter to a never-to-be-forgotten public humiliation he couldn't possibly recover from, sound the death knell of their relationship and completely ruin his parents' celebrations in the process.

For a long, excruciating moment she found herself frozen,

unable to speak. She tried to paste a shocked smile on her face while she struggled to comprehend what Peter had just done. The implications of either accepting his offer or turning him down were racing through her mind. The third choice, of gently asking if they could just go somewhere private to discuss this further, was a non-starter, judging by the hopeful faces of the crowd of people who had stopped everything they were doing to stare at her. That would be as devastating as a refusal.

The tension in the room was palpable.

Helen made her decision then.

She really had no choice.

'Yes,' she managed, and the room went wild.

Now Helen was sitting on the edge of the bath in the en suite bathroom, staring at her outstretched hand. The ring Peter had chosen was a little loose and would have to be adjusted. She knew she would have to be very careful not to let it slip from her finger in the meantime. It wasn't right either. It wasn't that the ring was ugly, exactly, it just wouldn't have been her choice, but then it wouldn't have been her choice to be proposed to abruptly at a party in front of everyone they knew.

This was the first moment she'd been on her own since she had accepted Peter's proposal of marriage. Helen had immediately been swamped by kind-hearted well-wishers, and there were hugs and squeals of delight from friends, all of whom mistook her slightly manic state for delirious happiness.

What had she done?

What had *he* done?

Why had he done it?

She couldn't fathom it at first. If Peter really knew her, he would surely understand that, if he was going to propose, she would prefer it to be in some private, hopefully romantic location, probably abroad somewhere, not on the edge of a packed dance floor in front of a crowd of friends and relations.

So why had he done it like that? Did he think it was the ultimate romantic gesture every girl dreamed of? Or was it because he knew she would find it virtually impossible to turn him down in front of so many people?

That was it. She was certain.

The realization hit her like a blow.

She felt like killing Peter then.

'Helen?' he called. 'Are you all right in there?'

40

'I do like a good preserve,' Peter told her earnestly over breakfast, holding up the tiny but expensive pot of jam that had arrived on a little plate with three others. He was inspecting it as if it were a precious stone. 'I honestly think that is one thing where you definitely get what you pay for, don't you?'

'Mmm,' she managed, not much caring about jam right now.

'I mean, there is just no point in buying cheap, watery jam with no fruit in it. Oh, look, there's Gavin.' And he left the table so he could greet Gavin and his wife. She'd heard a lot about Gavin lately. He was married to one of their old university friends and was 'a good contact', apparently, but Helen couldn't remember why.

Bradshaw had the hangover from hell. It needed ibuprofen, cold glasses of water, a long, hot shower and, eventually, a double bacon sarnie, which he just about managed to keep down. He was no less resolute about changing his life, however, even when the effects of the beer had worn off. Everything was now open to question and he was going to follow his heart.

He looked over at the dictaphone on his coffee table. He never need turn it on again. It was a tempting notion. If he chose to, he could ignore Wicklow and stay away from Durham jail. Soon the man would be dead and Bradshaw's recollections of him simply one of many unpleasant experiences during his time as a police officer.

But a nagging doubt remained. What if he *could* discover the secret behind Adrian Wicklow's crimes? Imagine if he was able to make the man tell him where the bodies of the children were buried? Wouldn't that bring some small solace to the bereaved relatives?

And then there was Susan.

Wouldn't it be so much more satisfying to walk away with this case complete? He told himself that was his prime motivation, but he also knew there was a less noble reason for finishing this one. If he left it unsolved, the mystery of what happened to Susan and the other children was likely to haunt him for the rest of his days. He couldn't turn his back on it. Not yet.

When Helen finally arrived home that night, the first thing she heard was Lena's voice. She was thanking Tom and sounded emotional.

'I haven't found her yet,' he countered.

'I know, but it's a start,' she said hopefully, 'and you have made such progress in only a short amount of time. I know you'll find her.' When Helen came into the room they ceased the conversation and broke free from their embrace on the couch. God, it really was as if Helen was Tom's mum and they were forced to stop canoodling because she had walked in on them.

'Hi, Helen,' said Lena.

'Hi.'

'How was it?' he asked her.

'It was okay,' she answered. 'It was good.'

'Oh my God!' said Lena. She was staring at Helen.

'What?' asked Tom, turning to face her.

'Haven't you noticed?' She nodded in Helen's direction, but Tom was none the wiser. 'The ring,' she said. Helen could see the surprise – or was it shock? – on Tom's face. 'Congratulations, Helen!' Lena beamed at her, while Tom stared dumbly. Lena came towards Helen then and enveloped her in a stiff hug she must have thought was sisterly. Helen didn't appreciate it. She looked at Tom over Lena's shoulder but couldn't read his face at all. He had turned it into a mask, revealing nothing.

'What great news!' squealed Lena. 'Isn't it, Tom?'

'It is,' he said. 'Congratulations, Helen.'

There would be no cheating this time.

Bradshaw had tried the scientific route, studying accounts of real murderers, the kind which had enabled organizations like the FBI to use psychological profiling to help identify killers before they struck again, but he had been wrong. Adrian Wicklow was a one-off. There was no recorded example of a killer doing what he had done, in the way he had done it, without there being other factors, such as a sexual motive or a diagnosis of some kind of psychopathic mental condition. Wicklow was different, so Bradshaw would have to think differently. To do that, he could no longer afford to ignore the man's own words. Instead, he would have to devour them, listening to them over and over again if he had to. He reached for the dictaphone and pressed play.

Tom was up early so he could arrive at the house before anyone left for work. Unlike Jess, her landlady *was* on the electoral role. Her name was Joanna Davis and the poster in the window was canvassing support – for her. She was the Green party candidate in the local elections. Joanna was registered as the sole resident in the house, but there were at least two other girls living with her. Tom watched them leave. They were both young, most probably students and renting rooms from Joanna on a cash-in-hand basis, just like Jess would have done.

Minutes later, a third woman left the house and locked the front door behind her. She was in her late thirties and Tom assumed this was Joanna. Before she reached her car, Tom intercepted her and explained that he would like to ask her some questions and mentioned Jess's name.

'I don't know anyone by that name,' she said curtly. 'Either name,' she added, for he had told her that Jess had also gone by the name of Eva.

He tried being reasonable. He explained he was an investigator hired by her sister and that he regularly worked with the police, but she was already opening her car door and dumping her shoulder bag on the passenger seat. Nothing he said seemed to move her. She went around the car, opened the driver's door, and climbed in. He had been going to let her go but her attitude annoyed him so much he grabbed the passenger door and opened it to lean in.

'Get out of my car,' she snapped.

'Declaring the income, are you? On the rent, I mean.' That stopped her.

'That's none of your concern.' she barked. At least she wasn't going to deny she had lodgers.

'Perhaps you think only little people should pay taxes, is that it? Personally, I feel quite strongly about that sort of thing. I've got a feeling most of the electorate will too, and the local paper is going to be very interested. Most local election candidates have a very low public profile but this will get you on the front page.'

'Oh, so it's blackmail. Is that it?' she blustered.

'I'm merely applying pressure, Joanna. How you choose to respond to it is your business.'

She looked at him then as if she was trying to work out whether he was bluffing.

Moments later, they were inside the house.

'I'm going to be late for work,' she muttered.

'Blame the roadworks.'

'I'm only on the other side of town.'

'Then blame the investigation into the missing person who has been living with you. It's your call.'

That shut her up.

Tom showed her the photograph of Jess then told her about Lena and her fears for her sister. When he was met again with the objection that Eva, as she was known to Joanna, was evading an old, violent boyfriend and for all she knew Tom was that boyfriend, he wrote Ian Bradshaw's number on a slip of paper and tore it from his notebook.

'Call the man. He's a detective sergeant. He'll vouch for me.'

She looked at the number and must have decided the offer was enough.

'Eva stayed with me only for a few weeks,' she began falteringly. 'I barely got to know her. I really don't know anything about her at all. I have to take in lodgers since my ex moved out. It's the only way I can pay the mortgage.'

'I understand,' he said, and she visibly relaxed, 'but the voters might not.' She gave him an evil look.

'I really don't know how I can help.'

'Eva lived here until recently. It's her last known abode. I need to know where she might be now. I'm not being overdramatic when I say I genuinely fear for her life if I don't find her first.' And he told her that Jess had run away from some violent people.

Joanna Davis looked genuinely alarmed then. 'I can't believe she brought this to my door,' she said. Tom realized he had found a way in.

'You could be in danger too,' he warned her. 'I found you easily enough. The next person who knocks on your door looking for Eva might not be so nice.'

'All I know is she left in a hurry. She told me that ex-boyfriend had found her.'

'Actually, it was a private detective.'

'We had a bit of a disagreement about the rent because she said she couldn't afford to give me proper notice, but I insisted and she paid up eventually. That was only fair,' she said, as if convincing herself. 'Eva was upset when she left and said she didn't know where to go or what to do. I advised her to try the refuges.'

'Is there one in Durham?'

'I told her if she got off the train in Newcastle and went to the Citizens Advice Bureau, they would give her the details and someone could help her.'

'Did she say if she was going to take your advice?'

'She said, "What choice do I have?"'

41

Helen was almost out of the door when the phone rang. She nearly let it ring but turned back, put down her bag and went back to answer it.

'Hello.'

'Helen Norton?' a well-spoken male voice asked her.

'Yes.'

'I'm Gordon Cassidy,' he said, 'Victoria's father. You left me a message to call you back. My wife and I have been away for a few days, visiting our son and his family.'

'Thanks for calling me back, Mr Cassidy.' She felt foolish for having contacted him now, having read about his unequivocal support for his daughter's boyfriend following the tragedy. The message she had left had been an intrusion and all for nothing, her questions now redundant. 'I was hoping to come and see you to ask you about the accident on Mont Blanc but I probably have everything I need now,' she said.

'Your message said you were a journalist but you were working with the police?' He seemed intrigued by that. 'Can I please ask what your questions were about?'

'Primarily, they were about Danny Gilbert and whether you had any' – she felt she needed to choose her words very carefully here – 'doubts about his involvement that day, but I have since learned you exonerated him of all responsibility in your daughter's death and thanked him for searching for Victoria.'

There was such a long pause on the line then that Helen eventually broke it with a 'Hello?'

'That was my view at the time,' he said cautiously.

'At the time?'

'When Victoria was lost on Mont Blanc, I naturally concluded that the sudden onset of a severe storm caused her death. Danny was in a bad way when they found him. He had hypothermia. I automatically assumed he had stayed on the mountain too long in order to look for her.'

'And you no longer think that?'

'No.'

Helen was shocked to learn about Gordon Cassidy's change of heart.

'Why not?'

'I changed my view when they found her body,' he said simply, and Helen felt a chill inside her.

'They found your daughter?'

'Yes, didn't you know?'

'No.'

'Then I suggest you come and see me, Miss Norton.'

'I knew you'd be back,' muttered the retired detective. It wasn't much of a greeting, but at least Meade left the door open for Bradshaw when he turned to trudge back into his home. 'Have you come to arrest me?' he called back over his shoulder.

'No, I just have a few follow-up questions.'

'Questions, questions,' mumbled Meade, and sat down in his usual chair. 'I spent my life asking them, now I get them from journalists and even fellow police officers, but they are more like insinuations. Some people would call that karma, I suppose.'

Bradshaw had a copy of the hand-drawn map Helen had found in the room full of files on the case at police HQ, and he spread it on the coffee table. 'I want to ask you about the area you searched when Susan Verity first went missing.'

'We searched everywhere,' said Meade, and he leaned

forward, took his glasses from the pocket of his cardigan, put them on and scrutinized the map. 'There were dozens of uniformed officers with dogs, plus loads of volunteers.'

'Where did you concentrate your efforts? Initially, I mean.'

'We started with the farm, because Susan Verity was last seen heading in that direction, We searched the whole place – of course we did. We examined the farmhouse, the barn and silos, and we spread men out so they walked over every field in a close line looking for any trace of Susan. We found her hairband a few yards from the farmhouse but had no way of knowing when she lost it. It could have fallen on her way out there that morning, when the kids fled from the hay bales or when she was on her way home again.'

'What about the abandoned factory? Did you take a look there?'

'Of course, and we found nothing in any of those old buildings. We also searched the church and the churchyard, and the quarry, in case she had fallen in there, but we'd have found her straight away if she had. We did house-to-house throughout the village and knocked on every door, we searched Susan's home and properties belonging to other family members or those close to her. We dredged the river and the flooded gravel pit down by the railway line. We followed the tracks for miles and searched every inch of undergrowth on either side of them in case a train had struck Susan and thrown her body some distance.' He rolled his eyes. 'Then we indulged Claire Voyant and her loopy notions, searching sites where our psychic could *sense* Susan's presence. Nothing. It was as if she had been swallowed up by the earth.'

'It sounds like you didn't miss anything.'

'We didn't.'

'That old lady you told me about?' Bradshaw asked him carefully.

'Which one?' Had he genuinely forgotten, or was he being evasive?

'You remember Miss Bowes?' When no immediate answer was forthcoming, he added, 'She ID'd Adrian Wicklow in the village on the day Susan Verity disappeared.'

'Oh yeah, her. I do sometimes struggle to remember the specifics after all these years, you know. We dealt with hundreds of leads.' Bradshaw said nothing. 'I think I do remember there might have been an issue with her as a witness because of her age and her eyesight.' He nodded as if in agreement with himself. 'Yeah, that was it, or so I was told.'

'How do you mean, *or so you were told*?'

'Well, I didn't actually interview the lady myself.'

'You didn't?'

'No, and don't sound so surprised. I told you about the number of leads we had going on. We were spread very thinly. I had DCs doing stuff I would ordinarily have liked to do myself, but it was the only way. I had to rely on them to give me a steer.'

'And someone gave you a steer that she wasn't that great a witness?'

'Yeah.'

'And who was that?'

'Honestly? I can't recall. I really can't. Can you remember every conversation you had on a case you tackled a year ago, let alone one that's twenty years old? Can you even remember where you *were* twenty years ago? At school and still in short trousers, I shouldn't wonder.'

'Fair enough. It's just I'm surprised she was dismissed as a witness so easily, bearing in mind what I now know about her after just a little bit of digging.'

'Which is?'

Bradshaw recounted the information Tom had relayed to him about Mrs Meade's time with the Royal Observer Corps.

'Well,' said Meade doubtfully, 'I don't remember anyone telling me that at the time.'

'And it's not something you'd easily forget, considering it directly affected her credibility as a witness.'

'No, well, exactly, I wouldn't have done,' he admitted. 'If someone had told me.'

'So no one did.'

'No.'

'You're sure?'

'Of course I'm sure.'

'Right then,' said Bradshaw, 'so there's only one question left. Was this a cock-up or a conspiracy? You tell me.'

42

The Cassidy family home was in the market town of Wetherby. It took almost ninety minutes to drive there from Durham thanks to the roadworks clogging the traffic going south on the A1. Helen spent much of that time wondering what it was that Mr Cassidy was so keen to tell her and why he couldn't just say it over the phone. Maybe he reasoned she was less likely to dismiss his concerns if he relayed them face to face, or perhaps he didn't fully trust her. Being a journalist, she was used to that.

Helen also wondered why Danny Gilbert had chosen to say nothing about the eventual discovery of Victoria's body. Helen was sure she had mentioned that the body was not found, and Danny hadn't said anything. Why wouldn't he have replied that it was eventually? Why would he want to keep that from her? Her initial research in the newspaper archive had yielded the facts surrounding the accident and that the search on the mountain had been called off. It hadn't occurred to her that, years later, a body could be found.

Gordon Cassidy's living room was dominated by the framed photograph of his daughter on the mantelpiece: a beautiful young woman dressed in graduation robes. He was seeing Helen alone, he explained, because, 'Her mother gets too upset raking over it all.'

'When Victoria died, we were all numb at first and grieved as a family,' he told Helen. 'Danny was very much a part of that family. We helped each other get through that terrible time.

'We kept in touch with Danny for three, perhaps four years.

He wrote a lovely letter to us when he met Janine, hoping we would understand that he wanted to continue with his life, and of course we did understand, completely. We even sent a wedding gift. Then, over a period of time, we gradually lost touch with him. That was only natural. We never resented that he wanted to get on with his life just as we tried to get on with ours. I have another daughter, and a son. We're grandparents now. The pain never entirely goes away, but we love our grandchildren and they have helped us to carry on.'

'Then they found our daughter,' he said finally, 'and that changed everything.'

'When was this?'

'Three years ago.'

'Did Danny know?' asked Helen.

'Of course. The French authorities contacted him at the same time as they called us. They brought her body down from the mountain and we made plans to bury her. We sent Danny a letter asking him if he would like to attend the funeral but saying we would understand if it was too painful. We knew he had moved on.'

'What did he say?'

'We never received a reply.'

'Danny didn't tell me that she had been found,' said Helen, and Gordon Cassidy's face told a story.

'No, I don't suppose he would.'

'Why not?'

'Because her body wasn't where he said it would be.' Gordon Cassidy said it calmly enough, but the words shocked Helen. 'Victoria's body was found years after the accident. Another climber located it. That's not entirely uncommon on a mountain – there are many stories of bodies not being recovered after accidents at that altitude – but this was different.'

'I don't understand,' said Helen. 'I thought she was lost on the mountain and fell and Danny didn't know exactly where. That's why he went back and forth looking for her.'

'That's right, but he should have had a vague idea where she went missing. When we asked for some details we discovered my daughter's body was found much further down the mountain than Danny said. He was four thousand feet out.'

'Wow, that's some discrepancy,' said Helen. 'Even on a storm-hit mountain. Did he explain why he was so far out?'

'I tried to speak to him about it and I wrote to him as well but he didn't respond.'

'What about the French authorities? They must have been suspicious when the body was located?'

'The official line is that Danny was a terrified novice alone on a mountain, disorientated by a severe storm.' He shrugged. 'They asked him after she'd been found about the location of her body. He told them he was confused and upset because his girlfriend had been killed so he made a mistake.'

'But you're not buying that?'

'No, and I think that, privately, the French have their suspicions. Proving that Victoria's accident happened differently to the way Danny described it would be very difficult. There are no witnesses, obviously, so it's his word alone we have to rely on. Danny told everyone Victoria died on her way down the mountain after they turned back because of the bad weather. That version of events would tally with a fall at nine thousand feet around the time he said, because that's where the storm was at its most violent, but it does not make sense if she died at five thousand feet, because the weather wasn't as bad at that altitude.'

'So you're saying they would have been through the worst of the storm by the time they were that far down the mountain?'

'Possibly,' he said. 'Or maybe she fell on the way up and not the way down.'

'Before the storm hit? But Danny got hypothermia.'

'He showed the symptoms – dizziness, confusion, head-aches, muscle cramps,' he said. 'And a heightened heart rate, which you would get from hiking up a mountain anyway.'

'You think he faked it?'

'I don't know,' he admitted, 'but the storm became his perfect alibi.'

'Why would he do that? I have to ask you, Mr Watson, why would he want to kill your daughter at all?'

'I have no idea. I admit that, and I never dreamed he had,' he conceded. 'Not until Victoria's body was found thousands of feet from the spot where he said it should be. Then I sought an explanation, any explanation, but Danny wasn't prepared to provide me with one. Surely that alone ought to be enough to ask him why?'

Tom drove to Newcastle and went into the library. He made his way to a table on which there were several clear files with leaflets in them. All were offering help of one kind or another. Some had images so you knew what the organization who had put them out were hoping to save you from. One showed a syringe, another a bottle of spirits; both listed dates and locations for meetings designed to help people with drug abuse and alcohol addiction. A third leaflet showed a young teenager sitting in a corner with her face buried in her hands and a number that could be called if you were being abused. Then Tom spotted a leaflet with an image of a distressed woman with a black eye. There was a speech bubble next to her which said, 'It's okay,' as if she had simply fallen. Underneath this, in big, bold letters were the words 'IT'S NEVER OKAY!' and the number of a women's refuge you could call for help. The accompanying text promised confidential treatment at a secret location in the city. This left Tom with a dilemma. As a man, he could hardly call the number and ask for access to the refuge in order to speak to a young woman who did not want to be found, but how else could he locate the place? He decided he needed Ian Bradshaw's help.

'Could you try and get me an address from your colleagues in Newcastle?' Tom asked when the detective picked up the phone. 'I'll be honest, it's a bit sensitive.'

Bradshaw sighed. 'Will I live to regret this?'

'When have you ever regretted anything you've done for me?'

'I'd answer that question,' Bradshaw told him, 'but I haven't got the time.' Tom told Bradshaw what he needed and why. 'Okay, leave it with me and I'll see what I can do.'

When the call was over, Tom realized he was left with time on his hands in Newcastle and, today, he was in no mood to waste it. The prospect of a pub lunch and a wander around the city was appealing. Maybe he'd even call into a travel agent and see what they had to offer. After all, if Jess was alive and well when she left Durham, she was more than likely okay now, which meant Lena might be in the mood to be impulsive.

Was Gordon Cassidy on to something, or was he just paranoid? Had his grief for his daughter tipped him into seeing murder instead of a tragic accident? If so, why wouldn't Danny Gilbert put his mind at rest by giving the man an explanation? Helen asked herself these questions, and more, on her drive back from Wetherby. By the time she reached home she was no clearer, but she knew she couldn't leave it at that.

Victoria's father had given her the right name, but it took an age to be connected. Helen attempted French but the woman on the line must have detected her accent right away and interrupted, telling her sternly, 'I speak perfect English.'

'Oh,' said Helen, a little taken aback by the woman's directness. 'Could you please connect me to the Peloton de Gendarmerie de Haute Montagne at Chamonix? I need to speak to a Monsieur Henri Gerbeaud.'

'Connecting you now.'

'So we've got a man who lied about the spot on a mountain where his girlfriend fell to her death,' said Tom. 'Or perhaps he was just disorientated by the storm. Then we have another man, Billy, who changed his story about the last sighting of Susan Verity after all these years of saying something else, though he may have just panicked because he was on TV. Finally, we have another man who likes to kill things and had a breakdown at sixteen, possibly caused by guilt or trauma.'

'It all sounds damning,' said Helen, 'but none of it proves anything.'

'And if one of them is guilty of something, then which one?' asked Bradshaw.

'Maybe it's all of them,' observed Tom.

'Or maybe none,' Bradshaw reminded him.

'And where does Adrian Wicklow fit into all of this?' asked Helen.

'That, I have yet to find out,' admitted Bradshaw, and it seemed there was little more to say for now. Then Bradshaw suddenly remembered something. 'Nearly forgot,' he said, and he handed Tom a piece of paper. 'That address you were after. I had to kill to get it.'

'You mean you owe someone a pint.'

'There are two other women's refuges in the city, aside from this one,' Bradshaw informed Tom. 'I've got you the addresses of all three, but the one you told me about is the biggest and most well-established. If someone was going to refer her in an emergency, they'd probably start there. They gave me this information on one condition: don't go waltzing in and scaring the life out of the poor lasses who live there. Some of them have been through a terrible time.'

'Understood, mate. I'll do this one from a distance.'

'You better had.'

When Bradshaw had gone, Helen asked, 'Can I have a word?'

'That sounds ominous. What's the matter?'

'Nothing is the matter. I've just been thinking,' she said. 'When this is over I should probably look for a job.'

'A job?'

'On a newspaper,' she answered.

'Why? I thought you were happy working with me.'

'I am – I was – I just feel, lately, that I am working for you, not with you.'

'What do you mean?' He sounded hurt. 'Is this because of Lena, because I'm helping her?'

'No,' she said. 'It's not about Lena.' But she had to admit to herself that her discomfort at living in a tiny bedroom in Tom's home had grown proportionately since Lena had appeared on the scene.

'We work together, Helen. We're a team. We write stories and we sell them, we get paid and share the proceeds, we're doing okay. I know things could be better, but we're just starting out.'

'But everything we do is through you,' she said. 'You sell all the stuff we produce.' Then she added, somewhat sulkily, 'Apart from my "parish magazines", as you call them.'

'Oh, Helen.' He was exasperated. 'Only because I have contacts in the industry. And I'm not trying to keep them to myself. Next time we have a story for Paul Hill I'll put you on the phone to him. You might get a better price.'

She shook her head. 'I know the reason for it, but I don't feel like it's *our* business, not really. It's yours. I just happen to work with you. You keep calling it Norton–Carney, like it's some in joke we have, but it's not real.'

'Of course it's real,' he said.

'Well, it doesn't feel real,' she insisted. 'To me.'

'Is this because of him?' he snapped.

She knew he meant Peter. 'No,' she said cautiously, 'but I suppose I have to accept that, one day, I should probably get a proper job.'

'*A proper job?*' He really did sound hurt now.

'Somewhere closer to home.'

'I thought this *was* home.'

'It is,' she said, 'for now; just not for ever. Things will have to change eventually. I'm engaged now. Not that you've ever mentioned it,' she chided.

'Nor have you,' he hit back, and they sat in silence for a time while they both contemplated this.

'You haven't been around much lately,' she said finally.

43

Thanks to Ian Bradshaw, Tom found the place easily enough. It looked like a run-down council office that tackled unimportant admin for Newcastle City Council, not a safe haven for women in desperate trouble.

There was a café across the road from it. He was glad he hadn't eaten. He managed to grab a window table and ordered an all-day breakfast with a mug of tea, keeping his eyes fixed on the doorway of the building opposite. Then he settled in to watch. He knew he could be in for a very long wait.

Helen's morning was just as frustrating. She needed to talk to Danny Gilbert about Mont Blanc, to ask him how Victoria's body had been discovered so far from the spot where he said she had fallen and why he wouldn't speak to her father about it. It seemed pretty damning, but she knew there were always two sides to every story, though she couldn't quite imagine how Danny was going to explain his version satisfactorily.

When Helen drove up to Danny's house, however, she was in for a disappointment. It was locked up and empty, with no car parked on the drive. His next-door neighbour came out of the house then, and when he saw Helen he challenged her.

'Can't you lot just leave him alone for one minute?' He must have assumed she was working for a tabloid, and she wondered how many times journalists had walked up Danny's driveway if even his neighbour was tired of seeing them. 'Anyway, you're wasting your time,' he told her as he climbed into his car.

'They've gone away for a bit.' He couldn't resist adding: 'To get away from you lot.'

He was gone before she could ask when Danny and his family would be returning; she assumed in any case that he wouldn't have told her even if he knew. As Helen got back into her own car she couldn't help wondering whose questions Danny Gilbert was really trying to avoid.

Bradshaw hadn't slept. He'd stayed up most of the night listening to Wicklow's memoir. Afterwards, he had tried to sleep but had terrible dreams that made him wake up covered in sweat. His sheets were drenched with it. Though he couldn't remember specifically what he had been dreaming about, he was in little doubt his subconscious mind had somehow been invaded by Adrian Wicklow. He didn't want to go back to sleep for fear of repeating them. Instead, he got up while it was still dark and started to formulate his plan before the sun rose. He couldn't keep doing this.

Ian Bradshaw decided he was going to confront Wicklow one last time. This had to end today.

It was nearly noon, more than two hours after he ordered his fry-up, when Jess finally emerged. Tom recognized her straight away and a felt a great surge of relief. He'd found her. His waitress must have been wondering what the hell he was doing there and why he kept ordering mugs of tea. He happily left the latest one untouched, pulled money from his pocket to pay for it all, along with a generous tip, left the cash on the table and went to the door.

Tom had watched five women leave the building already that morning before Jess, and had been beginning to doubt both himself and the validity of the information he had received from Jess's former landlady. He stood inside the door of the café now and watched through its window as Jess paused and looked about her. He noticed she was carrying a large shopping bag. Was this her routine to avoid anyone approaching suddenly without her seeing them? He stayed there until Jess seemed satisfied she wasn't being pursued. She turned to her left and went up the street. Tom opened the door of the café and started to follow her at a distance. Almost immediately, it began to rain. He kept his eyes fixed on Jess as she rounded a bend that took her away from the main drag of the city centre and into an area with offices and apartments.

He followed Jess for nearly ten minutes, being careful not to lose her but hanging back a way so that, when she turned to check behind her, he didn't arouse suspicion.

Then abruptly, she walked into a pub called the Golden Hind. Tom waited outside for a moment while he contemplated his next move.

He took out his mobile and called Lena. No reply. Maybe she had client meetings. He was disappointed he couldn't give her the good news.

He didn't have to go into the pub. He could just keep trying Lena, or he could go home. Tom knew where Jess lived and now, presumably, where she was working. He need get no closer to her than this, and Lena had been quite clear he shouldn't try until she was in a position to talk directly to her sister. The bungled approach from the private detective had spooked Jess enough for her to leave Durham city in a hurry, and they did not want to lose her again.

But . . .

Jess had never met Tom and had no idea who he was. If he walked in there like any other customer and behaved normally, Jess wouldn't even know he was there because of her. He'd order a pint and maybe some food to kill time. He could grab a newspaper from the shop across the road and pretend to read it. She would be none the wiser.

Tom wasn't entirely sure why he wanted to do this. He told himself it was because he wanted to be certain it really was Jess and he didn't want to take his eye off her, but there was more to it than that, and not just the prospect of getting out of the rain. Tom had taken the time and trouble to locate Jess. He wasn't used to finding people and not making any kind of connection with them. It would feel like the job was only half done if he called Lena, turned his back and drove away.

As long as he didn't speak to her directly, except to order a beer, then he wasn't actually approaching her, not really.

What harm could it do?

'You really want to do this again?' asked Wicklow once Bradshaw was seated opposite him. 'Sure you're up to it?'

'I wouldn't be here if I wasn't.'

Wicklow looked at Bradshaw for a moment and the detective stared back at the child killer unflinchingly. 'So you think you understand now?' he said.

'I think so, yes.'

'You look as if you actually believe you do,' conceded Wicklow. 'Care to elaborate?'

'Your world view,' Bradshaw told him, 'that irreligious stance you hold dear, the one you hide from Father Noonan – the atheistic creed which supports the idea that, once life is over, it's over, and there's nothing after it.'

'Okay,' said Wicklow doubtfully. 'Go on.'

'It shows how much is at stake and why you don't think returning the bodies is at all important.'

'It's not.'

'Not to you, only to the families. They want closure, a burial, Christian services, prayers and talk of meeting again in an afterlife to console them, but you don't believe in any of that so returning those bodies is irrelevant. But, in a way, death matters more to you,' he concluded, 'because it's so final.'

'You're right,' said Wicklow. 'Once life is gone, bodies are just empty husks . . .' He seemed about to continue on that theme, but stopped himself. 'So, why do I do it?'

'I once told you it was about power, and you said I was wrong,' Bradshaw reminded him. 'But, in a way, I think I was actually correct. I thought you relished the power you held over a small child while you killed them, but that isn't it, is it, Wicklow? In the end, the actual person doesn't matter. You stalked them for hours, sometimes for days, and you built up an idea in your head of who they were, but none of that really counts at all because it isn't about the personality of the individual, is it?'

'No,' admitted Wicklow. 'It isn't.'

'As long as they fit a broad profile, they qualify.'

'And that profile is?'

'They just need to be young,' said Bradshaw. 'But not because you get a kick out of that, and it isn't because you can overpower them so easily. You're a very strong man. There's only one reason you prefer children to adults.'

'And what's that?'

'They have their entire life ahead of them,' said Bradshaw, 'and you take it from them like that.' Bradshaw clicked his fingers, and Wicklow's eyes widened in excitement. 'That's what you enjoy — stealing all those years, taking their whole lives from them right at the beginning, robbing them of everything they are ever going to be.'

'Very good, Detective,' said Wicklow approvingly, and he beamed at Bradshaw. 'You are definitely on the right lines here. I'm impressed,' he added, 'but do continue, please.'

Bradshaw could scarcely say the words now. 'While you're

killing, to you, the real fascination is in the eyes,' he managed. 'Or at least what lies behind them. It's not about the body,' Bradshaw told him. 'That's why it has never been sexual. It's about the life force they have inside them and you taking it away.'

'Why the eyes?' asked Wicklow. He seemed genuinely moved by Bradshaw's mention of them. 'Tell me.'

'Because they are the windows to the soul,' said Bradshaw, 'and you like to look right into them while you're killing your victims.'

'Why?' He was almost pleading now. 'Why do I like to do that? Tell me?' he urged.

'So you can witness the life force being extinguished,' said Bradshaw. 'That's what you crave and it's why you have to see their eyes. You like to watch as the light goes out.'

44

Adrian Wicklow stared at Bradshaw with something resembling astonishment. His mouth opened but he seemed unable to find the words, then Bradshaw jumped as a sudden sound filled the room.

The single clap was loud and hard, and it went right through him. Wicklow waited till it died down before he followed it with another, then another, bringing his hands out wide and banging them back together, hard, each time. He repeated this slow clap four or five times before Bradshaw realized what he was doing.

Wicklow was applauding him.

'That is as good an explanation as I have ever heard. I wasn't entirely sure you had it in you. When you first walked in here, with your cheap suit and your bad attitude, I thought, *Well, we won't get very far here*, but you exceeded my expectations. No pseudo-intellectual bullshit from you. You looked into my heart and you understood!'

'Understanding is not condoning, Wicklow,' Bradshaw reminded him.

Wicklow sniffed. 'Pity. I'll miss our cosy little chats. Tell me, though – how come you understood when those supposedly clever souls with all the letters after their names couldn't?'

'They were comparing you to others,' said Bradshaw. 'I worked on the basis that you were unique.'

He liked that notion. 'Go on.'

'I did the same thing they did at first. I read the books and learnt about other serial killers and I tried to equate your behaviour to theirs. I tried to fit what you had done into a neat category that already existed.'

'But you couldn't do it.' Wicklow said this with some satisfaction.

'No, because there has never been anyone like you before.'

Wicklow seemed to radiate pride at this.

'You're a one-off,' said Bradshaw. 'And once I realized that I was able to go back into your book and listen to it differently, not like a doctor or a scientist but as an ordinary man. Then I understood why you did what you did.'

'Extraordinary,' said Wicklow. 'You're right, though. It is the life force that compels me to kill them. Some people say it's a destructive thing, but I don't agree. I'd say it's creative, in its own way.'

'You're creating an alternative reality,' said Bradshaw simply.

'Yes! Oh my, go to the top of the class, Detective! That's right, I'm creating a whole new world without them. Imagine the thousands, the millions, of tiny interactions they would have with others if I didn't end them? Those subjects of mine would go on and on, maybe for years, possibly into old age. They'd grow up, meet someone, marry and have kids, and those kids would eventually do the same until the subject would be an old man or woman with grandchildren, maybe even great-grandchildren. A whole family with years and years of combined experiences between them, out there in the world.'

'But you stop all that. You take it from them.'

'I end all those infinite possibilities with just a few brief seconds of applied pressure, and when their light goes out a whole alternative world that might have been is snuffed out with it, like a candle.' He held up a finger and blew on this imaginary candle to illustrate his point. Bradshaw could see the excitement in Wicklow's eyes. He was relishing this. No wonder he found prison agreeable. He could tap into the memory of every one of his victims at will, revelling in the enormity of what he had done to them, over and over again. 'Perhaps you were correct, Detective. It *is* the power. The power to alter the world, one subject at a time.'

'I'm prepared to talk more about this; today, tomorrow,' Bradshaw said reasonably. 'It's fine with me, but first . . .'

'But first?' He sounded put out that the detective had interrupted his speech.

'We had a deal, remember? I work out why you do what you do and you repay me by telling me where the bodies are buried, then you let me know what really happened to Susan Verity.'

'Oh yes, our deal.' Wicklow said it as if Bradshaw had suddenly reminded him of something grubby and distasteful. 'Well, that's going to be difficult.'

'Why would it be difficult?'

'It was all so long ago.'

The realization of his suspicion all along that Wicklow might not keep to his side of the bargain made Bradshaw no less angry. 'Don't try and wriggle out of this, Wicklow. You swore you would tell me.'

'I honestly . . . after all this time . . . couldn't tell you where the children are buried, and what good would it do you anyway? They have gone the way of all flesh, Detective. There won't be much left to bury.'

'Nonetheless, the families –'

'The families! That's all I ever hear about! The families and their suffering! What about my suffering?' he wailed.

'We had an agreement.' Bradshaw spoke low and with menace. Inadvertently, he tensed and made his right hand into a fist. Wicklow glanced at it.

'Well, I'm breaking it. I've changed my mind,' said Wicklow smugly. 'What are you going to do, Detective, beat me up? I

278

bet you'd love to do it. You policemen all do that in the end, don't you, when you don't get what you want? I'm a dying man, though, so really, there's very little you can do to harm me.'

'You bastard, Wicklow,' said Bradshaw. 'You're going to burn one day.'

'No, I won't. Neither of us really believes that. Don't try and con me that you do.'

'We had a deal,' said Bradshaw helplessly.

'And I told you that when you first came here, you should have been more courteous.' He smiled at the detective then. 'I'd love to help you, but there's nothing I can do.'

45

The pub was an old-fashioned place on the outskirts of the city, little more than a few tables, chairs, the beer pumps and the optics. Tom was one of only six customers, all of them male, all drinking pints, and no one was eating. A large chocolate Labrador snoozed at an old man's feet.

Tom approached the bar. Jess was on her haunches behind it with her back turned towards him so she didn't notice his arrival. She was busy placing small bottles of fruit juice and spirit mixers on a shelf and Tom watched her as she arranged the tonics in a neat line. When she turned around she seemed startled to see this stranger. 'Sorry,' she mumbled. 'I didn't hear you.' Her east London accent was just like Lena's. 'What you having?'

'A pint of bitter, please.'

She got on with pulling his pint and only spoke again to tell him the price. She took his money silently then handed him his change.

'Thanks,' he smiled. She did not return his smile. He couldn't work out if she looked like Lena or not. There was some resemblance, but it was superficial. She had the same slender frame, though she was shorter than her sister, and her features less striking but she was still pretty. She probably got hit on by every bloke who came in here. Tom took his pint and sat down in a corner. He opened the paper and laid it on his table, reading it while occasionally glancing up to observe her covertly.

Some barmaids like to chat incessantly to their customers.

They dispense a form of banter with their pints, either because they enjoy the craic or because they consider themselves part of the entertainment, knowing that many of the men are here for the chat as much as the beer. They befriend their regulars. They might keep them at a bit of a distance but they know their custom is the lifeblood of a pub like this one.

Jess was not that kind of barmaid.

She was efficient enough, he supposed, but she merely went about her job with the minimum of fuss, and offered no conversation. When he ordered food later she brought it to him without comment, then scooped empty pint glasses from another table before going quickly back behind the bar once more. This girl was keeping a low profile and Tom knew why.

He guessed that Jess worked a split shift and would be free for a couple of hours in the afternoon. At 2.30 p.m. on the dot, she finished emptying ashtrays and wiping tables then called through into the private section of the pub, 'I'm off now, Jim!' But she did not move immediately.

'You'll want paying,' said Jim, and he emerged, as if he had picked up the hint. The older man, who presumably ran the place, reached into the till and handed over her money, cash in hand. 'Would you be up for a few more hours the week after next?'

'I don't know, Jim. I might be moving on soon.'

She pocketed her money and left.

Tom drained his pint and followed her.

It was her tone of voice that had alarmed him, not just the words. A woman in her position, who was living hand to mouth, had turned down extra work, and she had just been paid, meaning nobody owed her anything so she had no reason to hang around. That bag of hers was pretty big. If she was travelling light, it might contain everything she owned. What if she got on a train now and left the city? How would he explain that to Lena?

Tom had assured Lena he would not approach Jess, but he might be forced to rather than let her skip town with no prospect of ever finding her again. He was discreet. He kept his distance. He followed Jess along several main streets, then she took a side street, and another. Where was she going? Not back to the refuge. Was this the direction for the train station? Tom knew Newcastle well but even he was disorientated now. If that was where she was heading, it was an unusual route to take. He held back and kept other people between them, ensuring that, if she looked behind her, he would not stand out. Then she took a right turn that led into a tiny backstreet no car would have bothered to navigate. Tom glanced down it as her back disappeared around a corner. One side was a building that had been boarded up for demolition so the site could be converted into flats. The other was a squat, grey building with residential apartments. The kind of place that is dead during the day because the handful of residents living there are at work.

What was she doing? Who was she meeting? If she disappeared into one of those flats, he'd lose her, possibly for good. Tom decided to risk it and followed her.

When he reached the front door of the flats there was no sign of her. She could have gone in, but he doubted she would have had the time to buzz one of the flats, speak into the intercom, wait for the door to swing open and step inside. Not here then.

Tom walked further on and went around another corner, which took him to the side of the vacant lot.

He was surprised to see Jess standing there. And he got an even bigger shock when he realized what she was holding.

'Don't fucking move,' hissed Jess. She gripped the gun more tightly for emphasis. Her face was set in a snarl and she did not look like a scared young woman no longer in control.

'Whoa!' was all he could manage at first. He froze and automatically put his hands up and to the side. 'Please don't point that thing at me.' He was terrified it might go off accidentally if Jess was scared and had no experience of guns.

'Don't move,' she commanded, and looked him up and down, as if trying to work out if she knew him. Her face told Tom she might have been expecting some other, more familiar figure.

'It's okay,' he told her. and he forced himself to smile. 'I'm not going to hurt you.'

'No, you're not,' she told him, 'because I have a gun.'

'Could you please put it down or point it away from me?'

'No chance. Who are you? Why are you following me?' She lowered the gun. 'This better be good, or I'll blow your fucking kneecap off.'

Tom could hardly believe what he was hearing. This was not the young woman Lena had described. This was some other woman entirely.

'Whatever you do, do not fire that gun.' He was trying to reason with her and to talk as calmly as he could. 'I'm on your side.'

'No, you're not. Why are you following me?'

'I was asked to find you.' Her immediate reaction to that was to cock the pistol and make it ready to fire. 'Not by anyone bad,' he assured her quickly.

'Who then?' She sounded as if she only knew bad people.

'Not the men who have been chasing you, Jess, not them.' When he was satisfied she was listening and not likely to fire the gun that instant, he added, 'I'm a friend. I was asked to find you by your sister.' If he had expected her to believe him and lower the gun straight away, he was disappointed.

Instead, she frowned and gripped the gun even more tightly. 'My sister?' she asked.

'Yes,' he assured her. 'She sent me to find you. She's so worried about you, Jess, and all she wants to do is make sure you're safe. She wanted me to look for you and bring her to you. It's what I do.' He didn't want to waste time explaining he was a journalist. 'Lena just wants to know you're okay, so I agreed to help her to find you, and that's exactly what I have done, that's all. I can call your sister now. She can be here very soon, so everything will be okay.'

'Nice try.' She aimed the gun at his head again now. 'But I don't have a sister.'

46

'You don't have a . . . what do you mean?' Tom asked her. 'Of course you have a sister.' He was confused now and wondering why she was acting this way. 'Lena. I'm talking about Lena,' he repeated helplessly. He knew he didn't have the wrong girl, so why was she saying this and still pointing that gun at him? 'You have a sister called Lena. I am seeing her,' he explained. 'She asked me to help find you.'

'I don't,' she told him simply. 'My sister is dead.'

'Dead?'

'She died seven years ago,' the girl said flatly. 'She OD'd.'

'But . . .' She must have seen the shock and incomprehension on his face then.

'Who have you really been seeing? That's what you're asking, isn't it?' She shook her head as if she couldn't believe it. 'I can probably guess.'

Tom didn't say anything for a while; numerous conflicting thoughts were running through his mind. This girl had to be lying. But a part of him already knew she wasn't.

'I don't understand,' he said. 'What's going on?'

'You have a photo of this girlfriend of yours?' she asked.

He shook his head.

'Describe her then,' she commanded, and he did, in detail. He could see the gradual realization in her expression. 'I know what's happened here.' To Tom's immense relief, she lowered the gun. 'Have you told her you found me, this woman?'

'I called her a while back,' he admitted. 'Before I walked into the pub.'

'Shit.'

'But she didn't pick up.'

This seemed to calm the girl for a moment.

'Then I have to go,' she said firmly, 'And so should you.'

'Why?'

'If you're as innocent in this as you say you are, your life is in danger too.'

There was a large part of Tom that wanted to simply let the girl go so she could disappear again and he could forget he ever saw her. Then things would go back to the way they were before, and he and Lena would pick things up where they left off. He could be happy again.

Of course, Tom couldn't do that; he was no idiot. He knew now that nothing would ever be the same again.

Your life is in danger too.

He couldn't just leave it at that. He had to know the truth – all of it.

'Don't go,' he pleaded, and she responded by pointing the gun at him again.

'You won't stop me.'

'Believe me, I'm not going to try. I just want to talk to you.'

'Why?'

'I want to know the truth.'

'What good would that do?'

'In all honesty, I don't know, but if you tell me I might be able to help you. You're clearly running away from something, and it must be pretty serious if you need to carry a gun.' The girl looked back at him doubtfully. 'I'm guessing life isn't too good for you right now, judging by those black marks under your eyes.'

'I don't sleep too well, so what?'

'Tell me what happened to you and I promise I will help you.'

'You can't help me,' she assured him.

'Why not?'

She hesitated for a moment. 'Because . . . I saw something I shouldn't have.'

'So that's why they want to find you – to shut you up.'

She nodded. 'For good.'

'Must have been something bad.'

'It was.'

'Someone killed somebody?'

She nodded again.

'And you can't go to the police?'

'They own the police.'

'They must be very powerful then.'

'They are. Biggest firm in London.'

'This isn't London.'

'Don't matter. They have powerful friends everywhere.'

'Okay, I get that. I understand why you ran, and you did a pretty good job of staying gone,' he said. 'But I found you.'

'So?'

'That means someone else could too, and sooner or later they will.'

Her face seemed to fall then and her whole body sagged. 'I am so tired,' she told him quietly. 'It's been so hard.'

'Then it's time to come in. I know someone who will be able to help you. I won't ask you to trust me. You shouldn't trust anybody, not even me, but I can set something up so you will feel completely safe.'

'How are you gonna do that?'

'I'll think of a way. Let me give you a phone number to call. We'll make it a public place so no one can harm you.'

He could see how conflicted she was. Eventually, she said, 'I don't know,' almost as if she were talking to herself.

'Let me help you, Jess. I'm your best chance right now of

getting out of this alive. Can I?' He moved his hand slowly towards his pocket to draw something out of it.

She nodded and he took out his tape recorder and showed it to her. 'Tell me what happened. Explain what you saw. Let me take this to the right people and I'll make sure they protect you.'

'No, I've got to go.' She was edgy again.

Tom had to prevent her from leaving. He wanted to protect the girl and he needed to know the truth about Lena.

In desperation, he called, 'Then take me with you.'

Helen made two more teas and handed one to Bradshaw. They were both on their second mug.

'I'm sorry,' he said. 'I shouldn't be banging on about this to you. I shouldn't be bending your ear.'

'Why not?'

'Because it's my problem, not yours. There's no reason to involve you. I should just deal with it.'

'Spoken like an entire generation of men who think talking about their problems is a sign of weakness. Women talk to each other all the time.'

'Maybe so but it's not as if I expect you to come up with a solution. Anyway, I'll be fine.' She sighed. 'What?' he asked.

'Ian, you're not fine,' she said. 'You're very far from fine, in fact.'

'What do you mean by that?'

'Have you glanced at a mirror lately? You look like you haven't slept in weeks.'

'Thanks.'

'You'd prefer me to say you look great? Can't do it, I'm afraid. I should have said something earlier, and I don't mind you banging on about it, as you call it, but my advice is that whatever game Wicklow has got you playing, you should end it soon, before it makes you unwell.'

He was going to protest, but something told him that would

be pointless. 'I do feel unwell,' he admitted. 'And I'm not sleeping, not really, and when I do sleep . . .' It was his turn to sigh. 'I usually wish I hadn't.'

'Bad dreams?'

His voice cracked. 'Yeah.'

'That's no surprise. Christ, Ian, you've been inside the head of a madman for days. What do you expect? There's no shame in it.'

'Maybe not, but I can't just walk away from it.'

'Even though he refuses to cooperate?'

'Nothing seems to get to him,' Bradshaw admitted. 'Everyone has tried, and I mean everyone – police officers, scientists, doctors, shrinks – and no one has managed to get him to give up his secrets or even rattle him.'

Helen took a reflective sip of tea then said, 'Well, I am clearly no expert, so you can disregard what I am about to say if you like but –'

'Go on,' he urged. 'No, seriously, I'm at a complete loss, so any suggestion is welcome.'

'Why do you think Adrian Wicklow won't tell anyone what happened to his victims or let anybody know where their bodies are buried?'

'He doesn't give a damn. He has no empathy for the parents, just as he had none for his victims when he killed them.'

'So, in short, he doesn't care.'

'That's right,' confirmed Bradshaw, wondering what she was getting at.

'So that's the solution then,' she said. 'In my view.'

'What is?'

'You have to find a way to make him care.'

Bradshaw contemplated her words for a moment. 'But we've just said he doesn't care. How can I make him?'

'That's the bit you'll have to figure out.'

'I'm not trying to be argumentative here, Helen, but how can I make him care about his victims or their parents when everyone he has ever met, including them, has failed to achieve that?'

Helen shook her head. 'You misunderstand me. I didn't explain it very well. It's not the victims or the parents he has to care about it. It's the outcome.'

'The outcome?' he repeated dumbly.

'He has to have a vested interest in the return of those bodies, or he won't give them up. You need to find a way to make him care enough to help you.'

'We can't offer him a reduced sentence. That's out of the question, and he'll be dead soon anyway.'

'I don't mean that. I'm not talking about anything specific, because I don't know what might work, but you have spent time with him, so maybe you can find the something that he does care about that will make him help you.'

'I see what you mean, but Adrian Wicklow doesn't care about anything. He never has. He . . .' Bradshaw stopped speaking then and Helen watched him as his face changed. She could tell that a thought had just struck him but was yet to take shape fully.

'What?' she asked. 'What is it, Ian? Tell me.'

'There is one thing' – he looked hopeful for a second, then his face darkened – 'but you won't like it,' he cautioned. 'I'd have to fight dirty. Very dirty indeed.'

'And you think I'd object to that?'

'Probably.' And when she said nothing at first, he added, 'this might be more Tom's territory than yours – no offence, to either of you.'

'Because I'm a woman?'

He shook his head. 'No. Tom has had more experience of this kind of thing than you, that's all.'

'This kind of thing,' she repeated thoughtfully. 'It's going to be bad, isn't it?'

'Yes.'

'Will it help you to find the bodies of those missing children?'

'Maybe.'

'Then do it.'

47

Jess made him drive her car while she sat in the back seat, the gun close to hand. 'Just head north,' she ordered, and he did as he was told.

'So why don't you tell me what happened?'

She made him drive for over an hour and, while they sped up the A1, she told him what she knew. By the time they reached Berwick, Tom had at least some pieces of the puzzle. The rest he would have to try to work out on his own.

She told him to pull over just south of the bridge that led towards the border for Scotland. He got out of the car and she climbed in, the gun tucked back in her bag now. Before she closed the door, he said, 'Let me at least give you that number.'

'You sure about that?' she asked him. 'Wouldn't you prefer just to walk away from this mess, now, while you still can?'

'I would, definitely,' he assured her, 'but I can't.'

'All right then.' She waited while he took out a pen and wrote down his mobile number, handed her the slip of paper then Jess pocketed it.

'If you do change your mind,' he said, 'call any time, day or night.'

He was standing on the platform at Berwick station waiting for the train back to Newcastle when his mobile rang.

'It's me,' Lena said. 'Did you call earlier? I couldn't pick up.' When he didn't immediately reply, she asked, 'What's wrong?'

'Nothing,' he said. 'I did call earlier.'

'I thought perhaps you'd found her,' she said hopefully. 'That you'd found Jess at the refuge?'

'No,' he said. 'I didn't. I cased the place out all day and watched the women come and go, but there was no sign of Jess. I'm sorry.'

Lena sighed. 'I really thought she might be there. I was so hopeful this time.'

'Yeah,' he said. 'I was hopeful too.'

'Tom,' she asked, 'is everything all right? You sound –'

'I'm just disappointed that I didn't find Jess, and I'm tired. It's been a long day.'

'Want me to come round and de-stress you?'

'I would love that,' he said, 'but I have to follow something up with Helen tonight.'

Tom did not want to see Lena again until he had fully digested everything Jess had told him. He wanted all the facts so she couldn't wriggle out of the situation. Most of all, he wanted to know who Lena really was.

'The cold case – of course. And I've got to go back down south in the morning. Another time then?'

'Another time. Listen, Lena,' he said determinedly. 'I am not going to give up, you hear me?'

'I hear you.' She sounded brighter now.

'There are other places I can try, and I've got lots of contacts in Newcastle. We will find her. I promise.'

'Thank you.' There was a grateful sob on the other end of the line that seemed to convey a series of conflicting emotions all at the same time: gratitude, worry, sadness and hope. His heart would have gone out to her, if he hadn't known she was a liar. This woman was some actress. 'You've no idea how much this means to me, Tom.'

'That's okay, Lena,' he said, *or whatever your name is.* 'I think I do.'

*

When he finally got back to Newcastle, picked up his car and drove back home to Durham city, Tom was tired, depressed and still experiencing a deep feeling of shock. He'd been an idiot. He had taken everything the woman he knew as Lena had told him at face value. He had been used by her and felt like a complete fool.

Most of all, though, he was angry, and that meant someone was going to pay.

'Are you all right?' asked Helen the moment she saw his face.

'Is it that obvious?'

'Where have you been?' asked Bradshaw. 'You've not been causing chaos, have you?' He was worried Tom might have provoked a scene, but his words were prophetic enough.

'Not at the refuge, no,' he said, 'but you could say that. Listen, Ian, I'm going to need a favour from you.' He sighed. 'And it's a pretty big one.'

'Oh,' said Bradshaw.

'What?' Tom asked.

Helen answered. 'I think you just took the words out of Ian's mouth.'

It took Tom some time to explain it all to them and it was growing dark by the time he had finished. Normally, by now, someone would have reached for the one of the selection of menus pinned to the cork board in the kitchen and ordered a takeaway, but listening to the tale Tom had to tell made them forget to be hungry.

'Oh my God,' said Helen when he was finally finished. 'So if Lena is not Lena, then who the hell is she?'

'That's what I'm going to find out, and it's why I need a favour from Ian. Jess had some ideas, and we've narrowed it down a bit, but even she can't be sure. I need proof. Could you get on to your guy at the Met?'

Bradshaw nodded. 'Of course, just tell me what you need. Are you going to confront her?'

'I'm aiming to,' said Tom, 'but I want to see if I can persuade Jess to come in first. She won't be safe til she does and I'm hoping she will realize that.'

Then Tom said, 'And what is it you want from me?' When Bradshaw hesitated, he prompted, 'Come on, out with it, man. My day couldn't possibly get any worse.'

'I think it's about to,' said Helen.

'I need your help,' said Bradshaw, 'to bury Adrian Wicklow.'

48

When they had finished explaining, the detective said, 'Things are about to get very interesting round here.'

'They are,' Tom agreed. 'One way or another.'

When Bradshaw had left, Helen asked Tom, 'Are you all right?' Then she said, 'Obviously, you're not – how could you be? What I mean is' – she hesitated – 'I don't know what I mean.'

'It's okay,' he said, in a voice that was surprisingly calm, 'I feel a bit like one of those old-age pensioners who has just been conned out of their life savings by a complete stranger but, apart from that, I'm fine.'

'Oh, Tom. I'm so sorry. I know you really liked her.'

'No,' he said, 'I didn't.' When she looked sceptical, he added, 'I mean, she wasn't real, Helen. I really liked the person I thought Lena was, but this person was not Lena. She was an invention. Lena died of a drug overdose seven years ago. I don't even know who this person is, but I'm going to find out.'

'It's chilling, isn't it? To be so intimate with someone then to find out you don't know them at all,' she reflected, then realised she was probably making him feel worse. 'Sorry.'

'No, that's an accurate description of my feelings right now. I keep churning it all over and trying to make some sense of it, but I can't, not fully, and do you know the bit I can't even begin to get my head around?'

'What?'

'She didn't approach us, Helen,' Tom said, '*we* approached her. You did, in fact. She was just sitting there in the hotel.'

'Reading your book,' Helen reminded him, 'which was a signal that was surely going to be noticed by one of us.'

'But she didn't know us. She couldn't have known we would be there in that hotel on that day.'

Helen frowned. He was right. How the hell could Lena have known they used the hotel? She thought about this for a long time, then a look of realization came over her face. 'That profile piece on you in the newspaper after the Sandra Jarvis case,' she announced. 'You said you worked as a freelancer but you didn't need an office. You just hung out in the bar of the hotel every day instead. The reporter even joked that it might harm your liver. They named the hotel. Thousands of people would have known where you spent your days after that. Lena was just one of them.'

'Oh dear God,' he said. She was right.

'All she had to do was turn up a few times and hold the book so that we could see it. That, and the way she looked . . . she must have figured it would be enough. Ironically, you came over all modest that day.' She looked guilty. 'But I went up to her for you, so it was all my fault. I'm really sorry, Tom.'

'You're the last person I blame. Oh, Helen, I am such an idiot. I believed every word she bloody told me. I've been conned, pure and simple, out-thought and out-bloody-smarted.'

'No, you haven't,' said Helen. 'And Lena is about to find that out.'

As promised, Ian returned the following afternoon to share his findings with Tom and to see what progress he had made on the favour he asked for. Tom seemed a lot calmer than Bradshaw would have expected.

'We always meet in pubs,' observed Bradshaw. 'Have you noticed that?'

'I figured I might need a drink by the time you'd finished,' said Tom.

'Fair enough.' He sat down next to him.

They were in the Market Tavern again. The last time Tom had visited the pub he had been asking the bar staff about Jess, desperate to help the woman he had thought of as Lena to find her sister.

'I used to drink here a lot,' said Tom, 'when I was young and carefree.'

'You're still young, you just don't feel it,' he told Tom. 'I spoke to my contact in the Met, described your friend then asked him to send me pictures of female associates of the Flynn family around that age.'

'And?'

Bradshaw handed him a long roll of thin white paper that had curled up on itself when it spooled out of the fax machine at Durham police headquarters. 'The pictures aren't great, but this was the quickest way. He sent me a dozen images.'

'Who are they?' asked Tom, scanning the pictures one after another.

'Con artists, pickpockets, coke dealers, hookers or immediate family members. All women in the close circle of the Flynn crew.'

'Christ,' said Tom when he saw her. 'That's Lena.' He felt foolish, since he knew that couldn't be her real name. She was younger in the photograph by a good five years and her hair was different, but he recognized her all right. She was staring out of a police mugshot. 'What did she do?'

'She was arrested as part of a long con involving an impoverished aristocrat, some bogus time-share properties in Spain and hundreds of thousands of pounds of missing deposit money from dozens of victims.'

'Did she do time?'

'Wasn't even charged in the end. The aristo suddenly copped for everything and claimed it was all his idea. She was just a girlfriend who hadn't realized it was a con. He got four years and she walked.'

'Someone must have had a word with him.'

'I reckon so. My man in the Met thinks he was a patsy. They used him to put a veneer of respectability on their scheme but she was the brains behind it. The Flynn family threatened him and he took all the blame.'

Tom exhaled, steadying himself. 'Okay then, so what's her real name?'

'That's the interesting part,' said Bradshaw, and he pointed at the photograph. 'This is Mia Flynn, daughter of Padraig Flynn and sister to Fergus and young Aidan.'

'Jesus Christ.'

'Sorry, Tom, but it turns out you've been sleeping with a mafia princess.'

Neither man spoke at all during the next pint. Instead they drank solemnly while Tom digested the fact that he had been seeing the daughter and sister of some of the most notoriously violent men in Britain. Even if Bradshaw had felt like consoling him, there really were no words that would have done the situation justice, so he tried the only two that made any sense at all right then.

'Same again?'

Tom nodded, and Bradshaw went to fetch two more pints from the bar.

Bradshaw reasoned that if he couldn't adequately console Tom, he could at least help him with his situation. 'I asked my guy at the Met about that private eye you told me about,' said Bradshaw, 'the one you said took a beating. I think I might know the reason why he got his legs broken.'

'I assume it was because he was stringing them along, and not getting any results,' said Tom.

'He has been known to play both ends of the game.' When

Tom didn't understand this, Bradshaw explained, 'Say you think your wife is cheating on you, so you hire a private investigator to catch her out, and he does. He's supposed to keep that private and report back to you without her knowing. You can then decide whether you want to confront her, divorce her, stay with her, whatever.'

'Right.'

'But instead of dropping her in it, our private detective approaches the wife and explains that her husband is on to her. He can tell the husband she is cheating, or he can say he never found any evidence against her and make this little problem go away, but she has to pay him.'

'Blackmail,' said Tom. 'My sympathy for that PI just evaporated. So you think he may have approached Jess and tried to extort money from the girl instead of shopping her?'

'He has a history of that kind of behaviour, according to my source at the Met. It's not such a high risk with a normal client, but perhaps he didn't realize which family was hiring him . . .'

'It would explain why he found Jess but let her slip through his fingers. Normally, you'd expect him to alert his client and let them approach her, but he spoke to Jess himself and she ran.'

'Understandably,' said Bradshaw. 'I think he struggled to explain that to his client and they were less than forgiving.'

'It would explain the two broken legs,' said Tom. 'Mia Flynn realized that I needed to know whether someone had searched for Jess already. I'd be following in their footsteps and I'd probably hear about someone else having asked questions. She made it sound like she was warning me to be careful.'

'You should be careful,' Bradshaw warned him. 'You've already upset half the gangsters in Newcastle, and the Flynns control large parts of London. If they come after you too, you'll need to dig a moat round that house of yours.'

'I hear you,' said Tom, 'and I owe you.' He fished into his

bag and brought out an envelope. 'I hope this goes some way towards paying my debt.' He passed it to Bradshaw, who opened it and slid out some printed pages.

'That looks amazing.' He marvelled at what Tom had created. 'You've even got the masthead with the paper's name on it. How did you do this?'

'Desktop publishing. I can write a story, give it pictures and borders, headlines and bylines, all thanks to our expensive computer.'

'Thanks for doing this,' said Bradshaw.

'Like I said, I owe you. I got you to help me aid a criminal family in finding a key witness. I almost made you an accomplice to a murder.'

'I won't be telling anyone about that, if you don't. If anybody asks, I'll say you had your suspicions about Lena . . . sorry, Mia . . . all along and asked me to check out her story for you.'

'But that's not true, Officer,' said Tom dryly.

'It's a version of the truth,' answered Bradshaw, 'and one I am significantly more comfortable with.'

'You'll make detective inspector yet.'

Bradshaw read Tom's work carefully then, taking in every word.

'What do you think?' asked Tom when he had finished.

'I think it's quite possibly the best thing you have ever written.'

'Thanks, but will it work?'

'I don't know,' admitted Bradshaw. 'Maybe. It was Helen's idea, by the way.'

'Helen suggested this?' Tom was shocked.

'Not specifically, but she said the only way to get Adrian Wicklow to give up what he knew was for me to make him care about the outcome.' Bradshaw held up the fake paper. 'And I think he'll care about this. I reckon he will care very much.'

49

A familiar figure was emerging from Durham jail as the detective approached. Ian Bradshaw had seen many distraught men in his time – men arrested for capital crimes then sent down for long prison sentences with little hope at the end of them, men who had lost loved ones to murder or some avoidable, tragic accident, men like Barry Meade, who had been ground down by years of stress and anguish – but Father Noonan looked as devastated as any of them when he left the prison that morning.

'Father Noonan?' he called, and the priest turned towards Bradshaw, looking as if God Himself had personally excommunicated him. 'What's wrong?'

Adrian Wicklow looked even more smug than usual that morning.

'I've just seen Father Noonan outside.' Bradshaw told him.

'Is he still upset with me?' That innocent voice again, as if Wicklow had no idea how he could have offended anyone.

'He said you had converted,' Bradshaw told Wicklow.

'That's right.'

'But not to Catholicism?' said Bradshaw. 'To Islam.'

'Yes.' There was a gleam in Wicklow's eyes.

'A little sudden, isn't it, this conversion to a completely different faith?'

'It may seem sudden to you, Detective, but I have very little time left.'

'How long has Father Noonan been visiting you here, Wicklow?'

'Twice a week for fourteen years now.'

'Really? And, from what I gather, he was the only one who bothered after your mother died.' He thought for the moment. 'That's about fourteen hundred hours the man wasted on you, and this is how you repay him? By giving him the big fuck-you then pretending you need an imam with you when you go? What a joke.'

'I'll tell you what's a joke; a supposed holy man latching on to a murderer, hoping to save him from the wrath of God Almighty and get himself to heaven on the back of it. Father Noonan wanted to be in here at the very end, holding my hand in one palm and a bible in the other while I drew my last breath. He hoped I'd make him famous. Now he knows the truth. He's been wasting his time.'

'Then I won't waste any more of mine.'

'I wondered when you were going to get to the point. I did leave word at the gate that I no longer wished to see you.'

'And yet here you are. I figured you would want to read this.' He handed Wicklow the envelope.

'What is it?'

'Your obituary.'

This was the first time Bradshaw had ever seen Adrian Wicklow look unsure of himself. He looked shocked, in fact. 'My. . .'

'Obituary,' repeated Bradshaw. He said the word slowly.

Wicklow stared at the envelope, then back at Bradshaw, who was regarding him calmly. The child killer opened the envelope and drew out the pages containing Tom's work.

'How did you get this?'

'My journalist friend was very interested when I told him I had listened to your story.'

'Journalists are not allowed access to my memoirs,' Wicklow reminded him.

'Not directly, but if someone were to listen to that book then leak information from it to a journalist, well, there really wouldn't be much that could be done about it, particularly with you dead and all.'

'What are you saying?'

'I'm saying my friend has already been privy to information no other journalist has had, which means he is the perfect man to write an obituary of the child killer Adrian Wicklow, one that will be so devastating every newspaper in the country will want to run with the story.'

'They can write what they like. They never understood me. Do you think I care what they say about me when I am gone?'

'Yes,' said Bradshaw. 'I think you *will* care.' And he seemed so sure that Wicklow began to read.

Moments passed. Bradshaw watched as Wicklow silently read Tom's article. The room was so quiet all Bradshaw could hear was the sound of a bird chirruping outside the window. Then, halfway down the page, Wicklow's head shot up. 'What the hell is this?'

'I told you, Wicklow, it's your obituary, the account of your life every newspaper will run with the day after they put you in the ground. I'm going to see to that personally.'

'They can't . . . you can't . . . this isn't right . . . I never . . . *ever* did that . . . you've got to tell your friend. He can't write this about me.' He jabbed the paper with his finger.

As Bradshaw watched, Adrian Wicklow become more and more distressed at the words he was now speed-reading. Bradshaw himself was experiencing a sudden deep inner calm. 'Which bit do you object to, Wicklow? Is it the part about killing the children or the bit about running the police and bereaved families ragged for years, offering them false hope then luxuriating in their distress?'

304

'You can't say this!' He was gesticulating wildly now. 'This isn't true . . . this isn't fair . . . it isn't fair on her.'

'Which bit, Wicklow?' asked Bradshaw innocently. 'Which part isn't fair, exactly? Show me.'

As Wicklow turned the paper so Bradshaw could see it, he pressed his finger on the offending passage, but he needn't have bothered. Bradshaw already knew which section of the obituary had upset him so deeply.

'Oh that,' the detective responded calmly, and he took the obituary back from Wicklow and began to read it calmly aloud.

'"Adrian Wicklow's father died when he was very young and he had no childhood friends. Wicklow was brought up almost entirely by his mother. In his own autobiography, written in prison, Wicklow describes an unnaturally close relationship that became more intense as the boy grew older and eventually became sexual. Wicklow has admitted sleeping with his mother regularly throughout his teenage years, even speculating that their incestuous physical relationship may in some way have been the root cause of his monstrous crimes."'

'But it's not true!'

'Isn't it?' asked Bradshaw. 'We've long ago given up trying to work out the difference between truth and lies, as far as you're concerned.' He shrugged amiably.

Wicklow was fighting to control himself now. Bradshaw could read the struggle in his face. 'I never did *that*!' He shook his head violently. 'Not with my own mother. How could anyone believe that?'

'They'll all believe it. Most people think every word they read in the newspapers is true. You know that. In this case, it's very straightforward. You grew up an only child without a father and were mollycoddled by your lonely mother. You admitted in your own memoir that you had regular sexual relations with her starting from the age of thirteen and continuing long into adulthood.'

'We did not! I never said that!'

'Maybe you did, maybe you didn't. But, really, who's ever going to know for certain?'

To Bradshaw's astonishment, Wicklow's eyes began to water. They were tears of grief and frustration. 'My mother was a good person,' he gasped. 'My mother never did anything bad to anyone. You can't slander a dead woman like this. You can't turn my mummy into a monster!'

'I can, and I'm going to.'

'Why?' roared Wicklow, and the tears started to really fall now, attracting the attention of the two prison guards, but they made no move to intervene. Instead, they seemed captivated by the spectacle. They'd never seen Adrian Wicklow like this before and were clearly enjoying it.

'Because it will hurt you,' explained Bradshaw, 'and it is the only way I can think of to get to you. I feel sorry for your mum, sure, but she's dead, and no pain I can inflict will ever be as hard as knowing she gave birth to a sick, twisted monster who delighted in killing little children. Compared to that, this is nothing. She's already gone. When you follow her, I'm going to go to the families of every victim so I can tell them how I watched you blub and plead with me not to tell the world that you fucked your own mother, then we'll all have a good laugh about it.'

'No, please.'

But Bradshaw was smiling at him.

'Are you finished?' asked the detective. 'Because I am.'

'You can't —'

'I can and I will.' He got to his feet. 'I only wish I'd thought of it sooner.'

'I'm begging you not to do this.'

'Go on, then, beg. I'd enjoy that. Your victims begged, and I know you loved it. Now it's my turn.'

In desperation, the murderer tore the sheet of paper into pieces and let out a howl of rage. Bradshaw laughed. 'It's not the only copy, you know.'

'Don't do this!' He was trying to get at Bradshaw now, but the two burly prison guards reached him just as he lunged. They grabbed the killer by both arms and dragged him away. 'No!' he roared. 'Let me go! No! Don't let him leave! He can't do this!'

Bradshaw waited til they had almost reached the door. He wanted to time it just right. Wicklow was shouting and howling and stretching out an arm to grasp the air in front of him, as if it were Bradshaw's throat.

'I'd love to help you, but there's nothing I can do,' the detective told him.

Wicklow let out a great bellow as he was bundled through the door.

50

The world seemed a happier, more optimistic place somehow. Ian Bradshaw's whole mood had lifted and he caught himself smiling at the unlikely nature of this victory. No one could have seen that coming.

It was amazing the effect a game of football could have on you.

'Four–one,' he said to Tom and Helen. 'Can you believe that?' He didn't even mind the pub blasting out 'Football's Coming Home!' at full volume for the thousandth time that summer. 'Four–bloody one.' He blinked in disbelief. 'England just beat Holland.'

'No, they didn't,' Tom corrected him. 'England just *thrashed* Holland.'

'I'm assuming neither of you was expecting that,' offered Helen, for they had both been jumping up and down and punching the air as the goals went in.

'No,' said Tom. 'Which makes you, officially, our lucky mascot.' He put his arm around her and gave her a squeeze. 'So you are not allowed to leave our side.'

'At least until England lose,' clarified Bradshaw.

'Stop talking about losing,' ordered Tom. 'England aren't going to lose. Be positive, man. Where are you going?'

'Home,' said Bradshaw, 'I can't drink with you on a school night, and I have a very big day tomorrow.'

'You sure about that?'

'No. Well, I don't know,' admitted Bradshaw. 'Maybe Wicklow will crumble or perhaps he'll realize we're bluffing.'

'A lot will depend on how convincing you were,' said Tom, 'playing a bastard.'

'Who said I was playing?'

The next day, there was no contact from Adrian Wicklow or from anyone representing him. Nor on the next. By the third day, it had become clear to Bradshaw that his final gambit had failed.

He had been so sure it would work, and his conviction had only been heightened by Wicklow's hysterical reaction to the fake obituary with its slur against his beloved mother. Now Bradshaw began to doubt there would ever be a way to persuade Wicklow to do anything against his will.

Just when he was beginning to feel very low, and as if things could hardly get any worse, Bradshaw was summoned to Kane's office.

'Have you cracked it yet then, lad?' his DCI demanded as soon as the detective sergeant was in his office. 'Wicklow's madness,' he added simply. 'Wasn't that what you were meant to be unravelling from his bloody life story?'

'Yes, sir,' said Bradshaw. 'I have.'

'Out with it then.' And Bradshaw was forced to somehow explain Wicklow's twisted motives to Kane. The DCI's frowns grew deeper with every word. 'Mad as a box of frogs,' Kane concluded when Bradshaw had finished. 'More to the point, will he now cooperate?'

'No, sir.' When Kane looked disgusted, he added: 'As predicted.' Bradshaw could have added the words *by me*, but he didn't.

'Jesus Christ!' exclaimed Kane, most probably with the chief constable's probable reaction to this gloomy news in mind. 'So what's your plan B?' he demanded, as if that were a simple matter.

'I'd rather not say, sir.'

'You'd rather not . . .' began Kane, who looked as if he was about to blow a gasket. 'What do you mean, lad? I'm not asking here!'

'Plausible deniability,' said Bradshaw calmly.

'What's that supposed to mean?'

'It's a political phrase they use in the States, sir. It means that if I don't tell you what I am doing, you will never have a problem denying you knew about it, should anyone ever find out.'

Kane looked at Bradshaw for a long, hard moment. Bradshaw realized the cogs were whirring. His DCI was irked at being kept in the dark but was starting to understand it might be best for his career at this juncture if he was.

'Wilful ignorance, you mean?' Kane was not an unintelligent man, and he was catching on quick.

'For now,' Bradshaw said. 'It's better this way.'

Kane exhaled. 'All right,' he conceded grudgingly. 'But I hope for your sake you know what you're bloody doing.'

'Yes, sir,' Bradshaw said, because he wasn't about to admit that he didn't.

'Get on with it then,' ordered his DCI when Bradshaw failed to leave.

'Actually, sir, there was something I needed to discuss with you about all this.'

'All what?'

'The Susan Verity case,' said Bradshaw, 'and some suspicious activity linked to it.'

'Suspicious activity,' parroted Kane, 'by who?'

'By us, sir.'

When the call finally came it was direct from the governor. 'Adrian Wicklow has taken a turn for the worse,' he told Bradshaw, then he added: 'Health-wise,' as if he couldn't have worsened in any other way. 'He's been in the hospital wing for a couple of days but is now stable. I'm calling you because he has been requesting that you go to see him – repeatedly.'

'Has he? The deterioration in Wicklow's health would explain the delay in contacting the detective, and that gave Ian Bradshaw renewed hope and a stronger hand to play.

'My staff report that they have never seen him so agitated. Could I ask what happened at your last meeting with him?'

'We discussed a number of things,' answered Bradshaw, 'and your officers were in the room at all times.'

'Yes,' said the governor, 'but they were surprisingly vague about it. It seems they can't recall too much of the conversation.' He waited for Bradshaw to speak but. when he shed no further light on the subject. he said, 'Anyway, he wishes to see you.'

'Well, my visiting him is entirely conditional.'

'Upon what?'

'Whether he has something for me.'

'I believe he has. I think he may even be prepared to tell you what you want to know.'

'What makes you think that, Governor?'

'His actual words were *call Bradshaw and tell him he has won.*' There was a tone of incredulity. 'That's not a phrase I am accustomed to hearing from Wicklow, Detective, believe me.'

An hour after he hung up the phone, Ian Bradshaw was back in the airless room at Durham jail, sitting opposite a pale, sickly and unhappy-looking Adrian Wicklow.

'I'm a very busy man, Adrian: people to see, villains to catch – you know how it is.' He looked at his watch. 'You have five minutes, then I'm out of here. I don't even know why I came back, to be honest. Our business is concluded.'

'It's not concluded.' Wicklow's voice was barely audible. Was he trying to control himself? 'You can't let that journalist print those lies.'

'Why not?' asked Bradshaw brightly. 'You've been lying to everyone for years: claiming you did stuff then saying you didn't, agreeing to meet the relatives then giving them nothing, saying you knew where the bodies were, then you couldn't recall their location, after all. You've led everyone on a merry little dance. One more lie won't hurt.'

'What do you want?'

'Me?' asked Bradshaw, and pointed at himself. 'You know what I want – the location of the bodies. But you didn't want to help, so it's too late now.'

'Then why are you here?'

'You asked me to come.' Bradshaw reminded him. 'And, to be honest. I genuinely enjoy watching you suffer. That's a pretty good reason, don't you think?' One of the prison guards smirked at this behind Wicklow's back.

'I can cope with dying,' Wicklow told him, 'but I cannot accept this. Not my mother . . . she never did anything . . . not my mum . . . please.'

Bradshaw savoured the child killer's distress. 'Why should I?'

'I'll do anything . . . please.'

Bradshaw waited until he was sure Wicklow meant what he said, then reached into the bag he had brought with him.

'I'm going to give you one chance.' He took out a map of the county. '*One!*' He emphasized the word then placed the map on the table and spun it so they could both see it side on. 'If you mess me about or lie to me, if you fail to cooperate, I swear I will go back to my reporter friend and we will make the current version of your obituary sound like an Enid Blyton story. Everyone who reads it will say your mother was the most twisted woman in history, got it?'

The child killer nodded weakly.

'You know what I want. Three bodies – their exact locations – and I want them now. If we find the bodies of those poor children, I might think again about that obituary we're going to run, but if we don't find them . . .' He spread his palms as if the outcome would be entirely out of his control.

'It's been years . . . I'm not sure I can remember . . .'

'You remember everything!' Bradshaw banged his fist down hard on the table, making Wicklow jump. 'You'll give me what I want today, then you can crawl back into your cell and die. No one will give a shit but at least they won't all be talking about your mum the day after you go.'

'All right,' Wicklow said weakly, and he transferred his attention to the map. 'But if I do this, you have to promise . . . you have to swear –'

'I swear that if we find the three bodies we will not print that obituary involving your mother.' Bradshaw paused then and looked Wicklow right in the eye. 'But there's one more thing I want, Adrian.' It was the first time Bradshaw had used the killer's first name.

'What?'

'The truth about Susan Verity. All of it.'

Wicklow looked Bradshaw directly in the eye then closed his own eyes and nodded, as if in surrender.

'Tell me what happened,' Bradshaw commanded. 'Were you there the day Susan Verity died?'

There was a long pause. Bradshaw wondered if Wicklow was trying to recall the events of that day or whether this was just born out of habit. Adrian Wicklow did not like to give away anything easily, particularly the Crown jewels.

'I was there that day,' he began. 'I saw her . . . I followed her . . . but I did not kill her.' He waited for a reaction from the detective and, when none came, said, 'That's the truth.'

'Well, if you didn't kill her,' asked Bradshaw, 'who did?'

51

1976

Wicklow kept going, despite the heat. He was a young man who could walk a long way under normal circumstances, but the sun was baking down on him. His collar was rough and itchy and there was a large sweat stain on his back where the shirt clung to him because it was flattened to his skin by his knapsack. He'd walked miles, it seemed, across fields and down lanes with deep, rutted tracks in them, caused by the wheels of heavy tractors that had carved their imprints into the land during the wet spring, and were now preserved in dried, baked mud.

He'd come too far. He knew that. Wicklow had left his car way behind him, at the other end of the village. If he were to act now it would be to invite the possibility of capture.

But it was also too far to turn back empty-handed.

He hadn't seen a soul apart from a solitary farmer who walked past him without a glance and an old lady at the entrance to the country lane who eyed him suspiciously, as if she knew what he was about. She seemed to see straight through him, right to his core.

But since then? Nothing. Wicklow had trudged on and on, reluctant to give in to the heat and his fatigue without reward for his efforts. The need burned deep in him that morning and he had to feed the hunger.

Then he saw them in the distance.

Five – no, six – of them. Three boys and three girls; he knew it was unlikely then. It was too difficult if they stuck together, but he could follow and watch them, looking for possibilities or signs of weakness. Something told Wicklow there was an opportunity here.

He almost gave up several times, but there were so many rows over this and that, and the children's raised voices told him there was no harmony here. Someone would storm off in tears in the end, he just knew it.

Then they all left the den together and headed back towards the village. He cursed. He'd wasted so much time watching them in this stifling heat and now they were all going home together. It was always possible they would split into smaller and smaller groups until one was on their own, but it was much riskier if it happened among the houses, where people might notice him and intervene. He thought of calling it off – until they went into the farmer's barn to play. He decided to give them a little longer then, and he got the stroke of luck he had been waiting for. They all came running out screaming, as if a demon were chasing them, not a red-faced, irate farmer who stamped and swore and scattered the children in the direction of the woods. This was more than he could have hoped for.

Wicklow followed. The terrain was perfect for him, so many trees and bushes and sections of high ground overlooking it all. It was as if the stretch of countryside here was designed for his purpose. What a pity he would only be able to take advantage of it once. He was determined to make the most of it.

One of the girls had disappeared and he reasoned she must have run off home on her own. Two of the boys were playing near the bushes, and they were soon joined by one of the girls, but that ended pretty quickly and the girl ran off. Wicklow followed her. He lost her for a while but caught up with her. She was walking with a boy.

They were heading for the quarry. What happened there would end in death, but not the way he expected.

Wicklow took up a perfect position behind some large clumps

of spiny bushes taller than he was. He was able to see everything through a gap in them, watching without being seen. He saw the two of them – the boy and the girl – and what unfolded before him was a fascinating little drama. He couldn't quite believe it at first and wondered if they had staged it all for his pleasure.

First came the dare, for that was surely what it was, the boy reluctant, the girl cajoling, the boy weakening, and then out he went.

But not for long. He didn't get far before he came back again, almost slipping to his death in the process.

He must have been rattled then, and what did the girl do? Wicklow couldn't hear all the words but he could tell she was mocking him for his lack of courage. 'You've not gone half a yard!' she shouted at one point. He moved closer so he could hear them.

The boy was desperately trying to get back on to solid land now. His feet were on the edge of the plateau but he was leaning backwards at an awkward angle and struggling to get himself upright again. One of his feet skidded and gave way, only his grip on the wire saving him. He let out a sound that was part cry and part sob. That shut her up. He looked terrified now, and used all his strength to haul himself upwards. His foot found a firm hold again and he finally pulled himself back to safety. He virtually fell on to the ground and, as he got to his feet, his relief turned to anger, and he lashed out at the girl who had mocked him.

'Ow!' she cried as his punch landed hard on her arm.

'That's for laughing at me!' He was furious, but she met his rage with her own.

'You don't hit girls!' she roared. 'You're not supposed to hit girls when you're a boy!' She brought her hand to the spot where he had punched her and angry tears flowed. 'You're horrible, and I'm going to tell everyone you hit girls!' But she wasn't finished yet. Whatever she said to him next was lost on the wind. Wicklow couldn't hear the words she hissed at him but he could see the spite and the relish in her face as she said them. The fury in the boy's face was just as evident.

'That's a lie!'

He took a step towards the girl and pushed her hard, stooped to scoop up a stone and hurled it blindly at her, letting out a roar as he did so. It struck the girl hard on the temple. A shot in a million.

She fell backwards with a shrill cry of pain and alarm and then slipped, falling first into then through the bushes that bordered the edge of the plateau. Wicklow thought she was lost. The bushes couldn't possibly have held the weight of an adult but the girl passed into them as if they were trying to catch her. Even from this distance he could hear the sound of branches snapping and leaves rustling as they were disturbed.

The girl went right over the edge, only the bushes keeping her from falling into oblivion, but they were giving way now. Wicklow's excitement grew. She flailed helplessly and tried to get back out, but she couldn't. She called something. It sounded like it might be the boy's name.

The boy scrambled towards her, desperate to prevent her from falling. He would reach out soon and might even be able to save her.

Then he stopped.

Wicklow watched in astonishment as the boy halted. He looked down at the desperate girl and did nothing.

The girl realized he was not going to help her. In that instant, she must have known she was finished.

The bushes parted and gave way and the girl slipped backwards through them and fell with a shrill scream that died on the wind.

Then there was silence.

Wicklow hadn't been expecting that outcome and his mouth fell open in shock when it happened. It was so stunning and glorious. One minute here and the next moment gone. The enormity of it would sustain his hunger for weeks. Even years later he would revisit the feelings of pleasure over and over again.

Wicklow watched the boy for a time, enjoying his shock and disbelief, then approached him silently.

'I saw it all,' he said through the fence, making the boy start and whirl towards him. 'I saw everything. I know what you did.'

'No,' the boy protested, and shook his head violently, the tears already there. 'No, it was an accident. I never did anything. I didn't mean it . . . it was an accident!'

Wicklow reached down then and peeled the wire fence back and upwards as if it were a piece of thin paper to be torn. He bent low and stepped through. He was on the plateau now and he walked right up to the boy then placed a hand firmly on his shoulder. The boy couldn't move. There would be no hope of escape.

'Yes,' said Wicklow reassuringly, 'it was an accident.' The boy could not hide his surprise. He must have been wondering if the man had really seen everything, after all. 'That's what you must tell them if they find out' – he peered over the edge, saw the girl's crumpled body far below and thought for a while – 'but they won't find out.'

For a moment, Wicklow contemplated pushing the boy over too, so he would follow the little girl and they'd end up down there together. Instead, they stood side by side, the child killer and the little boy, staring at the broken body of Susan Verity, united by their secret.

He turned and the boy peered up at him. Wicklow saw the fear and anticipation he always witnessed just before the light went out, but there was something else too.

Excitement.

He could see it in the young boy's eyes.

'Don't worry. No one will ever know what really happened here.' He smiled warmly at the boy. 'It'll be our little secret.'

52

'You're saying Susan Verity was killed by a little boy,' said Bradshaw in disbelief. 'One of her playmates?'

'Yes.'

'Why?'

'I don't know.'

'You said you witnessed it.'

'I did, but I didn't hear everything. I was too far away. I didn't want them to notice me. I was still hoping they would split up, like the others, and I could choose one to' – he spread his palms as if it was obvious what he had intended to do – 'but in the end I didn't need to. The boy did it for me.'

'There was an argument of some sort?'

'So it would seem.'

'And at the end of it the boy –'

'Threw the rock which hit the girl, but she might have lived if he had gone to her.'

'He didn't go to her. He could have saved her?'

'But he let her fall,' Wicklow assured him.

'Jesus, why didn't you reveal all of this before?'

'I enjoyed stringing you all along. I like to see the anguish on a copper's face, and it made no difference to me whether they thought I did it or not. I was already going down for the others. You can only serve a full life sentence once. They didn't even charge me in the end. There was no body, no proof of foul play, just a missing girl and her grieving parents.'

'What happened to the body?'

'Oh, I handled that.'

'What did you do?'

'I told the boy to wait, then I went back round the perimeter of the quarry. On the far side there was a way down, a tiny path. I had to climb over the wire fence to get to it. It was steep and completely overgrown. It took me a while to get down there.

'When I reached her, the girl was lying on the rocks not far from the water. I used it to wash away any traces of blood once I'd removed her. You wouldn't have known she was ever there.'

'But the body?' pressed Bradshaw. 'Where is the body?'

'I couldn't just leave it. She had landed on her back and I could see she had a bloody big mark where the stone hit her forehead. It was obvious that was the blow that had sent her over the edge. I took her body to a big clump of winny bushes. You know what they're like – the thorny gorse bushes with those sickly smelling yellow flowers on them. I figured anyone looking in the quarry would be expecting that the girl would have fallen by accident; they wouldn't be thinking she might be buried there. Even if they did, the smell of those bushes would disguise quite a lot. I found a nice gap right in the middle of the bushes, and I dug.'

'What with? Your bare hands? Don't tell me you carried a shovel around with you, Wicklow. I won't buy that.'

'I had my little bag of tricks with me.' Then he explained: 'A knapsack containing a lock knife, a length of rope, a little blanket for sitting on, sandwiches and a water bottle to make out like I was on a day's hiking, and a trowel for digging. All innocuous stuff but very handy. The trowel made relatively short work of the sandy soil. It was hot down there, but I managed.'

'So you did all this just to put two fingers up at the police?'

'That wasn't the only reason,' admitted Wicklow. 'It was the boy.' There was a look of amused pride on the killer's face.

'He was a protégé,' offered Bradshaw. 'Wasn't he?'

'Oh, very good,' admitted Wicklow. 'You're a lot smarter than you look, you know. I never had any contact with that little boy again but I saw something in him that I recognized in myself.'

'What?'

'Hurt and anger, resentment, the sadness that comes from knowing you will never truly fit in, no matter how hard you try.' He sighed, as if this realization were somehow new and fresh to him. 'The knowledge, even at that tender age, that contentment will always elude you.'

'That why you didn't kill him?' asked Bradshaw, and Wicklow nodded. 'Or hand him in?'

Wicklow smiled. 'I wasn't going to cage that little bird. What a waste it would have been. All these years, I have imagined him still out there' – he smiled – 'making mischief.'

'Which one?' Bradshaw urged him. He was so close to the truth now. 'There were three boys there that day. Who did it?'

Wicklow looked at him blankly then. 'I have no idea,' he said after a while, then, by way of explanation, added, 'No, really, I honestly haven't. I never even bothered to ask his name.'

53

It took Helen a while to get what Ian needed and, even then, it was from an unlikely source. There was nothing in the case files, she knew that already, so there was no point dredging through them all again, and she didn't want to ask any of the boys. She decided to call Andrea, but she did not have what Helen was looking for either.

She would just have to bite the bullet and go to the boys themselves, but Danny Gilbert still wasn't back and neither was Billy Thorpe.

In desperation, she went to Kevin Robson's home, and was greeted by his crabby grandma, who told her he was fishing at the gravel pit again. Helen wondered if he ever did anything else.

'Actually, I was wondering if you could help me,' she said. Helen told the old woman about her role with the police and how there was a new witness – she did not say it was Wicklow – who claimed to have information on the whereabouts of Susan Verity's body. Helen explained that they needed to ensure this witness was not a time-waster, and she wondered if Kevin's grandmother might have any old photographs of the boys they could use to see if he recognized them.

'I took a picture of them that morning,' she told Helen. 'With my old Box Brownie. They were explorers,' she explained, 'and wanted a photo.'

'Do you still have it?'

'Somewhere.'

'Would you mind if I borrowed it?' She fully expected the woman to say no.

'If it'll help you find out what happened to poor little Susan.'

'It will,' she said, though she did not want to tell the old lady her grandson was now one of the three main suspects.

'Come in then. It might take me a while to find it.'

It did take the old lady a while but, eventually, she re-emerged with a shoebox stuffed with ancient photographs. She went through them until she found the one she was looking for and handed it to Helen. Three young boys staring unsmilingly at the camera; in fact, they looked very serious. 'See,' said Kevin's grandma, 'explorers,' as if that explained the lack of smiles. Exploring was a serious business when you were ten.

Helen gazed at the photograph, a moment caught in time, three unknowing friends who would be involved in a tragedy just hours later that would shape their lives – but who was the cause of it: Billy, Danny or Kevin?

'Mickle Fell?' asked the SOCO in disbelief. 'Do you realize how big it is?'

'I'm not suggesting you dig up the whole mountain,' Bradshaw told him and the rest of the sceptical people gathered in the briefing room. 'There are large stone posts marking the walk up to it. Wicklow reckons he buried the bodies at the beginning of that walk so he wouldn't have to carry them far. I've marked the location on the map and the number of one of the first boundary posts. Concentrate on an area no more than ten paces off the track directly behind that post and you might find something.'

'Might,' scoffed someone.

'How did he bury these bodies without anyone seeing him?' asked another dissenting voice, from the back of the room.

'He claims he took them up there after dark and did it by lamplight.'

'And you believe him?' The newest voice sounded like its owner might have been asking him if he believed in fairies.

Bradshaw didn't want to say whether he believed Wicklow or not. 'We'll see, won't we?'

There was some further muttering, and more hostility than Bradshaw had been expecting. 'I know there is always doubt with Wicklow . . .' he began.

'Doubt? The only thing that's guaranteed where Wicklow is concerned is that he's lying.' It was the same man who had asked how Wicklow could have buried the bodies without being seen. There were murmurs of agreement.

'I know,' said Bradshaw, 'but I am asking you to give it one last try.'

And when it was clear the room was no more enthused by that prospect, DCI Kane intervened. He had watched and listened impassively until now. 'Bradshaw here is no bigger fan of Wicklow than you, me or anyone else,' he said, 'but he has been visiting the bastard for a reason and *this* is that reason. Now quit your griping and your moaning and go out there and examine that site like professionals, for the sake of the families of those missing children,' he ordered. 'Unless one of you has a better idea?'

Silence.

'On your way then.' The room swiftly cleared.

For once, Bradshaw was grateful for his DCI's intervention. 'And Susan Verity?' asked the DCI.

'A team is already down at the quarry,' Bradshaw told him, 'but there's a fair bit of ground at the far end and it's all covered by those bloody bushes. It'll take time, maybe even a couple of days, but all we can do is let them get on with it and wait.'

'That's always the worst part of this job, the waiting. Listen, I've been doing a bit of digging of my own.' When Bradshaw shot him a look, he said, 'I'm sorry, that's in poor taste. I'd like a word, though, on the QT. I have some information that will help you to focus on the right areas of your investigation.' He nodded towards his office. Bradshaw followed him there.

'This is a bit delicate,' said Kane, once they were inside with the door closed behind them. 'Deniable, in fact.'

'Deniable?'

'Meaning I will deny it if you tell anyone,' snapped Kane. 'Got it?'

'Er, yes, sir. Got it.'

'I asked around,' said Kane, being deliberately vague, 'about some of your . . . concerns.'

'The missing notes from the case files,' said Bradshaw, determined to be specific. 'The farmer not having his gun taken off him, his links with one of our senior officers and the eyewitness being a trained observer but dismissed as a batty old lady?'

'Whoa, whoa, whoa!' said Kane, as if Bradshaw were a runaway horse. 'One thing at a time. First of all, the missing notes and the failure to assist our helpful local MP, yes, it was a cover-up, of sorts.'

Bradshaw was stunned to hear this. 'Oh, right,' was all he could think to say in response.

'Look, things were very different in the eighties. You weren't even in the force, but back then it was entirely acceptable if a child killer got a few slaps or a dig in the ribs on his way into custody. In fact, it was expected. Now, obviously, times have changed, and for good reason; it undermines your case if a man like Wicklow can claim he was tortured, forced into a confession. That's all he banged on about in the interview room at first.' Kane looked sheepish. 'Someone wrote down more about that than they should have done.' He coughed. 'That's why the notes disappeared.'

'What about the farmer?' he asked. 'Keeping his gun?'

'It shouldn't have happened, of course, but it isn't what you think either. Our senior man knew him, but only because he lived down the road. He didn't have a cosy word with the magistrates – the opposite, in fact. No one spoke to them, because none of our lads turned up that day in court. That's why he got to keep his gun, because nobody bothered to attend to say he might be dangerous. It's like your RAF observer lady. She was interviewed, probably by a DC, and they are not always the brightest, as you know. She tells him what she did in the war and he doesn't bother to write it down or tell his superior.'

'Why not, when it was relevant?'

'I don't know why not, because I wasn't that DC, but he made a mistake. You see, Bradshaw, what you call a cover-up is rarely what you think. There usually isn't some huge conspiracy involving criminality or friends in high places. No' – he shook his head – 'it's invariably someone realizing they cocked things up and being desperate to protect themselves. We all make mistakes,' he continued. 'If those mistakes go back far enough, the people who made them can often have become quite senior since and have a lot to lose if they are uncovered.' He added significantly. 'Sometimes, they can be very senior indeed. You get me?'

And Bradshaw did. He realized that, in his own way, Kane was being as honest with his subordinate as he could, and there was a reason for that. Kane understood that what Bradshaw took at first glance to be unaccountably corrupt behaviour by the members of the police force was in fact a simple enough case of an arse-covering exercise by embarrassed senior police officers. Good old-fashioned incompetence, in fact, and that knowledge was strangely cheering when compared to the alternative. Of course, it also meant his DCI had lied to him when he said that everyone involved in the case had since left the force.

*

Helen could hear the raised voices as she walked up the path, and her heart sank. Tom and Ian were arguing, and it sounded heated.

She let herself in cautiously and closed the door behind her, just as Tom told Ian he was 'talking out of his arse'.

Helen walked into the house and said, 'Calm down,' to them both, continuing: 'Whatever it is, we can fix this. Just tell me the problem and let's see if we can't reach a compromise.'

Both men stared at her for a second then fell about laughing.

'Okay,' she said, when no explanation was forthcoming. 'What's funny? I could hear you arguing all the way up the driveway.'

'We weren't arguing,' Tom explained, 'we were just disagreeing about the finer points of the football.'

'Oh, yes, the football. I forgot it was on. Did England win?'

'Spain had two goals disallowed and two penalties turned down,' explained Bradshaw. 'We only beat them in a penalty shoot-out, and *he* thinks we are going to go on and win the whole bloody thing.' He jerked his head at Tom.

'Oh, come on, Ian, the cup *is* actually half full sometimes, you know. What about Stuart Pearce banging in that penalty in the shoot-out? It was glorious!'

'It was,' said Bradshaw, 'but I think we used up all of our luck right there, that's all.'

'Jesus Christ!' Tom was exasperated. 'It's like watching football with Eeyore. You're a proper gloom merchant, do you know that?'

'I do,' he admitted. 'It's called being realistic.'

'Well, it must be exhausting,' said Tom. 'You have to dream occasionally, and football is about the only place left where you can do that. We're the home side. It's Germany next in the semi-final, and if we can beat them –'

'That's a bloody big if,' Bradshaw reminded him.

'Keep believing, Ian,' Helen told him, 'I have a good feeling about it.' When they both stared at her, she admitted sheepishly, 'Obviously, I'm no expert,' then handed Ian the photograph.

'Oh,' he said when he saw it. She thought he seemed disappointed somehow.

'What's the matter?'

'Nothing,' he said. 'I knew they were kids when this all happened but we've been talking to the adult versions.' He tilted the photograph so they could both see. 'Look how young they are.' Not for the first time, Ian Bradshaw thought about Susan Verity and her supposed fall from the quarry's edge and wondered once again if a child this young was truly capable of causing it.

54

Bradshaw called the governor of the jail, only to be told that Wicklow was receiving treatment and wouldn't be available until that afternoon at the earliest. It was yet another frustrating delay in a long line of them.

Bradshaw occupied his time at HQ. The governor had promised to call him back as soon as he could be permitted to see Wicklow. In the meantime, there was no news from the site on Mickle Fell or the quarry. The SOCOs had been hindered by the absence of information about an exact location to dig in. Bradshaw had to admit it was not looking good. Either Wicklow had played him, or he really couldn't remember where he had buried those bodies, more than fifteen years earlier.

Bradshaw was in limbo and unable to do anything more to drive his investigations forward. It seemed his biggest decision that day was going to be whether to have ham or cheese in his canteen sandwich.

DCI Kane entered the room at that moment and marched purposefully up to Ian Bradshaw's desk. All eyes followed him, then turned to the detective sergeant. Was the younger man in for a dressing-down?

Kane halted by him. 'They've found a body.' He said it quietly, but everyone stopped what they were doing to listen. 'They have found a child's body on Mickle Fell, and it's right where you said it would be.' Then he corrected himself. 'Right where *he* said it would be – and you're the one who got that out of him.' Kane nodded his appreciation. 'So, well done, lad. You did it.'

Kane placed a hand on Bradshaw's shoulders and the

younger man felt entirely disarmed by the gesture. It was almost fatherly. Bradshaw was unused to physical contact these days and it threw him a little. His DCI withdrew his hand and Bradshaw could see the genuine emotion in the older man's eyes. Was it relief at finally finding one of the children after so many years? Bradshaw knew what it meant to the families, and maybe Kane appreciated that as well. His DCI might be a careerist, but he was human too.

Kane left Bradshaw's desk and then the room. Bradshaw felt self-conscious all of a sudden with so many eyes on him. The room was still silent but his colleagues were looking at him openly now and he didn't understand why they couldn't appreciate how uncomfortable that made him. He didn't know what to do or say, so he went back to staring at the screen on his computer, hoping they would get on with their own work before too long, but they continued to gaze at him.

He would never know who started it, but the noise was clearly audible in the otherwise silent room. A clapping sound. One person began it, then two, then a third until everyone in the room took it up. His colleagues – the men and women he had worked with, clashed with, failed to fit in with – were applauding him. The team he had never really felt a part of, the people he had at times come close to hating because they made him feel like such an outsider, were, to a man and woman, on their feet and clapping his achievement.

And how did he respond?

He didn't. He couldn't do anything. As raw emotion swelled up from some place very deep inside Ian Bradshaw he knew he couldn't even look up at them, for fear that he would completely lose it. This case – this bloody case that had taken so much out of him and countless other good men and women – was finally close to being solved. He had won.

'Well done, Ian,' said the colleague sitting closest to him.

'Thanks,' he just about managed.

Mercifully, the applause began to die down.

There was another hand on his shoulder then. 'Well done, Ian.' It was DI Tennant. 'You did a great job.'

When the governor finally called him to say it was okay to visit Wicklow, he was glad of the excuse to get away.

'We've found one,' he told Wicklow. 'At Mickle Fell. We're still looking for the others, including Susan.'

Wicklow said nothing. Bradshaw recalled his total disinterest in the bodies of his victims being found, so he reached into his bag and retrieved a brown envelope. The killer watched him intently. The detective withdrew a small, faded photograph from the envelope, placed it face up on the table, turned it one hundred and eighty degrees so it was facing Wicklow, then slid it across the table towards him.

Adrian Wicklow glanced down at the photograph and looked at it closely for a while, then he picked it up and peered at the three young boys. He looked at Bradshaw, who stared back at him, waiting for an answer, then Wicklow placed the photograph back on the table.

'Which one?' demanded Bradshaw. 'And don't give me the wrong boy, or I'll find out about it and you will suffer.' He didn't need to explain how.

Wicklow reached out a hand and held a stubby finger over the photograph. Bradshaw watched him all the while, not daring to breathe, but the finger didn't move.

'I don't know,' he said.

Bradshaw glanced down at the picture of the boy's faces then looked back up at Wicklow.

'I'm not lying,' said the killer. Bradshaw said nothing. 'I'm not. There's no point any more. I'm too tired, I'm too ill and I haven't got time for any more games. I don't remember – or, at least, I do remember him, but none of these boys looks exactly the way I recall. It was twenty years ago, and they all look the same.'

Bradshaw had to concede it was true. Three pasty-faced boys the same age, of similar height and build and all with dark brown hair, kept long because it was the 1970s. He hated to admit it but the boys did look very much alike.

'I can't help,' said the killer, and Bradshaw was struck by how ill he looked. Maybe he didn't have long. 'Do you know who it is anyway?' Wicklow asked, thinking the detective might just be stringing him along. 'What's he doing these days? I'm dying to know.' He laughed at his inadvertent joke. 'Quite literally.'

Bradshaw slid the photograph back into its envelope.

'Right, Wicklow,' said Bradshaw firmly. 'We're done.'

'Is that it? Don't you want to come back and see me again? You might want to verify things. I mean, he'll probably deny everything.'

'I'm sure he will.'

'There you go then. You'll need me to corroborate it all for you.'

'I doubt it. You've told me everything you saw that day, and when and where you saw it. I don't need anything else. I have everything I need from you.'

'I don't suppose I'm going to get a thank-you for helping you.'

'Are you serious?' asked Bradshaw. 'God, you are, aren't you? You actually think I should be thanking you because you finally stopped wasting our time after all these years. What do you think?'

'If that's how you're going to be . . .'

Bradshaw got to his feet.

'Wait a minute,' said Wicklow. 'Haven't you forgotten something?'

'What?'

'My book.' And he held out a hand to receive his dictaphone and the tapes.

'Oh yes, I did almost forget,' admitted Bradshaw. 'Your book, that self-justifying account you are convinced generations of criminologists will study in an effort to understand the infamous Adrian Wicklow.'

'They will,' said Wicklow smugly.

'No, they won't.'

'I think you'll find they will,' Wicklow assured him. 'I get letters every week asking for access to that manuscript.'

'You don't understand me, Wicklow. I know there are lots of people who want to hear your . . . memoir, for want of a better word, because they are keen to know your twisted mind or would just get off on it, but I'm afraid none of them will ever hear it.'

Wicklow straightened then. 'Why?' he asked, and when Bradshaw said nothing their eyes locked for a moment. 'What have you done?' hissed Wicklow.

Ian Bradshaw shrugged. 'I burned it.'

The silence that followed covered the time it took for Adrian Wicklow to try to read his opponent. He was attempting to work out if the detective was bluffing or not. Wicklow stared at the calm, implacable face of the detective then said. 'You burned the tapes? You're lying.'

'No. I didn't see why you should get to live on beyond the grave, Wicklow. That's what you want, isn't it? To be important. To think that, somehow, in the history of crime, you matter. Well, you don't. You're not even a footnote. You'll be forgotten by everyone except the relatives of your victims, and that's the way it should be. I couldn't have your memoir sitting in some black museum being pored over by students so you could infect their minds too. So I went outside, borrowed my neighbour's barbecue and made a little fire, popped the tapes of your rambling diatribe on it, set it alight and watched it burn.' He smiled at Wicklow. 'I enjoyed that. It was a good feeling. It made me feel warm inside.' He could see the rage building inside the child killer now. 'What's the matter, Wicklow? You upset that all those months of work have been for nothing? Now you know how the police feel.'

'You liar.'

'I'm not lying,' said Bradshaw placidly, enjoying the moment, 'and you know it. I can tell by the look on your face.'

'I'll have you for this. I'll sue you. I'll get you fired.'

'That won't happen,' said Bradshaw, 'because you don't have the time.'

Wicklow got to his feet. 'Sit down, Wicklow,' ordered the guard behind him, and Wicklow had to make an effort not to launch his weakened body at Bradshaw. He finally sat down.

'It doesn't matter,' Wicklow said after a while. 'They'll remember me anyway.'

'A few people, maybe, but there's a new psycho out there every week. There'll be interest in you for a day or two, but that's all.'

Wicklow remembered their agreement then. 'And you will change my obituary, just like we agreed?'

'Yeah . . . about that,' Bradshaw began. 'I don't know. I'm not sure I really have any power over that journalist. He can write what he likes. I mean, it's a free country.'

Wicklow's eyes widened. 'What about our deal?' His voice sounded panicked now. 'You swore you wouldn't use it if I gave you the bodies and told you what happened to Susan Verity. We had a deal!'

'And how many of those have you made before? How many deals have you negotiated over the years in exchange for . . . nothing?' Bradshaw reminded him. 'So now maybe I'll break this one. Then again, perhaps I won't. Since you'll be dead, you'll never know, will you?'

55

The SOCOs had descended on the quarry armed with nothing more than a loose description of the location of Susan's body; it was somewhere in a large area of thick gorse bushes. It was the third day before they made the breakthrough and human bones were uncovered.

News that Susan Verity's body had been found spread quickly through the village even though there was no official police statement confirming it was her. The local radio news cautiously mentioned that police were examining a site not far from the last known location of the girl, but none of their reporters could get near the place. Journalists from regional and national newspapers alike were kept back from the site, so they couldn't be sure if the police had really found anything. They waited impatiently at a perimeter fence set up by uniformed officers some way from the quarry; a few of them even adjourned to the nearest pub, safe in the knowledge they would soon get wind of any development because they had their contacts in place – tame police officers, some of them quite senior, paid to inform them if anything happened – but still there was no official notification.

None of this mattered. Soon the word got out. A body had been found. Everyone knew it had to be Susan.

Kevin Robson heard about it too, long before the news was official. 'They reckon they've found her,' he was told by an excitable neighbour. 'That's what they are saying, down in the quarry. They've actually found her.'

When Kevin heard that he turned and ran.

*

'That was Ian,' Tom told her as he ended the call. 'There's been a breakthrough.' His face showed the contrasting emotions experienced when there is a development in a case that brings comfort to no one. 'Human remains, right where Wicklow said they would be, down in the quarry, buried among the bushes.'

'Then it's true,' she said. 'It's all true.'

'Maybe,' he conceded. 'But if it really was one of the boys who killed Susan, he can just deny everything and say Wicklow did it. At the moment, it would be their word against that of a serial child killer.'

'Wicklow is known for playing games, but everything Ian told me about this makes it feel different. I think he did witness it. You can call it an accident, or a murder, but whatever happened, Wicklow saw it.' She sighed. 'Yet he can't, or won't, identify the killer.'

'We do have more than just a discredited witness,' he reminded her. 'Billy and Kevin both said they were the last ones to see Susan alive, and it was Billy who went after her, so he was the very last one to see her go. He and Kevin both said she walked off towards the farm and they never saw her again. She didn't come back that way and, when they went home in the same direction, they didn't come across her. It was only when Billy was on the TV recently that he slipped up and said otherwise. Danny and Andrea also said Susan walked away from them both before she met Billy and Kevin, back towards the village, not the quarry. Now we know she actually ended up dead in the quarry.'

'Which makes them liars.'

'Yes, it does, but who has been lying for who here? Danny and Andrea could possibly have seen Susan walk away from the quarry towards the other boys but, somehow, she ended up back there. There are three boys and one girl here who are all saying something that can't be true, but according to Wicklow, only one of the boys killed Susan. The others are either wrong about her movements –'

'– or covering up for the killer.'

'So we put pressure on them all to see if one of them begins to crack. We need someone to turn against the killer.'

'All right,' she said. 'Where do you want to start?'

'With the weakest.'

They found Kevin down by the lake. Tom knew he wouldn't have the nerve to flee from his village after a lifetime clinging to its familiarity for comfort. The flooded gravel pit by the railway track was the end of the universe, as far as Kevin was concerned.

They managed to get the car down a rutted dirt track that had been hardened by the summer sun. They parked it near a gate with a stile, crossed a field and found him sitting there, staring out. No fishing gear this time, and no rifle either. He was just gazing at the water.

'You'll not catch anything without a rod,' Tom said as they drew closer.

Kevin didn't say anything. He just shifted uncomfortably on the ground then drew his legs up and wrapped his arms around them, gripping his shins with his hands and drawing them closer to his body; a comfort gesture. He looked just like the little boy he would have been all those years ago when this began.

'They found her, Kevin,' Helen said. 'She was in the quarry.'

Kevin closed his eyes and lowered his head, turning away from her and resting the side of his head on his knees. He didn't want to see them. He wanted all this to go away.

'It's all right, Kevin,' Tom told him. 'You were only ten years old when it happened. No one will get into any trouble, not really. A few people might be upset with you for lying at first, but we can help to make them understand. You didn't mean it to happen, did you? It was just an accident. If you tell us how it happened, then we'll make sure everyone gets to hear your story so no one can lie or twist it, then you won't get all the blame.' He waited to see if Kevin would respond. 'But if you don't tell us, everyone is going to think the worst. Do you see that?'

'We want to help you, Kevin,' Helen assured him. 'If you did this thing, then tell us and we'll protect you. If you didn't do it, I can understand why you've kept it a secret all this time – to protect your friend – but they've found Susan, so the time for secrets is over. Wouldn't you feel so much better if you let it all out now and told us the truth?'

The high-pitched, mournful keening sound that came from him shocked them. They couldn't see Kevin's face because it was turned away from them, but there was no mistaking his reaction. Kevin Robson was sobbing.

He lifted his head then and started nodding it back and forth while he wept. 'Yes,' he agreed. Tom nodded at Helen to continue. Perhaps Kevin would see her as a more gentle, sympathetic presence than he was.

'Susan didn't run away towards the farm, did she?' Helen said. 'She went the other way, towards the woods and then the quarry.' When he didn't contradict her, she asked, 'What happened, Kevin? Did you go with her?' No reply. 'Was Billy there, or Danny? Did Susan fall, or was she pushed? Was it an accident, Kevin? Tell us, please.'

'It was an accident,' he said and it was as if a dam had burst. Kevin's crying turned into full-on sobbing that saw his chest rise and fall rapidly as he tried to draw his breath.

'Okay,' agreed Helen. 'You never meant to hurt her. No one really thinks that you did.' She knew they were close to the truth now. They just had to handle Kevin in the right way and he might tell them everything. 'So why don't you just tell me what happened. Who was it that actually hurt Susan?'

'He pushed her,' said Kevin. 'it was a joke, and he didn't mean to do it, but he pushed her and she got hurt.'

Tom and Helen exchanged looks once more. A surge of adrenalin ran through Helen. They were almost there.

'Who did?' she asked. 'Who pushed Susan?'

It seemed to take Kevin Robson an age to summon the words from deep within him. 'Billy,' he said finally. 'He pushed her and she fell.'

56

They didn't get a lot from him after that. They were hoping for details but all they got was more weeping and incomprehensible words. In among them were Kevin's denials but the story remained consistent. It wasn't supposed to happen like that. Nobody meant to hurt anyone. It was an accident. Billy had pushed Susan Verity and she fell.

In the end, Tom watched Kevin sobbing and said to Helen, 'I think that's as far as we'll get with Kevin for now,' and she agreed. Continuing with the questioning would only heighten his distress and possibly push him over the edge.

Better to get him back to the village, hand him over to Ian Bradshaw and let the detective take it from there. This was likely to be a slow process, during which the full truth would have to be coaxed from Kevin. But he knew what had happened.

And he had named Susan's killer.

Word of the discovery of Susan's body reached Billy in the pub. It started as a murmur from the lounge bar. Then the landlord came through from the lounge to the public bar and Billy heard him say, 'It's little Susan. They've only bloody found her.' One of the drinkers propped up at the bar asked him where. 'The quarry,' he replied and, slowly, all eyes turned to Billy.

For the first time in his life, Billy left a pint half finished. As everyone looked at the man who had repeatedly told everyone that he had last seen Susan heading away from the quarry towards the farm, Billy got up and started to leave before they could confront him.

'Where are *you* off to?' asked one of the regulars, who he had known all his life. 'In a hurry, are you?' And there were sneering comments from his fellow drinkers. Billy blotted them out as he walked swiftly towards the exit.

He swept past them all and had almost reached the door when someone walked through it towards him. A big, muscular presence blocked Billy's way. Robert Marsh was standing there, and he was glaring at Billy.

'You!' hissed the farmer. 'I've been looking for you.' He thrust out a finger at Billy, who stopped in his tracks, terrified now.

'Liar!' shouted the farmer's son. 'Liar!' he called again, and Billy whirled on his heel and ran for the back door.

'Billy Liar!' shouted the furious farmer as he fled. 'Billy bloody Liar!'

Billy didn't stop. he didn't turn around or look back.

Billy ran.

'Billy Liar!'

They managed to calm Kevin down eventually and coax him into their car so they could drive him back to the village. Not knowing how the villagers would react to the news that Susan had been found, and mindful of Kevin's safety, Tom called Ian Bradshaw, who came to meet them, along with a squad car, to take Kevin back to the station for more detailed questioning.

'You going to question him now?' asked Helen.

'You might need to give him a little time to calm down first,' Tom cautioned.

'He does look in a bit of a state,' said Bradshaw, as they watched the red-eyed and shaking figure of Kevin Robson being driven away. 'And he's not the prime suspect,' Bradshaw reminded her. 'Or so you say.'

'No, he isn't,' agreed Helen.

'Better round *him* up while we're here then,' said Bradshaw. 'In case he tries to do a bunk.'

'You ready to finish this thing?' asked Tom, and Bradshaw nodded.

Billy Thorpe was like a cornered animal.

He had to find Danny.

Danny would know what to do.

Billy ran through the village as fast as a man can when he hasn't done a minute's physical exercise in years or gone without cigarettes or beer for a day. By the time Billy reached Danny's house, he was panting, sweating and breathless. He thanked the god he didn't believe in when he saw Danny was back.

Danny had been expecting Billy. He let his friend in, and they waited together.

An hour later, they both heard it: the sound of a car driving up then slowing to pull over on the kerb outside the house. They must have driven straight from Billy's house once they realized he wasn't there.

Danny went over to his window. He pulled the curtain to one side so he could peer out. Helen, Tom and Ian stepped from the car.

'They're here,' he told Billy. His friend was trembling now. 'But it's okay. It's better this way.'

He meant that the car didn't have police livery, sirens or flashing lights on it.

'I'm scared, Danny,' Billy told his friend.

'I know.'

They took Billy to police HQ in Durham city. Bradshaw made him a cup of tea and brought it into the interrogation room for him. Helen and Tom waited outside. This was police business now.

Bradshaw thanked Billy for attending the police interview voluntarily.

Billy didn't respond.

'You've heard we found her?' asked the detective.

Billy nodded.

'It's not confirmed that it's Susan yet, of course, and won't be for some time. The body has been there twenty years, so formal identification of the remains won't be easy, but the first impression is that the body could be Susan and, since we were acting on information provided to us, we have to work on the assumption that it is.' He let Billy digest this. 'The thing is, Billy, we located the body in the quarry to the south of the woods, and you told the police that Susan walked away in a northerly direction, back towards the village.

Billy shrugged. 'Yeah, she did. She must have changed her mind and come back again.'

'Why would she do that?'

'Dunno.'

'How could she have come back without you seeing her?'

'Dunno.'

Bradshaw frowned at Billy's dismissive answer. 'I've just been speaking to Kevin Robson.'

Billy made no response.

'He's been telling a different story.'

Again, silence from Billy. 'And so has our witness.'

'Witness? What witness?'

'I'm not at liberty to say,' Bradshaw told him, 'but we have someone who saw what happened. Now, at the moment, all we have to go on is the testimony of that witness and what Kevin has been saying to us.'

'What's he been saying, like?'

'A number of things,' said Bradshaw, who wasn't keen to admit that they hadn't got much sense out of Kevin since they brought him in. He seemed to be in shock at the discovery of Susan's body after all these years and too upset to elaborate further on what had happened.

'He said it was you, though,' Bradshaw told him.

'Kevin said *what* was me?' asked Billy.

'It was you that killed Susan.'

Billy's eyes widened in alarm. 'Now wait a minute. I never killed Susan! I never touched her! Kevin's lying!'

'Why would he do that?'

'I don't know why! But I tell you, I never touched Susan.'

'That's not what he said, Billy. Kevin reckons you pushed her.'

'He reckons what?' Then Billy stopped for a moment and seemed to be thinking. 'Ha!' His reaction was unexpected. Unless Bradshaw was mistaken, it sounded like a snort of laughter.

'That you pushed her.'

'Well, I did.'

'You did?'

'Yes.'

'You pushed her off the edge of the quarry?'

'God, no!' said Billy, 'Don't be daft! I pushed her over, that's all. We used to do that all the time when we were kids.' When Bradshaw looked at him blankly, he added, 'Kevin crept round behind her and went down on all fours. I gave her a shove and she fell over him. That's when I pushed her, and that's what he's talking about.'

'That's ridiculous, Billy. Why would Kevin get so upset about it if all you did was push her over him?'

'Because we hurt her!'

Bradshaw stared at him then, as if Billy was having him on. 'I pushed her too hard and when she hit the ground she rolled and slid down the hill.'

Bradshaw frowned, and this unnerved Billy. Clearly, the detective didn't believe him.

'She rolled,' repeated Billy. 'She couldn't stop herself and she went right into them.'

'Right into what?'

'The nettles,' said Billy. 'She landed in them.'

Bradshaw looked at Billy to see if he was lying. You couldn't always tell – no one could – but Billy wasn't a very sophisticated witness and Bradshaw could detect no obvious trace of a lie there.

'Let's get this straight,' said Bradshaw. 'You're saying that Kevin is claiming you shoved Susan in some nettles?' Billy nodded. 'And you reckon that's all he means? I'll be checking, you know?'

'Yeah, that's all he means.'

'Then why is he so upset?'

'Well, we felt bad,' Billy explained. 'We never meant it to happen. We thought she'd just land on the grass, but I pushed her too hard and he was too high up, so she shot over Kevin and slid down the hill. She couldn't stop herself and she rolled right into the nettles. She got stung all over and she was really upset. She started shouting at us both and screaming, then she ran off, crying.'

'Right,' said Bradshaw. 'Assuming for one hypothetical second that I believe you, Billy, and here's hoping, for your sake, that Kevin can back this up, in what direction did she run?'

Billy looked a bit sick then, as if telling the truth would get him into a whole new load of trouble. 'Tell me what really happened, Billy. We've found her, remember?'

'She went to the woods,' he admitted reluctantly.

'Not to the farm?' Bradshaw queried. 'The opposite way to what you said?'

Billy nodded slowly.

'Then why have you been lying about it for the past twenty years?'

Billy Thorpe looked terrified.

'I know you were only ten years old when it happened, so you can't be charged with much, if anything, because you were too young,' he told the worried man in front of him, 'but it would help us greatly if you were to explain yourself now and give me the reason you lied.'

'I didn't want to get into trouble,' he protested. 'I pushed Susan, I hurt her and she ran off. Nobody ever saw her again.' Billy looked on the brink of tears; in fact, to Bradshaw, he strongly resembled a frightened child, which of course he would have been back when it happened. 'I didn't know what happened to her, but I knew that it wouldn't have happened if I hadn't hurt her. She only ran away from us, off on her own, because she was upset, see. I thought we'd get the blame.'

'So you said she was fine when she left you and that she walked calmly off towards the farm?'

'Yes.'

'Why?'

'I just told you I –'

'Why did you say the farm, Billy?' Bradshaw interrupted. 'She could have gone off in any direction, so why did you say she headed back towards Marsh Farm?' The guilty look on Billy's face provided Bradshaw with an answer. 'Because you didn't like the farmer?'

Billy took a long time to answer that question and, when he did, all he gave in response was a tiny nod.

'Jesus Christ, Billy. Have you any idea what that man went through because of you?'

'We all hated him. He was a right bastard.'

'But he wasn't a child killer,' said Bradshaw reasonably.

'Though quite a number of people in your village continued to suspect he might have been.'

'I didn't mean for that to happen,' sniffed Billy. 'We didn't understand, we were only kids.'

'But you never changed your story, did you, not once, in all those years, not until you let it slip in that TV interview, and by then Farmer Marsh had been dead for years.'

'How could we?' shouted Billy. 'We couldn't change our story! It was too late for that. The police had wasted loads of time searching the farm and all the fields. They'd have been furious with us. I was worried they'd take me away, into care or something, stick me in borstal.'

'So you were trapped in a lie.'

'Yes.'

'How did Kevin feel about that?'

'You know how it affected Kevin. He's never been right, not for years.'

'And what about Danny? Was he in on it too, or does he not know you've been stringing him along, like the rest of us?'

'Oh no,' he protested. 'It was his idea.' Billy immediately regretted saying that. 'He was trying to protect us, that's all — me and Kevin.'

'Was he now?'

57

'Sorry, but I'm really not hungry any more,' explained Helen, pushing her plate to one side, a half-eaten portion of fish and chips still on it.

'Me neither, to be honest,' admitted Tom. They were sitting in the village pub and it had taken them an age to be served. The place was packed with journalists and even some of Bradshaw's colleagues who had been down at the quarry earlier. Now they all wanted feeding and Tom had been told by the landlord, 'You can have fish and chips, 'cos fish and chips is all I got left.'

By the time their food finally arrived they were both past caring, deflated after the false alarm caused by Kevin's comments about Billy. *'He pushed her,'* mimicked Tom, in a passable imitation of Kevin's tearful voice. 'Yeah,' he added. 'He pushed her into some bloody nettles.'

'I honestly thought we might be there at last,' said Helen, 'that we might have made a breakthrough. Instead, I just feel like an idiot.'

'We were both taken in by it,' said Tom. 'It's not easy to think like Kevin Robson; he's a bit of a one-off.'

'He's been scarred by what happened to Susan, and we should have realized.'

'What about Danny?' he asked her. 'According to Ian, it was his idea to say that Susan had run off towards the farm.'

'So Billy claims,' she said. 'But if it was Danny's idea, even Billy is saying it was just to protect him and Kevin. None of them liked the farmer so they were trying to deflect the blame away from them and put it on him.'

'The poor bastard. Imagine the life he had after that. Half the bloody village thought he had something to do with it.'

'And the other half thought it was Adrian Wicklow.'

A familiar face entered the pub then. Andrea Craven looked around the room as if she was hoping to spot someone, then her eyes settled on Helen and Tom and she walked over.

'A little far from home, aren't you?' Tom asked her.

'I came as soon as I heard,' she told them. 'Is it true?'

'It's true they have found a body,' said Helen, 'and it's pretty certain it must be Susan. I'm sorry.'

'It's all right,' answered Andrea, though she looked shaken. 'I've been expecting this for so many years. What other outcome could there be? But still . . .'

'It's a shock.'

'Yes,' she admitted. 'Silly, I know.'

'But understandable.'

'Were you looking for someone when you walked in?' he asked her.

'Not really,' she said. 'I wondered if –'

'Danny might be here?' Helen completed the sentence for her and Andrea flushed.

'He does come here,' admitted Andrea. 'To be honest, I didn't know what to do or where to go. I just drove down because I wanted to be here. I would have felt so helpless sitting at home, watching it on the news.'

Helen thought of Andrea on her own in that little cottage and understood why she might want to be with other people, today of all days.

'So, what do you know?' she asked them, a look of trepidation on her face.

'Sit down, Andrea,' Tom told her. 'I'll get you a drink.'

She thanked him and asked for a Coke because she was driving. 'We have a new witness,' Helen told Andrea when he left the table, but she did not reveal who it was. 'That person told us where to find Susan. He also told us how she died.'

Tom went to the bar, leaving Helen to explain it all. He didn't have the energy to fill in the blanks for Andrea and the wait at the bar was a welcome moment of relative solitude. Eventually, he caught an overworked barmaid's eye and ordered, returning to the table moments later with three fresh drinks.

'He must be lying,' Andrea said, 'this witness. If he said one of the boys killed Susan, then he must be lying.'

'Perhaps,' said Tom, 'but he knew where we'd find her body.'

'I feel like we're still missing something,' said Helen. 'If there is anything else you can tell us, Andrea,' she prompted.

'There's nothing,' protested Andrea. 'You know everything already.'

'Let's just go over it one more time,' said Tom. 'You were all at the den, then someone had the bright idea to play on the farmer's hay bales, so you went there.'

'Yes.'

'The farmer spotted you and went barmy.' Andrea did not contradict him. 'So you scattered and ran off in different directions. Michelle went home, Billy and Kevin ended up together, you stumbled across Danny, then Susan arrived but she left you and headed home, then met up with Kevin and Billy on the way.'

'That's right.'

'Billy and Kevin always said Susan went towards the farm when she left them, but it turned out she went the other way, towards the woods.'

'What?'

'Billy's admitted it,' said Helen before she could argue against this, 'and we now know why.'

'Billy and Kevin played a trick on Susan,' said Tom. 'Billy

350

pushed her over Kevin's back and she rolled into some nettles. She was upset and in pain and she ran off towards the woods.'

'And died in the quarry,' said Helen flatly. 'We just don't know who did it.'

'Was it Kevin, Billy or Danny' – Tom sighed – 'or someone else entirely? Christ, it could have been more or less anyone in that area in roughly their age group, or it still could have been Wicklow.'

Tom's mobile phone rang then and he stood up from the table to answer it.

'Tom Carney?' It was a woman.

'Yes.'

'Can you talk?' He recognized the voice then. It was Jess.

'Yes, just a minute, it's a bit noisy here. Don't hang up!' He turned back to Helen then. 'It's her,' he hissed, and she immediately knew who he meant.

Tom started speaking urgently and moving quickly, squeezing past people as he made for the exit. He almost knocked a pint out of the hand of a big bloke by the door and got a 'howay, man!' from him as he shouldered it open.

You're not alone?' she sounded suspicious.

'I am now.'

There was no answer and he wondered if she had hung up on him then, after a moment, she said, 'I've been thinking about what you said.'

When she said nothing further, he urged her, 'Go on.'

'I've made my decision. I want to come in.'

'All right.'

'But we have to do this my way or we don't do it at all.'

'Okay,' he said. 'How do you want to play it?'

Jess was precise. She issued instructions, and Tom listened. She told him there could be no compromises. Behind the assertiveness, he could read fear, so he let her continue. There was too much at stake to jeopardize things by taking the initiative away from Jess. She needed to be in control. 'All right,' he agreed, and she immediately ended the call. Tom ran back into the pub.

'I've got to find Ian.'

Helen could tell it was urgent. 'She wants to come in?'

He nodded. 'But I can drop you home first.'

She shook her head. 'Just go,' she told him. 'I'm fine. I'll get a cab later. I should hang around here, don't you think?'

'Probably best under the circumstances,' he agreed. At least one of them should stay in the village. 'Keep me posted.'

'I will,' she promised. 'Likewise.'

He smiled at her. 'Thanks, Helen.' And, with that, he was gone.

Helen was left with Andrea, who had barely spoken since Tom had gone through the timeline with her. She hadn't said anything helpful and Helen didn't feel in the mood to make small talk with a woman who was not big on conversation in any case, so they sat in silence for a time while Helen thought about Susan Verity. Perhaps this would be one of those cases where opinions stayed divided, between those who blamed Wicklow and others who believed his story about one of the boys ending her life so abruptly. Without the proof they needed, twenty years from now they might still be talking about it and no one would be any clearer.

Andrea frowned then, and Helen noticed.

'No, that's not right,' said Andrea quietly, as if answering a question Helen had just put to her.

'What's not right?'

'What Tom said.'

'Which bit?'

'The order everything happened in.'

'Oh, right,' said Helen, who felt drained of energy by that

point. She took a sip of her wine and watched the barman pour a fresh pint for a journalist.

'Susan had the nettle stings when we saw her,' said Andrea, 'and red, puffy eyes because she'd been crying. She had them on her arms and legs and even some on her face.'

It took a moment.

There was a second or two while Helen processed the information, and at first she accepted it at face value, as an unimportant fact. Then something fell neatly into place.

Helen slowly turned to face Andrea. 'What did you say?'

Andrea was taken aback by Helen's tone. 'I said Susan already had the nettle stings when Danny and I saw her.'

'Oh my God,' said Helen.

58

'What are you doing back here?' asked an impatient Ian Bradshaw when he met Tom in the entrance at police HQ.

'I've been trying to call you, but I couldn't get through.'

'I am just a tiny bit busy right now. I thought you might appreciate that.'

'Well, you're about to get busier mate. Remember Jess?'

'Of course.'

'She wants to come in,' Tom told him, 'and I need you to arrange it.'

'Andrea, I want you to pay attention to what I am about to say, because I think it's important,' Helen told her.

'Okay.' Andrea looked a little worried then.

'When you ran away from the hay bales and everyone scattered, you said you ended up in the woods with Danny.'

'Yes.'

'And Susan joined you there soon after. Everyone has always said she left you a little while later then walked home in the direction of the farm. She met Billy and Kevin along the way. They were the last people to see her alive. But we now know that Billy lied about the direction she went in. He has finally admitted that, when Susan got stung in the nettles, she ran in the opposite direction, back towards the woods.' Helen let that sink in. 'Back towards you. You said she had the nettle stings when she reached you.'

'I suppose so. Yes, she did.' It was a reluctant admission.

'Andrea, I have to ask you this and I need you to tell me the

354

truth, because it is far better for you if I do the asking now than if the police get involved.'

Andrea looked even more nervous now. 'All right.'

'Did Susan Verity really walk away from you and Danny?' asked Helen, 'or did someone ask you to say that?' Andrea almost flinched. 'Did *Danny* ask you to say that? He did, didn't he?'

Andrea looked as if she was wondering how Helen could have possibly worked that out but, to Helen, it was the only reasonable explanation. She nodded dumbly.

'You left first, didn't you?' asked Helen. 'When you went, Susan was still with Danny, and they were on their own.'

'Yes,' admitted Andrea, 'but that doesn't mean anything, because Susan went home and she saw Billy and Kevin on the . . .' Her words tailed away. Helen could tell she was confused.

'No,' said Helen, 'it didn't happen that way. She met Billy and Kevin first, got stung by the nettles and ran to the woods. It was at that point she met you and Danny, not beforehand. Then you went home, leaving Susan and Danny alone in the woods, not far from the quarry.'

'I . . .' Andrea began, but she couldn't find the words. Helen knew she was wrestling with the notion that she had been wrong about everything all these years, and with the implications.

'Why did you leave first?' asked Helen, eager now to get Andrea concentrating on the facts.

'Susan was mean,' said Andrea, sounding like a child again. 'She teased me about being alone with Danny.' Her face took on a pleading look. 'Susan was pretty and popular, but she could be nasty too. I thought she wanted to be on her own with Danny, so I left.'

Helen could picture the young Andrea Craven being excluded like that and trudging disconsolately away.

'Why didn't you tell the police that?'

'Danny knocked on my door later,' she said.

'He came to your house?' The other woman nodded. 'Was everyone looking for Susan at that point?'

Andrea shook her head. 'Just her parents. They'd been round to see us all. No one was too worried about her yet. She'd not been missing that long.'

'Why did Danny come and see you?'

'He told me Susan had been mean to him too, saying nasty things about his father, so he left her and came after me but I'd already gone. He told me Susan went off in a huff after they argued and that Billy and Kevin had seen her go towards the farm.'

'And he asked you not to say he was on his own with ~~Andrea?~~ Susan? Why would he do that?'

'Because she stormed off and he didn't want the adults to blame him if she had done something stupid afterwards.'

'So you agreed to say you were with him when she left?'

Andrea nodded slowly. 'Yes.'

'Why, Andrea? Why would you do that? Because you liked him?'

'I loved him,' said Andrea. 'Even back then. I've always loved him.' She returned Helen's stare. 'And it didn't do any harm.'

'Because he wasn't the last person to see her alive.' Andrea nodded again. 'Except . . .' Helen weighed her words carefully: 'I think perhaps he was.'

Any doubts Helen might have had about the danger of confronting Danny Gilbert at his own home were eased by the scene that greeted her. There was a kid's bike on the driveway and laughter coming from the front garden, then Danny's young daughter raced by, pursued by a boisterous puppy that darted after her into the house. There was movement beyond the kitchen window too, his wife was in there, but Helen's eyes were drawn to the open garage door and the car that was protruding from it. As she drew nearer, Helen could hear a radio coming from the garage. She couldn't see Danny but it sounded as if he was in there.

'Hello?' she called, and when there was no immediate response she inched around the gap between his car and the frame of the garage door.

Danny was standing by a work bench fixing something. He had his back to the door.

'Miss Norton,' he said, without turning round. 'There's no one else that well-spoken around here.' He turned to face her, that boyish smile still firmly in place. 'Always a pleasure, never a chore.'

Helen squeezed passed his car and into the garage. 'Do you have a moment?' she said.

'For you? Of course. I'm sorry I'm so hacky.' He picked up a cloth and wiped the oil from his hands. 'My pet project.' He nodded towards the frame of the motorbike he was working on. 'She's a 1969 Triumph Trident, a beautiful machine. I'm doing her up. Hoping I'll get to ride her soon.' He grinned at her. 'With a name like Norton, I expect you appreciate a classic British motorcycle.' Then, as if he had suddenly remembered, he said, 'But you wanted a word.'

'It shouldn't take long,' she said. 'There are just a couple of things I want to clarify with you, Danny.'

She wondered if he would invite her into the house, but there were fresh oil patches on his overalls so he was probably reluctant to leave the garage.

'Go ahead,' he said. 'I'll help if I can.'

Helen's first inclination was to ask him about Susan Verity but, since her body had just been found and his friend taken away by the police for questioning, Danny would be expecting that. Instead, she wanted to see if she could catch him off guard. Danny had been away and she had never had the opportunity to ask him again about that day on the mountain.

'The first relates to what happened on Mont Blanc.' As she had expected, he seemed surprised by that. 'You never told us they found Victoria's body.'

'Didn't I? Well, they didn't, not at the time. It was years later. That's why I didn't say anything.'

'You sure it wasn't because the location of her body contradicted your version of the story?'

'Have you ever been on Mont Blanc, Helen?' He sounded impatient now. 'Well, I have, and when a storm comes down on you that suddenly, you can't see your own feet, let alone give an exact location of a fallen climber. You have no idea.'

'I'm sure there is quite a large margin of error, but you were several thousand feet out. I met with Victoria's father –'

'Oh, here we go. I should have known Gordon would be behind this.'

'He told me you kept in touch for years but when Victoria was found you didn't attend the funeral service.'

'Because I didn't want to go through it all again! Jesus,' he hissed, 'would *you* want to relive that horrific experience? I'd moved on. I just couldn't face . . .' He ceased trying to express his feelings. 'I can't believe he doesn't understand that.'

'Oh, he does,' she said, 'or at least he would have if you had explained it to him, but you never replied.'

'Well, I bottled that, didn't I, which makes me a bad person,' he said defiantly, 'but I always felt guilty about what happened that day and I couldn't face him again.'

'Why do you feel guilty about it? It wasn't your fault. It was the storm. Victoria was the more experienced climber. If anything, she should have known not to take you up the mountain.'

'Because I'm a man,' he snapped. 'Because we are supposed to take care of you and I didn't take care of Victoria.'

'Do you want to hear Gordon's theory?'

'You're itching to tell me.'

'He thinks Victoria died on her way up the mountain, not on her way down. He reckons something happened between you and her but you continued up the mountain until the storm hit and it gave you the perfect explanation for her death.'

'I don't believe this.'

'He reckons you hung around for a while to make it look as if you were searching for her but what you were really doing was providing yourself with a kind of alibi.'

'Helen, he is a grieving father who has never really got over the tragic death of his favourite daughter, and now he is looking for a reason why it happened. I was lost in the storm, I barely made it back down; Victoria slipped and fell. Gordon is the only one who believes I had anything to do with her death.'

'Not the only one, actually, Danny.'

'What do you mean?'

'I have been speaking to Henri Gerbeaud. You don't remember the name? He questioned you for hours about Victoria's death.'

'Of course I remember him.'

'Henri remembers you, and he reckoned you had something to hide.'

'Why was I never charged then?' he demanded. 'With anything? Explain that!'

'Insufficient evidence, apparently, but he was always felt your account didn't stack up. The storm that hit that day affected the section of the mountain where you said Victoria fell. It was far less extreme at a lower altitude and that's where her body was eventually discovered. When that happened, he went to his superiors and urged them to reopen the case, but they turned him down.'

'Well, then,' was all he managed.

'There was no appetite to reopen one old investigation when a hundred die on Mont Blanc every year, but he assures me that will change if there is any fresh evidence that makes you look like a killer.'

'How could there be?'

'Well, there is,' she told him simply. 'As of today, when they found Susan Verity's body at the bottom of a quarry.'

'You're not serious,' he scoffed. 'You think you can link Victoria with Susan? You've lost the plot.'

'They both fell.'

'Yes,' he said, 'they did, but Victoria died in an accident, and I wasn't the last person to see Susan alive, so you won't get very far with that.'

'You said you saw Susan for the last time when you were playing with Andrea.'

'That's right,' he agreed.

'But then Susan got bored and she went off on her own to play.'

'Correct.'

'She then bumped into Kevin and Billy. They spent some time with her and were the last two people to see Susan alive,' she recalled. 'The very last was Billy, who followed her for a short while and confirmed she was heading back towards Marsh Farm, presumably so she could cross its fields on her way home?'

'Yep,' he said. 'That's how it was. I've said it a thousand times and never deviated.'

'No, you never have,' she admitted, 'but Billy did, in that TV interview.'

'Billy was pissed. They shouldn't have allowed him to go on air like that. It was a scandal.'

'When the police spoke to Billy earlier he told them something new, which didn't appear in any of the case files or in the transcripts from the interviews with any of the children, because he had never mentioned it before.'

Helen let that sink in. Danny watched her. 'Right,' he said. 'What was that then?'

Did he look nervous as he asked that? If he was worried, it didn't show.

'Billy told us he pushed Susan and she fell. He said he and Kevin played a trick on her where Kevin went behind Susan and Billy shoved her so she fell backwards and tumbled down the hill. She ended up in a pile of nettles.'

'Did he?'

'Yes,' she confirmed. 'Did you know about that?' She watched him closely as he answered.

'Did I know about that?' he asked himself absent-mindedly.

'You and Billy were close,' she said reasonably. 'You still are. I imagine he would have told you about it at the time.'

'Probably,' he said airily. 'Possibly. I can't remember.'

'He didn't intend to push her into those nettles, but she got stung all over. Susan was quite upset and she ran off crying. Does that ring any bells?'

'Now you come to mention it, it does, but it was a very long while ago, so it must have slipped my mind. I obviously remember a lot about that day, Helen, but not every little thing. I've tried to forget, in fact.'

'But Billy didn't tell the police – at the time, I mean. Why do you think he kept quiet about it?'

'No idea.'

'He was worried he would get into trouble. Susan was upset. She'd been stung and she ran off and nobody ever saw her again, right?'

'Right,' he agreed.

'I think Billy was worried people would blame him for Susan going missing. She ran away and never came back and they might say it was his fault. Susan might have made a bad decision because she'd been hurt and upset, gone off with someone, or had an accident maybe.'

'Perhaps.'

'I think that sounds reasonable, don't you? I think I would have been tempted to leave that bit out, if I was Billy. He was only a child, after all. I think I'd have just said I saw her running off towards the farm, but I wouldn't let on I'd hurt her. I'd get Kevin not to mention it too, and I'd tell him that was for the best, wouldn't you?'

'Maybe,' he admitted. 'I suppose.'

'I wouldn't think it was significant at all, if it weren't for one thing,' she said. 'I spoke to Andrea, and do you know what she said?'

'How could I?'

'She said that when you both saw Susan, she had red, puffy eyes.'

'Really?'

'Yes, and Andrea also told me why she'd been crying. Susan Verity had nettle stings on her arms and legs, and even some on her face.'

'Right,' said Danny, and his tone was both puzzled and defensive. 'So what does that prove?'

'It proves that you both saw Susan *after* she'd fallen in the nettles. It shows you saw her after Kevin and Billy pushed her over and she ran away crying. It proves that Billy wasn't the last one to see Susan, like you've all been saying for twenty years.'

'Now hang on.' His face was twisted in confusion. 'I don't remember seeing any nettle stings on Susan.'

'No, but Andrea does. She recalls it like it was yesterday. Know what else she remembers, Danny?'

He shook his head dumbly.

'She remembers that Susan was mean to her about you.

Andrea remembers how she got upset because when Susan showed up and found you two together she teased you both about being boyfriend and girlfriend, so Andrea left.' Helen made sure to watch Danny Gilbert very closely. 'She went home, leaving you alone with Susan. She never gave that any thought at the time, because you and the other boys all said the last people to see Susan alive were Kevin and Billy, not you and Andrea, so Andrea thought Susan went off to see them again afterwards.'

'Did she?' His voice was a monotone now.

'The police checked with Billy. They asked him whose idea it was to say nothing about Susan falling in the nettles, and you know what he said?'

Danny let out a little laugh then, but there was no humour in it. 'How could I know what my old friend told them?'

'He said it was your idea. You swore them both to secrecy, because you reckoned they'd get into very big trouble if they told the truth. Billy said it was your idea to say that Susan ran back towards Marsh Farm too, so you could all blame the farmer for Susan's disappearance.'

'Good old Billy.' Danny shook his head as if attempting to clear it. He was smiling, but he couldn't hide his anger and fear now. 'I'm not sure what you think all this stuff about the nettles actually proves.'

'It proves one important thing,' she told him. 'It proves Billy wasn't the last person to see Susan Verity alive – *you* were.'

59

Danny just stood there with a big, false smile on his face, as if everything Helen had said was so amusing. 'I don't know where you are getting all this from, Helen,' he said, 'or why it is that you keep putting two and two together and coming up with five.'

'Is that what I am doing, Danny?' He nodded slowly. 'And I haven't even mentioned the witness.'

The smile faded away then. 'What witness?'

She knew she had to play this card just right, so she chose her next words very carefully. 'The one who saw everything and kept quiet about it all for years until now, the man who watched Susan fall and helped you cover it up.'

He snapped then. 'Who the hell is going to believe a word *he* says?'

'Why wouldn't they believe him, Danny?' She spoke quietly now. 'I never even said who the witness was, but you know it was Wicklow, don't you, because you were there. You reckon you'll be okay because it's his word against yours, but how could you know he saw everything unless it was you that he helped? You know, I wasn't a hundred per cent sure,' she admitted. 'Until now.'

Danny no longer bothered to deny. Instead, he asked, 'And what does Tom think about your theory, Helen? He's not here. Does that mean he reckons it's a load of old crap you've made up on the spot?'

'I haven't told him yet.'

'And you won't have had time to tell old Henri either,' he

said, 'because you just couldn't wait to come up here and have this out with me, could you?'

Before Helen could answer him, Danny took a step towards her and swung his arm. By the time she recognized it as a blow, it had already landed and Helen was sent reeling backwards. There was a tiny moment between the impact and its full effect. In that split second she knew he must have hit her over the head with something, because the pain was excruciating. Just before she dropped to the floor she saw the metal wrench in his hand.

Helen hit the ground hard and tried to get up, but she couldn't and crashed back down again, her face scraping against the cement floor. Her vision started to blur and she was in terrible pain. She felt liquid on the side of her head. It had to be blood. My God, he'd hit her. His family were only feet away, inside the house, but that hadn't stopped him.

'Fucking interfering bitch,' hissed Danny. 'Why didn't you just mind your own business?' He bent low so he could speak into her ear. 'You made me do this,' he told her, and he actually seemed angry at her for it. The force of the blow made her feel like she was going to be sick.

Danny Gilbert grabbed Helen by the lapels of her shirt and with a grunt hauled her to her feet but they gave way and she slumped back to the ground once more. 'Get up!' he ordered, and this time he pulled her into a sitting position then slapped her hard across the face.

Helen did not get up. She couldn't get up.

Danny let out a cry of frustration and let her fall back down to the ground, where she lay on her back, helpless and in immense pain. She was no longer in command of her body.

Helen was dimly aware of a sound as Danny wrenched open the boot of his car; then he came back for her. This time he grabbed her from underneath her shoulders and dragged her towards the car.

'I am going to bury you,' he promised, and her fear became even stronger than the pain.

He was going to kill her. He was going to murder her and bury her somewhere no one would ever find her. She tried to move, to struggle against him, but she could do nothing. Danny was dragging her closer and closer to the car.

When they reached it, he hauled her upwards into a sitting position once more and was about to lift her into the boot when Helen heard a new voice, shrill and panicked.

'Danny!'

It was a shriek.

It was Andrea Craven. Because Helen didn't have a car, Andrea had driven her over to Danny's house. She'd offered to come in with her but Helen had told her it would be better if she waited outside while she asked Danny some questions. She must have wondered what was going on. Thank God her curiosity had got the better of her.

'It's all right, Andrea,' stammered Danny. 'She's trying to frame me and I'm . . .' Even Danny couldn't find the words to explain why he was holding a badly injured and bleeding Helen upright so he could bundle her into the boot of his car.

'Oh, Danny!' she gasped. 'I never would have believed it!'

'Then help me, Andrea,' he urged the woman who had loved him since they were children. 'Help me to stop her.'

'Help you?' she said. 'To kill her? Like you killed Susan? My God, did you murder Victoria too?' She looked at Danny as if she finally understood him then. 'What's wrong with you, Danny?'

Helen wanted to cry out, to scream at Andrea to run, but she couldn't manage it – and how would the poor woman be able to outrun Danny, even if she tried? Helen's vision was blurred and she was in great pain still; it felt like there must be a lot of blood and she wondered if she might die from the blow.

'Please,' he pleaded.

When Andrea finally answered, her voice was cold and hard. 'No, Danny.' Then she said, 'What will you do now? Kill me too?'

The look on Danny's face was her answer and she instinctively stepped away from him. Danny let Helen fall back on to the floor. Her head slumped to one side and her vision cleared enough to witness him pick up the wrench again. He advanced on Andrea.

'Daddy?' The voice was confused and frightened. No one had heard the door from the house to the garage open. Danny Gilbert's daughter was standing there, staring at her father. She was young but old enough to understand there was a woman on the ground with blood on her head.

'Sweetheart.' Danny's voice was almost as high as his daughter's now. 'It's all right,' he said, against all the evidence before her. 'This lady,' he began, 'she's a bad woman. Daddy just has to . . .' He looked down at Helen then and his voice trailed away. In that moment, perhaps, he realized it was over.

Danny didn't look at his daughter again. Instead he slammed the boot shut and walked robotically towards the other woman.

'Get out of my way, Andrea.'

Andrea Craven took a step back and moved to one side. He was still holding the wrench when he walked passed her but a second later there was a sharp, metallic sound as it hit the ground where he dropped it.

Danny Gilbert climbed into his car and drove away.

When Helen opened her eyes the first thing she saw was Tom looking back at her. It took her a moment to remember what had happened and to understand why she was in a hospital bed. Tom got out of his chair and came closer, his face all concern. 'Are you all right?'

It was a stupid question. She wanted to say, *I've been hit hard over the head with a heavy metal object. Of course I'm not all right*, but she didn't have the energy so instead she just said, 'Yes.'

Tom exhaled and said, 'Thank God,' which was an unusual utterance from a committed atheist. 'I was so worried about you.'

'I'm okay.' She wasn't okay, and her head throbbed. She vaguely remembered being helped into an ambulance and examined by concerned paramedics then ending up in the hospital, but the rest of the experience was fuzzy.

He smiled at her then. 'I leave you on your own for five minutes and look what happens.'

'It was Andrea,' she began. 'When you left –'

He silenced her with his own explanation. 'She called me when you got here. I was with Ian but we came as soon as we heard. They wouldn't let any of us see you, but this morning . . . I hope you don't mind . . .'

'What did you say?'

'I told them I was your fiancé.'

'Oh,' she said. 'Not my brother, or something less complicated.'

'First thing I thought of, and what's-his-name is 250 miles

away. Anyway, it worked, and they let me in. I didn't know what to do. I was going to call him but . . . I wasn't sure if that's what you would want. The doctors told me you'll more than likely be all right, and I know he frets about you.'

Oddly enough, Tom had done the right thing not calling Peter. He did fret about her and would use this incident as one more reason for her to leave the area and her profession. Even Helen had to concede that, this time, he would have a point. 'It's fine,' she said. 'I'll call him later. I don't want him to worry about me.'

'I thought you'd say that,' he said cautiously.

'I feel much better now,' she lied.

'They're keeping you in for observation. It's not like the movies, where you get to check yourself out so you can go and catch the bad guys.'

'So I'm stuck here.' She had to admit to herself that the idea of not moving for a while did appeal to her. 'But what about Danny Gilbert?'

'Gone,' he said. 'Drove off after he hit you. Andrea phoned the police after she had called you an ambulance. He won't get far. Every police officer in the north-east is looking for that big German car of his. Don't worry about him. He's finished.'

'But can we prove it all?'

'Helen, we don't have to. He lost the plot and tried to kill you. You're the victim of a serious assault – attempted murder, in fact – and Andrea is a witness. Why do you think he did that? Because he knew you had enough information to make his life hell. Being present when two people are killed then lying about both incidents means he's through. You heard what they were like to the farmer, and that was with hardly any evidence against him. Everyone would think Danny had killed two people, whatever the outcome with the police, so he had to silence you. He didn't know Andrea was with you.'

'You had the car so she drove me.' Then Helen realized. 'If I'd walked across the village instead, I'd be dead now.'

'I'm so sorry I left you. That was stupid.'

'Not as stupid as me confronting a murderer on my own,' she said. 'But I honestly thought . . . I mean, his family were inside . . .' She still couldn't believe he'd attacked her while his wife and child were close by.

'Fuck him,' said Tom. 'Leave him to the police.' She seemed to sag in relief then. 'I got you something on my way home yesterday.' He fished in his bag. 'The bookshop was just closing but I explained it was an emergency.'

He handed her a copy of *The Secret Garden*.

She took it and looked at the cover. 'My favourite book when I was a girl.'

'You mentioned that once,' he said dismissively.

'And you remembered.'

'Thought you might like a trip down memory lane, since you're going to be stuck in here for a few more hours at least.'

'Thank you, Tom. That's lovely.' She gave him an apologetic look. 'But I'm not sure I'm up for reading just yet. My head really hurts.'

'Oh no, I didn't mean that,' he said. 'I'll read it to you. I'll do it quietly so we don't disturb anyone else.'

'You can't stay,' she said. 'You're really busy, and they won't let you.'

'I filed copy last night,' he said. 'An article about Danny going on the run, for which we will be paid. I also charmed the nurses,' he said in a whisper. 'They don't seem to mind. I am your fiancé, after all,' he reminded her.

'But what about Jess?'

'That's all in hand,' he told her. 'There's plenty of time.' And when she had run out of arguments, he said, 'Now then, Chapter One,' and he began to read.

61

Helen was allowed to go home late that afternoon. Tom insisted she spent a couple of days doing nothing but getting well, and she was happy enough to comply. Nothing more could be done about the Susan Verity case until the police tracked down Danny Gilbert. As soon as she got home, she read Tom's article.

POLICE SEEK MISSING FRIEND IN SUSAN VERITY CASE

Exclusive by Tom Carney

Police are anxious to trace the former playmate of tragic schoolgirl Susan Verity almost twenty years after her death.

According to a police source, a credible witness claimed Danny Gilbert, now 30, could have been the last person to see Susan alive when they played together at the edge of the quarry close to where her body was recently found. Gilbert's whereabouts are currently unknown. Danny's friend, Billy Thorpe, has admitted that he misled detectives at the time, and since, telling them that he saw Susan walking in the opposite direction, a piece of information that significantly derailed police efforts to find Susan after her disappearance in 1976. Billy Thorpe will not be charged with wasting police time, since he was a minor when the girl went missing.

A police source said, 'We urge Daniel Gilbert to get in contact so he can assist us with our enquiries.'

In a further twist, French police also wish to question Danny Gilbert about the death of his former girlfriend Victoria Cassidy.

Miss Cassidy disappeared while on a mountaineering holiday on Mont Blanc with Gilbert. The incident was treated as a tragic accident by French authorities but her body was not found at the time. It was discovered years later, at a considerable distance from the location identified by Mr Gilbert as the spot where he had last seen her.

Danny Gilbert's wife, Janine, the mother of his two young children, pleaded for her husband to hand himself in at the nearest police station. 'Whatever has happened, we just want him home,' she said.

Tom could have made the story sound even worse by mentioning the assault on Helen, but he had known she wouldn't want that. Her family and fiancé would be upset if they learned how close to death she had been, and Tom might prejudice a future trial if he reported the assault before Danny was arrested or charged for it.

Helen re-read the article. None of it was untrue. At no point had Tom stated that Danny Gilbert might be responsible for the death of his girlfriend or for that of Susan Verity. All he had reported were the bare facts. Danny was missing and two police forces in separate countries wished to re-interview him about two deaths, separated by more than ten years. Despite the absence of anything overtly linking Danny to their murders, or even the use of that word, the article was damning. Anybody who read it would understand the truth. Danny Gilbert was in big trouble.

'I've got another piece lined up about the discovery of the bodies on Mickle Fell. They found all three of the missing children there, thanks to our good friend Detective Bradshaw.' said Tom. 'Which reminds me – will you be okay on your own if I nip out early tomorrow morning? I wouldn't ask, but it's important. We're bringing Jess in.'

'Of course,' Helen assured Tom. 'Can you think of a safer place for me to be?' Danny Gilbert was unlikely to come after Helen now that he was officially on the run and probably wouldn't be able to break into this house, even if he tried.

Tom went to the desk, picked up a large white cardboard box and handed it to Helen. It was a deep, squat container the dimensions of a cake box, and she noticed that it had both their names above the address. 'What's this?' she asked, and lifted the flap on the box to look inside. A series of smaller boxes was stacked neatly, two layers deep and three rows across. Twelve mysterious little white cardboard boxes. Helen looked at Tom questioningly.

'They're for you,' he said. 'Well, half of them anyway.'

Helen reached for one of the boxes and opened it. She examined its contents carefully and felt a surge of emotion. To combat this, she carefully removed a business card from the top of a large pile of them. It was high-quality work, a firm card with a deliberately mottled textured that felt good to the touch. The lettering on it was in three separate colours with the name of the business embossed in gold above the address and contact numbers.

NORTON–CARNEY
Journalists

'Why is' – she cleared her throat then continued – 'my name first?'

'Practical reasons,' he assured her. 'It scans better. Carney–Norton doesn't have the same ring to it.'

There was a long pause while Helen regarded the card in her hand and tried to calm the emotion she was feeling. Tom misunderstood the reason for her silence.

'Look, it's something I've been meaning to do for a while,

but you don't have to – I mean, if you still think you want to go and get a proper job.'

'No,' she said quickly.

'Then stay, Helen,' he pleaded. 'Please. I've seen an accountant. It will all be fifty–fifty.'

'It shouldn't be fifty–fifty,' she demurred. 'Without your contacts . . .'

'That's a shame,' he told her, 'because fifty–fifty is the only partnership I'll consider.'

The next morning, Tom left the house before it was light, picked up Bradshaw then drove him into the city centre. The detective was full of questions about Helen and Tom answered them all. 'She's resting today,' he assured the detective.

Satisfied by this, Bradshaw exhaled and looked out of the window at the empty streets. 'If this lass doesn't turn up, I'll bloody kill you,' he said.

'Not a morning person then?'

Bradshaw regarded the dark skies above them. 'It's not morning yet.'

Tom drove them to the top of the hill and parked to one side of the grassy square between the castle and the cathedral. Jess had demanded somewhere public, but it had to be early too, so there wouldn't be many people around. It was barely five o'clock in the morning when Tom turned off the ignition.

'What now?' asked Bradshaw.

'We wait.'

'Is she coming by car or on foot?'

'Didn't say.'

'But she *is* coming?'

Tom sighed. 'So she said.'

'Right, well, good, because this is not my idea of fun, I can tell you. Not after the week we've had.'

'Been busy, have you?' he asked innocently, as if the discovery of four bodies and a dash to the hospital to check Helen was all right was normal enough.

'Shut up.'

'Like a good moan, don't you?'

'Yes,' said Bradshaw, 'I bloody do. Why does it have to be this early?'

'Because that's how she wants to play it and I daren't give her an excuse to change her mind.'

'Yeah, well, she's late.'

'Seven minutes,' said Tom glancing at his watch. 'She's seven minutes late. Christ, you'd be a hopeless hostage negotiator, you've no bloody patience.'

'No patience? I put up with you, don't I?'

'Shhh.'

'Don't bloody shush me.'

'*Ssshhh!*'

Despite himself, Bradshaw went quiet. Sure enough, he could hear the distant, low murmur of a lone car engine. A moment later Jess's car came into view.

'Is that . . . ?'

'It's her,' Tom assured him.

They got out of Tom's car and Jess pulled up some distance from them. Her car was facing theirs. She put the headlights on full beam, dazzling them both, and they heard her climb from her car but couldn't make out much beyond a blurred shape behind the headlamps.

'Stay there!' she ordered. 'Don't come any closer.'

'It's all right, Jess,' said Tom. 'This is Detective Sergeant Ian Bradshaw from Durham Police. He's here to help you, just like I promised.'

'Don't move,' she said. 'Not yet. Take out your ID and throw it to me.'

'Okay, Jess,' answered Bradshaw.

'I hope you haven't got that gun with you, Jess,' said Tom.

'Gun?' asked Bradshaw, wondering why Tom had neglected to mention this.

'What do you think?' was her answer.

'Just be careful, all right,' said Tom. 'We don't want anyone getting hurt.'

'No,' she agreed. 'We definitely don't.'

Bradshaw threw his warrant card carefully towards her. It landed just in front of the car and she stepped forward then bent to retrieve it. She examined it closely then said, 'So you're a copper, bully for you. I've met a few of them in my time and half of them were bent.'

'Well, he's not,' said Tom.

'But I'm not sure how I'll be able to prove that to you, Jess.' Bradshaw folded his arms. 'So how do you want to play this?'

She took her time answering. Tom and Bradshaw were left standing silently between the two cars, the only sound coming from a cawing bird who sounded just as aggrieved as Bradshaw to be up this early.

'Take me to the police station,' she told them.

'Okay,' Bradshaw agreed. 'Get in.' He gestured to Tom's car.

'No chance,' she told him. 'You get in. I'll follow you. We do it that way or not at all.'

Helen heard Tom leave the house at what seemed like the middle of the night and couldn't get back to sleep. Instead, she lay awake thinking: about Danny Gilbert almost killing her; about Victoria Cassidy and Susan Verity; how she was the lucky one; and what would have happened if Andrea hadn't walked in when she did. Most of all, she thought about her life right now.

It was still barely light outside when she gave up on sleep and got out of bed. She showered, dressed, then looked in the mirror. The blow had been towards the top-left-hand side of her skull and, although it had broken the skin and almost knocked her unconscious, she hadn't needed stitches. Helen had promised Tom she would take it easy and she fully intended to, but there was something very important she had to do first.

Helen had discovered that a near-death experience concentrates the mind wonderfully and draws everything into sudden, sharp focus. She headed for the train station.

The three of them sat in the empty canteen at police HQ. Jess had insisted on it. She wanted a room that was large and open, with more than one exit, and it had to be a public place even in the station, although no one was there this early, not even the canteen staff. She also made it clear that Tom had to be there while Ian asked the questions.

'So, Jess, I understand you wish to make a statement?' asked Bradshaw.

Jess looked at Tom as if seeking guidance then said, 'Yes.'

'You witnessed criminal activity?' probed Bradshaw.

'Yes,' she said. 'Yes, I did.'

When she failed to elaborate, Bradshaw asked, 'And what criminal act did you witness?'

'Murder,' she told him. 'I saw someone kill a man, so yeah, murder.'

'You saw a murder?' Bradshaw repeated. 'You actually witnessed this taking place with your own eyes?'

'Yes.'

'And who was the victim?'

'Ronnie Byrne, a member of the Byrne crime family.'

Bradshaw and Tom exchanged glances. 'And who was the killer?'

'Aidan Flynn,' she said. 'The youngest brother in the Flynn family.'

Ian Bradshaw's eyes widened. Jess seemed to be offering the youngest of the infamous Flynn brothers up on a plate. This was a huge scalp. Bradshaw needed a moment to let this sink in. Then he asked, 'And how did this killing take place? What was the method?'

'Knife,' she said simply. 'Aidan lost his temper and stabbed Byrne in the neck.'

Bradshaw realized that, if Jess's story was true, she was handing them gold. 'Did you know the victim?'

She shook her head. 'That night was the first time I'd seen him, but I'd heard of him, obviously.'

'Obviously,' said Bradshaw. 'And what was your relationship with the alleged murderer?'

'I was seeing him,' she said simply. 'He was my boyfriend.'

'And yet now you want to provide a witness statement saying that he is a murderer. Why is that, Jess?'

'Well,' she said, as if it were a stupid question, 'he's trying to fucking kill me, isn't he?'

62

'Because I like jam?' wailed Peter. 'You're calling off our engagement because I like jam?!'

'No!' Helen was exasperated, as much at herself as Peter. She had tried to lay out her reasons calmly and logically, visiting him at his home while first ensuring they would be alone. He still hadn't seen this coming. She would not be steamrollered into marriage by a public proposal, she told him. Peter was, understandably, upset. They then somehow got off track, arguing about the many little ways Helen felt they were incompatible, and now they were arguing about a Tiptree miniature, instead of breaking up like adults who had once cared deeply for one another, and it was all her fault. Helen had prepared a speech about them going in different directions but his panicked, emotive response threw her into a rant about his love of the carpet shop, tweed jackets and miniature jams.

'It's not the bloody jam,' she reiterated, 'that was just a tiny example of how we have grown apart.'

'But I only mentioned it once,' he protested.

'Forget about the jam, all right!' She forced herself to calm down while Peter watched her as if she were going mad and this was all a very bad dream. 'We are different people, Peter, that's all. I've changed. You've changed. Surely you can see that.'

'You're upset,' he offered. 'You injured yourself and you're not thinking straight.'

'That's not it,' she told him. Peter had noticed straight away that she didn't look well and when he had moved closer to greet her he had seen the damage to the skin near the parting of her hair. A closer examination had her floundering for a lie. 'I left the kitchen cupboard door open and banged my head on it. I'm fine.'

'But . . .' He was struggling to find the words now. 'Don't you love me any more?'

She let out a deep, exhausted sigh then: 'No,' said Helen. 'I'm sorry, Peter. I don't.'

Peter sat down suddenly, as if someone had abruptly pulled the plug on him. He hadn't seen this coming at all. Helen knew she had hurt him terribly and felt enormously guilty but she was determined to banish those thoughts until this was finished with. It was something she simply had to do.

Then she witnessed a new emotion forming on Peter's face. Anger.

'It's him,' Peter snarled. 'Isn't it? You're sleeping with him!'

'I am not sleeping with Tom,' she told him firmly.

'Oh, really,' he sneered. Peter really believed it. Just because she may have spoken a bit too much about the man she respected, admired and had a passing attraction to in the past.

'Dear God,' she said, 'you just can't see it, can you? This has nothing to do with Tom.'

'It has everything to do with Tom. We were fine before you moved in with him.'

'No,' she said. 'we weren't. We really weren't.'

'Well, you never let on!' he bawled at her. 'You never said a bloody word, not even when I proposed to you. I hope you're happy, making a fool out of me – in front of your family, my parents and all our friends. I told you I loved you and wanted to marry you and you've thrown it all back in my face.'

That just made her angry enough to tell him how she had really felt about his romantic gesture. 'You deliberately engineered it so I had no choice but to accept you. You didn't even discuss it with me beforehand.'

'Discuss it with you?' He was outraged. 'How could I discuss a secret, romantic gesture that every girl is supposed to want, in advance?' he hollered.

'You didn't even hint to me that you were going to ask me to marry you. Not once.'

'But . . . we've been together so long . . . I just assumed that . . . what was the bloody point otherwise?'

She felt flustered now, because she couldn't really take issue with that. A couple of years back she would have said exactly the same thing. 'All I could feel was everyone in the room staring at me, waiting for an answer. What choice did you give me?'

'What choice? You could have just said no!'

'And ruin the whole evening? Your parents' big night? How could I possibly say no in those circumstances? You'd have been –'

'Humiliated?' he said coldly. 'Yes, I would have been,' he admitted, 'but at least it would have been better than this.' He turned his head away from her and stared out of the window. 'Christ, what am I going to tell Dad?'

'What has he got to do with it? This is about us. When I first met you, Peter, you had plans of your own. You weren't too fond of your dad in those days, and none too keen to run his little carpet empire for him.'

'Well, I couldn't get a decent job,' he spluttered. 'Not one that paid what he pays me, not one with prospects like this one.'

'He bought you off!' she shouted. 'Can't you see that? He made it too easy for you to join him and too hard to go anywhere else. Now you are stuck there for life and you'll never see the real world or have an opinion of your own.'

'I have opinions,' he protested.

'And they are almost exactly the same as his. You could have tried harder. You took the easy option.'

381

Criticism hurts the most when it's at least partially true, and she could tell by the punch-drunk look on Peter's face that she had hit home hard, which was why he suddenly lashed out.

'You're a cold one, Helen. Let's see how long Tom puts up with it then, shall we, before he's had enough?'

'Stop talking about Tom. He has nothing to do with this.'

'He has everything to do with it.' There was a look of contempt in Peter's eyes. 'You really have had a blow to the head,' he sneered, as if that could be the only reason why she would give up a prize catch like him.

She glared at him then. 'Thank you for making this so much easier.'

Lena wasn't meant to be back for a few more days but when Tom left her a message to say there'd been a breakthrough, she called him straight away.

'I think it might be significant,' he told her, 'but I'm going to need to run it by you.'

'So tell me,' she urged him.

'I can't,' he said. 'At least, not over the phone. It's too . . . delicate.'

'Okay.' She didn't seem to mind that he might be inferring that speaking over the phone could incriminate them both. 'Well, if it will help you to find Jess, I can come back this afternoon. Where shall we meet?'

He gave her the name of a pub in Durham and Lena agreed to meet him there. He wondered if he had played this right or whether he had made her suspicious and might never see this woman again.

63

Danny Gilbert was parked down a country lane miles from Maiden Hill. He had chosen it because the rutted track was the kind of place he never would have normally driven his new car but an ideal location to hide from the world. He managed to get the car hidden behind an old caravan that was parked near some woodland. The caravan had green algae growing on it and looked as if it had been abandoned long ago.

Danny knew he could live in his car for a while but he didn't dare drive it anywhere. He knew the police would be looking everywhere for it and he knew he couldn't go on like this. All he wanted to do now was explain it.

He'd written it all down in a long letter addressed to Helen Norton. He'd used some of the stationery samples he always carried in the car to tell the whole story. That day with Susan, the expedition with Victoria, why he did what he did, everything that was wrong with him. He wanted them to understand and for some reason thought Helen might be the one to tell his story without distorting it, even though he had tried to kill her.

The first had died because of a rush of temper. He could recall it all so clearly even now, after all these years: inching out on to the quarry ledge from the plateau and instantly feeling terrified, desperately trying to get back to safe ground and almost falling to his death. And how had Susan reacted? By mocking him. 'You've barely gone a yard,' she told him, and when he was back on firm ground he had hit her and she'd gone crazy. It wasn't the telling-off for hitting girls that did it. It wasn't her telling him he was a coward that had pushed him to go too far. It was what she had said when she lowered her voice and hissed at him in spite, 'And your daddy's going to prison, Danny Gilbert. He's a crook. Everyone knows that.'

The stone was in his hand before he realized it, and he launched it at her, then she fell backwards through the hedge.

He could have saved her then.

He chose not to.

He had loved the feeling when she fell.

The second had died because he had rowed with his girl-friend and just wanted to shut her up. Victoria had gone on and on, moaning about his slow progress up the mountain, comparing him unfavourably with her former boyfriend, belittling him at every turn until, finally, he'd snapped and shut her up for good. He had to concede that he never would have pushed her off that mountain if he hadn't killed Susan Verity ten years earlier. He had known exactly what would happen. More to the point, he had known how it would feel and had gloried in the sense of power and fulfilment as he sent Victoria off that ledge and watched as she screamed all the way down.

God, it had felt wonderful.

Somehow, he had managed to keep his impulses in check for another ten years. Maybe he would have been able to go through the whole of the rest of his life without killing anyone, but he doubted it. He'd almost finished Helen off, and had even experienced a feeling of murderous rage towards Andrea.

The feeling when he killed was so intense, far more satisfy-ing than anything else he had ever experienced. Forget drink or drugs or sex – forget them all. None of them ever came remotely close to the surge of adrenalin when he watched Susan's shocked face as she fell backwards over the edge or heard the cry of terror from Victoria as she went flying from the ledge and plummeted on to the rocks far below.

It was glorious.

Telling the French authorities Victoria had fallen from the ledge during the storm on the way back down had been his mistake, but he had also known that the likelihood of her body being spotted so far below was slim, and he had to explain her death somehow. He had calculated a fall on the way up from a wide ledge in glorious sunshine was far less likely to be believed than that she had slipped during a storm on the descent.

Helen Norton wouldn't let it lie, though. With Susan Verity found at the bottom of a steep quarry, it would be enough for the French authorities to reopen their investigation and he would have to answer for Victoria's death. It had been just his luck to have a woman like Helen poking her nose in. He'd liked her at first; she was beautiful, sharp and clever – too clever by half – but in a strange way he was almost glad he hadn't killed her now.

He wondered what his life would have been like if he had never come across Helen and Tom Carney and that bloody detective. He might have had another forty years.

Bad luck, then.

Maybe they really were all cursed after all.

It took Lena five hours to make the journey north from London but she made it to the pub half an hour after Tom. She smiled at him from the doorway and went over to sit with him.

A second later Ian Bradshaw joined them from the bar.

Lena looked uneasy and her face seemed to freeze when Tom calmly announced, 'This is Detective Sergeant Ian Bradshaw from Durham CID. You might remember his name from my book.'

'Yes,' she said. 'A friend of yours.' She nodded at Bradshaw.

'That's right. We work on cases together and, from time to time, he is able to help out with one of mine. I've told him all about you, Lena, and he knows I'm helping you to find Jess. He's been doing a bit of digging on my behalf.'

'Great,' she said brightly, but he could see the uncertainty in her eyes. 'You said there's been a breakthrough.'

'I think so,' said Tom.

'I've got some photographs, Lena, and I'd like you to take a look at them,' said Bradshaw.

'Photographs,' she parroted back at him. 'What kind of photographs?'

'Pictures of people we think may have come into contact with your sister. Could you take a look and let me know if any of them rings a bell?'

'Sure.'

'What about this lady here?' asked Bradshaw, and he turned over a photograph of a middle-aged woman who looked respectable enough. 'Do you know her at all?'

Lena regarded the photograph closely for a while, as if she were really concentrating on it, 'No, I'm afraid I don't recognize her,' she said.

'You're sure of that, Lena?' asked Bradshaw. 'Have another look. Take your time and make absolutely certain.'

Lena did as she was instructed and gazed at the photograph til none of them could be in any doubt as to how seriously she was taking this.

'No, sorry,' she said finally. 'I really have never seen this woman before. I don't recognize her at all.'

'You're absolutely positive?'

'Yes,' she said firmly.

'I'm a little surprised by that,' said Tom.

Lena looked up into his unsmiling face. 'Why?' she asked. 'Who is she?'

'That, my dear,' he told her, 'is your mother.'

64

Lena knew it was over then. She must have realized now why he had chosen this table. When Bradshaw sat down next to her, she was hemmed in by the wall and couldn't possibly leave. It didn't stop her trying to get to her feet, but Bradshaw took hold of her forearm. 'Sit down, Lena,' he said. 'Or should that be Mia?'

She let out a lame little humourless laugh then, as if unconcerned she'd been discovered, but she was fooling nobody. 'Oh, well done, Tom,' she said. 'I have to admit that's a good one.' She sat back down and her body sagged. She appeared to be trying to control her emotions but then she looked as if she were going to be sick.

'I thought you'd like to know that I found Jess,' Tom told her. 'And, since you are so concerned for her well-being, you'll be pleased to hear she is alive and well. She's also cooperating fully with the police – and what a tale she has to tell.'

There was a flash of anger in Mia's eyes then. 'So what happens now?' she asked.

'It's bothering you, isn't it, Tom?' she asked him once they were at police HQ. 'You're wondering how much of it was real and how much was an act. Your fragile male ego can't cope with it, and you're dying to ask the question. You're desperate to know just how much of this I've been faking, aren't you?'

'Actually, Mia' – he used her real name – 'I'm more concerned with the fact that I've been sleeping with a bunny-boiler. Whether you've been faking it or not doesn't really figure on my list of problems right now.' That wiped the smile from her face. 'I'll tell you what I am interested in though,' he said. 'Why me?'

'That article in the paper,' she replied. 'I read it one day, and it was so . . .' She thought for a moment. 'The woman who interviewed you, it was like she'd fallen for you in about ten seconds flat – you, the handsome young investigative journalist, so bright, so clever.' She smiled archly. 'So good at finding people.

'We'd tried, of course, but we don't have as much influence up here.' Tom could see Bradshaw stiffen slightly at her hinting at bent coppers. 'So we got in a private detective, and you know how that worked out. You were plan B. There was something about you. I remember looking at your picture in the paper and I just knew I could play you, even before I met you. All I had to do was show up with a copy of your book and wait, then you would do the rest. I sat there for hours before you walked in. God, it was dull. Did you really think I enjoyed your boring bloody book?'

'I wouldn't have approached you,' he countered. 'Just so you know. That's not really me. It was Helen who came over, acting the matchmaker. If it hadn't been for her, I'd have left and you'd have had a wasted journey.'

'I'd have found another way,' she said. 'I always do.'

'Maybe. And I'll admit you were very good. I never suspected you, even when you told me not to contact your mother or to speak to Jess, in case I scared her off. That all seemed very reasonable under the circumstances. You're a great actress, Mia.'

'Thank you.'

'And it was a good plan. Trouble is, the plan is always the first casualty when real life intervenes. You thought you had it all worked out. You were playing me, and you were right, I did find Jess – but you didn't foresee that I might follow her because

I was worried she'd duck out on you. You couldn't have known she would pull a gun on me in broad daylight in the middle of the city either. It's amazing what a scared woman with guts will do.'

'She's the bunny-boiler,' sneered Mia.

'Takes one to know one,' said Bradshaw quietly.

'You've been a bit smug, Mia,' said Tom. 'You're very pleased with yourself and the way you played me but the sad fact is that Jess and I are on the winning side, not you. She told me everything and I persuaded her to come in and testify. Where does that leave you now, eh?'

Mia looked defeated then. 'You haven't got anything on me,' she told them. 'If you had, you'd have charged me by now.'

'You were trying to find a girl who didn't want to be found,' Bradshaw reminded her. 'And certainly not by you.'

'She was my brother's girlfriend,' she said defiantly. 'We were all really worried about her.'

'I'll bet you were,' said Tom. 'But why pretend to be her sister?'

'Because if I'd told you the truth you wouldn't have helped me. My family name carries a lot of baggage.'

'You're telling me!' said the detective. 'So you were simply reuniting a couple of lovebirds. The fact that she witnessed a murder had nothing to do with it.'

'What murder? I don't know anything about a murder. Had she reported one when I asked you for help?'

'She didn't dare,' said Tom. 'And I don't blame her.'

'So I asked you to help me find her,' she said. 'So what? That ain't a crime.' Mia was enjoying herself again now.

'Maybe not,' said Bradshaw, 'but murder is, and so is conspiracy. Then there's perverting the course of justice.'

'You haven't got a chance of making any of that stick. I'm clean. It's not my fault my surname is Flynn.'

'Maybe you're right, Mia,' admitted Tom. 'Perhaps you'll walk. Maybe they won't even charge you.' She looked very satisfied at that. 'Your brother, though, that's a different story entirely. They have a body, a motive and now, thanks to you, they have an eyewitness, safely tucked away where you can never touch her.'

Bradshaw spoke then. 'If you hadn't involved Tom, if you'd left Jess alone, she might never have come to us. Thanks to you, Jess was so terrified, you left her with no choice. When your brother asks the Met how they caught up with him, I'll make sure they lay all the credit at your door.'

Mia was furious now. Her eyes were wild and she set her face into a snarl. She looked angry, hurt and beaten all at once. 'Screw you!' she hissed. 'Both of you.' She jabbed a finger in Tom's direction. 'And you'd better watch your back from now on.'

'Join the queue, love,' he told her.

65

When Helen finally returned home, Tom was sitting in the lounge, watching the TV.

'Are you okay?' he asked.

'Yes, I just had to nip out for a bit. What happened?'

'Don't you know?' he asked, sounding a little indignant.

'How could I?'

'The Germans won' – she hadn't been expecting that answer – 'on penalties . . . a-bloody-gain.' His exasperation was all too apparent.

'Oh,' she said. 'I forgot it was on.' He looked at her like she was a madwoman. 'Well, I have had a lot on my mind lately.'

'If you weren't talking about the football, what were you asking me about?'

'Well – Jess,' she said. 'And Lena, obviously.'

'Not her name,' he said sulkily. 'It's Mia.' And Tom recounted the interview with Bradshaw.

'Good,' said Helen. 'She deserved it. Feel any better?'

'Marginally, but I've not had the best of times. Let's see. I got involved with a woman who was really using me to track down her brother's ex so he could kill her and now England have just crashed out of the semifinal on penalties.' Helen couldn't understand how he could link those two things and was even more surprised when he added, 'I hate football. I *really* hate football.'

She went to make them both a coffee and, when she returned with them, he asked, 'So, are you going to tell me what happened?'

'What?'

'Your engagement ring.' he said. 'You're not wearing it.'

'Oh. I'm sorry – please don't get angry.'

'Why would I be angry?'

'Because I went to see Peter.'

'Instead of resting?' She nodded. 'Well, it must have been important to you.'

'It was. I think this is for the best.' And she gave a little nod then, as if agreeing with her own point.

Helen was dreading his questions. She was emotionally drained, and maybe Tom sensed this because he simply said, 'I think you did the right thing,' so calmly he might have been commenting on the purchase of a new pair of shoes. 'Why don't you get some sleep? You look like you need some.'

She opened her mouth to answer him but the phone rang.

'I'll get it. If it's your ex, I'll tell him to fuck off.' He said that with some relish.

She told herself that Tom probably wouldn't do that, but she knew that he might. He was gone before she could protest. She heard him say 'Hello', closely followed by a surprised 'Oh, hi, yes, nice to speak to you . . . of course . . . I'll go and get her,' and wondered who it could be.

He leaned around the door and said, 'It's your sister.'

'That went well,' said Helen when she came back into the room forty minutes later. 'I've not heard from my big sister in a while but she felt the need to call up and give me a pep talk. Apparently, I'm being rash and impetuous in calling off my engagement and it isn't really me. This from a woman who has had at least two affairs with married men – that I know of.'

'It's your life,' he reminded her.

'It is.'

'Look at the pair of us,' said Tom. 'The woman who binned

her fiancé after the shortest engagement imaginable . . . and the man who's been dating a dead girl.'

'That sounds a lot worse than it was.'

'Either way, I feel like a class-A, prize-winning chump.'

'How could you have known?'

'Helen, I fell for a conman.' He corrected himself. 'Conwoman.'

'People do,' she reminded him. 'All the time. Every day, in fact. Conmen . . . and con-women wouldn't last very long if they weren't extremely good at it. I bet you're not the first to fall for her lies.'

'But I still feel like one of those middle-aged ladies in America who fall for a gold-digger and lose all their money.'

'You didn't lose any money.'

'Actually, I did.'

'No! You gave her money?'

'Not directly. I booked a week's holiday for the two of us. It was meant to be a surprise. I didn't realize she was planning a bigger one.'

'Oh God. Can you get your money back?'

He shook his head. 'It was non-refundable, from a travel agent in Newcastle. So now I have a week in Crete that I don't want and no one to go with.'

'Are you going to go? On your own, I mean.'

'I could do with a break, but it will feel a bit strange going there like Billy-No-Mates.' Then he looked at her intently.

'What?'

'Why don't you come?'

'Very funny.'

'I'm serious. You deserve a break every bit as much as me – probably more so, after what you've been through.'

'I don't think that's a good idea.'

'I know you don't do spontaneous.'

393

'I do spontaneous,' she objected.

'Not usually,' he said, 'but why not this one time? Come on, say yes.'

'But . . .'

'But what?'

'Presumably, you and . . . her' – she couldn't say *Lena* when that wasn't her real name and didn't want to call her Mia – 'were going to be sharing a room?'

'Well, yeah, but you *have* lived in my house for months. If you like, I can ask them to change it to a twin room.'

'That might be awkward.'

'You mean when the grandkids ask how we got together?' And despite herself, Helen laughed at this. 'I promise not to tell them about the dickhead in the tweed jacket if you don't mention the conwoman.'

'That's probably for the best.'

'Say you'll come.' He was serious again now, and Helen so wanted to say yes, but fear gripped her. She knew she could lose Tom for good if the week went badly, and he was pretty much all she had left now.

'I can't. I'm sorry.'

'At least think about it.'

'I have.'

'Then think some more. I fly out the day after tomorrow at four o'clock in the afternoon. Tell you what I'll do. I'll take the pressure off you and I won't mention it again. Remember that nice pub we drove past the other day, the one with the seats outside? I'll have a pint there at noon before I drive to the airport. I'll wait there for an hour –'

'Please don't.'

'– in case you change your mind. It won't kill me to have a pint before my holiday. Just don't forget your passport. I'll get the booking changed into your name –'

'Don't do that.'

'I won't be taking anyone else,' he told her, 'so either you'll be on that plane with me or the seat will be empty.'

'Tom, I can't do this, and I won't change my mind in forty-eight hours.'

'You might.'

'I won't,' she told him emphatically.

66

HERO COP PERSUADES CHILD KILLER TO GIVE UP BODIES:

DETECTIVE URGED MURDERER TO DO THE RIGHT THING

By Tom Carney

The bodies of three children missing for years have finally been found. In a dramatic move, police forensic teams examined a field in a quiet rural location and gently uncovered the bodies of three children aged between nine and twelve. They had been in the ground for more than fifteen years.

Grieving parents are now able to give the victims of child killer Adrian Wicklow a proper burial, thanks to a lone police officer who refused to give up. Detective Sergeant Ian Bradshaw was hailed a hero last night for repeatedly visiting the self-confessed murderer, who has incurable cancer, and urging him to cleanse his conscience by doing the right thing before he died. According to a police source, a delicate game of cat and mouse ensued, during which Detective Bradshaw managed to gain the trust of the murderer while pretending to befriend him. 'Ian Bradshaw fooled Adrian Wicklow into believing he was a sympathetic ear. In the end, the killer told him everything. I don't know how he did it when so many others have failed but, whatever he said to the killer, it worked.'

The murderer's last-gasp conversion to Islam has also been cited as a possible factor in Wicklow's about-turn. Imam Fasri has been credited with helping to persuade Wicklow to save his immortal soul by giving the detective the information he needed. A Catholic priest, Father James Noonan, previously spent fourteen years visiting the murderer weekly, but failed to get any information on the whereabouts of the missing children. Imam Fasri, who has known Wicklow for less than a month, refused to take credit for the dramatic development. He said, 'It was God who made Adrian Wicklow give back those children, not me.' Father Noonan refused to comment.

Bradshaw finished reading the article. 'Who hailed me as a hero?' he asked sceptically.

'I did,' grinned Tom.

They were standing outside Bradshaw's flat. The detective had been loading up his car when Tom arrived to show him the piece he had written.

'Don't panic. I told your press officer what I was going to write.'

'Really? Was he happy with it?'

'He was the police source. He knew the alternative angles were far worse. I could have told the truth.'

'That would never do. What if he hadn't liked it?'

'I'd have sent it anyway.'

'And that bit about Father Noonan?'

'Added it later. I thought he deserved it.' Then Tom said, 'What's going on? Are you leaving?'

Bradshaw hauled a bag into the boot of his car. 'Just for the weekend. The Lake District,' he announced. 'I wanted a bit of time on my own.'

'You're always on your own.'

'Thanks for that,' replied Bradshaw dryly.

'And I didn't mean now. I meant, are you leaving for good?' He pointed at Bradshaw's flat.

'Oh, that,' said Bradshaw absent-mindedly, as if he had forgotten the large For Sale sign on his home. 'I've decided to make some changes.' The first of Ian Bradshaw's changes had come about when he called the number on the flyer that had been pushed through his door by a local estate agent. 'Big ones.'

'Any interest yet?'

The detective imitated the spiel in the bland tones of an estate agent: 'In a desirable location, this property would make an excellent starter home for a young couple. It's our property of the week!'

'Then why sell?'

'Don't know,' Bradshaw said quietly. 'I fancied a change and I was tired' – he noticed Tom was looking at him closely now – 'of the place,' he added quickly, then he shrugged. 'Nice to do things on a whim now and then.'

'Is this the only thing you'll be changing?'

'Nope. As soon as I sell this place I'm going on holiday. I'm going to go out more and not sit at home obsessing about things I cannot alter.' Bradshaw put a second, smaller bag in the boot. 'Oh, and I rejoined the gym.'

'You'll never go, you know that, don't you? What about the job? Any changes there?' he asked gently.

'I haven't decided yet.'

'Don't do anything hasty.'

'You're only saying that because I am literally the one person in Durham Constabulary who thinks you're worth the hassle.'

'That's true,' admitted Tom, 'but you're quite good at it too, though I'd never say that publicly, of course.'

'Of course not.'

'And now all the bodies have been found, you must be the chief constable's blue-eyed boy.'

'Not so much,' answered Bradshaw. 'Latest word is the

current head of the Met is staying put, so he has no chance of getting the job after all.'

'Even so,' said Tom. 'It wasn't entirely about that, was it?'

Bradshaw caught Tom's eye in a manner that managed to convey that police resources would not have been expended on a cold case like this one for any other reason and Tom was a fool if he thought otherwise. He managed to do all this with just a look.

'DCI Kane must be happy with you, though,' Tom said, a little desperately.

'I think he genuinely is, for once. Kate Tennant wants me back in her squad as soon as. They've got another gangland murder to solve. A bloke was washed up on the banks of the Tyne with most of his face and fingers missing.'

'Nice,' said Tom. 'Good that she wants you back, though.'

'They're actually treating me like I'm not entirely a fuck-up.' Then he added, 'For the time being. Funny thing is, now that I have a bit less to prove –'

'You wonder if you can be bothered with any of it at all?'

'You're a perceptive fellow.' Bradshaw closed the boot of his car.

'Heard anything from Wicklow?'

'I've had messages from his solicitor requesting a visit,' Bradshaw told him. 'There won't be one. I have no wish to hold that man's hand on his death bed.'

'He must be desperate to see you.'

'He is. He wants my guarantee that we won't print that obituary. I'm not prepared to give it.'

'Let him suffer like they suffered,' Tom told Bradshaw. He meant the families of Adrian Wicklow's victims.

'After fifteen years in the prison system, Wicklow has finally reached a point where he is no longer enjoying himself. Why should that change? I'm not always sure I know what justice is these days,' Bradshaw admitted, 'but this feels a bit like it. We're not running it though' – Bradshaw looked worried then – 'are we?'

'Defame a dead woman who did nothing but give birth to a monster? No way,' said Tom. 'But he doesn't know that.'

'He thinks all journalists are scum.'

'It comes to something when your chosen profession is looked down on by a child killer. Are you okay, Ian?'

'How do you mean?'

'You've been interacting with one of the most evil men imaginable,' Tom reminded him. 'I wouldn't fancy that.'

'I've had the odd night of interrupted sleep, but I'll be fine,' said Bradshaw, even though he wasn't sure about that.

'Okay then.'

Changing the subject, Bradshaw asked, 'So what will you do now? You could probably use a break too.'

'I'm taking one.'

Bradshaw smiled slyly. 'Who with?'

Tom nodded his head towards Bradshaw's now packed car. 'I'll not keep you, mate. Enjoy your weekend.'

67

BUNGLING DETECTIVES FIND MISSING GIRL – 20 YEARS TOO LATE!

TRAGIC SUSAN VERITY LAY JUST YARDS FROM SPOT WHERE SHE WENT MISSING IN 1976

CHILD KILLER WANTS TOP COP BEHIND BARS

Exclusive by Nina Williams, our crime correspondent

The body of missing schoolgirl Susan Verity, who disappeared twenty years ago, has finally been located in a disused quarry, less than a mile from the spot where she was last seen by friends. In a damning admission, it was revealed that the site was originally searched by police back in 1976, shortly after she went missing.

A police source tried to explain the astonishing oversight. 'Susan's body was hidden, because it was buried between clumps of wild gorse bushes, and the intelligence police were acting upon was that she was last seen heading away from the quarry.'

Police are now working on the assumption that young Susan may have fallen from the edge of the deep quarry, or that she was pushed. They wish to interview Danny Gilbert, 30, urgently, in connection with Susan's death. Detectives had pinned the blame for her death on a multiple child murderer. Adrian Wicklow admitted killing Susan but later claimed he had been forced to confess after being tortured by police officers. Wicklow's solicitor is demanding that Detective Inspector Barry Meade, now retired, should face criminal charges for the handling of his client's arrest. He said, 'Adrian wants justice and is prepared to take this to the European Court, if necessary. His human rights were violated. He was tortured by men who behaved as if they were in the KGB, not the British police.'

Durham Constabulary has promised a full enquiry. Asked to comment on rumours of possible criminal charges against him, Detective Inspector Meade said, 'I wouldn't be surprised if they hang me out to dry.'

Helen spent an hour at the Metro Centre trying to cheer herself up, but bought nothing. Instead, she wandered around listlessly, looking at clothes she didn't really want and knew she would never wear.

She reached a new clothes store with a shopfront dominated by a single long glass window incorporating a display of beachwear. There was a male mannequin dressed in a checked, sleeveless shirt and beige shorts, with a straw hat and sunglasses. What looked like a cocktail had somehow been wedged into his hand. Next to him stood a female mannequin dressed only in a bikini. She had sunglasses too, but they were pushed back on top of her head, and there was a beach ball at her feet and fake sand beneath her toes.

The bikini was quite nice.

It would have suited her figure.

But she didn't do spontaneous.

Tom had told her that.

She wasn't rash or impetuous either.

Her sister had told her that.

Helen marched into the store.

Retired Detective Inspector Barry Meade had just finished mowing his front lawn when the journalist approached. He could tell the man was a reporter just by looking at him. It was the way he walked hastily up to Meade, anxious to get a word in before the policeman could dash back into his home. He didn't like the idea of leaving his lawnmower out here unattended so he unplugged it from the extension lead and began to twist the cable quickly into loops around his elbow.

'Have you heard the news?' gasped the reporter, who couldn't wait to tell it to him.

Meade did not bother to reply. He'd been expecting it, but he didn't want to give this little scrote the satisfaction of confirming that his world was about to implode. All those years as a police officer, and it had come to this.

Criminal charges.

Criminal?

How the hell could they allow this to happen? All those villains he had put away, they were the real criminals; he had spent his life in service to a legal system that ought to be giving him medals now, not scrutinizing a solitary case he had presided over which hadn't gone so well. Maybe they had gone too far with Wicklow, but didn't he deserve it?

Police brutality?

That was a laugh. What about the brutality meted out by Wicklow on those poor little children? Who really cared about a couple of digs in the ribs and a few hard slaps around the face? Christ, it was a different era back then.

'I've heard nothing,' he said defiantly, placing the rolled-up cable on top of the lawnmower. 'And I've nowt to say to you.'

'But surely this is a big day for you, isn't it? After all these years?'

'A big day?' He rounded on the man then. 'Are you serious?' In his temper, he lost his usual caution where journalists were concerned. 'I can defend myself against anything they throw at me. I did my job to the best of my ability and, if they don't like it, then fine, but I am not guilty of anything!'

The reporter shook his head. 'No. I'm not talking about any of that,' he said dismissively. 'None of it will go ahead now anyway. You can relax, Detective Inspector Meade.'

'Relax?' The detective had no idea what he meant. 'Just what are you banging on about then?'

'It's Adrian Wicklow.'

'What about him?'

'We've just heard,' said the reporter. 'He's dead. He died this morning.'

Barry Meade froze. He stood stock still while he processed the information he was receiving. 'Wicklow is dead,' he said disbelievingly. 'Are you sure about that?'

'Prison issued a statement about an hour ago,' confirmed the reporter. 'It's all over the news, but I guess you were mowing your lawn.'

'Then it's finally over?' asked Meade quietly.

'Yes.' The journalist didn't fully understand him. 'They won't be charging you with anything to do with Wicklow now he's dead and gone. There's no point.'

'He's dead,' said Meade once more, and the journalist looked at him questioningly, wondering if the retired detective was in shock or had gone prematurely senile.

'That's why I came to see you. I wanted to get your reaction to the death of the man you hunted for so long. How do you feel now that your nemesis has finally gone for good?' He brought his pen to his notepad in readiness for Meade's words.

The retired detective didn't say anything. Instead, he took a sideways step to stand on his path then turned his back on the reporter, but he didn't go into his house. Instead, he immediately span back round so he was facing the young man again. This caught the reporter by surprise. Next, Meade put his hands out wide as if he were using them for balance and span round again.

To the reporter's astonishment, it soon became apparent that retired Detective Inspector Meade was dancing. While the man watched with his mouth open and his pen poised for words that never came, Meade performed a perfectly executed soft-shoe shuffle, his arms moving out wide in exact synchronization with his feet, which seemed to have been borrowed from a younger man for the occasion. A slight but beatific smile was on his face.

The man from the tabloid lowered his pen as the retired detective finished his dance with one last spin, clapped his hands together firmly to signal that it was over and slid to a halt, before smiling warmly at the reporter and going into his house without a word.

68

Helen pulled up outside the pub but didn't get out of her car. She was still in time, but there was no sign of Tom. He had specifically said he'd wait for an hour and would be sitting outside the pub, but he wasn't.

She would have blamed him for this, but Helen had emphatically and repeatedly told Tom she would not be coming, so he must have, quite understandably, given up waiting. He had been there, though. Even from her car she could see the remnants of his time here. The little table by the door had an empty pint glass on it, along with a neat pile of the day's newspapers. Next to one of the folded papers were those bloody sunglasses of his. He'd left them behind again.

She almost got out of her car to retrieve the sunglasses for him but he would know she had turned up after all then and she didn't want that. It would be simpler this way. The shopping bag with the bikini in it was next to a hastily packed travel bag containing a few summer dresses and her passport. They mocked her now from the passenger seat.

A few thoughts went through Helen's head while the engine of her car ticked over. Some of them involved the practicality of attempting to dash to the airport in time to catch up with him. Then she contemplated booking a later flight and turning up unannounced, like in some sort of rom-com. She quickly dismissed those notions, telling herself she was actually very tired and in need of a few days on her own. She would sleep late and go for long walks, browse bookshops, sit in tea rooms, read a little. She would get her head around the break-up with Peter and allow the dust to settle. Her family would get used to it, or they wouldn't. That was their choice. She would stay up here in the north-east. It was her home now and her job mattered.

In a little while, Tom would return from his holiday and they would go on, much as before, as partners – at least in one way.

Helen glanced at the empty glass, the newspapers and Tom's sunglasses.

'Wasn't meant to be,' she said quietly to herself, and she edged the car away from the side of the road and drove away.

Epilogue

The whisky bottle was more than half empty but he could still feel the cold so he took another huge swig. It burned his throat on the way down.

Danny Gilbert was determined to go through with this, but the shock of the waves as they lapped around him at chest height was breath-taking. He stopped and looked around as the water buffeted him: no one on the jagged stretch of north-east coast line where he had entered the water; nobody out at sea. Perfect. They'd probably never even find him. He'd simply disappear, just like Susan Verity.

It had to end this way. He'd been naïve to think otherwise. That article in the paper by Carney had finished him. It told you everything you needed to know about Danny, right there, in less than three hundred words. He had killed two people. There was no denying it, and now he had to account for what he had done.

His old man had always said that Danny would make something of himself and end up in the newspaper. He took another step and the water came up to his chin. He hurled away the whisky bottle and it disappeared into the water. Danny Gilbert threw his arms up into the air and shouted, 'Made the front page, Dad!' Then he laughed, took another big step forward and disappeared under the waves.

Acknowledgements

Thank you to everyone at Penguin Random House for publishing *The Search*. In particular, I'd like to say a huge thank you to my brilliant editor, Emad Akhtar, for all of his help and great ideas. A very big thank you to publishing director, Maxine Hitchcock, for her support and faith in me. I am also very grateful to Eve Hall, Beatrix McIntyre, Sarah Day, Jenny Platt and George Foster for all their hard work on my behalf.

I would like to thank my brilliant literary agent, Phil Patterson at Marjacq, who has helped me to publish seven books now. I could not have done any of this without him. Thanks also to Sandra Sawicka at Marjacq for handling the foreign-language versions of my books.

Thanks to Peter Hammans and all at Droemer Knaur in Germany, and a very big thank you to the brilliant Ion Mills at No Exit.

The following people have all helped or supported me in different ways at key times in my writing career: Adam Pope, Andy Davis, Nikki Selden, Gareth Chennells, Andrew Local, Stuart Britton, David Shapiro, Peter Day, Tony Frobisher, Eva Dolan, Katie Van Sanden and Gemma Sealey.

To my lovely wife, Alison, I have to say a huge thank you for believing in me all these years. Your support kept me going.

My amazing daughter, Erin, makes every day brighter, particularly when the words aren't flowing across the page like they are supposed to. Thank you, Erin, for your love and inspiration. I couldn't have done it without you.

When she woke to find herself imprisoned in a large metal box, the only thing that terrified her more than the prospect of her captor returning was the thought that he might not. Then she would be trapped, at least until she ran out of the things she needed most: food, water, air.

THE DISAPPEARED

Book 4 in the Ian Bradshaw, Helen Norton and Tom Carney series

DS Ian Bradshaw and investigative journalists Helen Norton and Tom Carney must combine once more to unravel a chilling secret that links two generations of women who vanished without trace or explanation.

These are not teenage runaways or drug users, vulnerable prostitutes or victims of domestic abuse; there is no strife at home or problems at school. There are no leads or explanations and, crucially, no bodies are found. The only thing that links these ordinary women is what they leave behind; distraught families, devastated partners, shocked friends, all longing for the same answer; what could have happened to The Disappeared?

The disappearance of seemingly normal women.
The blackmail of someone with a dark secret.
The mind of a reluctant killer twisted by years of abuse.
***The Disappeared* is the dark and compelling new novel from Howard Linskey and is available to preorder now.**